Undying Lands

Book 2.5 of The Unraveled Fate Series

Every villain has a past...

& not every queen dreamed of being one...

UNDYING LANDS

KARA DOUGLAS

THE VALON
WILD LANDS
LYNGVI
THE AMASVARTNIR ISLE
ANDRONICUS SEA
CIMMERIAN FOREST
ZENTIA MOUNTAINS
RUNNSWICK

Empire
Syreni
Drogheda
Baile
Lilium Glade
Nox Grove
Palace
Viridian
Astern
Andronicus Sea

Pronunciation Guide

Names:

Evelina: Ev - ah - lēn - ah
Daimon: "Day" - mon
Annora: Ah - nor- uh
Maliena: Māh - lēn - ah
Neve: Nēe - v
Cyprian: "Sigh" - pre - in
Seretha: Se - "rath" - ah
Gloriana: Glōr - ē - ah - nuh
Carwyn: "Care" - "win"
Keir: "Keer"
Khaline: K - al - "line"
Leda: Lēe - dah
Eurydice: Yer - i - duh - sē
Vidaris: Vy - dār - is
Astoria: Ay - stor - ē - uh
Xenos: Xē - nōs
Zephyr: Zeh - "fear"
Lunaria: Lu - nah - rē - uh
Aegis: Āy - giss

Places:

Andronicus: An - drōn - ah - cus
Baile: B - ale
Lilium: Lil - ē - um
Penyth: "Pen" - ith
Crea: Crē - ah
Valon: Vāl - un
Caelum: Kāel- um
Cimmerian: "Sigh" - "mare" - ē - un
Drogheda: Drōg - hed - ah
Zenovia: Za - nōv - ē - uh
Viridian: Verr - id - ē - un

Valon Empire Field Guide

The Fae

Woodland fae
    The Leaders
    Born of the earth
    Territory: Unmarked
    Light manipulation
    Nature & growth
    Healing abilities
    Link to creatures of the land
    Magic gifted from Azmara

Aegis fae
    The Protectors
    Born of blood
    Territory: Drogheda
    Strength
    Control over fire
    Mind manipulation
    Skilled in battle & war
    Magic gifted from Zillah

Undine Fae
>The Defenders of the Sea
>Born of the water
>Territory: Syreni
>Water manipulation
>Influence over creatures of the sea
>Magic gifted from Xenos

Nocturna "Nox" fae
>The Protectors of the Subconscious—Both in Shadows and Dreams
>Born of the shadows
>Territory: Viridian
>Dream influence
>Dreamwalkers
>Shadow manipulation
>Magic gifted from Nyx

The Divine

Goddesses of the afterlife:

Eurydice
>Goddess of the Moon and the Keeper of Souls that make it to Caelum

Vidaris
>Goddess of Vengeance and Ruler of the Vale
>In the triad of Dark Gods

Lesser Known Gods and Goddesses:

Azmara
Goddess of Growth and Nature

Nyx
God of Fear and Dreams
In the triad of Dark Gods

Zillah
Goddess of Chaos and War

Astoria
Goddess of Hope

Xenos
God of the Seas
In the triad of Dark Gods

Celeste
Goddess of Wisdom

Author's Note

This book contains depictions of anxiety, depression, grief, images of war and fighting, blood/gore, death, death of a loved one, and explicit sexual content with light bondage. If any of these may be triggering for you, please read carefully. Feel free to contact the author for further explanation.

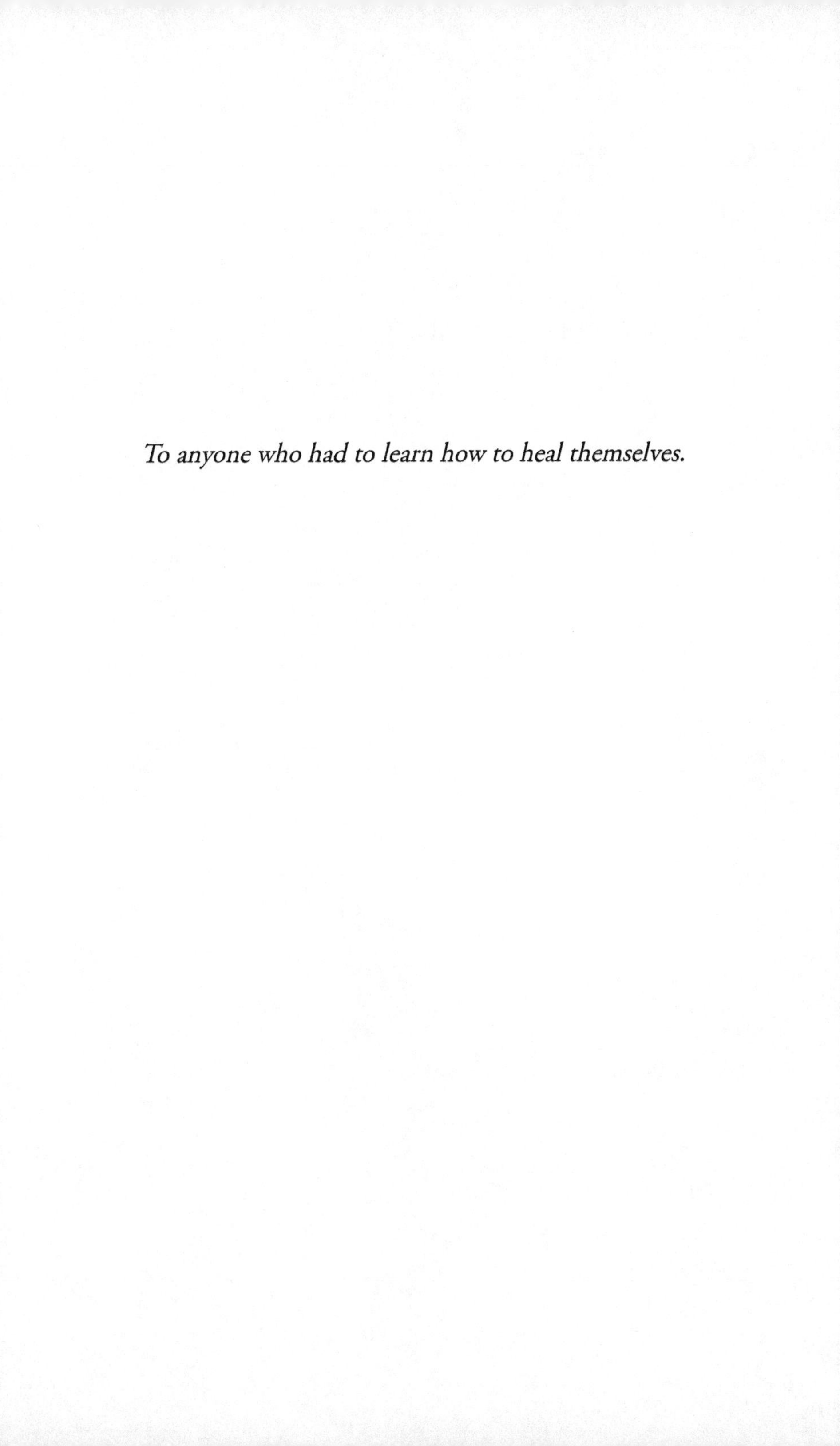

To anyone who had to learn how to heal themselves.

PROLOGUE

EVELINA

EVELINA WAS ONCE A GIRL WHO SPENT HER DAYS FILLED with the warmth of the sun against her face and laughter tumbling from her lips. She dreamt of her future, of her friends who would always be there, and the boy with midnight eyes.

But one day, her dreams changed. It was the same thing that haunted her sleep now, the same memories of the little shadow boy who left her behind. She would wake up each morning with sweat-soaked sheets twisted around her legs, wishing there was something to make her forget.

Each night, she fell asleep praying to Eurydice that the memories wouldn't come. They always did. Even the good ones —few as they were—hurt. Because all her dreams were his, and every reminder of his absence was a pain she could do nothing to fix.

A Nox so young shouldn't have been able to enter another's dreams yet, but he had found a way. The first time was by accident, when they had fallen asleep beneath an oak tree in the middle of the day. Neither of them realized they were dreaming —they thought perhaps they had died and awoken in Caelum. Then their eyes went wide with the possibilities, feverish with childish delight. They were unstoppable—best friends who could explore not just the woodland in the day, but whole universes in their dreams.

After that, they dreamt together every chance they could get.

They were too young to understand the heaviness growing on her mother's face, the way her father's lips seemed to struggle to smile. Too naive to the world around them to see the darkness rising.

Soon, even their dreams would not be safe.

If she were lucky, her haunted dreams would end there by the time the sun rose. But sometimes, the memory would keep playing out. Flashes of her crying beneath the Mother Tree after an unsuccessful day of training with the healers. The shadows that swirled gently around her, holding her until he was there, and it was his arms wrapped around her.

His shadows would always find her.

But that was before it all changed.

Before, the humans still lived in harmony with the fae, and her mother was still married to a human king. Then Moros killed Evelina's father. He had been raising a rebellion, preparing to overthrow her family's rule, and he took his opportunity to strike on the darkest day of the year.

And her father did as he'd always promised, protecting the queen with his life.

At the lux, his warm face was turned to stone, his calm gaze empty.

Moros's betrayal was felt throughout the entire empire, pushing some to join the rebels, and some to reaffirm their support of the Manors. What had once been the unified Valon Empire split almost neatly in half.

The realm descended into chaos. The rebels wielded swords charmed with dark magic, lumps of iron shot out of cannons into villages, and an endless sea of human soldiers grew larger and larger with their ease of reproducing.

The fae were strong enough to protect the palace, but they were still forced into the fray. Aegis trained every race of fae in

Drogheda. Woodlands learned to weaponize their growth and animal affinities, Undine to make water as dangerous as a sword, and Nox to wield shadows on the battlefield.

Evelina thought the rebels would be taken care of quickly, but her hope was drained day by day.

The wyverns arrived shortly after, signaling the start of the war.

And that's when they took the last thing she called her own.

A wyvern had claimed her shadow boy for the war, taken him away to the Zenovia Mountains to train with the Riders.

Away from her.

This was the dream she hated most of all, where she waited for him to return, watching the forest edge from the palace.

He said he would be back. He always came back.

She awaited the comfort of her shadow boy in the wake of all she had lost. As the months turned into years, the memory of his smile faded.

For the first time, he didn't come.

PART ONE:

BLOODBORN

ONE

EVELINA

Twenty Years Later

It had been three weeks since the last slaughter. The death that came along with the war was inevitable. But Evelina still mourned when lives were lost.

A soldier screamed in pain, his cries as mangled as his leg. Evelina quickly pressed crushed linndula root to the open wound.

"Please pass out," she whispered—more a prayer to Eurydice than anything else. She pressed harder, quickly wrapping his calf in bandages with her other hand. The scream abruptly stopped. She glanced at his face, finding his eyes closed and his breathing shallow.

Relief and adrenaline swept through her body, one after the other. Relief that the soldier had passed out and was no longer in agony; adrenaline as she pressed her two fingers just below his jaw to ensure he still had a pulse.

Her shoulders relaxed when she found the faint tapping rhythm of his heartbeat—slow, but there.

Taking advantage of his unconscious state, she used a salve imbued with the lead healer's Essence to keep him unconscious.

She rubbed it into each temple, careful to avoid the thick gash oozing blood from his cheek. Then she rifled through her satchel until she found another salve, this one thicker, a pale blue color, and layered it over the soldier's open wounds. The remedies might all be temporary—needing reapplication often—but it would heal their bodies ten times faster than a fae struck with a ferrum blade could usually heal.

As she looked around the room, it struck her that these were the lucky ones. The ones who had survived. They were all lined up in this small wooden cabin, cot after cot. A Mother Tree was painted on the door, the symbol of a healer's ward that housed the wounded.

Unfortunately, this was only one cabin of many, full to the brim with wounded fae. This refugee camp had nearly been full before the latest arrivals had shown up. Soon, she didn't think it would be able to house any more wounded.

Once she was satisfied the soldier wasn't going to slip away to a blissful afterlife in Caelum, she moved on to the next victim. She paused, taken aback at how similar he looked to a boy she once knew. The pointed ears poking out from shaggy, dark brown hair, the midnight eyes, and the way he looked at her as if she held all the answers in the realm.

"Will they follow us here?" the boy asked. His eyes were wide and filled with worry. He was so young. The clothes he wore told the story of a boy who lived in a farming village— Woodland, most likely.

She cleared her throat, shaking off the memories. "Doubtful. Word came about an hour ago that Viridian forces stopped the rebels from advancing. They pushed as far south of the palace as they could, but we held strong."

The boy opened his mouth to reply but was instead accosted by a wet, bone-rattling cough.

Evelina had seen her fair share in her time as a healer, and this one was simple. She quickly got to work, mixing rennew powder into a cup for him to drink, and to his credit, he downed it in a few gulps—even without it being warmed. She had him lie down and sat with him for a few moments to make sure the effects of the rennew started to work. It was fast-acting, his cheeks already filling with color and his cough calming.

It was often humans who needed the magic of a healer, their bodies unable to mend themselves in the way fae could. But fae weren't exempt from pain. Immortality didn't protect them from a ferrum blade, or curses from another, especially if their Essence was drained.

The need for healers only seemed to grow as the war dragged on. Evelina's time was split between tending to the wounded in the refugee camps and mixing and replenishing tonics in the infirmary at the palace. She wanted nothing more than for this war to end, but for as long as there were those needing healing, she hoped she could always be here to help them.

The walk back to the palace felt longer than the walk to camp. A few other healers trailed silently alongside her. When she thought of the incoming people seeking healers and shelter, her adrenaline carried her all the way to the camp. But now, with the sun starting to set and the forest quiet, her thoughts were too loud, her eyes too heavy.

Attacks close to the border were pushing more and more fae toward the palace, forcing them to relocate with their villages burned or destroyed. Moros and his endless human army were not the only threat anymore. A fringe group of dark god worshippers had morphed into something far more dangerous within the borders themselves. Unlike the human soldiers mindlessly pillaging towns and heckling villagers, these fae rebels knew the land.

They were lethal. Calculated.

At some point, they had started leaving the symbols of the dark gods in the wake of their destruction: orange flame enveloping a tree for Vidaris, white flame over a star for Nyx, and blue flames atop cresting waves for Xenos.

Before the wyverns arrived, Evelina had so much faith in life, so much pride in bearing the Manor name. But now it felt like the whole world was turned against them. And even though she knew the empire had to fight back to protect the realm…death was death. A life was still lost. Perhaps it was her years in training as a healer that made her understand how precious life was.

Her steps faltered as she arrived at the lunaria garden by the palace, the other healers going ahead to return to the infirmary. Evelina paused in the garden. It rested alone on a small patch of soil, nestled between pine trees and lined with wooden stumps along the perimeter.

The boy from earlier had looked just like the boy from her dreams. Flashes of her and Daimon sitting between the lunaria flowers as younglings, of midnight eyes that watched her so closely, filtered into her mind. It was always the place she felt safest with him. Though the flowers looked the same, somehow it felt empty now.

"Why these flowers?" Evelina asked, her voice unsure.

Daimon grabbed her hand and pulled her behind him. "Because no one comes out here. We can dream for hours without being found."

She didn't have to be convinced after that. She walked alongside him, her dress swishing against the leaves on the ground.

He stopped abruptly in the middle of the garden and sat down.

"What are you doing?" she laughed.

He tugged on her hand, motioning for her to sit down beside him.

"And get my gown dirty?"

It was his turn to laugh. "Since when have you ever cared about that? You spend more time in the herb garden than anywhere in this realm."

She smiled. He knew. Of course he did.

"Fine, but only for a little bit today." She lowered herself to the ground, seeing now that the tall lunaria bushes covered them from the outside world.

"See?" he whispered. *"No one can see us here."*

Evelina's heart beat wildly in her chest. She shook her head to push the memory away, quickly making her way through the rest of the garden, through flowers and tall pine trees. It took the rest of the walk to the palace to calm her racing heart.

Finally, she made it to the healer's garden. She paused by her favorite section and took in her handiwork. If anything could clear her head after visiting camp, it was this, being here. The ground was damp from last night's rainfall, water collected in some of the tiny, cuplike petals that were scattered throughout.

It only took a few breaths before her hands were caked with dirt, her golden-brown hair spilling over her shoulders as she checked on the growth of her plants. An attack on the other side of the Zenovia Mountains had her planting clover this time. A raid on Syreni's coast for the sea-holly beside them, and snowdew flowers beside those. Sweat had worked its way onto her brow, causing her to rub the back of her hand across her forehead.

The three-week-old seeds were growing well, now formed into small sprouts poking up from the damp soil. The grass around her was vibrantly colored, bringing out the green in her hazel eyes. She squinted, trying to soak in a few fleeting moments of quiet. She knew she had little time to linger before Gloriana found her.

This was the only way Evelina knew how to honor the dead. With every loss of life she heard about, she would plant something while praying to Eurydice that they found peace in Caelum. The tradition started after her mother planted an oak tree to honor her father.

Evelina was twelve when her father died, and she would

never forget sitting beside the growing seed, watching it turn into a sapling, hoping her father would magically return. But he never did. She and her siblings would visit the tree often, but Evelina sat in commune there the most. It was the only way she knew to mourn. While Ren honored him in battle, and Carwyn by being the perfect Manor heir, Evelina offered anything she could of the woodland itself back to him.

Planting a variety of jade vines, middlemists, and tea flowers—anything she could get her hands on at the time—made her feel closer to her father while she honored those who had been killed. He'd always called her his flower child, since the lilies outside the palace had bloomed the day she was born. He shaped so much of her love for the natural world; renovating the gardens for her first birthday, gifting her herbal pouches and tea blends at every festival, and stealing what moments he could away from the palace to hear her gush about everything she'd learned from Gloriana out in the healer's herb garden.

Seeing his remains turn into the great oak tree that shaded her now reminded her that everything always grew back in its own way. It was the same reason she hoped each of these seeds could make these deaths, one day, mean something.

The sun had nearly sunk beneath the horizon, its golden light illuminating the sky.

"Evelina!" a familiar voice shouted from the palace entrance. "I could use your help before you head off to sleep."

"You got it, Gloriana!" Evelina yelled back.

Gloriana was a brilliant healer and self-appointed mentor. When they first met all those years ago, Evelina had been struggling to figure out the difference between the hundreds of herbs they used. Gloriana marched right over and started rattling off rhymes to help her remember the names and their uses. She didn't bat an eye at Evelina being a Manor princess—and she had no qualms about correcting her when she was wrong. It's the only reason Evelina became so specialized in herbs.

Gloriana stepped into the garden with Evelina, her soft blue eyes fiercely determined. Her ashen hair was pulled into a low knot, just as it had been every day since they first met all those years ago. A few strands always seem to escape, falling around her face in odd directions.

"We'll debrief your camp visit if you have the time," said Gloriana. "May want to tally up what supplies we have with the influx of new refugees coming in these days."

Evelina frowned and set down the flower she was holding. She had been officially training as a healer since the war started two decades ago, but she had been learning herbs and mixtures long before that.

But now, it wasn't learning how to grow and nurture herbs for fun; it was a life hanging in the balance between her hands—her skills.

She loved being a healer, finding strength in knowledge when her Essence was found...*lacking* to others. Her affinity was that of light, her gift so different from those of her siblings. Some lightwielders could mend bones and seal flesh back together—like Gloriana—but hers was just delicate strands, not quite strong enough to heal. Some saw it as a weakness not to have a defensive affinity, but she didn't mind it. She saw how power burdened the Manor household firsthand. And she was content to stay out of all the dangerous games they were forced to play because of it.

"I won't be long," she told Gloriana.

Gloriana nodded, her eyes lingering on the ground where Evelina had knelt. She gave her a small smile and left her in the garden.

Evelina stood and tried to get the dirt off her gown, but it was no use. By now, everyone was used to her being perpetually covered in soil.

One of the gardeners—a human—waved and smiled at her as she passed by. Ian had always been one of her favorites. They met when she was merely a child and he treated her like family.

But now, Ian's eyes crinkled in the corners when he smiled.

His arm that was lifted in the air shook slightly, and the other hand supported his back. Still, he always had bright eyes and a wide smile, determined to live his short life to the fullest.

She'd watched him age over the years, while she stayed frozen in time like the rest of the fae. By fae standards, she was still a child—even though it'd been just over thirty years since she'd been born.

"Anything I can get you?" Ian asked with a smile. "You've been spending more and more time at the camps lately." She didn't miss the lilt of loneliness in his voice.

"The refugees have been pouring in every other week, it seems," she said quietly. "We'll manage."

He nodded, his eyes tired and worn. "Good luck out there. You'll need it."

She smiled sadly at him. Ian was the hardest-working man she knew, kind to everyone he met, even those who didn't always deserve it.

She hurried through the garden and stepped into the palace. Warm light glowed from the ceiling of the corridor, illuminating the path with its flameless glow. No lamps or fires were used; the palace didn't need them. She had once loved how magical her home had felt, how safe and free it was. But even the warmth that seeped from the walls didn't reach her chilled skin.

The walk through the palace was bustling, and, as always, people were running around frantically. The corridors used to brim with all sorts of people. It would always feel strange to see so few humans in the palace; so many of them had migrated to the other side of the Zenovia Mountains to stay with the rebel stronghold.

Her exhaustion caught up on her walk to the infirmary. She felt the heaviness of the day, having been healing and aiding the refugees since before sunrise. Once she finally made it back, she felt the chill on her skin start to warm.

The infirmary wasn't anything grand. A room within the palace that used to be for storing fabric had been cleared out.

They mixed herbs, made medicinal salves, and had several workstations for the soldiers brought here to be healed—if they weren't too wounded to make it this far.

There were rows of shelves partially filled with herbs and tinctures, their stock running much lower than it used to. A few cots were crammed into the center of the room, long enough for a fully grown Aegis to lie down on. Other times, they used it to spread their herbs out when mixing tonics.

The room was empty now, save for Gloriana.

"We're running low on stinging nettle," Gloriana said from behind a shelf, her body hidden. Jars clinked together from where she stood, and she whispered softly to herself as she listed off her items. "Lorene said several in the eastward camp haven't been healing as quickly as he would like, so he took most of the stock with him this morning."

Lorene had been a healer nearly as long as Gloriana. He was a soft-spoken Woodland who tended to fade into the background, but he came to life under pressure, shouting orders at the younger healers on where to go and what to do when the situation grew dire.

"The batch growing in the garden will be ready within the next few days," Evelina said. She walked over to one of the wooden tables and set her satchel on it. Disappointment bit at her as she counted how much supply was left after her visit. "Looks like we'll need more linndula root soon too." She glanced over at the far-right shelf, finding the top two shelves nearly empty. She frowned. "And blood-replenishing brews."

Gloriana poked her head from around the back shelf. Her hair had come more unraveled, large pieces now falling out of the knot. She looked over Evelina's shoulder to where the empty jars were piling up, her mouth pressed into a thin line.

"How much longer until the roots in the garden are ready?" she asked slowly.

Evelina sighed and turned to put her half-empty jars back on the shelf. The top row for linndula root—only a few jars remaining now—the middle row for stinging nettle—even less of those left—and the bottom two for an assortment of mixed tonics. "Longer than what we need," she answered.

As she worked her way through the first shelf, taking stock, she tried to shove away her frustrations. The list of needed items grew longer each week—the demand much greater than the supply, which was alarming considering how vast the healer's garden was. It took up a large portion on the west side of the palace, filled with every herb imaginable. But if it weren't for the Woodlands using their Essence to speed up the growth process of the herbs, they would've run out years ago.

She started to wonder how much longer the empire could sustain things the way they were. The rebels were pushing more and more refugees toward the palace as they burned, looted, and destroyed villages. Camps were reaching capacity, and the soldiers were stretched thin even with the aerial units helping to cover more ground with patrols.

Those who traveled to and from where the Riders trained brought back word of how the wyverns were growing restless. Of how their lead commander was fighting so hard to keep spirits high.

Daimon was good at that when they were young, too.

Evelina cursed as she lost track of her place, rereading the list. The days were long enough without adding worry over how he was or if he survived yet another battle. There were so many lives lost and *everyone* was exhausted. Her empire needed her to do her part—to heal and soothe those she was able to help.

So, she pushed her fatigue aside and moved on to the next shelf.

Two

Daimon

Even in the daylight, darkness lay like a heavy blanket across the faces of the soldiers. The lack of any real progress was wearing on them day by day. Daimon was constantly in strategy sessions with other commanders, preparing for Moros's next move and the rising power of the rebels.

Everything changed when the wyverns started to show. Ancient texts talked of the beasts and how they flew beneath Eurydice's blessing, only arriving in a time of need. No one had seen the war coming. It was a shock when the beasts arrived, the rebellion building right under their noses.

The empire was able to easily defeat the rebels in the early days, when they were still a regular human army. They grappled for power through praise of the dark gods, looting villages and burning innocent homes to instill fear. That was before Moros realized his advantage over the fae: the ever-replenishing resource of human soldiers. He no longer cared for the death toll, but instead the damage they could cause. Then they found a way around fae magic, using malicious spells to curse their swords and weapons—at the expense of their own souls—maximizing their damage while depleting the Essence of nearby fae. This high-risk advantage severely tipped the scales in favor of the rebels.

It didn't help that the dark gods seemed to be pushing the rebels closer to victory, using the war to fuel their power. What they would do with that power was harder to guess. Vidaris could be playing the long game for something that wouldn't come to an end for centuries—long after they'd all ascended to Caelum and a new generation had been born.

All he knew for certain was now, each time one of the beta fleets brought a report of their patrols throughout the empire, their shoulders slumped a little more.

Aegis were stretched thin throughout the realm, and no matter how many of them there were, the mass of land was far too vast to fully patrol every single village. Even with the Undine, Woodland, and Nox joining to train among the Aegis, it wasn't enough to cover *every* corner of the realm.

Most of the ground soldiers fighting with Daimon's fleet were Aegis, their fire affinities invaluable. They were on the border with him and his Alpha Fleet, tasked with stopping Moros and his human army from advancing past the Zenovia Mountains.

He scrubbed a hand down his face, his skin rough and lined with stubble along his jaw. Daimon always spent his mornings the same way no matter where he was—with a steaming cup of rhodiola to calm any lingering nerves, meditating beneath the rising sun. When he was young, a talented little herbalist had brewed a cup for him. Said it'd help to center himself before the day.

He couldn't bring himself to stop drinking it long after he'd left her.

The trees around him shook, swaying violently with a gust of sudden wind. Daimon jumped to his feet, his Essence surging to life in his veins as he felt his wyvern draw near.

He could feel her restlessness, could sense her unease.

She blasted out of the sky and landed in front of him. The gust of her wings sent the trees into a whirl of motion like a coming storm as the ground cracked and splintered, spreading out in a web beneath her taloned claws. Her golden eyes seared into him with a warning.

Wordlessly, he gripped the knotted rope on her side and jumped onto her back, settling himself into the leather saddle with ease. She pushed off the ground, barreling into the sky. He held on, determination coursing through him as the view below turned from pure forest green to dry, cracked lands, then clouds. After a half-hour flying north, he could finally hear the screams —could smell the flesh that burned.

A horn blared, followed by a softer blow several miles away. The horns would blow across the entire kingdom, alerting each village of the attack. There were different cadences for each warning; the first blare to alert which territory, the next to indicate which direction from the centermost point of the territory, and the last to tell how many miles away it was.

He paused, listening intently to the horns—a pattern only the warriors had been taught. And as the first horn blew again, he knew.

Drogheda was being attacked.

The outskirts of Drogheda dipped into the western waters of the Andronicus, where the rebels must have finally broken past, overwhelming the naval unit with their sheer size. They'd been trying to advance further past the border for years, hauling cannons, swords, and weapons of all kinds, pushing countless amounts of fae onto this side of Zenovia in their campaign north. But so far, Daimon, his fleet, and the ground soldiers stationed at the mountains had kept them at bay. Each force had its own stronghold firmly planted on either side of the long mountain range that split the continent.

Making it this far into the border was their boldest move yet. Usually, any one of the fleets should have seen the ships coming… Daimon cursed this morning's foggy weather blighting any chances for that.

Zephyr roared, an alpha calling her unit to the skies, as Daimon directed their flurry of motion toward the coast. He would kill every damned one of the traitors he came across. His nostrils flared and his blood rushed in his ears.

Coming down from the clouds, water came into view. The Andronicus Sea thrashed with the onslaught of vengeance and fury, the wind tossing waves and the current violently sweeping ships side to side. The empire's fleet was chasing the rebel ships to shore, the Undine aboard manipulating the currents to push them back. One of the rebel ships had already made a clean break from the skirmish, anchoring near a shoal. Soldiers were exiting on a wide plank, carting cannons through the shallow water onto the beach. The Valon soldiers jumped from their ships, fighting to take down the cannons being brought to shore.

The rebels held fast to their weaponry, circling it and raising their swords. Cries of the wounded pierced the air, mingling with shouts of rage. Where one rebel fell, two more took their place, blade in hand. In mere seconds, bodies lay scattered along the shore, some still and lifeless while others writhed in pain.

Daimon hovered with Zephyr above the water's edge, calculating to determine what his first command would be. The calm he felt in this moment always accompanied him before a battle. His heart beat swiftly in anticipation, but his mind was quiet. Ready. Zephyr perched them atop a rocky cliff, large enough to spy on the chaos below but covered enough that they weren't spotted. She shifted beneath him, growing restless as the screams intensified.

The rebels fought relentlessly, most of their troops at sea but close to anchoring more to breach land. Their clothing was simple, not even a cheap metal armor to cover them. But one thing they all had in common: they were *furious*, their faces twisted with rage.

Death came swiftly in these battles—enough to make any

male second-guess running into the chaos—but that wasn't why Daimon always paused before entering the fray. It was because his shadows seemed to hum in anticipation every time he was close to a rebel, a reminder of the same darkness inside him.

Zephyr stretched her wings out, sending a shot of restlessness into Daimon's chest.

"The fleet is almost here," Daimon soothed, then, quieter, said, "Come on, just hold on a little longer." He could feel them, and from the way Zephyr kept glancing behind them, he knew she felt their nearness, too.

They were the Alpha Fleet, the head aerial legion he commanded. He was in charge of ten beta fleets, most of them closer to the palace, but this was his pride. The finest weapon of the Valon Empire. And the closest thing to family he'd ever had.

Early in the war, the fleet didn't have a solid strategy. Whoever made it first to the battle would charge in to save as many as they could. Without hesitation, they rushed into the fray to keep the enemies at bay until the rest of the unit arrived. Fearless against any opponent. For a time.

Before Graddock.

The ground troops had been held back trying to save those aboard a sinking Valon fleet, leaving Graddock to face the long lines of archers alone. His wyvern was felled, struck alone by at least a hundred arrows. The rest of the fleet arrived just in time to watch their comrade plummet out of the sky, falling into the Andronicus below.

Graddock died with his wyvern in the graveyard beneath the waves.

It was the hardest lesson Daimon had to learn in the early days of the war. Now, they waited for the rest of the unit to arrive, no matter how their instincts screamed to jump into battle. The wind whirred in a loud, unnatural groan, and the clouds grew darker beneath the shadows of soaring Riders. He rolled his neck, cracking it from side to side. Zephyr stretched her wings out, preparing for action.

His flight had arrived.

Vero—Brielle's wyvern—was the first beast to descend from the clouds, a solid wall of leathery muscle and the biggest of the flight. The rest of the unit quickly emerged from the misty white clouds, their wings swirling the air around them as they lowered out of the sky.

With a grim look of determination, Daimon patted Zephyr's neck and said, "Wings up, Z."

She shot into the sky, eager to join her fleet. Brielle guided Vero over to settle on Daimon's right, her cropped hair covered by a wyvern-scale helmet that formed into a sharp point down the middle of her nose.

Keir, leader of the Aegis, joined just behind Daimon on his left on the wings of Codax. Keir was brash, ready to fight at every breath. He was Daimon's third, ready to listen to his every word.

"Ranick and Elias, take the beach to help any of the wounded," Daimon barked over the wind, and then turned to his left. "Keir and Willow, take air above the reef as the naval units roll in."

"Yes, Commander!" the four shouted as they broke apart from formation, diving downward in pairs of two as they always did.

Always watch your partner's back—those were the rules.

"Aster and Brielle, you're with me."

Aster nodded as he pulled up on the other side of Daimon, lowering his black gaze to the scene of destruction below.

"Heard," affirmed Brielle.

The trio nose-dived off the cliff, soaring above the waves toward the beach. He glanced at Aster. The usually steady Undine was wide-eyed—frantic. The rebels making it past the border shook them all, but these were his people. Daimon felt for him, but he couldn't afford any of his Riders going into battle unprepared.

"Focus!" he yelled. "We don't save anyone if we're distracted."

Aster and Brielle closed in tighter, prepared to follow Daimon into any terror. Daimon cataloged everything he could see in the blur of motion happening beneath him, trying to look for an opening.

The rebels had docked several cannons on land while the rest were protected in small cutouts on the sides of their ships. Their weapons were not to be underestimated, but their position wasn't great. With the Valon fleet to the west and the ground troops of Drogheda coming from the east, they were caged in, both by sea and sand.

Still, they needed to be taken out quickly if they wanted to win this. The Valon soldiers were far more skilled than the rebels, but they were no match against the might of their cannons, which wiped out the fae in large clusters, forcing the wounded to retreat and give up their position. If they could just remove the cannons from the battle, they could force the rebels to retreat.

He focused his attention on the cannon closest to him, currently being loaded. His pulse increased as he realized it was covered in dark runes. There was no way of knowing the power it was capable of if it was cursed. Daimon raced for it, praying Zephyr would be quick enough.

A loud crack split the air, and the side of one of their ships was quickly blown to bits. It groaned loudly as it collapsed against the shore. More screams followed; a few Undine manipulating the water at the stern were caught in the blast, their bodies torn apart from the impact. Wood splintered into a thousand pieces as those aboard scrambled to abandon it.

Zephyr swooped down, closing her talons over the barrel of the cannon and dragging it off the ground. Rebels attempting to protect it were forced back, diving and covering their heads as wood splintered off in all directions. Daimon steered his wyvern back over the sea, relieved to hear the heavy splash of the weapon sinking into the depths of the Andronicus.

A line of rebel archers stepped forward, sending a flurry of arrows into the skies. Zephyr flew higher, her wings beating rapidly against the air as the weapons soared beneath them. Many of the arrows found their targets if Daimon counted by screams alone, but it did little to slow the cannonfire. The second a rebel ship docked, they flocked to the cannons.

Aster and Brielle spread out beside him. "At least fifteen more cannons left!" Aster shouted.

"They're all marked with dark runes, Daimon," Brielle added.

He ground his teeth together. "It's starting," he growled.

Whatever curses the humans tied to their weapons were affecting everyone's magic, likely drawing on any Essence it could find to fuel itself. These were the times Daimon worried most about the outcome of a battle—when their magic felt dampened, weaker. It wasn't just the curses maximizing the weapons' damage; it also severely weakened any fae's magic in the vicinity. Between that and the rebels' overwhelming numbers, it made the battles longer—more deadly.

"Use your Essence sparingly and keep close to our soldiers. Most of them will be relying on their blades until this is over."

If Daimon didn't hate the traitors so much, he could almost admire the idea. All they had to do was set the curse. Then, once they got around fae, it would latch onto their magic like a leech draining them dry—their own Essence became their enemy.

But they paid a hefty price. The humans among the rebel forces couldn't withstand using Essence; they had to martyr themselves with each weapon they bound in darkness. Even with the fae on their side, it wouldn't be enough for the constant stream of dark objects they used in combat. Moros tricked the humans into believing in his power, and many died in the glory of his mission. But not all who fought were his followers. With the fae magic depleted, the lands south had grown fallow.

Joining the rebellion was for some the only way to get rations for themselves and their families.

Daimon could feel it now, like a chain was wrapped around his chest, squeezing him—choking him. He glanced over his shoulder at Brielle, noting the way the fire in her hand flickered against the wind.

They needed to find a way to end this. Quickly. Or they were going to lose.

THREE

DAIMON

THE TRIO CIRCLED BACK AROUND TO THE BEACH JUST AS the naval forces made it to land. They were already drawing their swords, reserving their Essence for various shields instead of using it for offense.

Aegis formed walls of flames around themselves, while Undine pulled from the sea to keep a torrent of water circling them. They were outnumbered three to one, leaving the battle a race against time as their magic waned.

Zephyr dove, her talons aimed at another cannon resting on the edge of the rebels' lines.

"On your left!" Brielle shouted from behind.

Zephyr flanked right, narrowly missing. Aster grunted in frustration, swooping down to the beach below. Brielle immediately followed him, the pair skimming along the surface of the sand. Even with their magic weakened, they still had their wyverns.

Brielle let Vero eat everything in his path. His jaws were brutal, mouth open as he tore apart three rebels at once. Aster and his wyvern did the same, careful to avoid the iron spears being thrown at them from the ground.

The rebels had reacted quickly to the wyverns, forming a line of archers around each cannon. They only had small windows for attack now with the number of arrows being shot at them, rotating between swooping down and then shooting high into the air to avoid getting hit. The rebels' numbers were beginning to thin, but the Valon soldiers were slowing with their dampened Essence.

A cannon close beneath Daimon rotated, aiming at one of the Valon ships still full of people. The rebel ships had blocked most of the beach, leaving them stranded in the water; those escaping were forced to swim in plain sight toward the shore. He called on his shadows, but felt the hold on his magic tighten. Not enough to stop him from using it, but enough that he didn't trust it to get the job done.

"Looks like it's your show today, Z," Daimon shouted, feeling his stomach bottom out as Zephyr dove to the ground again.

With her wings tucked in tightly to her sides, they were freefalling, hurtling toward the ground so quickly that the group of rebels manning the cannon beneath didn't see them coming until her teeth were clamped around their necks, eating them one by one.

The closer Daimon got, the more he realized they weren't all human. Some of them were fae, fighting against their own kind. More and more seemed to be aiding the rebellion these days, dark god worshippers enticed by Moros's vengeful message.

The traitors hurled various types of magic their way—fire blasts, raining rocks, tidal gusts of water—but it all bounced off the wyverns' scales. They were creatures of war for a reason.

Daimon ducked down so hard he cut his chin along Zephyr's scales, narrowly dodging an iron-tipped arrow.

It was the Rider who was at risk.

Aster went for another cannon from behind, so Daimon pulled Zephyr across their line of vision to distract the rebels pressing in. A new rank of soldiers flooded in around the cannon, barely casting a glance at the bloodshed Zephyr left behind. They loaded the massive weapon up with a lump of iron the size of Zephyr's head and aimed it at them.

The crack of the cannon sounded and they dove down, all the way to the tips of the waves. Water sprayed onto Daimon's face as Zephyr's wings brushed against the sea, just in time for the iron missile to soar safely over them. He heard the crunch of bones and wood and briefly glanced at where the weapon *used* to be just as Aster's wyvern, Ryug, finished off the next cannon.

Daimon assessed the scene. Along the beach, he caught a flash of a familiar face framed with chin-length sandy hair. He was clothed in a white linen shirt and light brown trousers. The shirt had an image of the Mother Tree sewn into the front and back of it—the sign of a healer. He was swimming out to the wounded still in the water and dragging them onto the beach, one by one. Even from his height, Daimon could see the healer's hands shaking. He shouldn't be out in the open alone, not with how unprotected the area was. This was why they had their codes. Riders went in pairs and waited for their fleet. Healers were meant to seek protection behind the front line. If they couldn't find protection, they were supposed to flee.

It might have seemed cowardly to some, but it was common sense. A coward could do more than a dead man could.

A flash caught Daimon's eye; two rebels had spotted the healer and were heading straight for him. Jarrett was a brilliant trauma healer who'd accompanied the Alpha Fleet in multiple battles. Still, he wouldn't be able to fight two rebels at once.

Daimon's eyes flicked to where Keir and Willow were flying over the rebels' ships, their wyverns shredding the sails with their talons while Undine from another ship pushed the rebels further out to sea. The cannons were slowly dwindling, swinging the momentum in the direction of the empire.

Just as the two soldiers reached the healer, Daimon made his decision.

"Go to Jarrett!" he shouted to Zephyr, and her head snapped around.

Jarrett's head twisted up, his eyes finding the rebels charging him. He scrambled to his feet and drew a sword.

Daimon and Zephyr raced above the shoreline, but the rebels got to Jarrett before they did. One of them lifted a shimmering sword and swiped it along his stomach. Jarrett spun, clutching his abdomen and raising his sword just as the other rebel brought theirs down.

Jarrett was barely holding on, his white healer's shirt blooming with blood. Just as the rebel raised his arm for the final blow, an Aegis came from behind, his sword driving through the rebel's chest. The other rebel screamed—her grotesque screech sounded like that of a dying sea creature. The cry abruptly ended when Zephyr ripped her head from her body.

Jarrett looked up and nodded, his gaze filled with appreciation. But the moment his eyes met Daimon's, his body fell to the ground. Blood pooled around him, the waves washing it away as quickly as it seeped out.

The Aegis fighting with him kneeled beside him.

A healer's life never should've been lost—not when their goal was to save, not kill.

Daimon gritted his teeth and turned his attention back to the battle. Death waited for no one, and if he had any hope of keeping the rest of his people alive, he had to keep going. He learned he had to move ahead or more lives could be lost.

Aster and Brielle had taken out several more cannons, leaving only three. He hadn't seen Ranick or Elias the entire time, which was either a very good thing or a very bad thing. If they were able to get a few of their wounded to safety, then that was good. If they weren't seen because they weren't *alive* to help—

Zephyr flung herself to the right, nearly tossing Daimon off her back as an iron spear shot past them. He shook his head and focused on the task of getting rid of the rest of the cannons as Zephyr leveled them back out.

His team was made up of only the best Riders; they could handle themselves.

Brielle flanked Daimon, her chest heaving as she said, "Keir and Willow took care of the last of the rebel ships." Daimon looked to confirm, seeing downed rebel ships and tattered sails hanging from the talons of wyverns flying above. "They're working their way toward us now."

Aster flew in close to his other side, rejoining them.

Daimon nodded and leaned forward. "Then we make our final push. Brielle, flank right; Aster, take the left."

They broke away from him while he took the middle. Aster would take on the mostly unmanned cannon half-sunk in the sand, while Brielle would target the one more securely placed on the rocks, shooting cannonfire into the ground soldiers. It was heavily guarded, but he wasn't worried. Brielle was his second for a reason.

That left the last to him. It was the largest and deadliest, the last of the rebels mostly abandoning their other pursuits to protect it. Every one of their archers had returned to its side.

The Aegis ground commander from before was yelling out commands beneath him. The rebel archers surrounded them, shooting iron-tipped arrows in relentless waves. Daimon waited for the Aegis to retreat, preparing to dive in.

But before Daimon could get to the next cannon, the Aegis general charged.

His swings were quick—confident. Three more Aegis closed in from the other side, taking several of the archers down and distracting the others.

It was enough to buy Zephyr time to yank the weapon off the ground, joining Brielle and Aster in the sky as they raced to the sea, tossing the final of the cursed cannons into the heart of the Andronicus.

Just as the cannons sank below the water, Keir and Willow came into view in front of them, sweeping across the last of the rebels, who had quickly turned their backs in retreat, sprinting toward the Zenovia Mountains. Willow was bleeding profusely from her shoulder, and Keir's wyvern had one of his legs tucked into his body.

It was over—for now. The traitors were defeated, but it took far longer than Daimon would've liked.

He brought Zephyr to the ground, slipped off, and jogged toward the Aegis commander. He could already feel the dampening on his magic lifting. But he was one of the fortunate ones. For some of the others with weaker Essence, it would take days, sometimes a week, for the magic to return.

The Aegis commander stood straight, his eyes blazing. "We had no chance against the cannons. If your flight hadn't been here, who knows how this would've ended."

Daimon looked at the scattered bodies of their enemy, and they looked so…normal. He knew he'd have the gruesome task of searching their remains, looking for any helpful information.

The Aegis's gaze dropped to the bodies too. Waves lapped at their feet, causing their boots to sink into the sand. Further along the beach, somewhere, was Jarrett's body—soon to be swept away. The Aegis frowned, his face splattered with blood, covering the scar that stretched from eye to jaw. "He was a brave healer to go out into battle."

Daimon nodded tightly. "He was a good man." He had become so hardened to tragedy that such deaths no longer moved him. A brave healer wasn't what they needed—bravery wasn't worth anything against forces as dark as Moros's. They needed order against their chaos.

"Cyprian," the Aegis said, sticking his hand out and breaking the mounting tension. "It was an honor to fight with you, Rider."

Daimon clasped his arm. "Daimon," he replied. "Commander of the aerial legion."

Cyprian smiled, the scar stretching across his face. "I know." His eyes flicked to where Zephyr stood behind Daimon, but it wasn't fear in his gaze. It was awe.

The whirring in Daimon's ears finally stopped, his pulse quieting enough to hear the cries of pain from the wounded.

The pair walked down the beach, joining the aerial fleet and other ground soldiers. They searched the bodies. Though he found nothing new, Daimon couldn't shake the feeling that this was only the start of something. They were too close to losing today, much closer than he was comfortable with.

The fae rules of war protected healers from the heat of battle, but the human rebels didn't honor the same code. He saw that today with Jarrett.

The closer the rebels pushed past the border, the closer they made it to the palace. And Daimon was trying—but failing—not to think about Evelina being in their crossfire.

It left him feeling hollow after a fight, like each step forward was three steps back.

He watched as the ground soldiers pulled the remains of those who had been killed by the cannons from the wreckage in the water, their faces unrecognizable. After all this time, it was still hard to say the end of a battle was a win. The loss was always there.

The rebels were different this time, stronger—it would've been a lot of effort to curse the number of cannons they had brought. Their aura was sickeningly dark.

When a life was ended, their souls passed into Caelum. But where did *these* demons go? Daimon could only hope they were sent back to the pits of darkness from which they had crawled out. If it was by his hand, even better.

FOUR

EVELINA

EVELINA WASN'T A STRANGER TO HEARTACHE. WAR HAD made her more accustomed to death and pain than most fae her age were used to dealing with. The Valon Empire wasn't perfect, but it was a place of wonder and peace—until the rebels decided to taint the land with their chaos and destruction.

Gloriana burst into the infirmary, nearly causing Evelina to drop the two tonic jars in her hands. "The rebels attacked the grove."

Breathless and frantic, she started stuffing herbs and tonics into a leather crossbody bag. Evelina quickly reshelved the jars and joined her in packing. Her heart was racing as they slung their bags over their shoulders.

Lorene hurried into the room next, his chest rapidly expanding. He pushed his light brown hair out of his eyes and said, "We don't have time to wait on the other healers. We need to go now."

Gloriana nodded, briefly glancing at Evelina.

"I'm going," Evelina said before Gloriana could say otherwise. Just because she was a princess didn't mean she was going to stay behind. "You could use the extra hands; we don't know what we're walking into."

Gloriana only hesitated a moment before slinging her bag across her chest. "Follow our lead and keep your eyes on your surroundings."

The three of them rushed outside to the stables. They saddled their horses and rode as fast as they could. An attack on the grove was the closest attack to the palace yet.

Evelina had been to the refugee camps countless times, but she had never been to the actual scene of a battle before. Her heart thundered as quickly as the trees zipping by. The horses' hooves pounded against the ground, loud enough to rival the piercing bells that rang their warning of the attack.

As they approached the grove, the horses skidded to a stop, dirt flying from the ground. They heard the screaming first. Shouts of panic and soldiers ordering people to clear out. The moment they got close enough to see through the trees, Evelina's blood drained from her face.

An Aegis close to them spun around, his eyes wide. He rushed toward them and said, "The rebels left the moment we got here. There's two that need help but—" A piercing cry came from the forest behind him, cutting him off. The soldier swallowed. "I don't know if anything can be done for them."

Lorena slid off his horse, nodding. "Take us to the wounded."

A flurry of motion disturbed the grove. Trees were singed and smoking, creating a thick fog that settled over the forest like a blanket. Undine frantically put out fires, while Nox bent down to check the fallen dream orbs and Aegis set up a safety perimeter.

Evelina's jars clinked together in her bag as they followed the Aegis soldier to the wounded. They skidded to a halt, finding two Nox lying beneath a tree.

Lorene and Gloriana dropped to the ground, quickly assessing them.

The sound of flapping wings descended from the skies, and

Evelina glanced up, overwhelmed. The trees were too thick to see more than a blur as they passed.

"Beta Fleet Six and Nine just arrived." A soldier ran up, his chest heaving as he reported to the Aegis.

"Are there any more wounded?" asked Gloriana, an odd look on her face.

The Aegis shook his head. "They were alone when the rebels came."

"We've got this," Lorene said without looking up. "Go."

The Aegis nodded sharply, casting a final glance at the two fae lying on the ground in front of them. Lorene paused, his hands folded together in front of him. He wasn't moving, wasn't reaching for any tonics or cloths for mending. He was a skilled healer; he should be doing *something*.

Evelina rushed over to him and Gloriana, dropping to the ground beside them. "What's needed?" she asked. She started on the wounded fae closest to her, her eyes drawn to a large pool of blood beside their shoulder.

"Evelina," Lorene said gently.

She turned to look at him, her eyes wide. "Lorene, why aren't you—"

Gloriana rested an arm on her shoulder, crouching down on the other side of her. "They're already gone," she said gently.

Evelina examined them, refusing to believe it. But their chests weren't rising and falling; their eyes were open and unmoving. Still, it wasn't until she placed her finger on the inside of their wrists that she believed they were gone. No pulse, no signs of life.

"There's nothing we could've done," Lorene said gently. "They're in Caelum now."

They walked back to their horses, a flurry of people still moving around them. Evelina had seen death before, had lost refugees who'd shown up with wounds beyond fixing. But the wounded at the refugee camps had always been survivors, people who had been brought to her. This was her first time being too late, her first time seeing all the ones left behind—the ones who never made it to her door.

As Evelina was saddling back on her horse, she heard a group of soldiers recounting the attack.

"They came out of nowhere," one said.

"If they can attack here, they can attack anywhere," another said with a rising panic.

Evelina closed her eyes, focusing on the feel of her horse beneath her, the smooth, spotted coat and coarse mane. She opened her eyes, feeling a little steadier.

"We were lucky it was only two," a third said.

Only two. That was two more who didn't deserve to die. Two was too many.

Every death cut into her like a dagger slowly twisting into her heart. She felt every soul they lost, every family that was left behind to pick up the pieces without their loved ones. The children who lost parents, the siblings who lost their sisters and brothers. It wasn't fair—wasn't right. Panic filled her chest, and her breathing started to come out in small gasps.

This was when her stress would become too much to bear. When her knowledge of healing would be of no use, because the patient was too far gone. She felt focused when she had a task to do, more in control. She had to find a moment to grieve for her people alone.

Her arms wrapped tightly around her waist as she counted the trees they passed. She didn't stop until she reached one hundred and ten—when her breathing evened out and her heart didn't squeeze as tightly.

Gloriana occasionally looked over at her, her eyes filled with worry. But a healer knew loss. It might not lessen the weight of each one, but they all knew it nonetheless.

FIVE

EVELINA

SHE PLANTED HER SEEDS BENEATH THE OAK TREE, ONE FOR each who had died.

Today, she didn't linger. Instead, she floated through the small lunaria garden in Lilium Glade. Their silvery coin-like pods glowed against the setting sun.

She sat on the ground in the center of the shimmering plants. The tallest ones were higher than her head and left her tucked away in the safety of nature, hidden away from the world.

The glade made her think of Daimon, of all the times she hid away here with him. She hadn't seen him since they were children, and now could pass right by him, not realizing it was him.

Of course, she didn't know what she would say even if she *did* see him.

She grieved in silence and focused on a game she'd always played. Daimon had taught it to her when they were children— for when she needed an escape. It wasn't a complex, thought-provoking game. But she could play it anywhere, anytime.

. . .

"A game of pretend," he said one night. Carwyn had just scolded Evelina for wearing the wrong shoes again. "For when I'm not here to give you a dream."

"Isn't that just daydreaming?" Evelina countered with a raised brow, but it was her eyes that gave her away. The glimmer of interest that came to life in her gaze when he was near.

"This is just for us," he said with a grin, his hair long and mussed from running around Nox Grove all morning. "Something no one else can have."

Evelina opened her eyes, flustered by the memory.

Letting her mind wander to these things was easier than thinking about the deaths of those she couldn't save. Easier than knowing the rebels were getting closer to the palace. With her family being targeted and her people killed, the thought of the rebels growing stronger was terrifying.

"I know you're here, Evelina." Annora's light and gentle voice called into the garden.

Evelina could already hear the soft pad of boots against the dirt. Flowers rustled and shook, disturbing some of the butterflies that had stopped to rest on them. Annora's bright eyes and slender frame appeared. She sat down in front of Evelina, and her hands fidgeted, her fingers tapping against her black gown. Silver stitching had been woven into swirls across the skirt.

"Did you hear about the attack?" Annora whispered.

Evelina reached out and grabbed her hand. "I went with Gloriana and Lorene. We tried to—" She took a deep breath. "I'm so sorry we couldn't save them."

And she was. Sorry that no progress had been made, that the war was dragging on for so long, and for all the lives lost.

Annora gripped her hand back as fiercely as Evelina held hers. They sat in silence together, not needing to fill the quiet with small talk. What was left to say?

Instead, they sat in the comfort of each other. Together in their grief and frustration.

Annora pulled her knees to her chest and picked at a blade of grass. Evelina watched her quietly.

"I'm starting to get why you and Daimon always came here as kids." Annora gestured to the flowers around them. "I forget how quiet the world can be sometimes."

There were other larger and more ornate gardens in the glade. This one was small—forgotten. But for them, it was a place of hope and tranquility, without worry or interruption.

"Evelina, I need your help," Annora said abruptly.

Evelina immediately nodded her head. "Anything."

Annora took a deep breath. She was never one to shy away from being honest or saying something that would make others uncomfortable—that was one of the reasons Evelina trusted her so much.

"The autumn equinox is tomorrow night," Annora whispered.

Evelina nodded again. The autumn equinox was sacred. Cherished. It was the night soulbonding ceremonies were held— when two mates decided to accept the soulbond.

Annora looked down to the ground, her fingers picking apart blades of grass into tiny pieces. "The war has been stalling for years now," she continued. "No side is making any real gains. And with each battle, we lose someone."

Evelina nodded. She knew all of these things but didn't understand what it had to do with the equinox. "We've lost a lot of lives—too many," she agreed.

"Exactly!" Annora threw her hands into the air. "We're immortal to the natural aging process, and yet we've been to more luxes than the average human."

Evelina missed the time when years would go by without a lux, without having to attend the celebration of a fae passing onto Caelum. There had never been a time where more fae passed than humans—not until the war.

Annora reached forward and gripped Evelina's hand. "While our lives may not be short, they are numbered," she said softly. "And that's why I need your help."

Evelina's gaze shot back to Annora, and she found determination across her friend's face. She knew that look; it was one she'd seen Annora use on countless fae.

"I've been keeping a secret from you," she whispered. "About Aldric."

The corners of Evelina's mouth twitched upward. She'd been watching Annora and Aldric sneak around for nearly a year now. She'd noticed the way their eyes sought each other out the moment they entered the same room, how they found small excuses to touch each other, and how his eyes never left her.

And then everything Annora had been saying clicked into place.

This time, Evelina did smile. The first real one in a week. In this desolate, war-ridden land, her friend had found happiness— had found the purest form of love.

"You're going to bond with him." Evelina's chest warmed, the heaviness against it briefly lifting.

Annora's eyes widened. "Yes," she breathed out. "You knew?"

Evelina laughed, her joy mixing with her tears. "I saw you two in the Radix Room, way up at the top of the Mother Tree."

"But we haven't been to the Mother Tree in months..." Realization cut across Annora's face. "You've known this long?"

Evelina shrugged. "I knew you would tell me when you were ready." She gave Annora a comforting smile, one that said she understood why her friend kept it to herself. Then she raised a brow, a soft smile still tilting her lips up. "So I'm guessing you need my blood to get you in."

All of those with Manor blood had access to the Celestial Temple, where bonding ceremonies took place. She and her siblings took turns helping with the ceremonies at each equinox. Queen Embry would often be there, just to be near her people during such a sacred ritual. Evelina had just had her rotation during the most recent spring equinox. She could remember the fae coming to the doors of the temple, unable to stop themselves from touching their mates even in the presence of others.

But Annora's parents—as lovely as they were—would never approve of their daughter bonding with Aldric. The stories of those who chose the wrong fae—thinking they were their bonded when they weren't—haunted every forest, village, and fae alike.

To go before Eurydice on the night of the equinox and try to bond one's soul with the wrong person led to forever being separated from one's true mate. There was only one chance to get it right, and it was partly why fae couples often chose to not bond.

"But more than that, I need my friend there," Annora said quietly, the tips of her ears tinged pink.

There were days Annora felt more like family to Evelina than her own siblings. She loved her siblings deeply, but Annora was someone she *chose* to be her family.

Evelina lurched forward and gathered Annora into a hug. Annora squeezed her back, both of them laughing and crying.

"I'm so happy for you," Evelina said through the tears.

"It pains me to do this behind their backs, but my parents would never let me risk it," Annora said softly, pulling back from Evelina. "They can't break a soulbond once the ceremony is complete. And I need Aldric like I need air. My body sings when he's around, and my heart is already his. He's the other half to my soul." Her voice broke.

Evelina gave her a reassuring smile, but Annora didn't smile back. She had a contemplative look on her face. As sacred as this ceremony was—happiness in its purest form—Annora's eyes were heavy, sad. A cool wind swept through the glade, rustling the flowers around them.

"I'll do it," Evelina promised. "Of course, I'll do it."

"I never would've thought I would be lucky enough to find my soulbonded," Annora whispered.

Truthfully, Evelina understood Annora's parents' fears. But

she found it easy to trust in Aldric and Annora's connection, because she knew the feeling too. That absolute certainty that stilled all the worry and stress, a love like the lunaria flowers that hid them away now in safe protection.

She and Annora sat in the glade the rest of the evening, reminiscing on their childhood and all that had changed. Their conversation was a mixture of sadness and joy. They talked until they both felt a little less empty inside.

A hollow ringing bounced in her mind, the memory of the grove still haunting her. She could still hear the warning bells piercing the air. Each time the Riders sang their cries of battle in the sky, Evelina's heart would thrash in her chest. When she heard that awful warning, her mind drifted to a certain aerial commander, wondering if he would be racing into battles of his own.

Six

Daimon

Blades clanged against one another in constant opposition as Daimon walked through the camp. Though the fae had their Essence, Keir ordered everyone to learn how to wield weapons too. If one's magic was drained in the middle of a fight, then they would need to know how to use a sword.

Zephyr flew above him, landing behind the cabin, over which a large cavern loomed. It only took them the first few nights of being bonded to realize they had to build their cabin where the wyverns could sleep close by. The creatures were fiercely protective, needing to be close to their Rider. But if Daimon were honest, he couldn't stand being far from her for very long either.

All seven of the wyverns huddled beneath the rock cliff, sleeping on top of one another even though there was plenty of space for them to spread out. Hills and rocky cliffs surrounded the camp, resting on an outer valley before the larger slopes, on the outskirts of the Zenovia Mountains, so they used this as their base. It was a short enough flight from the palace that they could go back and forth easily while still maintaining patrols on the border.

Daimon walked into the fleet's cabin, his shoulders slumped.

It was times like these that he missed privacy. *Why* did it have to be his idea for his unit to share a cabin? At first, it was just a way for them to bond as a team, but then it turned into something more. Something stronger. And here they were years later, still sleeping under the same roof.

Well, slightly the same roof, since Willow and Aster built an entire new wing of the cabin to make more room. No one wanted to have a room next to those two; they'd be kept up all night.

Brielle was studying a map spread across a small wooden table. Aster was beside her, drawing with charcoal.

"Ranick and Elias just started their watch on the glade's border," Brielle said without looking up. "We'll be lucky if they manage to stay out of trouble."

Aster grunted his agreement, scribbling away on the yellowed parchment. His snow-colored hair was pulled back into a knot at the nape of his neck, strands loosened and falling into his face as he sketched.

Daimon plopped down on a worn, cushioned chair. He stared out an open window at the snowcapped mountains glinting in the clear evening. Heaviness sat against his chest, as it always did following a battle. Visions played in his mind: the cannons destroying their ships, his people being blown into pieces, spears piercing their chests before he could save them. Loss was inevitable, but he still replayed every detail he could remember.

"They had twice as many cursed weapons as they normally do," Aster said, pulling Daimon back to the present. He stopped sketching to give Daimon a pointed look. "We did the best we could given the cannons, too."

Daimon glanced back at him. Aster was one of the quieter of the flight, the only Undine among them and somehow drawn to the only Woodland. Within a week of the flight forming, Aster and Willow were attached at the hip. Not long after, they ventured back to the temple during the spring equinox to be bonded.

"They would've had to in order for them to break past the fleets," Daimon said with a sigh. "They never should've been able to do that."

"Something was different in the way they fought today," Brielle mused. "Perhaps the curses they cast on the weapons are starting to do more damage to them than harm to us. Warping them somehow."

The best-case scenario would be that their own weapons worked against them, but thinking about the ships that had been hit and the scattered bodies... It felt as if they did plenty of damage.

"We know Moros is willing to grapple at anything for power, no matter how corrupt the means to get there is," Daimon said slowly. "I'll send a messenger to the palace."

Daimon spent the rest of the afternoon listening to Aster scribble on his paper and bouncing ideas of new rotations off Brielle. It slowly developed into a more relaxing evening, a reprieve from the weight of the attack.

But more than anything, it felt like the calm before the deadliest of storms.

The entry door rattled as it opened, and Keir stepped in. His eyes were red with lack of sleep and his brows were pinched tightly together. Daimon leaned forward in the chair, propping his elbows on his knees as Keir paced in front of them.

"The rebels attacked Nox Grove," Keir rushed out. "This morning, right around the attack on the edge of Drogheda. Beta Fleet Two brought word that they were after the orbs."

"They've never made a move so close to the palace." Brielle gasped. "And at the same time as the other attack?"

Daimon stood and walked over to the frost-tinted animal pelt that was fitted over the shutter. The mountains looked peaceful from this distance, stoic and ancient. Half the time, he wondered if their presence helped keep the rebels out, or if it kept them *in*. The attacks happening simultaneously couldn't have been a coincidence, and that worried Damion more than anything.

Keir blew out a deep breath. "I need you to investigate the grove while I go to the palace."

Daimon had known this was coming, but the confirmation still made his pulse race. It had been so long since he had gone that close to the palace. Since he had been so close to Evelina.

"Then we better pack," Daimon answered tightly and turned away from the shutter. He nodded to Brielle and added, "Care for a trip to the grove?"

Brielle smiled and placed a fist over her heart.

He looked to Aster next. "Keep the rest of the flight in line while we're gone."

Aster gave a curt nod.

They packed quickly, using sacks that could be secured onto their backs. Once they were done, they found Ren waiting for them outside, a bag over his shoulder. Ren was one of the Manor heirs, the responsibilities of which he often liked to avoid. Daimon knew Ren had been stationed on the western coast, not far from camp, but it still sent a ripple of shock through his body to see the heir standing in front of him.

Ren's sandy-colored hair was lighter than Evelina's, but his eyes were the same mixture of green and brown as hers. So much so that it took Daimon's breath away. But his eyes weren't filled with the same wonder.

Daimon silently shook himself, trying to get it together.

"It's been a while," he said roughly.

"Too long." Ren looked just as uncomfortable, even regretful. "I'm on the western coast now."

"I know." Daimon still hung on to every whisper of Manor news, anxious for the day Evelina would find her future consort. But he sighed, resigned to go face it in person this time.

Daimon closed his eyes and pulled on the connection deep in his chest. He could feel her within him, always beside his heart no matter how far she was. The moment he tugged at their bond, he could hear her wings shifting from behind the cabin.

The sound of wings beating in the air came before she did. Ren shifted on his feet when he heard them. Anyone who wasn't a Rider tended to be uncomfortable in the presence of wyverns. They weren't trusting creatures—monsters of the night that gave their trust over to a singular person. Their Rider.

Ren shuffled his feet again, his eyes darting nervously to the sky. "I'll see you when we get back—"

"You're riding with us," Daimon interrupted. "There's no use in traveling by ship when you can get back in a day."

Ren opened his mouth to protest, but froze when a dark mass broke through the clouds. Zephyr flew over the cabin, her dark scales shimmering against the sun. For a moment, she hovered above them as she flapped her wings and sent dust flying into the air. Ren coughed and took a step back, careful not to be too close to Daimon when she landed. Slowly, she descended from the sky. Then, with a heavy thud, she slammed into the dirt, stretching her leathery wings out before tucking them into her sides.

Daimon smiled as the golden-eyed wyvern looked him over.

"I'm fine, Zephyr," he assured her.

She huffed, unimpressed, the hot air from her nose sending a new wave of dust into the air.

"Mother hen," he muttered, but he couldn't help the smile that tugged at his lips. "The edge of Viridian was attacked, right near Nox Grove." He gestured to Ren. "He's coming with."

"I'm not getting back on one of those." Ren took a step back, his eyes wide and hands raised as he sputtered out another protest. "I can ride a horse—"

"And you'll get there long after we're done if you do that," Daimon said. "Come on." In one swift movement, he mounted Zephyr and patted her neck. Zephyr turned her massive head to Ren, her blazing eyes set on him.

Ren swallowed thickly. "Fine," he relented.

Daimon nodded, watching with faint amusement as Ren moved much slower than necessary to climb onto Zephyr's back. Just as they got settled, another wyvern descended from the sky. Vero landed beside them, his eyes immediately focusing on Brielle. The beast stretched his head out toward her, a light clicking noise coming from the back of his throat. Brielle ran her hand along his jaw and rested her forehead against his.

"Ready for a ride?" she said to him, and Vero dutifully stretched out his wings and lowered himself to the ground so she could climb up.

They said their goodbyes to Aster, asking him to fill in the rest of the flight when they returned from patrol.

As Zephyr took to the skies, Daimon thought back on memories he tended to keep locked away. Memories that he preferred to hide in a box and toss into the Andronicus rather than revisit.

He hadn't been to Viridian in *years*, and even the faces that resided there had faded in his memory. But it was still his home, his origin. Even if he didn't have any blood family there anymore, it was still his. And a part of his heart would always be there.

Every flap of Zephyr's wings took him closer to Nox Grove. Before he'd left, he'd never imagined growing so far apart from Evelina. Not when she was his best friend; not when seeing her smile became the reason he climbed out of bed each morning.

But that was before everything went to shit.

SEVEN

DAIMON

DAIMON WAS SILENT AS ZEPHYR FLEW THEM CLOSER AND closer to Nox Grove, the night sky shining with the moon and stars above them. With each flap of Zephyr's wings, Daimon felt the growing sense of unease weighing against his chest.

"Will it be strange for you to be back after this long?" Ren broke the silence.

Daimon wanted to say, *Yes, because your sister most definitely hates me for not returning in twenty years, and she may try to stab me in my sleep, even if she is a healer.*

Instead, he said, "It'll be an adjustment."

Ren snorted.

"The rebels have gotten smarter with every passing year, even if the others don't want to accept it. I think they're trying to run us dry," Daimon mused before Ren could ask him any more questions. "Like tiny cuts all over the body to make us lose just a little bit of blood each time, and by the end, we won't even have realized we've been fully drained."

Clouds filled the sky, giving them coverage from anything that might lurk on the ground.

"They have to be just as tired as us," Ren said. "Even if there are three times as many of them as there are us, we have wyverns and stronger magic."

Daimon tightened his hand into a fist and held it until his nails bit into his skin. "And still we haven't been able to rid our land of them." He placed his palm against Zephyr, her scales rough and warm.

"You don't think they can keep up the curses forever, do you?" Ren asked, his brows bunched together. "It has to be running the rebel humans into madness by now. They can't sustain themselves using dark magic."

Daimon didn't have an answer for that. He thought back to the battle at Drogheda. They didn't seem diminished; if anything, they seemed more empowered the darker their magic grew. Like they were monsters instead of people.

He shook off the thought. Humans couldn't contain that much dark magic. They'd collapse if they went any further.

"Maybe we'll find something out at the grove."

"Terrifying to think about them getting their hands on the orbs," Ren said with a shudder.

Zephyr took a sharp turn and Ren yelped. He made a noise of distress with every turn she took. But Daimon had a feeling Zephyr was doing it on purpose. Each time Ren would make a noise, a burst of amusement would shoot through their bond.

"You know she's pleased when you show fear," Daimon said with a faint smile.

Ren huffed, crossing his arms. Zephyr flapped her wings, jolting them forward a little faster. Ren's hands flew to hold onto her spikes.

"How do you deal with this thing all mixed up into your emotions?" Ren muttered.

Zephyr banked again, straightening back out once she was satisfied she'd scared Ren again.

Daimon often tried to think about what his life was like before he was bonded to his wyvern. As hard as he tried to remember, there wasn't a day he could imagine not having her emotions entwined with his.

"I'd be careful what you say around her," Daimon said. "She's far smarter than people realize." She purred, the sound more of a growl, but one Daimon could easily distinguish.

Communicating mind-to-mind wasn't all that rare, as it happened among stronger Aegis or soulbonded. But the connection made with a wyvern wasn't *talking*; it was feeling everything they felt, hearing as they heard, seeing as they saw. Only the other Riders could understand the connection that was made with the beast, and there were never enough words to try and explain what it felt like. It simply existed.

"Maybe they'll go back to wherever they go soon," Ren mumbled.

The thought of Zephyr leaving made Daimon's stomach clench. All he knew was the Riders who lost their wyverns—or the wyverns that lost their Riders—were never the same after the loss. To have such a deep connection abruptly severed was something he prayed to the moon goddess he'd never have to experience.

Wyverns were only paired with a Rider in a time of war, and from what little texts there were on their history, they would return to where they came from until called on again. The stories rumored that their retreat into slumber was peaceful, a gentle parting that left the bond to fade over time rather than the way death cut it off.

Still. He didn't want to accept either of those as a possibility.

Zephyr lifted her right wing into the air and caused them to hit a hard left, pulling him from his thoughts.

"Does she have to keep doing that?" Ren groaned.

Daimon's mouth twitched, the closest he got to a smile most days. "You know she's only doing it because she knows you don't like it."

The twisted trees of Nox Grove came into view. Even in the

darkness, the sight of it wiped any traces of the small grin off Daimon's face. This had been home for so long, and it looked the same, but also…different. He no longer recognized the trees or the faces of the Nox present.

Zephyr tilted her nose down and dove out of the sky, landing between two large, crooked trees, the trunks warped from growing at odd angles. She shifted between her legs and tucked her wings in tightly to her sides, a sign Daimon knew well from years of being with her. She was on edge.

He slid off her back, and by the time he landed, Ren had already scrambled off and stopped a few paces away.

"Watch from above while we look through the grove," Daimon said to Zephyr. Her golden eyes flicked to the grove behind him. She studied the area and searched for any possible threats, a flash of defiance radiating from her. "You'll have the best vantage point to warn us if something is coming," he assured her. She let out a huff of frustration and bolted into the sky, a shot of annoyance piercing his chest as she settled above them.

Their journey had only taken a few hours. People were still helping clean the grove, counting orbs and gathering snapped branches.

Daimon turned to Ren, his skin clammy. "You'd think as a Woodland you'd be the most comfortable with creatures," he said with amusement. All of the Manors had a deeply rooted connection to the land and the creatures that roamed it. The crowned ruler especially.

Ren huffed and turned away to walk toward the swarm of fae gathered in the grove. He called over his shoulder, "But my affinity is for nature, not creatures. *Especially* not airborne ones."

Daimon shook his head as Ren stalked off, his gait already stiff from the ride. It made Daimon huff out a laugh devoid of joy. He remembered how his legs would ache when he first learned how to ride. The legion would have to fly for hours, sometimes entire days from sunup to sundown. They had to figure out how to fly not only with their wyvern, but as a unit.

"Check the dream orbs again," a raspy female voice hissed ahead of him, jolting him back to the present. "We need to ensure nothing was missed."

His eyes roamed over the smoldering branches of the grove. The orbs that stored fae dreams were glowing brightly through the haze. Each one of them held a fae's subconscious as they slept, watched over by the Nox in the grove to ensure no beasts or darkness would corrupt the dream.

He hadn't seen them in years. It took his breath away. He stepped closer, seeing familiar faces leaning in close, whispering furiously to one another.

"Maliena," Daimon said. He cleared his throat.

Maliena turned to him, her slender arms folded firmly across her chest. Her black hair was pulled back into a tight knot at the nape of her neck, showing her sharp features. She froze when she saw him, her blue-gray eyes widening. A look of relief passed over her face and his chest warmed.

"You're back," she whispered.

He hadn't seen her in twenty years, the woman who nearly raised him when he had no parents to take care of him as a boy. She knew his mother before she died and, in a way, Maliena was pieces of his mother that he deeply wished he was able to know. He had never met his mother before her soul moved on to Caelum.

In the blink of an eye, Maliena wrapped her arms around him.

"Any updates on what happened?" Daimon asked as she released him. He noted the way the fae beside her shifted on his feet. Neve, her soulbonded. His hair was just as dark as the twisted trees around them, his eyes as brown.

"Nothing was left behind and nothing seems to be out of place," Neve said. "It's good to see you back."

The warmth in Daimon's chest dulled with the icy guilt that

nipped at it. They looked just as they had twenty years ago. He wondered how different he looked to them, having gone from the quiet little moppy-haired Nox boy to a commander clad in wyvern-scale leathers and covered in scars.

If he ever got the chance to rise high enough in the ranks to be considered a council member—the highest regard among the fae—then he would be like them. Kind and fair, calm and wise.

Neve motioned Daimon closer. "They never should've gotten a chance to be this close to the orbs."

"Did we lose anyone?" Daimon's gut twisted as he asked it. Neve was right—the rebels never should've gotten past the border. And there should've been soldiers patrolling here too.

"Saige and Gracelyn were in this part of the grove when they hit," Maliena said with a shake in her voice. "We found their bodies near the entrance."

Daimon waited for more. When the silence stretched, his shoulders sagged in relief. "Only two?"

Maliena cast a wary look at him. It took him a moment too long to realize why. *Only two*—it was insensitive. But only two was a relief when it came to how many lives *could* have been lost. Daimon swallowed the guilt that stabbed his heart at the thought.

"Where were the patrol when they attacked?" he asked.

"We had to send the group south toward the western coast after the attack near the mountains," Neve said, regret thick in his voice. "No one knew how far the rebels would make it. They were spread thin."

Daimon gritted his teeth together as frustration ate at him. Patrols were spread thin for this exact reason, not to be sent away at every distraction. He couldn't lead the Riders *and* tell the ground troops how to do their jobs. How could they have gotten sloppy enough to leave an area unguarded, a weak spot the rebels were able to find?

Especially Nox Grove. There could have been endless reasons for them to attack here. The forest of dreams was precious. Infiltrating a direct link to any number of fae's minds could be disastrous.

"I should've been here," he said through gritted teeth.

Neve placed a large hand on Daimon's shoulder. He was massive, even by fae standards, a lean and muscular male who also happened to be a head taller than the majority of the Aegis.

"You can't be everywhere all at once, Daimon," Neve said gently. His eyes shone with understanding.

A muscle ticked in Daimon's jaw. He broke Neve's gaze, unable to stand the pity in his eyes.

"What about Annora? Is she safe?" Ren asked, returning from a discussion with another Nox.

Daimon knew that their daughter was their entire world. They'd trade their seat on the council in a heartbeat if only to spend more time with her.

"She refused to stay behind when we were told about the attack," Maliena said with a sigh. Her voice was frustrated but resigned. "She wanted to help any way she could."

Daimon remembered Annora as one of the shy council children who always had a quiet strength. He remembered catching her dragging Evelina around the palace, the pair sneaking around together and getting into trouble.

He wondered how much of that remained the same. She was likely as stubborn of an adult as she had been as a youngling. If she wanted to do something, no one could stop her. That's probably why she and Evelina were attached at the hip.

At least, they used to be. He had no way of knowing what they were like anymore.

"Keep an eye on her for us?" Neve asked, pulling Daimon from his thoughts. "We've been pulled in a thousand directions since we got here. She'd be glad to see you again."

Daimon gave a firm nod. "Keir called me back to look into this attack, so my second and I will be here for the time being. I'll have Brielle patrol this area with a beta fleet to make sure the rebels don't decide to come back for another try at the grove."

He glanced up at the sky, barely able to make out Zephyr above them with thick, lingering smoke.

"Thank you, Daimon." Maliena sighed with relief. "I know the legion is stretched thin with patrols, but I'm glad you're back."

He lowered his gaze back to them, his eyes determined as he said, "We do what needs to be done for our people."

EIGHT

DAIMON

DAIMON MOVED THROUGH THE GROVE SOMBERLY. Carvings had been etched into the crooked trees, marks of the rebels. This time, the symbols they'd left showed support only to Vidaris. Flames had been carved into a handful of trunks. Their devotion ran so deep that they *stopped* at some point in their attack and risked getting caught to leave the symbols.

He roughly scratched his jaw, the stubble itchy and hot, studying one of the markings, a jagged outline of flames. He would be expected to brief Keir after he surveyed the area. So, as he examined, he stopped to speak to several witnesses. Mostly Nox, but other races had come to help after hearing about the attack. Most of the stories were the same: they saw flashes of light—fire, he had gathered from another—coming from the trees. Shouts from the two Nox tending to the area were heard before silence followed and the flashes stopped. According to the Nox present, all orbs were still here and accounted for.

The rebels certainly proved a point in making it this close to the palace, but it was odd for them not to make a stand. Up to now, they seemed focused on inflicting the most damage possible. If they weren't looking to make an attack, then what were they after?

None of the stories answered that question, which only spurred on the unease in his gut.

It meant they had gotten what they came for.

Daimon passed through Nox Grove a final time, sweeping the perimeter. He stayed for hours to ensure there wouldn't be any rebels returning to the grove. The deeper he moved into the grove, the thinner the crowd got. He heard a soft voice, familiar and quiet, from a few trees away.

Annora.

A flood of memories he hadn't expected came rushing to the surface, bringing unwanted reminders of how many years he'd missed. And an even more painful reminder of who else had changed while he was away.

Annora might hate him for being away for so long, or she might not care at all. Even though they weren't blood siblings, her parents had been like parents to him. And he still treasured the moments they'd shared, almost like he really had a sister, too.

Glimpses of the palace peeked through the trees. His veins turned into ice at seeing it again. This was the closest he'd been to Evelina in years. She was likely within the walls, roaming the corridors now.

Unlike Annora, there was no doubt in his mind that Evelina hated him for never returning.

He shook his head and turned, and the moonlight cast just enough light to see. Annora's face was older, more mature, and her frame petite but fuller. When he saw who was with her, he paused, far enough back that they hadn't noticed him yet. Aldric, another Nox, had her gathered in his arms. His hand stroked her hair as he murmured into her ear.

Daimon had met Aldric when he came to train at Zenovia's edge. He was a fine soldier who talked of a fae he couldn't wait to get back to. Judging by the way he was planting kisses on Annora's forehead, it was clear now who that fae was. Aldric grabbed a strand of Annora's long, onyx hair and tucked it tenderly behind her pointed ear. He had a quiet but authoritative presence that clung to the air around him wherever he went.

Daimon smiled to himself. He was glad that someone could find a glimpse of happiness in this dreadful war, even if it seemed they had to keep it to themselves.

He turned and backed away silently to make his way back to Maliena and Neve, finding Ren talking quietly with them. They turned to him, an air of expectancy hovering around them as he approached.

"I'll find Keir and give him a brief on what I've seen so far," said Daimon. "But it may be wise to spend a few more days here to make sure nothing was missed."

Neve nodded. "That would probably be for the best. Queen Embry has already called for the council to gather this evening to continue discussions on the recent attacks."

"We were just about to go to the meeting," Maliena added.

Daimon nodded, eager to get the brief over with and find Keir so he could spend some time in the night sky with Zephyr. Despite it being a long day, he was wide awake. "I'll be back before sunrise for another walkthrough." He turned, his eyes already drifting to the clouds.

Neve cleared his throat, making Daimon pause, but his eyes were still set above. "The queen thought it would be best if you debriefed everyone at the same time."

Daimon was fairly certain his heart stopped beating at those words. His gaze slowly lowered to Neve, Maliena, and Ren. Maliena was staring at him, her brow raised as if waiting for him to say something. It took him much longer than necessary to collect himself.

"What was that again?" Daimon breathed.

"They want you to come back to the palace tonight."

NINE

EVELINA

AFTER GRINDING THE FEVERFEW LEAVES AND REPLENISHING their jars, Evelina cleaned up the quiet healing room. It was so late in the evening that the other healers were likely in bed or on a night trip to one of the camps. She straightened a few mortars and pestles and called it a night. The corridor that she stepped into was quiet but filled with a soft, warm glow that the palace provided at all times. This was one of the rare occasions where the palace felt like it used to—safe and cozy. She could almost pretend it wasn't the place of discomfort and worry that it had turned into. It made her want to turn around and go back into the infirmary, to soak up the last dregs of comfort within these walls.

Walking through the empty halls, she neared a private door to the throne room. It was cracked open, enough to see a sliver inside, and she could hear the council in session on the other side. The meetings weren't a *secret*, but she never went to them. It wasn't where her talents were best suited. She was the fourth in line with the weakest magic, leaving her to serve her realm by healing. And taking a fae consort chosen for her when the day came. That was something she had no control over—arguably the biggest decision in her life was to be made by someone else.

Evelina had always resented that Manors were the only royal fae line, but the human rulers used to be elected by the empire. It was how Moros was able to squeeze his way onto the throne. He was just a simple farmer before he became king; after quickly gaining attraction from his alluring speeches and promises of maintaining peace, he won the votes of the humans to be the next king.

A fae's immortality didn't grant them their life to rule, only the life span of the human monarch they shared the empire with. Otherwise, the Eternal Crown would never tie itself to a new fae. But now that the human monarch wasn't someone they shared the crown with, it remained with the Manor ruler, only changing to each predecessor by death of the fae wearing it, or by abdication. The land needed strength replenished, slowly draining each fae who wore it until the moment it left them.

It kept their land safe—strong. Which meant the Manors had to be strong, too.

Love was an afterthought to Evelina's family. Their duty was to breed heirs with their chosen fae consorts. How was that fair? All in the name of a pure fae lineage, she supposed.

Voices filtered through the crack in the wooden door, and just as she was about to continue on, she heard a deeply familiar voice. She pressed in closer to get a better look. She had to rotate at an awkward angle to see the room through the small crack in the door. The entire council had already gathered. All three of her siblings were present and accounted for, seated in order from eldest to youngest—with a notably empty seat at the end, where she should be. Carwyn, seated at the front with her sandy blonde hair pulled into a tight bun on the top of her head. Ren to her right, his long hair brushing his shoulders as he leaned over to whisper to Carwyn. He wore soldier leathers—though he tended to more often than not since joining the naval fleet on the western coast. Lastly, there was Lyria—soft and gentle Lyria. She was older than Evelina, but could easily be mistaken for the youngest.

The rest of the council was there too. Keir, the Aegis council head and member of the alpha aerial legion; Seretha, the Undine council head; and Maliena and Neve, leaders of the Nocturna.

She spotted a broad-chested soldier in his naval uniform sitting in the second row of chairs—dark blue leathers with gold thread sewn into the cuffs of his sleeves. His hair was tied back in its usual low knot and his skin was slightly tanner since she had last seen him.

Senna. She smiled, glad that her friend was home. He had only been gone a few months, but he was close with all the Manors, returning often from commanding the naval fleets to bring reports back to the palace.

And another soldier, too—possibly a commander or high-ranking officer from the looks of it—one she didn't recognize. He was standing at the front of the table, everyone's rapt attention fixed on what he was saying.

Something hot curled in her core when she looked at him.

His frame was filled out from what had to be years of training, his face shadowed with a beard that hadn't been trimmed. Her eyes trailed down the expanse of his broad shoulders, down his muscular back and trimmed waist. He still wore his uniform, light armor made of black wyvern scales, and a thick metal plate covering his left shoulder and crossing down to his right side to protect his chest. A Rider.

His body was perfectly toned from years of training. She couldn't see his thighs from where she was standing, but she could guess that they were just as strong as the rest of his body.

So strong that he could probably pin her to the ground and—

"Nice of you to join us, Princess Evelina." Seretha's sharp voice snapped her attention back to the present.

Everyone in the room turned to look at her and her cheeks flared red. The heat that had filled her core vanished and turned into embarrassment.

"Care to join?" the soldier added.

She opened the door and stepped in, having no other option after getting caught. She looked *anywhere* but at the soldier she had just been caught staring at. Which was a mistake, seeing as Carwyn was smiling brightly at her.

"She'd love to join." Carwyn motioned for her to take a seat.

If Evelina made an excuse about being too tired, or having healing duties to attend to, no one would be surprised—likely wouldn't even try to stop her. But without her approval, her feet were moving, pulled forward by the curiosity of seeing what this soldier was here to say.

"The rebels have been growing in strength and numbers, the attack on Nox Grove—"

The door shut behind her and made a loud snap as it closed. The soldier stopped talking and glanced up at her. He looked as if he had just been in battle, his face smeared with dirt and hair askew.

"Sorry," she muttered, finding an open seat in the back instead of next to Lyria. The Rider's eyes followed her to her seat, his gaze lingering. She tried to ignore the way he was affecting her; she shouldn't be thinking about *any* of the soldiers in this way, not when her consort would one day be chosen for her.

"The rebels have been aiming to take the crown for decades now and are growing more bold. With the attack on Drogheda and the grove, the tides are changing," the soldier continued.

The Woodland queen hummed, drawing the attention of the room. She shook her head and said, "Or they're growing desperate. Perhaps it isn't boldness that's making their moves now, but a need for this to end."

Others echoed their agreement. Queen Embry stood, switching places with the soldier to stand at the front. Evelina's eyes wandered to where the soldier took his seat beside Keir. His back was to her, and his dark hair was long and unkempt.

"Evelina." Her mother's voice cut through the room. "Do you agree with your siblings?"

Evelina's face heated as every head in the packed room

swiveled toward her. It heated further when the soldier slowly spun around with an unreadable face. He was looking at her *again*. She shifted in her seat, flustered beneath the heat of his gaze.

There was something familiar about him.

"Agree?" She knew better than to blindly agree without knowing what it was she was agreeing to.

"That we need to focus on restoring the faith of the crown," the Rider offered, his voice somehow smooth and rough at the same time.

Evelina shot him a look, not quite a smile, for saving her the embarrassment of admitting she hadn't been listening. Only his face was smug, annoyingly amused.

"May I?" he asked. Queen Embry nodded, giving him the floor again. "We've yet to discover new information on the rebels." His voice rang through the room. "And we can't win against an opponent that we don't know. The realm knows that —otherwise, we would've put a stop to this years ago."

He paused and took his time to meet the gazes of everyone in the room. His face was calm, his voice even and strong. "I've seen the defeat that weighs on everyone's shoulders." He paused again. "On the villagers that are relocated after an attack, on the soldiers that haven't had a reprieve since the war started."

Evelina could agree with that. The refugees she visited seemed to have long given up the spark of fight within them.

Carwyn stood, her angular, foxlike face stoic as her icy blue eyes flicked around the room, confident in every muscle she moved. Ren stood with her, the only other Manor sibling who had a chance at the throne. But Carwyn was eldest, and the only sibling to have two affinities, making her the obvious front-runner as the next fae ruler.

Carwyn cleared her throat and turned to Keir. "The progress to fully squash this rebellion has stalled for quite some time."

Keir nodded, every bit an Aegis. His skin was riddled with

scars and burns. He had been a council head longer than any of the others, his experience invaluable.

"Progress has been slow in making any significant gains," he said in a gravelly voice.

Silence fell over the room, a reminder of what had been lost.

Carwyn broke the tension. "We need a secret weapon, something that the rebels won't see coming. We need an edge."

Keir leaned forward and braced his elbows on his knees, a jagged scar along his neck stretching as he tilted his head. "And what is this secret weapon?"

"We'll know it when we find it," said Carwyn firmly. "Eurydice will make sure of it."

Keir burst into laughter, joined by other council members.

"What you're saying is, we should find a secret weapon, but you don't know what that weapon is?" Keir's eyes danced with amusement.

Carwyn raised her chin, refusing to be belittled by the Aegis leader. She was the most brilliant fae that Evelina knew, her strength matching her cleverness. It was the thing that set her apart from the rest of Evelina's siblings. Ren was nearly as strong, but Carwyn was far more calculated. It was the only reason Keir still allowed her to speak.

"The Goddess of the Moon always provides," she said without hesitation. "We need only to be steadfast in our faith."

Evelina had always admired Carwyn's confidence in Eurydice. When everyone seemed to doubt the goddess who watched over them, Carwyn was firm in her belief that they had not been abandoned. But Evelina had seen a lot of lives lost and too many people uprooted from their homes, forced to relocate to overcrowded refugee camps. It was hard for her to stay as confident as Carwyn more days than she could count.

Keir cleared his throat, bringing the attention of the room to him. "The losses were heavy during the attack on the edge of Drogheda. They killed our flight's healer as he was tending to the injured."

The other Rider nodded his head, a deep frown tilting his mouth down. "We'll need a new one quickly. Especially if the rebels keep pushing further past the border."

"Healers shouldn't be a target on the battlefield," Maliena hissed. Neve placed an arm around her, grunting in agreement with his wife.

Senna shifted his weight and said, "Perhaps we should instead station the healers at the camps. We're too overwhelmed on the battlefield now to protect them, and we can't afford to lose any more."

The queen turned, her gaze landing on Evelina. "Two of the best healers in the realm reside in the palace," she said slowly. Heads turned, following the path of her gaze. "Gloriana and Evelina have been working with refugees for years."

Queen Embry paused, pulling her gaze away from Evelina, redirecting it firmly toward Keir. "They will accompany the Alpha Fleet as their healers on the border."

Keir bowed his head. "It would be our honor to host them."

Evelina blinked. Her mother was already going over the details with Keir and the other Rider, but Evelina couldn't hear her. Her pulse pounded—from fear of being on the border or exhilaration from being able to heal in such a way, she wasn't sure.

The Rider beside Keir was watching her, his eyes widening a fraction.

"We'll keep them further from active battles," Keir assured the queen. "Perhaps to tend to the survivors after."

The soldier's face was blank again, but a muscle ticked in his jaw. "The princess may not be the best healer to utilize."

Queen Embry's eyes narrowed at him. "She and Gloriana have worked in tandem for years," she said sharply. "We all have a duty in this war."

Evelina was being sent to heal on the border. Not *asked* by her mother, but commanded by the queen. She often felt the crown's heavy weight more than her mother's tenderness.

"It's greatly appreciated, Queen Embry." Keir nodded and turned to the Rider. "We leave after first light tomorrow, Daimon."

It was as if Evelina had been hit with a boulder; the wind knocked out of her instantly with a single name. A name she'd been avoiding for twenty years.

Because it couldn't be him. *He* couldn't be *here*.

Her blood drained from her face, her breath catching. She knew why the Rider felt so familiar now.

He glanced at her, only for a moment. She could see it then —a face she didn't recognize right away—but the midnight eyes… They were *his*.

Her once closest companion. The one who had always been there when she needed him. If she called, he would answer.

Until the day he didn't.

It had been nearly twenty years since he'd left the palace. Since he had left her without an explanation or even a goodbye. She dreamed of seeing him again so she could yell at him for leaving so quickly—so she could demand to know *why* he left the way he did, without ever returning.

But sitting here, looking into the eyes of a man that didn't reflect the boy she once knew, she was frozen. Her heart raced with excitement at seeing her old friend again, mixed with a heated anger that he'd left in the first place—a wound that never quite healed.

There was a time when she would have killed to have the chance to speak with him again, but things were different now— *he* was different now. This Daimon's smile was harder, joyless— cruel, almost. His voice was different, too—devoid of emotion even within the lilt of his tease. There was no crinkle in the corners of his eyes, no real smile. His smirk was just as emotion- less as his eyes.

The war had changed him the moment it sank its teeth into his heart. The once kind eyes had hardened, so much so that she had to stare at him for a moment to be sure it was really him.

The Daimon she knew died the day he left.

She didn't hear anything else that was being said. She wanted to bolt out of the room, to run and hide in the infirmary. But she also couldn't look away from him.

He was *here*. She would have to work with him for the foreseeable future. And she had no idea what to do with that.

Because truthfully, it didn't matter that he had changed. Because war hadn't just hit him—in the time he'd left, it had ravaged her people, her home, her family.

He wasn't the only one who had changed.

The day he left, the Evelina he knew died too.

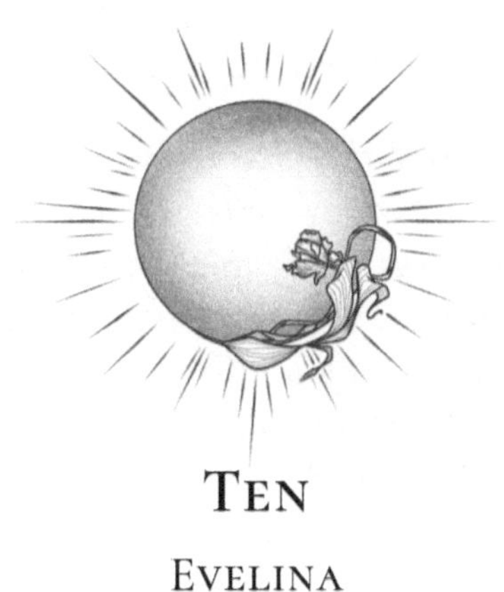

TEN

EVELINA

EVELINA DIDN'T TRY TO SLEEP THAT NIGHT, BUT SHE hardly ever did. Especially now that she knew Daimon was back. And not only that, but now she would be stationed with him.

She went straight to the infirmary after the meeting, eager to avoid running into him. She wasn't ready to face him yet—didn't even know what she would say. The last time she had seen him, they had still been so full of innocence, two bright souls still clinging to hope. Even though she had just lost her father, she thought his sacrifice would be the first and last of this war. But then the losses kept coming, and Daimon—her only friend— left.

A warm arm draped across Evelina's shoulders. She was trembling so violently that the arm had to tighten to hold on.

"I'm so sorry, Evie," Daimon whispered.

The sun was setting over the quiet lunaria garden, the sky glowing a soft orange. Evelina hated how the land was bright and flourishing on a day like this. There should be clouds in the sky, perhaps even a thunderstorm. The land should be grieving just as Evelina was. Didn't it know it had just lost its king?

Even though her father wasn't bound to the land as her mother was, it seemed wrong for the skies to be so peaceful.

"Why are the rebels doing this?" she sobbed. "There's been more and more attacks, Daimon." She buried her face in her knees, her body curled in on itself.

"I don't know," he whispered. "It isn't fair."

His arm stayed wrapped around her shoulders as she cried. Her tears didn't dry until the sun was nearly set and it was time for her to go back to the palace. He walked her back, glancing her way every few minutes.

When they reached the entrance, she turned abruptly toward him. "Can we meet back in our garden tomorrow?"

That's what it had become—theirs. He was her closest friend, the one she could count on to always be there.

He nodded quickly. "As long as you need."

She met him in the garden every sunrise after that day. From sunup to sundown, they hid away in the flowers. All of her siblings were a wreck. Carwyn hid away at the temple to pray, Lyria stayed by Mother's side without fail, and Ren left to train with Aegis soldiers. Her mother was even worse off. She might have donned the mask of queen to lead her realm in this difficult time, but Evelina could see it wearing on her day by day.

They all were seeking their own safe place to heal from the grief.

All Evelina wanted was Daimon.

Evelina slammed a jar down harder than she meant to, the shelves rattling. She cursed and straightened it, checking it over for any cracks. She tried to ignore the pain in her chest, the deep wound that had been sliced wide open. No matter how she willed her thoughts elsewhere, the memory still came.

• • •

He was late this morning.

They had fallen into a routine for the past several months, meeting at the garden, sharing dreams for hours on end.

She paced the garden, her stomach twisting and heart racing the more time that passed. He was never late, and on the days they didn't meet, they always talked about it the day before. He had told her yesterday he would see her tomorrow, but tomorrow had come and he wasn't here.

Before the rebels, she wouldn't have thought much of it. But since then, villages had been attacked, people had gotten hurt, and wyverns had descended from the sky to choose fae as their Riders. Any one of those options wasn't something she wanted to consider happening to him.

When she finally heard the crunch of his boots behind her, she whirled around and flung her arms around his neck.

"I thought something had happened to you!" she admitted with an embarrassed laugh as she let go. "Don't scare me like that."

When her eyes met his, she didn't see the gaze of her friend staring back at her. There was a glint in his eye, a mixture of determination and guilt.

"What's wrong?" Her mind raced with thoughts of what could've happened, who she might've lost this time.

He hesitated, his midnight eyes shining with an apology she didn't understand.

"I was chosen, Eve." His grin was lopsided, and the unmistakable lilt of excitement seeped into his words.

"What do you mean?" she breathed.

He looked up at the sky, a sense of longing swirling in his gaze. "A wyvern chose me. She's incredible, you should see her—"

"But—" Her voice broke. "You're not old enough to be a soldier!"

His smile dropped.

Evelina's hands began to shake. He couldn't leave to go be a Rider. She knew fae of all kinds were being recruited to go learn how to fight, but he couldn't be one of them. They were still children.

"Well, I won't be a soldier yet," he said slowly. "I'll get to learn how to bond with Zephyr with the other young Riders. We won't get to be soldiers until we pass our trials."

He reached out and laid his hands over hers, soothing the tremble in them. His thumb glided over her fingers until the shaking lessened.

She shook her head and took a step back. "Don't go."

He scratched the back of his head. "I'm sorry," he whispered and looked down at the ground. "I have to. This is my chance to actually do something worthwhile—to be someone others respect."

Evelina turned away from him, wrapping her arms around herself. "But you don't have to prove anything to me. You're already doing something worthwhile. You're my friend."

"And I'll still be your friend while I'm gone," he whispered. "But the rest of the empire isn't you. Eurydice picked me, Evie. I'm gonna help them end this war, and when I come back, I'll be someone you can be proud of."

"Please," she begged.

He pulled her into a hug and whispered, "I'll be back to visit often."

"Promise?"

"I promise."

Her chest squeezed at the memory. She needed a distraction from her own mind. So, she did what she did best and worked. Her thoughts wandered to what it would be like on the border, of all the ways war could harm yet another soul as she restocked herbs and mixed pain-relieving tonics. Did Eurydice even let those who killed and destroyed into Caelum?

The rebels were a puzzle that no one had been able to piece together. There had to come a day in this darkness that light was able to shine through the pain and death. But despite the grief that swirled in each day since the war started, tonight would be a reprieve from that.

Evelina checked the moon's position out the window, seeing that it had already begun to cast a soft glow on the dark forest below. The autumn equinox moon was bright and round, not a single cloud in the sky.

Annora had told her of their plan to wait until the very last moment, until all of the other bonded couples had completed their ceremonies and no one would see them as they caught the last stream of moonlight.

But Evelina was late. As usual. She was supposed to wait on Senna to escort her, but he wasn't here yet—and she didn't have any more time to spare. The window of time they had to complete the ceremony was ticking away.

"Are you nervous to be on the border?" Gloriana asked. She was the only other healer still in the infirmary—she hardly seemed to leave.

Evelina paused and swallowed. She was. But not entirely for the reasons Gloriana would have guessed.

"A little," she admitted. "Less so with you there too."

Gloriana smiled. Evelina's eyes darted over to the window nervously. She needed to go before it was too late. She waved goodbye, slipping out before she missed the ceremony entirely.

With soundless footsteps, she padded barefoot through the dark palace. The stone floor was warmed by the palace itself— the Essence from all the sleeping fae keeping it alive. An orb of light formed in her palm, the glow guiding her path. It was second nature to call on her light.

Why she possessed the light affinity was beyond her. Didn't the moon goddess know she preferred to be in the background? Instead of being one of the rare fae able to wield light, she would rather have a normal nature or animal affinity like her siblings.

Plus, it wasn't usable in a way that was interesting like more powerful fae would have wanted.

Evelina slipped out of the palace and into Lilium Glade. The glade had been here long before her and was sure to stay long after—a forest brimming with warmth. The moon was shining brightly, proud almost, feeling more like a taunt than a comfort.

Evelina wasn't happy with the Goddess of the Moon right now. Eurydice had seemingly left her people behind, their land stuck in war with no end in sight. She has been silent without a single sign of comfort in the midst of the empire crumbling to pieces.

The sound of hushed laughter caught Evelina's attention. It echoed through the forest, disrupting the quiet of the night. But she knew that laughter.

She couldn't help but smile a little at the sound of her friend's happiness.

"She'll be here soon." Annora's light voice filtered over to Evelina from somewhere deep within the forest. Evelina's fae hearing caught every word.

"She's late," came Aldric's warm tone.

A soft sigh followed. "She's *always* late."

Evelina crept through the forest. The night was the darkest it'd been in a long time, offering her friends a chance to let their love escape the bounds that society was attempting to tie them in. She neared the couple and found them standing beneath a narrow willow tree. Its branches were long and wispy, so light that they swayed against the smallest breeze.

Their hands were clasped together, their eyes wide. Annora's lithe body was draped with thin lavender fabric, while Aldric wore a deep amethyst tunic—the color worn during a bonding ceremony. A sign of one's devotion to their bonded. Aldric was like most Nox, tall and spindly. His deep olive skin shone in the night.

They were so immersed in each other that they didn't even notice Evelina watching them.

"So, you're finally ready to do it?" Evelina said.

They spun around, their eyes wide with surprise.

Annora's face split into a wide smile. "Took you long enough." She ran over to her friend and threw her arms around her neck, embracing her tightly.

"Me? I've been here for hours," Evelina teased, hugging her back.

"Aldric might've tried to get Lyria to help if you had taken any longer," Annora said with a final squeeze.

Evelina grinned, knowing good and well they wouldn't have placed their bonding ceremony in the hands of Evelina's sister.

"So, how long have you two known you were soulbonded?" Evelina asked, looking between the two of them. Finding a mate wasn't considered a rarity, but the bonding ceremony was. Oftentimes, a fae would find their mate, but they wouldn't choose one another. Even worse, one might choose the other, who wouldn't want to go through with it.

When a soul was discovered to be connected to another, it didn't make someone *belong* to the other. It had to be chosen and accepted by both parties, a mutual agreement to bind one's soul.

"I think we were the last to know," Aldric said with a laugh. "It seemed those around us caught on far sooner than we did."

He wasn't wrong. They were different when they were around each other, brighter.

"Well then, we better not waste any more time." Evelina gestured to the path to the Celestial Temple.

Annora grabbed Aldric's hand, and the pair clung to each other as they made their way to Eurydice's temple.

Against her own will, Evelina's mind wandered back to Daimon. To where he was sleeping and what he was doing. If he had never left, he would've been right alongside them, joining to watch the ceremony. There was a chance, even, that *they* could've been bonded.

She shook her head, shaking the useless what-ifs from her

mind. He *did* leave. If they had been meant to be, he would've stayed.

It didn't matter anymore what they could have been. All that mattered, tonight, was that at least someone in her life could find their happy ending.

Eleven

Evelina

A small tunnel ran along the insides of the temple. It was mostly empty save for the spiders that spun their webs. Like much of the glade, it'd been here since long before Evelina—even before her mother and her mother's mother.

No one knew who built Eurydice's temple all those years ago. Perhaps it was the moon goddess herself. That was partly the reason the tunnels were a mystery, for the only key to opening it was the blood of a Manor.

The front entrance would be far easier to go through, but that would increase the chance of them being seen—and caught. Evelina led Annora and Aldric to a back gate, one that was often abandoned and unused.

Evelina had seen the obscenely ornate building more times than she could count, the height of it imposing in the forest. She glanced up, her eyes running along the triangular tip of the temple. The walls of it were grooved and covered in ivy, tiny white flowers blooming from the green stems.

Priestesses milled about as they always did, sprinkling freshly picked lily petals onto the ground—the flower of the moon goddess. They ensured the tributes were always prepared properly, stoking the burning herbs from the Nox and prodding at the coals the Aegis burned on a never-ending flame, resting atop the pillars that sat on either side of the entrance. They also kept the natural springs of water clear so it would reflect the temple on its surface—the Undine gift. Last, they tended to the flowers the Woodland brought to be placed in the gardens.

Evelina slipped past the priestesses, smiling and saying her blessings to Eurydice. They nodded to her, their eyes shimmering with a knowing only the priestesses could possess. While they were loyal to the crown, they honored Eurydice's blessing above all else, and a soulbond was the most precious of blessings the moon goddess could give.

Still, they needed to be careful until the ceremony was complete. The Woodland queen had a sixth sense for what was happening in her realm, and she wouldn't look kindly upon their covert ceremony.

At a stone door carved into a small alcove on the back half of the temple, Evelina stopped, turning around to face Annora and Aldric as they trailed behind her.

"Are you sure about this?" Evelina asked, her first show of hesitation.

Aldric wrapped an arm around Annora's waist, tugging her in close and giving her a kiss on the top of her head. Evelina's heart squeezed in her chest at how well he cared for her friend. Aldric might not have been considered a match for Annora, but no one could be her equal in the way he could.

But still… To be wrong about this was to prevent them from ever finding their true soulbonded. They only had one chance, and they had to be certain.

"There's no one else I would rather do this with," Annora reassured her, tears shining in her eyes. Aldric gave her a grateful smile.

Evelina turned back to the door and took a steadying breath. Trailing roots had overgrown across the stone, encasing the entrance so tightly it was hard to make out where it was. But

Evelina could feel it in her bones, her blood that sang out to the ancient magic of the temple.

She pulled out the small blade she brought with her, running it along her palm until blood rose to the surface. With a steady reach, she wiggled her hand through the thick roots until her palm was flat against the cool stone. The wound from her blade stung as it met the door, but she could feel magic coursing through her already.

It was different than when she helped with the bonding ceremonies. It was as if the magic here was slower, a rusty hinge that needed a tug before it would open.

Annora shifted in Evelina's periphery. "Why isn't it—"

Like a broken instrument coming to life, the door groaned and creaked, opening of its own accord until it was cracked enough for Evelina to push. With her knife, she cut through the thick roots still blocking their path and pushed the door to reveal the tunnels beyond. She turned around to face Annora and Aldric, a mischievous grin on her face.

"Letting me do all the hard work?" she teased to lighten the mood. She could feel their heaviness and nerves lift like a blanket being pulled off of them.

Annora placed a hand on Evelina's shoulder with a soft grin. "You know that we're indebted to you for this."

Evelina waved them off, ignoring the tears welling in her eyes. "Thank me when it's over."

She squeezed through the small tunnel, praying to the goddess that no one other than the priestesses decided to come back here. It was unlikely anyone would know who Aldric was, but Annora would be recognized immediately, almost as quickly as Evelina.

Icy drops of water slid down the walls and pooled onto the ground, slicking their path and causing her steps to slow as she led them through the tunnels. She was careful to pause every few steps with her ears straining to find something on the path ahead, but it was empty.

They crept through the dark tunnel until Evelina was certain she was just behind the wooden altar that sat on the other side of the wall.

She stopped at a small cutout in the wall. It was boarded up, slants of light filtering through the cracks. But she knew of the loose board that would swing out far enough for someone to squeeze through. She and Lyria had found it after trying to sneak in when they were children.

They paused, straining to listen. Silence met them and they all relaxed simultaneously.

"Through here and into the ceremony room you go," she whispered.

Annora looked to Aldric, her face unreadable in the dimly lit tunnel. "What if the Sacred won't do it?"

Evelina pushed the board open for them. "We all know the Sacred isn't going to question those that have the call to be mated. We've heard the stories of how she can sense a bond."

With a final push in the direction of the boards, Aldric crouched down to slide through.

Before Annora followed him, she turned to Evelina, gripping her shoulders. "Promise me you'll stay to watch so I know we aren't alone."

Evelina pulled her into a hug, whispering into her ear, "I wouldn't miss this for the world."

The board thumped back into place after Annora made it to the other side. With the cracks so small, Evelina searched for a way to watch. She blindly reached her hand out and pressed it to the wall. Her fingers caught on the jagged stone, her fingertips becoming numb from the frosty bite of cold. She ran her hand along the wall until she found what she was looking for—a single loose stone in the center. Once she slid the stone from its resting place, she was offered a front-row seat to the ceremony.

An orange flicker danced against the opening, and she leaned in until her face was level with it. Inside the temple, she saw

Annora and Aldric, their hands clasped tightly and their eyes sparkling with delight, the hesitation gone.

Their luck resided in the fact that the Sacred didn't question those who came to her—it wasn't her job to. She was nothing more than a conduit for Eurydice to speak through, both an empty vessel and a temporary house for the Goddess of the Moon.

Evelina drew in a sharp breath, her solace in staying hidden within the thick stone walls. The only time she'd been in front of the Sacred was when she was given her affinities. It was the only time she'd ever spoken to the goddess directly.

Being in that room felt like a vortex. A person's focus was on nothing but the Sacred and the goddess. Even with fae hearing, senses were dulled within the blessed walls. That was how younger fae had gotten away with spying on temple readings for so long. Even if it was a known rite of passage, no one tried to stop it from happening.

"The goddess has agreed to see you tonight," the haunting voice of the Sacred said. Her white hair shone and the hollow blue ring on her forehead glowed brighter than the torches around the room. From where she was hidden, Evelina couldn't see her haunting eyes, but she shivered at the thought of them.

A rock skidding across the tunnel floor caught Evelina's attention. She froze. Her pointed ears twitched as a hushed whisper floated toward her. Someone else was here.

She stiffened against the wall and attempted to press herself into it. There was no use in trying to run, because there was nowhere else to go. That was the risk of entering the tunnels—there was one way in and one way out...and she had left the door wide open.

TWELVE

EVELINA

THIS FAR INTO THE TUNNEL, NEARLY AT ITS END, EVELINA was faced with a dead end, nothing more than an abrupt stop in the path. Meaning there was no way out if someone was coming from the other side.

She braced herself for the inevitable moment she got caught red-handed.

But then a deep, familiar voice floated through the tunnel and echoed off the walls. It was Keir. "They couldn't have gone far; the tunnel can only be so deep."

Evelina relaxed. But who was he talking to?

"We should get a few hours of sleep before we leave in the morning," Keir whispered angrily. "And why would we care who's in the temple this time of night, Daimon?"

Evelina froze at his name, still undetected from where she crouched.

"Don't you want to know why the door was left open?" Daimon whispered. "Whoever opened it didn't use the front entrance for a reason—they didn't want others to know." His voice was tense.

"And maybe they don't want others to know for a *reason*,"

Keir muttered. Their voices were getting closer. "If a Manor is here, *then there's a reason.*"

Evelina curled into herself, hoping they wouldn't investigate any further.

"We need to be rested for the flight. Let's just—" Keir's voice cut off.

Evelina stared down at two pairs of boots. She looked up reluctantly, and two *very* large fae stared down at her.

Keir let out a long, frustrated breath and said, "Should've known it was you."

"What are you two doing here?" Evelina whispered. Her stomach bottomed out as she looked at Keir and *only* Keir. She hoped they couldn't hear her heart as it pounded in her chest.

"We could ask you the same thing," Keir huffed.

Evelina narrowed her eyes, not wanting to give up Annora and Aldric. But then the unmistakable voice of the Sacred filtered from the other side of the wall.

"A final bonding beneath the equinox moon," the Sacred began.

Daimon and Keir shuffled closer to the wall.

"Who is it?" Daimon asked softly, and turned his head until his gaze found hers.

Her breath caught as she realized how close they were standing. Everything she had wanted to say to him for twenty years sat on the tip of her tongue. To ask why he never came back, to yell at him or tell him how much he had hurt her.

Instead, she dropped her gaze and said, "Annora and Aldric."

Daimon and Keir exchanged a glance, a silent conversation passing between them. Keir made a face, seemingly conveying something, and Daimon shook his head, his eyes flashing with anger.

Keir had bonded with his wyvern early in the war and joined the Alpha Fleet not long after. She didn't know how he managed to be the Aegis council head *and* on the fleet, but he did come back to the palace often. Daimon did not.

"Are you really all having fun without me?" a light voice said.

Evelina held back a grimace as one of her sisters popped up in the tunnel. She didn't even hear her approach, though that wasn't much of a surprise. Lyria had always had the stealth to sneak about more than the others—especially if she was trying to remain hidden.

"Lyria, go home," Evelina whispered. While Lyria was years older than Evelina, she always acted younger than her.

"Make me, Evie," Lyria said, sticking her tongue out. "Don't be such a downer."

Evelina sighed and turned away. Lyria always had a grin on her face and her wide, brown eyes were soft and inviting. Evelina would never understand her desire to be the center of attention, but she still had more in common with Lyria than any of her other siblings. Their eldest sister, Carwyn, was the strong and confident leader—but she was next in line for the throne, so it came with the territory—and Ren was the glue that held them all together.

"You can't tell Carwyn we came here." Evelina spoke quietly, but her words were firm as she turned to eye Lyria.

Lyria gasped. "I wouldn't do that. Now, who is it?"

Daimon rolled his eyes and Keir held back a smile. Everyone knew that Lyria couldn't keep a secret. If the saying was *Loose lips sink ships*, then she could sink a whole fleet. But even when they all bickered and got on each other's nerves, they were there for each other. Always.

"Annora and Aldric," Evelina repeated. She was beginning to grow restless.

Lyria's eyes grew wide and a grin split across her face. She opened her mouth as excitement danced in her eyes. Evelina lunged forward and slapped her hand over Lyria's mouth before she had the chance to speak.

"I *said* to keep your voice down," Evelina hissed, knowing her sister was about to speak far too loudly. She never had been able to control her eagerness. "This is likely their only chance."

Lyria muttered something unintelligible beneath Evelina's hand. Evelina slowly removed her hand and gave her a pointed look.

"I was just going to say it's about time they figured it out," Lyria mumbled. "I *am* capable of keeping quiet, you know."

A small tremble rolled beneath the temple and caused loose stone to crumble and dust to rain down.

"Eurydice is here," Daimon whispered.

The group crowded against the small opening, eager to try and see Eurydice. It wasn't often they were able to see the Goddess of the Moon. Evelina was squished into the middle, with Daimon on one side, her sister on the other, and a reluctant Keir in the back.

Every brush of Daimon's shoulder against hers set her skin aflame. She hated it. She hated that she loved it.

Lyria gasped and said, "Maliena and Neve don't know Annora is doing this, do they?"

"You have to keep this to yourself, Lyria, please," Evelina whispered quickly. "Just until they decide to tell everyone. It's too late to be stopped now."

Lyria shuddered and shuffled closer to Keir. He stiffened and kept his eyes fixed ahead.

"And what if they're choosing wrong?" Lyria pressed. "What of the empire if it's a mistake?"

Evelina's anger rose to the surface, but she fought to keep it at bay. She trusted Annora had made the right decision—besides, it was still *her* mistake to make.

"What *of* the empire? We don't know how long the empire can fight the rebellion—or what will even be left of the empire once it's done," Evelina said bitterly. "At least one of us deserves some semblance of happiness."

Evelina turned back to Annora and Aldric, ignoring her sister's frustrated sigh and the weight of Daimon's stare. Instead, she watched as the Sacred handed a small blade to Aldric.

"You deserve happiness too, Evie," Lyria said softly.

The words hit Evelina deep in the chest, piercing a tender place in her heart. Her eyes darted to Daimon, but he was pressed as far away as the small space would allow, his eyes firmly fixed ahead as if he hadn't heard their conversation.

It was an odd thing to have someone she once called her closest friend now feel so foreign to her.

She cleared her throat, setting her attention on the ceremony.

"*Are you so certain that her soul mirrors your own?*" The Sacred spoke to the couple in a voice that did not belong to her. It sounded like a hundred fae speaking at once. It sent a chill sliding down Evelina's spine knowing that meant the goddess was here. She wondered if Eurydice knew she was watching.

"I'm certain, Goddess," Aldric said confidently, his voice strong and unwavering.

Eurydice turned to Annora and said, "*And you are so certain that your souls are merely the same, just cleaved in two the moment they were conceived?*"

"I'm certain, Goddess." Annora beamed, reciting the vow back.

"*If you do not share a soul, the ritual will expose your false hope.*" The Sacred's head tilted to the side, puppeteered by Eurydice. "*And you understand that you can only make this declaration once—even if you are wrong—forever to be separated from your true mate by falsely choosing another? You are so confident in this decision?*"

Annora and Aldric turned to each other, their gazes wide and their hands clasped tight. Aldric nodded his head and Annora smiled.

"We're certain, Goddess," the two vowed in unison.

"*Then only the blood willingly given beneath the moon will tell,*" Eurydice said and raised both of her arms. "*Both of you are to cut down the length of your palm and let the blood fall to the ground. The scar of the bonded will remain.*"

Aldric made the cut first, not even flinching as the blade

sliced his skin open—a ferrum blade to stop the fae healing process from immediately closing the wound, just like the one Evelina had used to cut her palm to open the tunnels. He handed the blade to Annora and she took a deep breath. She made the same cut across her palm until the blood welled to the surface of her skin. Both of them extended their arms and squeezed their hands into fists.

"*The blood will make known if you are truly mates,*" Eurydice said as the blood trickled onto the stone. "*If the blood seeks the other's out and becomes one on the sacred grounds, then you will know. But if it does not, and instead flows parallel to each other, then you have chosen poorly.*"

Annora and Aldric looked so unequivocally in love, so deeply intertwined with each other. Even with the hint of accusation in Eurydice's words, their gazes didn't falter from each other.

Evelina held her breath as the blood on the ground began to move. Her hand started to shake—something it tended to do when she couldn't hide her nerves. But it was dark enough in the tunnel that no one would see.

The separate streams of blood got closer to each other but started to slow down, not quite touching. Evelina felt her tremors increase, fear that her friend could be jeopardizing her true mate overwhelming her. She loved Aldric and how kind he was to Annora, but what if they were wrong?

From the corner of her eye, she could see Daimon lean toward her, his gaze still set on the ceremony. Her body froze when she could feel the heat of his body warm her shoulder. Her heart began to beat wildly as she remembered the ways he used to be there for her. She hadn't been this close to him in so long, hadn't remembered the smell of frost and cedar that wrapped around him.

But things were different now. She knew better than to let her mind race with the possibilities of why he was doing what he was doing. He probably wasn't leaning toward her, her eyes seeing something that wasn't there. She could pretend in her mind, but not in reality.

They all watched in anticipation as the blood of Annora and Aldric melded into one singular puddle. Eurydice clapped once, and Annora threw her arms around Aldric.

"*And so it seems the blood of one flows through the blood of the other,*" Eurydice declared. "*This bond is unbreakable, unable to be unwoven or erased. The pull that you feel for each other will only intensify as the bond permanently settles. Your pain will be their pain, your thoughts will be able to be heard within their thoughts, and your joy will overflow with theirs.*"

Annora and Aldric held each other so close that their noses touched and smiles stretched onto their faces. Eurydice nodded her head at Annora. "*Do you accept this bond, Annora, daughter of Maliena and Neve, Nocturna with an affinity for dreams, protector of the vulnerable as they sleep?*"

"I accept," Annora said breathlessly, her eyes not moving from Aldric's.

"*And Aldric, son of Odessa and Nolan, Nocturna with an affinity for dreams, protector of the vulnerable alongside your mate, do you accept this bond?*"

Aldric held fast to Annora, his eyes alight with hope as he said, "I accept this bond."

"*Then I, Eurydice, Goddess of the Moon, bless this bond,*" she said firmly, and another tremble shook the ground of the temple. "*For these two souls now become one, no longer a mate calling to another but a soulbond forever bound.*"

Annora and Aldric gasped simultaneously, and their eyes widened as an unforeseeable force hit them at the same time. Aldric held a palm up, examining it closely. He held it out to Annora. A stark white scar was burned into his palm. Annora held her palm up, now etched with the same scar.

"*The mark of the soulbond will stay with you until your dying breath.*"

Evelina smiled. Their love was true. Someone in her life had managed to find a glimpse of happiness within the endless war. She began to lean away from the opening, finally feeling as if she could sleep for the night. Daimon and Lyria had already pulled away, Keir several steps away as he began to exit the tunnel.

But then something shifted in the air around her and she paused.

She watched as the body of the Sacred turned her head toward Evelina, and then the eyes of the moon goddess herself were set upon her. The glowing white eyes and hollow blue ring on her head blazed through the room, and she found that even if she wanted to move, she couldn't.

Annora and Aldric were too wrapped up in each other to notice, but Evelina was frozen.

In Eurydice's eyes, there seemed to be a warning. Evelina waited for her to speak, but then the goddess's eyes dulled, as if it had never happened.

THIRTEEN

DAIMON

DAIMON PAUSED THE MOMENT HE REALIZED EVELINA didn't emerge behind Lyria. His skin prickled with heat, and his heart raced at her nearness. He hoped he hadn't looked as off-kilter as he'd felt when he and Keir found Evelina in the tunnel. The moment he saw those bright hazel eyes, he felt like his world turned upside down. But when he realized she wouldn't look at him—only at Keir—he felt the heaviness of the guilt that came along with not returning.

And now she would be coming *with* him to the very border he had chosen to stay at. The moment Queen Embry suggested Evelina should be one of the Alpha Fleet's healers, the memory of Jarrett being cut open with a rebel's sword flashed into his mind.

If anything happened to her...

"Come on, we can still manage a quick rest before sunup, Dai," Keir grumbled. His eyes drifted to where Daimon's focus was set on the opposite end of the tunnel.

His ears strained for her footsteps. Just as his heart began to race, he heard the light, quick pattern of her steps—a cadence he didn't realize he still knew the rhythm of. His shoulders relaxed, but it wasn't until her face peeked around the corner that he assured himself she was okay.

"Don't stick around on my account." She shot him an icy look, gaze narrowed and lips pressed into a thin line. Her eyes blazed with sparks of anger.

He opened his mouth, but couldn't find the words. What was there to say after he never returned home all those years ago? Her choice of words about waiting on her wasn't lost on him. His stomach twisted at her glare.

It took everything in him not to grab her hand and make sure she was real. To touch her, to feel her hand in his. She was so different, but still so much the same that it took his breath away. He couldn't help but to be curious, to want to know this version of her.

Daimon cleared his throat and said, "Keir and I can walk you back to the palace."

Keir snorted and started to walk away. The corner of Evelina's mouth tilted down, and his gaze tracked the movement of her lips, but she was already looking beyond his shoulder. She quickly shuffled past Daimon to follow behind Keir.

But even as she moved to brush past him, he couldn't help leaning in—just slightly.

He couldn't stand it—he *hated* that this was their first conversation after all this time. It nearly drove him to madness, his anger rearing its head to match hers.

He shook his head—pushed the daydreams away—and followed after her.

The walk back felt longer than usual to Daimon. He lingered behind Evelina as they walked through the forest, her arm looped through Lyria's. She was quiet and lost within her mind, while Lyria's dainty laugh drifted back to him every few moments.

"Did I miss it already?" a deep, unfamiliar voice asked as they neared the palace.

"Senna knew and not me?" Lyria turned to Evelina, slamming to a halt.

Evelina grimaced apologetically and waved to the Woodland as he jogged up to her. His hair was a dusty brown, tied into a low knot. He was long-limbed, slender but lean. He wore the leathers that most of the soldiers wore, but there was gold thread sewn into the cuffs of his sleeves. A commander, then.

His smile was relaxed, somehow looking fully at ease. He slung an arm around Evelina's shoulders, the familiarity in his touch making Daimon's stomach twist.

Evelina recounted the ceremony for him, his gaze intensely set on her.

"Senna can walk them back," Keir said with a yawn. He looked up. The sky was beginning to light with the soft glow of the sun rising. "We'll be lucky to get an hour of rest before it's time to pack up."

Senna turned toward them as if noticing their presence for the first time.

"Keir," he said with a grin. He walked over to him, shaking his hand. "You're headed back to the border from what I hear."

It wasn't a shock Keir would know this soldier; he was the war commander, after all. But something prickled in Daimon's chest regardless.

"We'll need your unit to be fully prepared along the Andronicus," Keir responded. "Think you can handle that?"

Senna nodded, his shoulders set and eyes confident. He turned to Daimon next, sticking his hand out. Daimon hesitated, but clasped his hand. "I'm Senna, commander of the western naval fleets." His eyes dropped to Daimon's uniform. "Rider, I take it?"

"Commander of the Alpha Fleet."

Senna's eyes widened and briefly flicked over his shoulder to where Evelina stood. He nodded and spun back to Lyria and Evelina. "I can meet you later—"

"Thanks for walking us back to the palace, Senna," Evelina said quickly.

Keir released an appreciative sigh, yawning again. "We'll see you at first light, Princess Evelina."

Senna paused, his eyes lingering on Daimon. But Evelina and Lyria were already walking back toward the palace, and he spun around to catch up with them.

Daimon's chest tightened as he watched the three of them walk away.

FOURTEEN

EVELINA

WARFRONT HEALER. IT WASN'T A TITLE THAT EVELINA EVER thought she'd be given, and now it filled her mind with every breath.

Her entire life was about to change. She was going to be on the border, thrust into the war front alongside Gloriana. Nerves swirled in her stomach, but her hands were steady. Confident.

"Each of you will ride with us on the flight back," Brielle said. Evelina vaguely remembered the Aegis, introduced by Keir during a council meeting a few months back. "The rest of the crew is still at the camp, but Keir, Daimon, and I should be able to make it a quick ride. Whoever doesn't have one of you with them will carry your supplies."

Evelina wasn't ready to be alone with Daimon in *any* capacity, let alone riding atop a wyvern all the way to the border.

"I'll ride with you," she rushed to say to Brielle.

Gloriana hummed to herself and said, "I'll ride with Keir."

Brielle nodded. "As you like."

"You know the food isn't like it is in the palace," a warm, deep voice called out through the trees.

"Neither are the beds," muttered another male voice.

Evelina rolled her eyes, a smile spreading across her face.

"Don't tell me you two are coming?" she teased. She twisted from where she was kneeling on the ground, satchel still in hand.

Ren stared down at her with crossed arms. Another soldier Evelina didn't recognize stood beside him, a curious look on his face as his eyes bounced between brother and sister.

Evelina's heart warmed at the sight of Ren, hoping against all else he was coming on this mission too, even if he was stationed on the western coast.

"Couldn't let my little sister show me up," Ren teased. "We're heading out to the coast in a week or two. Don't get into too much trouble while slumming it with the Riders."

He hugged her and she breathed him in, searing the final taste of home into her mind, before he and his friend disappeared into the distance.

It wasn't about *showing his little sister up*. Ren looked out for his siblings, especially Evelina. They all had it in their heads she needed their protection, but now *she* would be the one to help *them*.

A dark mass appeared in the sky, shaking the trees and blowing the grass back as it lowered to the ground. It was followed by two more masses, their wings spread so far that they blocked out the morning sun. The three beasts landed, the ground trembling beneath Evelina's feet in their wake. Her heartbeat sped up and she took a step back along with Gloriana. Evelina had only been around wyverns a few times—mostly in passing—and even less this close up.

Daimon and Keir sat atop their wyverns, while the largest one was without a Rider. It walked over to Brielle, each step of its clawed feet shaking the trees around them. Brielle smiled as it lowered its head in front of her. She patted it between the eyes and turned to Evelina.

"This is Vero." Her voice was filled with pride as she introduced her beast. It turned its head toward Evelina, the eyes as red as rubies. "He's a little grumpy, but there's nothing to worry about when you're with me. We'll give you two plenty of time to bond with them once we get settled in camp."

Keir slid off his wyvern and Evelina tracked the movement, avoiding looking at Daimon atop his.

"Gloriana, that's Codax." Brielle jutted her chin out toward the wyvern. Its scales were a deep green, so dark he appeared black. "He's a little more friendly, but I hope you don't have any gooseberries in your pockets, otherwise he'd go straight for them."

Keir motioned for Gloriana to come over. She shot Evelina a nervous glance. It wasn't every day a healer rode a wyvern, but if they were to be the Alpha Fleet's healers, they'd have to be comfortable being around them.

Evelina took a step forward. A growl sounded from her left and froze her to her spot. Her eyes darted over to the third wyvern, the beast's teeth showing as it growled again.

"Z," Daimon said sharply, patting her neck. He looked down at Evelina, his eyes soft and curious. "She wants to be introduced too."

The wyvern stopped growling and her ears perked up. She tilted her head to the side, her glowing golden eyes assessing Evelina.

"That's Zephyr." Brielle stepped up beside Evelina, waving off the creature. She leaned in and whispered, "She's the moodiest. Like her Rider."

"I can still hear you," Daimon said gruffly.

Evelina swallowed, her nerves increasing as Brielle led her over to Vero. This wyvern was *massive.* Most were, but this one… It was bigger than a small cottage, longer than the tallest oak sitting on the edge of the healer's garden.

Keir helped Gloriana onto Codax, while Brielle helped Evelina onto Vero. She showed her how to place her foot on a thick rope with knots that hung off just beside her wing. Evelina grabbed the rope, placed her right foot on the knot, and hoisted herself up. The transition was awkward and horribly uncoordinated. But Brielle was patient, giving her a push from her left foot so she could get a better position.

Once she was seated, she tested out the saddle, feeling Vero's scales beneath it. His scales were smoother than she thought they would be beneath her fingers. But soon, her stomach dipped as Vero flapped her wings and lifted from the ground. It was terrifying seeing the wyverns up close, but now that they were breaking above the tree line, the fear was being replaced with pure exhilaration. She couldn't help but admire her realm stretching out around them. The sights of the tops of trees, the palace behind them, and even the healer's garden—from this height, it felt like she was dreaming.

Zephyr and Daimon took the lead, flying in front of Keir and Brielle. Evelina was transfixed by him, mesmerized. He looked as if he belonged there—so sure in every movement he made—all the while seeming entirely relaxed.

She still couldn't believe she was going to be on the border with him. Her heart was pounding for ten different reasons, but having to come to terms with the pain of him leaving her was at the front of her mind.

FIFTEEN

DAIMON

IT WAS EVENING WHEN THEY FINALLY TOUCHED DOWN AT the camp. They were greeted by Aster and Willow just landing from a patrol, but Evelina and Gloriana didn't linger. Brielle led them to a cabin beside the fleet's, the healer cabin Jarrett used to sleep in. It was stocked with herbs, tonics, and tinctures. Still, Gloriana and Evelina came with sacks filled with more supplies. Evelina didn't so much as look at him, but he found himself stealing glances in her direction every few breaths.

He yawned while he paced outside of Evelina's cabin. Something in his chest buzzed and burned with warmth, his magic answering a song he couldn't hear. A primal magic poking at his chest. Zephyr seemed restless too, her head following Daimon as he started to stalk around the camp.

"Up for a ride?" he asked her. Her ears perked up, eyes glowing in the dimming light.

He glanced out into the thicket of forest outside the camp, where a fire was crackling. He knew Brielle slept less than anyone else, her need to keep others safe driving her to stay up all hours of the night. She was usually who he reported to when taking flight, a way of keeping track of the Riders in case something went wrong while in the air.

He left Zephyr behind, the trees too closely packed to let her follow, unless he wanted to wake the entire camp with her knocking them over—a feat she would be all too eager to do. He crossed over the fallen trees and pushed through the bramble bushes until he found Brielle seated by the small fire.

"I'm headed up for a quick sweep," he said by way of greeting.

She grunted and nodded her head, her eyes focused on the pines around them. "I'll be here."

Brielle was brilliant, a talented warrior with her skill and her mind. Daimon didn't doubt she likely knew he was doing more than just a perimeter sweep. They were both Riders, both needing to take their beasts to the skies when the world got too heavy.

He walked back to the center of camp and tugged at the bond nestled in his chest. Zephyr flew from the back of the cabin, her wings fluttering in preparation for the flight she was always desperate for.

He wasn't the only one who longed to be beneath the stars and among the clouds.

With a quick jump, he hopped on her neck, barely having time to hold onto her spikes before she launched off the ground. He huffed a breathy laugh, feeling a burst of excitement flow through their bond. Her joy settled his worries, mingling with his emotions.

They soared through the clouds, a slow and steady pace that started near the camp and then got further away—until the moon was high in the sky. He made sure to settle his shadows over the campfires below, blocking their light so he couldn't see the fires they made no matter how close he was. No chances would be taken, not with Evelina here.

Zephyr's ears flattened against her head as a low rumble moved through her throat. Daimon's attention snapped into focus, searching the forest below. But all was quiet. No rustles of branches or scattering of birds to signal any kind of movement.

And then he felt it. The hairs on his neck standing on end, his blood thrumming like something was trying to pull it out of his body.

"I still marvel at how magnificent these creatures are," a deep voice rumbled from behind them. "Though I do prefer dragons."

Daimon whipped Zephyr around, the misty clouds swirling as her tail spun. It was too hazy to see, the voice seemingly coming from thin air. He knew all the Riders, each and every one of them. This was not a Rider.

His pulse pounded against his temple. He knew the voice, though—it was one he could never forget. There was always something dark in each syllable he spoke, a crackling of energy that filled the air around him.

"Show yourself, Nyx." Daimon held his voice steady, though his insides were quaking.

"I suppose I shouldn't be surprised you recognized me." A deep sigh followed the words. Through the clouds, an outline appeared as the figure got closer. With the moonlight shrouded in haze, Daimon couldn't see the man's face until he was hovering a few paces from Zephyr. He floated in the sky, no beast with wings to hold him up and no wings of his own.

He watched Daimon for a moment, his face still partially shadowed in darkness. Zephyr angled herself so that Daimon was partially shielded by her.

"I know it's been quite some time since we last spoke," Nyx said with a grin. "I've gone by many names over the years, but Nyx has always been my favorite."

Daimon clenched his jaw, his insides twisting.

Nyx laughed, a deep sound that scattered like thunder through the clouds. "You are always far too serious."

Nyx hovered a moment before floating closer, the shadows lifting from his face as he paused within hand's length of Zephyr's nose. She sniffed him, her neck stretching out. He lifted his gaze to Daimon's, one of his eyes a midnight blue and the other bright green. There had always been variations as to how he was depicted, but the color of his eyes remained the same in every painting. That was how Daimon had recognized him all those years ago.

The dark god, Nyx.

"A pleasure to see you again, Daimon." The god's mouth curved into an eerie smile.

Daimon didn't return the smile. If Nyx was here, it couldn't mean anything good. The tales involving the gods showing their faces to mortals never ended well, and Daimon knew all too well what Nyx was capable of.

Nyx tilted his head to the side, his navy hair rustling in the wind. The hue matched the navy iris of his right eye. "Problem?" he asked.

Daimon remained silent, willing his heartbeat to stay even.

The stories about the gods were endless, as well as the abilities they harnessed. While he didn't feel any aggression behind Nyx's visit, he was still a god. Many stories told of the way all gods could sense what any fae or human was thinking and there was nothing they could do to stop it.

Some said it only took one thought from a god to take any fae's magic away. Not to mention their cunningness, how they all had their own selfish agendas, no matter how neutral their magic seemed. Daimon had no way of knowing what legends were true. The gods were still a mystery—and it had been years since he had last spoken with Nyx.

Nyx's smile turned feline, his gaze making Daimon more unsettled.

"Smart of you to stay silent." Nyx laughed, the sound like metal grinding against stone. "I would expect nothing less of my offspring."

Daimon's spine straightened at the word, his blood boiling. *Offspring*—the word callous and without emotion.

But then again, Daimon did not consider himself his son. And no matter the true story of their blood, he would never accept Nyx, the God of Fear and Dreams, as his father.

Sixteen

Daimon

"The war needs to end. Your power alone could change it, could prevent future deaths," Daimon hissed, unable to stop himself. The night sky was deceptively calm, a stark contrast to the chaos in his mind. "You're a fucking bastard."

Nyx laughed, the sound deep and warped. "Technically, *you're* the bastard."

Daimon squeezed his hands into fists, trying to rein his anger in. He hated Nyx. Hated him for the constant reminder as to what stood between him and Evelina, at the cavern of space that separated her light from his darkness.

"We could use you and that rage of yours," Nyx said with a heavy sigh—more bored than holding any real emotion. "But Vidaris is patient. As am I."

She sure as fuck was going to be patient. Daimon didn't know what exactly the Goddess of Vengeance had planned for him, but he didn't care to know. Because it was never going to happen.

"The war isn't over yet," he snarled.

Nyx watched him closely, quiet for long enough that it made Daimon fight the urge to squirm beneath his scrutiny.

"Do not forget your birthright, Daimon," he said slowly.

"Vidaris is the ruler of the Vale for now, but with her interest in *you* as the Lord of Shadows, it could tip the power back in my direction if we play our cards right. I grow bored of watching her rule the Vale."

Daimon held back a laugh, reminding himself he was in the presence of a god. Nyx had been pushing him to become the Lord of Shadows for years, wanting him to play his part in whatever scheme Nyx had concocted to steal Vidaris's rule over the Vale.

Nyx had been forced into servitude to Vidaris centuries ago, a vassal to her power. Nyx's son taking the helm of Lord of Shadows would be an ultimate show of loyalty, perhaps enough cover to finally buy him the freedom to rebuild his power.

Even if Vidaris suspected anything, she remained vulnerable as long as she couldn't find a being of two worlds—both fae and god—to guard the realm outside the Vale.

Which left Daimon pretty much screwed, wrapped in their webs of power.

"Your power has matured enough for you to take the Shadow Realm." Nyx tilted his head to the side. "Why delay the inevitable?"

"If it's inevitable, why rush?"

Nyx chuckled and flung his arms around wide, looking up at the stars above them. "You are the son of a *god,* while also being the son of a fae woman. To take up the helm as the Lord of Shadows, one must have a foot in both worlds, blood of man and god."

As far as Daimon knew, there weren't any others like him. Both son of god and fae, making him halves of each and never quite whole.

"Man will not accept who you are." Nyx bared his teeth in a smile that looked more like a snarl. "Or have you forgotten how eager men are to burn those who are *different* at the stake?"

Daimon could never forget it, even if he wanted to. Zephyr whimpered beneath him, feeling his pain.

"Perhaps a reminder would be of use," Nyx said with a sigh, as if the burden of this responsibility weighed on him. He turned his back to Daimon, waving his hand—the god of dreams himself painting a mirage across the sky. Like looking through a mirror, Daimon watched the memory play out before him.

A woman held her hand to her round belly, her hair as dark as night, falling in wild waves down her back. She sang a broken melody about a boy who would change the fate of fae and man alike.

Daimon took a deep breath, the image of his mother almost too painful to bear. Yet he found himself unable to look away.

The woman sat with her legs folded beneath her, a white cotton nightgown snug on her stomach. She placed short sticks in a ring around an oak tree one by one. After, she took a black-bladed knife and carved symbols into the bark. She hummed her somber tune while completing the steps, not once breaking its pattern.

A leaf crunched behind her and she froze, fingers still wrapped around the blade, the point touching the tree. She briefly closed her eyes, still humming.

"Aurora," a light, feminine voice said shakily. "Aurora."

And yet Aurora still carved, eyes closed as she etched the symbols from memory. The footsteps grew closer to her, but she didn't break stride.

"You're with child." The woman's voice was pleading. "You promised you would stop this madness."

Aurora sliced the dagger sideways and then again from the opposite side, creating a jagged X in the bark.

The woman crouched down beside Aurora, revealing her face.

Annora—no, Maliena. She looked so much like Annora that Daimon had to take another deep breath. Nyx still had his back to him, his hands folded as he watched the memory.

Maliena's typically warm smile was tilted into a frown as she watched Aurora still cutting symbols into the tree. She reached out and placed a hand on Aurora's shoulder. She flinched at the contact, Aurora's shoulder icy to the touch, as if she had been out here for hours.

"If anyone catches you worshiping the dark gods, they'll cast you into the wilderness," Maliena tried again.

This might have been well before the time of the rebels surfacing, but worshiping the dark gods was unheard of—or at least carefully hidden. Simply being related to someone who worshiped them would make any fae an outcast.

Aurora paused, her humming halting and hand stopping. She slowly turned her head to Maliena, the side of her face now visible.

Daimon's breath caught in his throat as he saw her hollowed-out cheeks and the deep circles beneath her eyes. He knew what would happen next, but that didn't make it any easier. This was Nyx's favorite memory to show, after all.

· · ·

"I love him, Mali," Aurora said in a scratchy voice. "He has to know I still believe in him."

Maliena's lip wobbled as she took in Aurora's tearstained cheeks. "Please, just come back to my cottage with me. Let's get you warmed up."

Aurora shook her head fiercely, jerking back from Maliena's touch. "There's hardly anyone left who prays to Nyx," she said harshly, her voice as sharp as the blade in her hand. She wrapped a protective hand around her stomach as she added, "I want our son to know him."

Maliena was the only friend Aurora had told of who fathered the child. To everyone else, he was an unnamed man she had met on a journey.

"This child is killing you, Aurora," Maliena said softly, her eyes welling with tears.

Aurora turned her attention back to the tree, resuming her etching with swift and deep cuts.

Maliena shifted, trying a new tactic. "Stop this for the sake of the child, then. He'll be outcasted for his entire life if anyone learns that his mother worshiped Nyx instead of Eurydice."

Aurora snorted a joyless laugh. "Eurydice hasn't answered a prayer in decades, while Nyx is here, helping where he can."

"And what of the child's Essence when it's born?" Maliena pushed. "Someone will find out if we don't—"

"No one will know if you're the only one present when it happens," Aurora said quickly. "No one will find out."

Every child released their parents' magic back to them; it would separate and seek out the place from which it had originated. Even if a child's parents were dead, their Essence would flow directly up, straight to Caelum. Since Aurora was a Nox, shadows would flow to her. But since Nyx was not fae, his Essence had nowhere to go.

The severed line would reveal Daimon was not blessed by Eurydice; that he was an abomination.

The memory rippled, like a rock dropping into a pond, and shifted into another.

Aurora was screaming as Maliena coached her breathing and yelled at her to push. "I can see the babe's head!" Maliena shouted. "Another big push!"

Sweat had collected on Aurora's brow as she pushed again. The door to the worn cottage burst open and a young midwife ran in, carrying a bowl of warm water and cloths.

"No," Aurora said breathlessly. "She was supposed to wait until after the babe came. She can't—"

There was no stopping the baby as it came out. A cry filled the cottage as Maliena wrapped it into a blanket.

"Please, you must leave. Come back later—"

But it was too late. The babe's Essence was already flowing from its tiny body, returning to its parents.

A line of shadows returned to Aurora, just as it should. But the midwife gasped as the other line of shadows dashed around the room in a frantic search, spreading and blooming around the walls in an inky darkness. Then it broke above the babe, splitting in two. One side dissolved back into light, while the other line grew, then suddenly dropped, severed, bleeding shadows like a snake with its head cut off.

"What is this madness?" the midwife demanded. The shadows around the babe abruptly vanished, the magic dispersing around the room. "A cursed child! Not blessed by Eurydice," she hissed and backed out of the cottage.

Maliena stood, cradling the babe, as the midwife ran from the cottage screaming.

"Save the baby, Mali," Aurora said breathlessly. "Get out of here, now!"

Maliena stepped forward, her eyes wide. "I won't leave you Aurora."

Men and women gathered outside the cottage, holding torches and farm tools they brandished as weapons.

"We will not have a child of evil in this realm!" a man shouted from the doorway. "Burn the house!"

Maliena panicked, looking to Aurora.

"Go," Aurora pleaded. "And let him know his father will always hear his call."

Daimon turned around, unable to watch what happened next. The memory dissolved, the cloud behind it returning to a gray haze. Icy pain stabbed at his chest.

"You see what happens when men are told things they do not understand?" Nyx turned back to Daimon. "Her loyalty to me was unmatched. You could learn a thing or two about that."

He hoped Nyx couldn't tell the way his chest was heaving, or the way sweat had collected against his temple. "You could have saved her."

Nyx shrugged, seemingly unbothered by the way Aurora's life had ended. But Daimon always saw past the facade. He could see the flash of pain in Nyx's eyes, could see the way his mouth briefly pinched tighter.

"Matters of the gods are not your concern," he said simply. "But as my heir, your rightful place is a creator of pain, a wielder of darkness and demons. Whenever you're finished with this little detour, you will have much to do. The path is being laid for you, Daimon. And when fate chooses, you will wear the crown of darkness."

"No one knows what fate has planned," Daimon said half-heartedly. But even as he said it, he could feel the nauseating unease swirling in his stomach.

Nyx chuckled as he began to disappear into the clouds. "You can only play soldier for the wrong side for so long."

Daimon's rage and guilt consumed him. He had begged in prayer to Nyx to change the tides of this war, to tear down the rebel forces. Had offered everything he could think of in exchange for his help. But Nyx didn't like deals—nor did he care to involve himself in matters of fae and humans. And even if he cared, Nyx was too weak to take on Vidaris. Vidaris grew stronger with each day, the war fueling her power as despair filled every living being in the realm.

He could put faith in his father to overcome Vidaris one day in their competition for the Vale. But it would mean swearing allegiance to the one being responsible for all this pain and suffering—not to mention Nyx was a dark god too. Daimon didn't like to think about choosing between the lesser of two evils. If it could save the empire, he would trade himself a thousand times over. But he couldn't risk being a puppet for the powers of darkness without a guarantee.

But the facts remained the same. He was an abomination. He would be forced into the role one day or another. And anyone bound to him would be chained to the shadows with him.

Every visit Nyx paid him reminded him of the day the god first revealed himself, when Daimon first found out the burden of his birthright. The day his life changed.

The same day he gave up his dream of ever returning to Evelina.

SEVENTEEN

DAIMON

TWENTY YEARS EARLIER

AFTER HIS WYVERN CHOSE HIM, DAIMON HAD COME TO camp in a valley alongside the Zenovia Mountains. He was placed in the only omega fleet in the entire camp, a training purgatory for anyone under the age of sixteen. Even so, the council head of the Aegis was among the Riders training here, something that amazed Daimon each and every day. He was learning how to be a Rider from the best of the best, training day in and day out.

Instead of sleeping, he lay awake in his cabin most nights, thinking of Evelina. After Evelina lost her father and Daimon left, he vowed to himself to become the best Rider. He might have started with tasks like fixing roofs and cleaning leathers, but he would be the best at doing it until he was strong enough to join a real fleet and see actual combat. Strong enough to protect Evelina from ever feeling that kind of pain again.

So, he trained harder than any other fae, only stopping long enough to get a few hours of sleep and shovel food into his mouth. Some of the Riders were being formed into units composed of eight to fifteen Riders. He made it his mission to be among the best, to hopefully even be in the lead fleet with Commander Keir.

But at night, when his body was still and his thoughts were running rampant, he ached to go back home to her. Tonight, Daimon felt a pull so deep in his chest that he couldn't ignore it.

It had been a few months since he had last seen her, and he just wanted to make sure she was okay. The omega fleet wasn't allowed to travel out of camp without permission from their cohort lead—and definitely not without some kind of chaperone —but Daimon had already gotten away with short trips through the forests at night.

If anyone found out, he'd be in deep trouble. But it was worth the risk for Evelina—even if for just one night.

He crept out of the cabin and jogged around back to where Zephyr was asleep. As swift as he could, he got her up into the skies before anyone could see him leave.

The flight at this time of night was peaceful—quiet. Cloud coverage was thick, leaving Daimon and Zephyr flying in near-total darkness. He didn't mind it, not when there was hardly a quiet moment in the camp.

Zephyr slowed, her ears pinned back against her head. Daimon scoured the forest beneath them, looking for the source of the disturbance. Everything was dark and still, the moon covered by thick clouds. His hair stood on his arms, and his neck prickled with the sensation of being watched.

Blood pounded in Daimon's ears, his chest tightening. Something was off. He focused his breathing and tugged on his Essence, calling on his shadows and letting them wind around his wrists and arms.

"Sorry for the dramatics," a deep voice said from behind. "I prefer to meet in the skies."

Daimon looked over his shoulder, his eyes finding nothing but empty clouds. His heart thrashed in his chest. He didn't know if this person was friend or foe, but he would be prepared if it was the latter. It could be another Rider; there were more than seven fleets now, and some were still being chosen.

"Show yourself," he demanded, turning back around to find a dark figure within the clouds.

The figure moved closer. It was as if he simply floated, no wyvern to ride on and no wings to hold him up. The closer he got, the more Daimon could feel his pulse pound. There was something dark that radiated from this man, something that had Daimon's instincts screaming at him to run.

A rumble worked its way through Zephyr's chest, and she bared her teeth. Daimon raised his chin, expecting the figure to retreat. But he didn't—instead, he came *closer.*

Daimon held his ground as the man came into view, taking in his appearance. He was impeccably dressed, hands folded behind his back. He wore a black coat, fitted perfectly to his shoulders and arms. Beneath the coat was a black linen shirt, threaded together with shimmering silver strands. His trousers were also black and tailored without blemish.

He wore clothing suited for a king.

"I've been waiting for the right time to meet you," the man said.

"Who are you?" Daimon demanded, letting his shadows grow around his hands.

The man stepped closer, his eyes dropping down to Daimon's shadows. He smiled. When his gaze lifted to meet Daimon's, a chill ran down his spine. Daimon knew these eyes— one the color of midnight and one bright green. They were the eyes of Nyx, the God of Fear and Dreams, the way he was depicted in every text.

"I think you know who I am, Daimon," the man said. "It's not often a god takes interest in man."

Daimon's blood ran cold as the man smiled again, flashing his teeth.

"You're—" His voice caught, his mind rushing to process the being before him. "You're Nyx."

Nyx winked. "In the flesh."

Daimon reined Zephyr back a bit, feeling like his shadows were wholly useless now. The god who gave Nocturna shadows was standing before him.

His smile was dark. Sinister. He was every bit of the god of fear at this moment.

"Why are you here?" Daimon pressed.

Nyx sighed and leaned against a tree. "To tell you the truth."

Daimon's brows pulled together, trying to make sense of what truth the God of Fear and Dreams might have to share.

"What do you know of your parents?" Nyx asked.

Daimon paused, even more confused. He never talked about his parents. His chest tightened as he tried to keep his mouth closed. But the words came out before he could stop them, like there was a gravitational pull yanking the truth out of him.

"My mother never told my father she was with child," he whispered.

"And your mother?" Nyx said slowly, his eyes expectant.

Daimon gritted his teeth, trying to hold the truth in. But again, the words came out despite him not wanting to speak them. "She died during childbirth."

Nyx nodded and hummed to himself. "In a way, I suppose Aurora did."

Daimon's eyes widened, the tightness in his chest loosening. "You knew my mother?"

"I knew her very well," Nyx said with a smile. His tone was teasing, like there was a joke only he knew. "In fact, I would say I knew her in a way I have known no one else. A way a god shouldn't know a mortal creature. Fae may be immortal to time, but you all die eventually. Nothing is truly immortal unless you're one of the Divine. Aurora knew that, and yet she chose to be with me regardless."

Daimon felt as if he had been hit by a brick wall. His breath caught, his mind racing at Nyx's words.

"You're a liar," he hissed.

Nyx tsked. "Haven't you ever wondered why your shadows are stronger than the other Nox? Why they developed from such a young age? You're only thirteen and you have better control than half the Nox alive."

He was a liar, a trickster here to cause chaos as the gods so often did. But Daimon didn't know of a fae that could float in the skies.

"Some have stronger Essence than others," he said with his chin lifted. But doubt swirled in the back of his mind. "That doesn't make me the son of a god."

Nyx laughed and shrugged his shoulders. "I suppose that alone doesn't. If my words are not enough, perhaps a memory will be."

Daimon's vision went dark. Though he was still seated atop Zephyr, his eyes now saw a different place entirely.

He saw his mother just as she was depicted in one of Maliena's paintings. There were flashes of Aurora with Nyx, of them meeting in the forest close to the Zenovia Mountains. She was praying to him when he appeared to her, and she fell at his feet when he spoke.

Memories flew by: Nyx visiting her when she prayed. Then she was in front of a tree, talking of her love for Nyx with her hand on her round belly. Maliena was with her, warning her of the danger that came with worshiping one of the dark gods. The last memory was of her being dragged out of a small cottage while Maliena ran out the back door, cradling a newborn.

Daimon swayed as his vision returned to him, now back in the skies with Nyx watching him. His face was bored, his hands resting in his pockets.

"Why show me this, why now?" Daimon choked out. He couldn't be Nyx's son. He was a normal fae, just like everyone else.

"Your inheritance awaits you," Nyx said. "The Shadow Realm is yours to take. Vidaris grows stronger each day with the war fueling her. She presides over the Vale, torturing the souls of the damned. But the in-between, the Shadow Realm, rests with a stronghold in both realms. A foot in the Vale and a foot in the living world. The ruler of it must be able to survive in both, which only someone born of god and man can accomplish."

Daimon's throat constricted with each word. He couldn't breathe—couldn't wrap his mind around his new reality, let alone the idea of ruling the Shadow Realm one day.

"Think on it," Nyx said, breaking Daimon out of his thoughts. "You'll be the heir of darkness soon. It would be best to take up the helm before others learn the truth of who you are."

Nyx disappeared into the shadows, leaving a cold wind in his wake.

Daimon's head spun. If Nyx was telling the truth, Daimon wasn't just the son of a god… He was the son of a *dark* god. The dark gods were not welcome among fae.

Perhaps if he raised his station high enough, no one would hold it against him if they learned the truth about him. If he could garner the respect of the people and prove himself worthy of Evelina in the eyes of the crown, then that would solve all of his problems. People would know he wasn't who his father was —they would see past his bloodline.

But deep down, he knew the truth. People would try and kill him for it just as they had his mother—they would be terrified of a dark god's heir. They burned his mother alive just after giving birth for what she had done with Nyx. The effects of people knowing would ruin his life, or that of anyone close to him.

And if he were to go back to Evelina…

Shame washed over him, consuming every inch of his being. What if there was darkness in him? There could be a chance of corrupting her, of whatever pieces of Nyx that resided in him somehow hurting her.

That was when he knew he couldn't go back to her, even to visit. He couldn't risk her life, her people turning on her the moment they found out she knew about him all along. Nor could he risk his weakness in breaking down and telling her everything, which he would do with a single look at her bright hazel eyes.

So he didn't go back. Again and again, his shame of himself and his fear for her won out.

Years passed.

In all that time, he kept hoping for a day he could change his fate, when he would finally return to her and prove he was worthy of her hand.

He passed his trial, the harvest moon bright in the sky as he sealed his immortality beneath it. He and his training cohort met in a small temple outside a cluster of villages, a single priestess presiding over the trial.

Daimon's trial was odd, the stories of his peers not aligning with his. They all spoke of three separate parts: mind, body, and spirit. His, on the other hand… It was composed of a single thing: slaying a dragon with three heads.

He thought it was strange that his experience was so different, but then again, the trial was specific to the fae taking it. Instead of dwelling on it, he chalked it up to how he had always been the odd one out his whole life.

His days shifted from being *too young* to do any real training to learning how to fly with other Riders. More and more he got invited to fly with some of the best, Commander Keir even joining some days. Zephyr seemed to fit seamlessly into their flight, teaching Daimon more than Daimon could teach her.

After that, Commander Keir told him he would be joining the main aerial unit—the Alpha Fleet. It was everything he had worked for, a real chance at making a difference in this war.

However, even that wasn't enough for Daimon. He set his sights on being commander. After a few more years of sweat and tears, he secured that position too. He was *almost* the man he wanted to prove he could be.

But Nyx returned again and again with the reminder of Daimon's heritage, and each success felt more like a lie. He had always hoped a day would come when he *finally* felt like he was worthy of Evelina. Over the years, that hope faded like fire being snuffed out by rain. The work, the titles, the training—none of it changed his blood.

Nyx was right. He would only serve to hurt her.

He was so close to being the man he fought so hard to become, only to question now if he deserved to be that man at all.

EIGHTEEN

DAIMON

DAIMON'S CHEST HEAVED AS HE SHOVED THE PANIC AWAY. Zephyr landed outside the camp, restless as he slid off her back and strode into the darkness of the forest. He didn't know where he was walking to, just that he needed to clear his mind after seeing Nyx again.

He could feel the tightness in his chest start to ease with each step he took. He passed a patch of flowers—lunaria, rare in this part of the realm. He paused, a wave of memories washing over him of a simpler time when he and a girl sat in a small garden together. They would sit in the middle of the lunaria path, laughing and playing pretend. She was his best friend, his closest ally.

But that girl—now a woman—had become a stranger.

He started walking again, running a hand through his hair as he blindly forged a path through the trees. It wasn't until he got to the edge of a pond that he realized he wasn't alone any longer.

Evelina was pacing in front of the pond with strands of light winding around her fingers. Her light affinity was almost as rare as his uncanny ability to manipulate the shadows. It was what drew them together as children. It drew him to her even now.

It took his breath away to see her like this. She had grown up into a fearless woman—and he had missed it all.

A waterfall was flowing into the pool of water behind her, the rushing so loud that she hadn't heard him approach. For a moment, he stood there, spellbound, watching the way her hands twisted around each other—something she did when she was anxious. There had been a time when he would've reached out and laid his hands over her fidgeting. He raised his hand now, almost as if by instinct, reminded that he had changed, too. More than just who he had become, but even his body. His hand was large, weathered—the skin of a Rider—and could likely envelop both of hers now in a single grasp.

Instead, he cleared his throat and tucked his hands into his pockets.

She stopped moving and looked up at him. A gentle breeze pulled small pieces of her hair across her face. Her hazel eyes swam with tears.

There was a tense pause, neither of them speaking. If he were honest, he had no idea what *to* say. The memories Nyx had played for Daimon were too fresh. It was too painful to be seeing Evelina right now.

"I was just about to bathe," she whispered, as if to explain herself. He had no way of knowing if she was scared or over-whelmed. The face he once read so clearly was indecipherable to him now. She took a step forward, but Daimon didn't miss the way her hands trembled and her lips wobbled.

He had so much to say. An explanation sat on the tip of his tongue; how he'd chanted her name like a prayer every second he was gone. He couldn't tell her why he'd stayed away all these years—still couldn't.

He could handle her anger, her fury and rage.

But her heartbreak? It was like a sword sliced him in half when he saw it flash through her eyes. He wasn't surprised to find it there, but it hurt all the same.

He turned away from her, his heart pounding in his chest.

He heard the rippling of water as she stepped into the pond. He didn't know if they would ever be on speaking terms again, didn't even know where to start.

And despite everything Nyx had reminded him of tonight, he walked away, wondering if every decision he'd made over the past twenty years had been a mistake.

PART TWO:

MASK OF THE COMMANDER

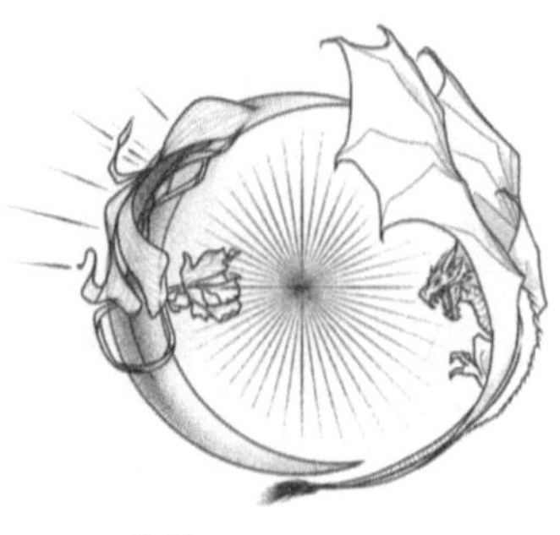

NINETEEN

EVELINA

THE CAMP IN THE ZENOVIA VALLEY HAD ITS OWN RHYTHM. The first few days, Evelina mostly stayed in her cabin with Gloriana. They went through every single jar that was stocked along the wall, familiarizing themselves with the healing mixtures and memorizing the location of each tonic so they could access them easily in a hurry. The entire living room had been transformed into a place suited for mixing herbs and making tonics. Most of the walls were lined with shelves to house the jars, bandages, and other supplies.

The valley nestled beneath the mountains was forested and rocky, the plush trees doing little to block the icy wind that breezed through the camp at night. Small cabins and tents were scattered around the healer's cabin, while a tall cavern rested behind what she now knew to be Alpha Fleet's dwelling. Theirs was the largest, but not by much, making her wonder how well seven soldiers fit inside. She hadn't been in yet, nor had she drawn closer than a hundred paces, her fear of crossing with Daimon only slightly outweighing her want to see his life here.

When the days were warm enough in the valley, she would open a sliding shutter covered in animal pelt to keep the heat in when the sun wasn't out. She'd note the way the Alpha Fleet worked in perfect unison in all that they did. They trained together on the ground outside the cluster of cabins, sparring and testing one another. Occasionally, one of them would have to come to her cabin for a mending salve—usually Keir or Brielle. They were the Aegis of the group, so that didn't come as a surprise.

Then she would watch as they mounted their wyverns, taking their practice to the skies when they weren't patrolling. She watched Daimon leading them, not shouting orders but laughing along with them.

It was odd to see him this way—relaxed and in charge. They had hardly said a word to each other since being here, but he seemed fully at ease with his fleet. She thought she'd be relieved seeing he was doing well now. But seeing how his life had moved on without her hurt more than she realized.

Today, she and Gloriana were still arranging the last of the supplies, tidying up the shelves and tying each bottle off with a label. Then, the door to her cabin burst open. A soldier came in carrying a Rider Evelina hadn't met. Her eyes were closed and her head was cradled against his chest.

"Willow was hit while patrolling the west region of the border," the soldier said quickly.

Gloriana bustled past Evelina and met them beside the nearest cot. Evelina helped the soldier lay Willow down, careful of the wound on her thigh.

"She's lost a lot of blood," Evelina said as she examined her. "Blood-replenishing tea?"

Gloriana nodded sharply and Evelina ran to retrieve it from the shelves. She quickly grabbed a heated kettle that hung in a fireplace on the other end of the room. Her head snapped up as the open shutter rattled and jars clinked together. The wyverns were restless, pounding the ground and beating their wings. As the water heated, Evelina moved toward the door to check outside.

On the other side was organized chaos. Foot soldiers were

running about, gathering weapons and saddling their horses. The Riders were mounting their beasts, hastening to take to the skies. She saw a flash of Daimon before he disappeared into the clouds.

Her heart thundered in her chest, but she promptly closed the door and set her attention back on the tea. Gloriana was using her light to mend Willow's wound on her thigh. Her eyes fluttered open, a painful cry emerging from her lips.

"Help me sit her up," Evelina commanded the soldier. "She needs to drink this tea; it'll speed up the process of her blood replenishing itself."

The soldier nodded, hoisting Willow up and causing her to whimper. Evelina held the cup to her lips, careful to make sure she drank the lukewarm liquid.

"She should rest here so we can watch over her for the next several hours," Gloriana said, her light dimming as she finished mending the gash on Willow's leg.

"She might not be the only one who needs healing soon," the soldier said tightly.

Gloriana and Evelina exchanged a look.

"Find us more cots and bring them in here, maybe even a few out front just in case," Evelina said. "We will prepare for the worst and hope for the best."

She found herself sending a prayer to Eurydice for the soldiers' safety, adding an extra one for Daimon as he led them. She may have always known he was on the battlefront, but seeing it with her own eyes made her realize the weight of it—to realize what was at stake. How afraid it made her to allow her heart to care more for him.

Daimon

The battle was quick—only a handful of rebels attempting passage through the mountains. They had caught Willow off guard with a ferrum arrow while she was patrolling, slowing down her healing ability. Daimon's fleet took care of them before the foot soldiers even arrived. But they captured one of the last remaining rebels.

Daimon landed further out from the cabin, ripping off his scaled armor so he could breathe. Keir landed beside him, his wyvern clutching the rebel in his talons—a fae, a traitor to his own crown. Codax slammed into the dirt, pinning him to the ground and caging him in.

Daimon stalked over, his shoulders stiff. Keir raised a hand, fire winding around his arms and blazing with the promise of death.

The rebel hissed, baring his teeth and thrashing beneath Codax's talons.

Keir sneered at him. "Sickening one would abandon their crown so easily," he said as Daimon stopped beside him.

"Fuck the crown," the rebel spat.

Daimon took a step forward. The rebel's head snapped toward him, watching him curiously. The trees danced above them as a wind swept through the forest. They stood in silence for a moment, leaves floating through the air around them.

Daimon jutted his chin out. "Think we'll get any information out of him?"

"Probably not, but it's better we try now that we have one." Keir's gaze traveled over the rebel, barely holding back his disgust. "He might change his mind come sundown."

Daimon wasn't surprised. Keir didn't shy away from using more…questionable methods to get an edge in this war. He was the commander of the Aegis, after all.

Keir turned to walk away, Codax in dutiful pursuit when he paused.

"Well, come on, commander." Keir's fire grew brighter as a smile stretched across his face, the flames highlighting his scars. "You're doing the interrogation with me."

TWENTY

EVELINA

A BREEZE TWISTED EVELINA'S HAIR AROUND HER FACE, whipping the strands wildly. But despite the chill, a sweat had begun to work its way onto her brow. Some color had already started to show in Willow's face, her breathing less erratic and growing steadier by the hour.

Evelina walked outside to the back of the cabin to clean her bloodstained leathers and hang them out to dry. A sound broke through the trees, making her pause. It was loud enough that Evelina could place it almost immediately, catching the distant outline of three figures between the trees before she heard the whimpering of a man. She took a cautious step toward the tree line.

Another cry of pain was all it took for her feet to move. She ran through the forest, the cries getting louder until she was a few paces from the figures. She squinted, trying to make sense of the scene, then held back a gasp as she realized what was happening.

The cries weren't of their soldiers in pain—it was a rebel, clothed in tattered cotton tunics and linen trousers, along with the dark runic weapons they wielded.

Evelina jumped behind a bundle of shrubs and lowered

herself to the ground to stay hidden. The sunlight was fading, though she could still make out the unmistakable broad-shouldered Aegis commander, and the man standing beside him.

Daimon and Keir.

Both were facing her, though their eyes were trained elsewhere. Keir's face was harsh, his mouth pressed into a thin line, but Daimon's face was shrouded in shadows.

She had never seen him like this. He looked…deadly. Terrifying. A sharp smile stretched across his face and he tilted his head to the side, studying their hostage. He had a rope of shadows around the rebel soldier's throat, binding him to a tree. With the evening sun illuminating the man's face, she could see his veins popping and straining against the shadowy rope.

Daimon was choking him—yet he wasn't *saying* anything. He wasn't questioning the rebel or demanding answers; he just stared down at him while his shadows tightened around the man's neck.

Evelina's chest began to expand rapidly. She pressed her hand against her mouth, masking her quickened breath. She knew the soldier was a rebel—the enemy that had threatened everything the empire had built over centuries. Her mind understood why they needed information from him, but it didn't erase the nausea in her stomach.

Daimon had been closed off since arriving, his commander mask firmly in place. At first, she thought there was some of the boy she knew still left underneath.

But now she realized he was every bit the ruthless aerial commander he presented.

Daimon took a step toward the man. "Are you ready to talk now?" His voice was rougher than she had ever heard it, dark in a way that made her skin crawl.

The man immediately snarled when the shadows loosened around his throat, spit flying from his mouth. "*Fuck* the crown and each and every Manor."

"Wrong answer." Daimon's shadows tightened once again, causing a gurgling sound to come from the man.

The rebel gasped for air, baring his teeth between short breaths. Slowly, the shadowy tendrils relaxed again. He coughed until blood dribbled down the side of his mouth.

"We follow our king," he whispered hoarsely.

Keir burst into laughter. "You call your little rebel leader a king?"

The man lifted his gaze to him, his eyes hollow. A shiver crawled up Evelina's spine.

"He will be king of all one day," he spat.

Daimon crouched down to eye level with the soldier, catching a ray of setting light. His eyes were hardened and dark, nothing familiar in the gaze she once knew so well.

"He will be king of none," Daimon whispered.

The soldier spat in his face. "May the empire die and a new king be reborn. May the land of the empire succumb to darkness. May every ounce of blood be drained from every Manor until their rule is over once and for all."

Evelina could not help the gasp that escaped her. The rebel's head snapped in her direction. His eyes widened in recognition, as if he could recognize a Manor by scent alone. He snarled and fought against his restraints.

Keir and Daimon whirled around, following his line of sight. Evelina rose, locking eyes with Daimon. He clenched his jaw and took a step toward her.

The rebel lurched forward, a torrent of fire gathering around him. Daimon twisted back toward him just as he shot the darts of fire directly at Evelina.

A wall of shadows formed in front of Evelina like a shield, covering her from sight. The rebel's magic slammed into it, but the shield held firm, dissolving the fire into mere puffs of smoke. She had never felt Essence this strong; it radiated with anger.

She felt her own magic flare in answer to the protective magic around her, light drawn to shadows.

The wall was thin enough that she could partially see through it, just enough to see Daimon as he crouched down to the rebel. He placed his hand on his shoulder, as if the soldier wasn't thrashing against the ties around his throat. Daimon held up his right hand, looking down at his fingers until a dagger made of darkness appeared in it.

The dagger writhed in his grip as tendrils of shadows wound around the blade—then he drove the point into the soldier's chest.

The onslaught of the rebel's magic halted against the shield in front of Evelina. His arms strained against the restraints of darkness he was still bound in, then went slack. Daimon held the man's gaze as his life drained from his eyes.

Evelina heaved, her hand flying to her stomach as she willed herself not to throw up.

The last thread of hope she had that there was anything left of the boy she once knew snapped.

TWENTY-ONE

EVELINA

EVELINA WAS AT A LOSS FOR WORDS. SHE WAS A HEALER, sworn to help and do no harm. She *knew* there was loss in war, knew that people died. But it didn't make it right.

"I'll clean up here," Keir said softly as his gaze caught Evelina's.

"Evelina," Daimon rasped, his eyes still bloodthirsty and hard. "What are you doing here?"

It wasn't every day Evelina found herself in the position of eavesdropping, but she had been caught doing so more times than she cared to admit. Daimon took a step toward her, but she was already turning to walk back to the healer's cabin. He caught up with her in a few strides.

"Princess Evelina."

She spun around, her eyes blazing.

"I'm sorry you saw that." He cleared his throat, avoiding looking directly at her. "Are you okay?"

"You killed him," she stated, as if it weren't obvious—even saying the words aloud felt odd. She was not surprised he was capable of such harm. He was the Alpha Fleet's commander—of course he had killed. But this was a different thing entirely. This was no battle. And the rage in his eyes…

"He would've killed you without blinking had I not shielded you," he said bluntly. "Dark god worshipers deserve what they get. He was too far gone."

Her nostrils flared, her anger rising. "Maybe he was too far gone. But that doesn't give you the right to stoop to their level," she argued. "These rebels have turned to the gods because they feel abandoned. They blame my family because they don't know who else to blame."

Daimon shook his head and ran his fingers roughly through his hair. "It wasn't worth the risk to keep him alive."

Evelina threw her hands into the air and angled her body away from him. "Isn't worth the *risk*?" she asked in disbelief. "We might lose a lot in this war, but once we lose our honor… We prove the rebels right." She couldn't help the frustration seeping into her words. She was exhausted, her patience as fragile as the twigs beneath her feet.

"Evelina, there is always death in war." His voice was deep and gravely. "It's inevitable—you know that."

She twisted back toward him, but his gaze was set intently on the water. "It doesn't mean a life should be taken like that. He had already lost—had no way to fight back."

"Fight back?" Daimon huffed a hollow laugh. "You have no idea what we've gone through while you've been at the palace— no idea what we see every day at the border. The rebels are barely human—barely have a soul. They've sold it all to Vidaris. Death is a favor to them."

"And what about honor?"

At this, he finally looked at her, a roiling fire in his eyes. "He tried to kill you."

A shudder rolled down her spine from the intensity in his gaze. Warmth filled her chest, a spark of shock nestled beside her anger.

"Nothing about this is easy. Certainly not using my Essence to harm another. You have no idea how much I've fought against what I was born to—" He clamped his mouth closed.

"Born to what?" Evelina asked, narrowing her eyes.

His eyes flickered, seemingly wrestling with something in his mind. He spun around, ready to walk away—but Evelina wasn't having it. She reached out for him, pulling him to a stop. He looked back at her, his chest heaving.

"What do you mean?" she asked.

He pulled away from her, but she held on firmly, digging her nails into his arm.

"Nothing." He looked at the ground, his face heartbreakingly open. His emotions had been so distant and hard to read since being here, but here was his pain now—on full display.

This time, she let him go. His stride didn't falter, and he didn't look back as he walked away.

Twenty-Two

Daimon

He had been bred for blood, reborn beneath sharp edges, and told to never show mercy. And he often never did. He was comfortable hiding behind the mask of commander while his heart shattered.

Seeing Evelina's face after he killed the soldier—the way her eyes showed the fear she wouldn't admit—was something he would never forget.

His father had told him it was his fate to one day sit at Vidaris's right side as her sword. The gods didn't know the future, not fully. But the truth of his heritage remained the same. And he refused to soil Evelina's name with his dark and tainted bloodline.

He stalked along the water's edge, sensing Zephyr in the trees watching him. It had been at least an hour since his conversation with Evelina, and yet his pulse hadn't calmed.

"Well, come on out and stop hovering," he muttered.

Slowly, he could hear the weight of trees bending and branches snapping as his wyvern trotted out of the forest. Zephyr whimpered, nudging him with her nose. A shot of her sadness spiked in his chest as she nuzzled his side.

"You overheard us?" He sighed, running his hand along the leathery scales of her neck. "She hates me, Z."

Daimon found himself wishing for the thousandth time that Zephyr could talk back. But he could still feel her through the Rider bond, and he hated that she was feeling so sad.

"It's better this way," he assured her.

Zephyr abruptly nudged him, pushing him forward and cutting him off.

"I *can't* tell her, you know that."

Irritation bolted down their bond. Daimon shook his head as her golden eyes narrowed in suspicion.

"I'm not scared of her not taking it well. I just don't want her to get hurt."

Zephyr tilted her head to the side, and he knew the beast well enough to know this was her *I don't believe you* face.

Daimon waved his hands in the air. "You know just as well as I do why I can't risk her being tied to someone like me. Our fates were pulled in different directions." He frowned, patting Zephyr's head absentmindedly. "To put it lightly."

Zephyr whined and laid her head on the ground behind him. Daimon sat down beside her, leaning his back against her neck.

It was a good thing Evelina hated him now. Especially when she was everything he had ever dreamed of. She was stunning in her element when healing, and had grown into a woman he couldn't take his eyes off of. It was already taking every ounce of his restraint to keep his distance.

But now that she saw him for the monster he was… He was as relieved as he was devastated. If he was too weak to stay away, at least she could be strong enough for the both of them.

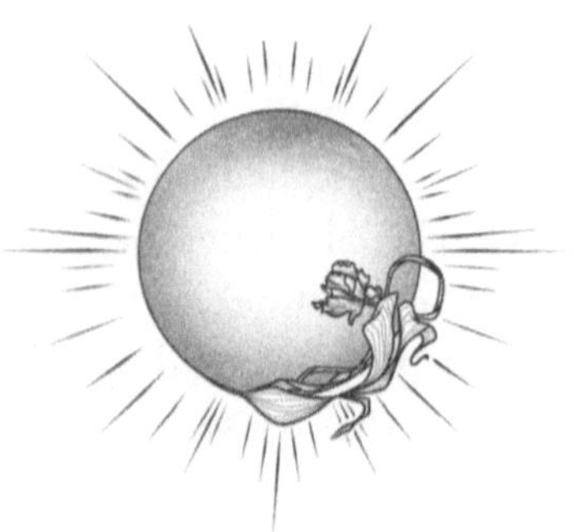

TWENTY-THREE

EVELINA

EVELINA DID A FINAL CHECK OVER WILLOW THE NEXT morning and cleared her to go back to riding.

"Take it *easy* the next few days," she said firmly. "Gloriana mended the wound, but if you push it too much, it may reopen. Your body needs time to fully heal."

Willow nodded her head, eager to get back. She rested a hand on Evelina's shoulder, her eyes crinkling at the corners with her smile. "Thank you." Her voice was as warm as honey. "This isn't the way I expected for us to meet, but it's nice to see a few more Woodland around here."

Gloriana came in through the front door, holding a large basket filled with bandages, herbs, and beeswax for mixing salve. "New foot soldiers arrived. They brought a few baskets that Lorene packed."

Gloriana set the basket down on a cot. She smiled at Willow and put the back of her hand against her forehead.

"No fever still." Gloriana hummed. "Stop back if you notice any changes with your wound."

Willow nodded and gave her thanks again before slipping out. Evelina helped Gloriana separate the new supplies, shelving them and recording the stock on scrolls of parchment.

"Brielle thought it would be beneficial for us to take turns riding with each of the wyverns over the next several days," Gloriana said as they finished the last of their organization. "She wants the wyverns to be comfortable around us—in case we need to fly with them to an active scene. Plus, they won't try to bite our heads off for getting close to their Rider while they're wounded."

Evelina nodded, knowing how vital this was as the healers of the Alpha Fleet. But she wasn't ready to see Daimon yet, not after their last encounter in the forest. "So one of us will stay here while the other is riding?"

Gloriana nodded. "Same as at the palace. One healer should always man the healer's room. You can ride with Brielle today and I'll go with her tomorrow."

That she could do. Evelina was most comfortable with Brielle and had already ridden Vero once on the way here. She turned to leave, a little more eager than the last time she had to ride the beast.

But Gloriana stopped her before she opened the door. "Are you doing all right? You haven't seemed to be sleeping much since we got here."

The reminder alone made Evelina yawn. "It's a big adjustment," she answered honestly. "And pressure. The soldiers are counting on us."

Gloriana smiled softly, her eyes shining with understanding. "Just remember we can't heal others if we're not healed ourselves."

Evelina nodded slowly. Gloriana always knew what to do and say—when to be soft and when to be firm. No one could understand better than Gloriana could. She wasn't only her mentor; she was her friend. Evelina couldn't have done any of this without her.

Slipping out of the cabin, Evelina found Brielle feeding Vero large slabs of raw meat behind the fleet's cabin. The wyverns all slept there, nestled into a cavern tall enough to fit each of them. Zephyr and Codax were nowhere to be seen, but the remaining four wyverns slept in a pile behind Vero and Brielle.

"How's Willow faring?" Brielle said as she threw another piece of meat. Vero snatched it out of the air, his massive jaws snapping with a loud crack as they closed around it.

"She'll need to take it easy for a few days, but she's mostly in the clear."

"Good." Brielle nodded, then added with a laugh, "Though I doubt she'll take it easy." She held the meat out to Evelina. Veros's eyes tracked it closely. "Toss him this and he'll warm right up to you. Mountain goats are his favorite."

Evelina hesitated and shuffled her feet nervously. Vero could bite her hand off in the blink of an eye.

Brielle shook the meat. "Come on, he won't grab it until you throw it."

Evelina slowly reached out for it, her attention set firmly on the wyvern. Vero *looked* ready to bite her hand off. But he sat perfectly still.

"Now toss it in the air toward him," Brielle encouraged.

Evelina took a deep breath and slung the meat up. Vero snapped it out of the air before it could descend, causing Evelina to jump back a step.

"Wonderful." Brielle patted his neck. "Now we ride." She pointed to the rope, reminding Evelina where to step to leverage her body up. It was smoother this time, but still awkward as she flung her body into the saddle. Brielle sat in front of her, motioning for her to hold on.

"Wings up, V," Brielle commanded, not giving Evelina any time to adjust before Vero spread his wings out and pushed off the ground. She felt her stomach bottom out again and she closed her eyes as a wave of nausea rolled through her body. The trees beside her blurred and wind whipped her hair across her face. Once they reached the clouds, Vero straightened out, his wings smoothly flapping every few moments.

"We'll make a small circle around the camp before we head back," Brielle shouted over the wind. "Just hold on!"

They glided through the clouds until Evelina began to feel at ease atop the beast, the wind calmer with their relaxed flight.

Vero's head snapped to the right, his ears flattening. He growled, seeing something Evelina couldn't.

"What is it?" Evelina whispered, her heart racing.

Brielle pointed down through a break in the clouds. Evelina squinted. It was hard to see from so far, but it looked like figures were moving through openings where the trees didn't cover.

"A rebel group just behind the ridge," Brielle hissed. "They're headed in the direction of the camp."

Evelina froze.

Brielle turned Vero around, dropping altitude to take a closer look. "I'll take you back to the camp and—"

"We have to stop them," Evelina said quickly. From what she could see, there were at least twenty rebels. Not enough for a strategic attack on the camp, but enough that one of them could run off and tell more rebels where they were.

Brielle bit her lip, clearly torn. "I have to take you back," she said, but her eyes were glued to the rebels fast approaching their hideout.

"No!" Evelina gasped. "There's no time, you know that."

There was a pause as Brielle considered, and Evelina waited for her to realize the inevitable.

"Daimon's gonna kill me," Brielle muttered before letting out a sharp breath. "Vero, call for backup."

Vero ascended higher into the clouds and released an ear-piercing screech. The figures beyond the ridge scattered, losing them the element of surprise. Brielle patted his side twice and he flew higher until the clouds covered them completely.

"Daimon and Keir are on patrol," she explained. "We wait on them before attacking. Stay behind me at all times and keep your eyes on what's happening below us. If you see anyone attacking, you shout their direction, okay?"

Evelina's hand trembled where it was still wrapped around Brielle's waist.

Brielle twisted around to face Evelina, her eyes hard. "Daimon and Keir will take the lead. I won't let Vero get too close with you riding."

The sound of wings flapping came from their left. Vero shifted, his ears rotating toward the sound. He let out a small chatter and the flapping wings instantly moved closer.

"We have the advantage here," assured Brielle, as if thinking out loud. "Three wyverns against twenty rebels will be a quick fight."

Zephyr and Codax broke through the clouds with Keir and Daimon atop them. Daimon's gaze landed on Evelina, the small metal accessories of his armor glinting in the sun with the movement. The wyverns forced themselves to hover as they formed their natural formation with Daimon at the center.

"What is she doing here, Brielle?" Daimon demanded, his eyes wide with anger.

"No time," Brielle said quickly—firmly. "There are about twenty rebels beyond the ridge. They've already heard Vero and will likely be preparing for a ranged attack."

Daimon hissed in frustration but nodded his understanding. He wouldn't even look at Evelina, as if unable to bear her presence there.

"Keep her as far back as you can," he said sharply. "We drop down once they're directly below us. If we're quick enough, we can end this in one strike."

Keir and Brielle nodded. Daimon's eyes flicked to Evelina before turning and patting Zephyr.

She struggled to decipher the difference between his disdain and his desperate care for her, fumbling around the mixed signals of his concern and his disregard.

But there was no time to think.

"Keir." With the one word, Daimon had the attention of the

Aegis, his eyes sharpening as he maneuvered Codax beside Zephyr without hesitation.

Evelina watched with a mix of horror and awe as the two wyverns nosedived out of the sky simultaneously. Vero flapped his wings restlessly.

"Steady," Brielle whispered.

Screams sounded below, followed by a roar from one of the wyverns. The roar wasn't a battle cry—it was a screech of pain.

"Hold on!" Brielle shouted. Vero dropped out of the sky, his wings tucked in tight to his sides. Wind hit Evelina so hard she could hardly open her eyes. Her hair whipped behind her as she squeezed Brielle's waist as tightly as she could.

The battle had made its way to a clearing in the trees—or one that had been burned away, at least. Keir was shooting fire at the group while Codax swept them close to the ground. Brielle brought Vero beside Codax and released a torrent of fire.

"No magic suppressant!" Keir shouted over at them. "My fire is holding strong."

Evelina's shoulders relaxed a fraction. She glanced up, looking for Daimon. Zephyr hovered high above them with Daimon on her back, dodging arrows from all sides. His gaze flickered to Evelina, his eyes sweeping up and down her body like a soldier assessing another for injury. Concern tugged at his brows as his eyes met hers. Her throat constricted as she caught a glimpse of what was coming; an arrow headed straight toward him.

She opened her mouth to scream—to warn him. But it was too late, the arrow slicing across his chest before she could make a sound.

Daimon slumped against his wyvern, his arm dangling over the side of her neck. If he had already passed out, he had to be losing blood—fast. Panic clawed at Evelina's chest. Her healer training kicked in, her mind already working through the small window of time they would have to get the bleeding under control.

Zephyr reared back and exposed her belly more, shielding Daimon almost entirely.

"I need you to get me to Daimon," Evelina shouted at Brielle.

Brielle looked up and growled in frustration. "We have to take care of these—"

"On your right!" Keir shouted.

An arrow flew straight at them. Evelina screamed, her life flashing before her eyes as the arrow flew toward her head. She closed her eyes and waited for the searing pain, for the few breaths it would take for her to bleed out and die.

But the pain didn't come. Maybe it happened so quickly she had already passed on to Caelum.

"Princess," Brielle breathed.

Evelina slowly—cautiously—opened her eyes.

The arrow was hovering in front of her face, frozen in midair, the tip inches away from her forehead. Brielle reached forward, her fingers trembling as she plucked the arrow from where it was stopped. The iron-tipped head was carved with dark runes, a soft, pulsing glow emanating from it.

"How did you do that?" Evelina gasped.

Brielle held the arrow out and then looked back at Evelina, eyes wide. "I didn't do that," she said slowly. "You did."

Vero roared and dropped out of the sky, hurtling toward the ground as another cursed arrow whizzed past them. Evelina didn't have time to process Brielle's words. There were only a couple of rebels left now. Brielle and Keir took them out within minutes, but Evelina's head was still spinning.

Keir guided Codax to the trees, doing a final sweep to ensure they got them all. Once he gave the all-clear, Brielle raced up toward Daimon. Zephyr whined. Evelina could swear she saw panic in the beast's golden eyes.

"Daimon," Brielle shouted.

He stirred, groaning and holding his shoulder.

"He's alive." Evelina sighed with relief. "I need to see his wound."

Brielle nodded. "Meet us at the healer's cabin," she told Zephyr.

Keir brought up the rear while they all raced back to camp. Evelina prayed to Eurydice that Daimon could hold on long enough for them to make it back.

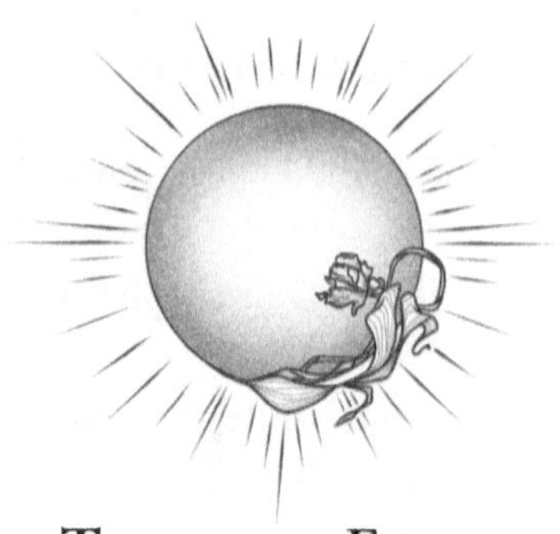

Twenty-Four

Evelina

Keir and Brielle helped Daimon off Zephyr and dragged him into the healer's cabin.

"Put him on the table," Evelina instructed. She called for Gloriana, her heart racing. Gloriana emerged from the back hallway, her eyes wide.

"We encountered rebels while riding," Keir grunted. He hissed, clutching his leg as they laid Daimon down. His pants were stained with fresh blood.

"Lie down over here so I can check your wound." Gloriana pointed to a cot across the room. Keir opened his mouth to protest and Gloriana shook her head firmly, adding, "*Now.*"

Evelina hurried by the hearth, where a bucket of fresh snow from the mountainside had melted into clean water. She washed her hands, careful to be thorough but quick. Then she hurried to Daimon and checked his breathing, finding it shallow but steady.

Evelina pushed his shirt open, swearing when she saw how deep the wound was. It started in the center of his chest and stretched up to his right shoulder; the ferrum arrow cut a deep slice in the skin, exposing muscles beneath.

She quickly dressed the wound with clean cloth. Then she

raked her fingers down his arms, feeling for any other deep wounds with her fingertips. When she got to his hip, she paused. A tattoo peeked out from his trousers; the hilt of a sword diagonally placed in line with his hip bone. Next, she had Brielle help her roll him to his side to check his back. All of the cuts were surface-level, his skin already knitting itself back together. They laid him back down, his eyes still closed and body limp.

"I need to clean the chest wound," she muttered.

Brielle, clearly anxious for her commander, asked, "How can I help?"

Evelina turned on her heel, grabbed a pair of scissors off the shelf, and returned to his side. She sliced the fabric of his shirt, starting at the bottom hem and working her way up. "Heat a bowl of water for me over the kettle and grab a sterile cloth off the third shelf, far right side."

Brielle immediately disappeared to do as instructed. Evelina applied pressure to the cloth covering his chest, waiting for the blood to stop. She had to replace it with bandages three more times.

By the time Brielle returned, the bleeding had finally slowed. She set a bowl of boiling water beside Evelina and handed her more sterile cloth. Evelina nodded her thanks and scooped a spoonful of crushed elonia leaf into the bowl. Once it was dissolved, she dipped the cloth in.

"I need you to stand across from me and hold him still while I clean the wound." She looked up at Brielle and nodded to the side of the cot she wanted her on. "He's going to wake up when I put this on him. Keep him as still as you can."

Brielle and Evelina switched sides. Brielle braced her hands on his good shoulder, while Evelina took a deep breath and pressed the cloth over as much of the wound as it would cover. Daimon immediately jerked against her touch, screaming in agony. Brielle pushed against his chest and grabbed the arm closest to her.

"Shh, I know." Evelina didn't bother telling him to stay still;

she knew it was no use. She had pleaded with enough soldiers at the refugee camps to know it wouldn't do any good.

He was still thrashing as she pressed the cloth against him, his eyes squeezed shut. Her hands worked quickly, letting the cut soak up the warm elonia water. Once she counted to sixty in her head, she took it off, and his body finally relaxed.

"You good, Evelina?" Gloriana called from where she was tending to Keir's injury.

"All good," she called back. She reached over Daimon and grabbed a small tin, unscrewing the lid. Now that the wound was clean, she could put a numbing salve on it to ease the pain. She scooped a generous heap onto her hands and smeared it across his chest until the gash was covered.

Daimon had fallen unconscious, his breathing even. Evelina nodded to Brielle and blew out a deep breath.

"He may be out for a day or two. The wound is deep and he'll likely need several blood-replenishing brews," Evelina said. "There's nothing more we can do for him right now, but he needs to stay here until he's healed."

Keir walked up to them, a small limp in his step. "We should brief the others and take a group for an extra patrol around the area," he said to Brielle.

Brielle looked at Evelina, her eyes flashing, likely remembering what Evelina did with the arrow during the fight.

"There's much to debrief on." She cast a final glance at Daimon and nodded her head. "Call on us if he worsens."

"Of course," Evelina promised. Once Keir and Brielle left, she bandaged the wound while Gloriana cleaned.

"We'll need to get him to drink the replenishing brew as soon as he wakes," Gloriana said from across the room. "But he needs rest for now."

Evelina hummed her agreement and pulled a chair up beside Daimon's cot. Gloriana bustled over and examined the wound. She focused her light on the deepest parts of the cut. Even with the strength of her light being able to heal most wounds, it barely made a difference with this one.

"It's too deep, but I'll try again in a few hours." She frowned, her brows knitting together as she tried one last time. When the wound didn't heal, she added, "I can wait with him. You should get some sleep after the day you've had."

Evelina shook her head. "I want to stay. He's my patient."

She couldn't sleep if she wanted to. Adrenaline was still pumping through her veins, her mind racing with thoughts of how the arrow had stopped before it touched her, her ears still ringing with Daimon's screams.

Gloriana moved about the cabin, checking in on Evelina every few hours. Evelina kept a bowl of room-temperature water at her side, dipping a cloth in and pressing it to Daimon's face often. He was sweating, but his body was shivering. She laid the back of her hand against his forehead, finding it warm to the touch. It wouldn't be good if he caught a fever with a wound like this.

She grabbed a cooling mixture and poured it into a bowl of clean water, then stayed by his side throughout the night, wiping his head and neck until his skin was no longer burning with heat. Her eyes began to grow heavy, her head bobbing as she fought against sleep now that the adrenaline was wearing off. It wasn't often she prayed to Eurydice anymore, but the moon goddess had answered her prayers. Daimon had made it back to the cabin alive.

"Thank you for saving him," she whispered.

It wasn't until then that she realized she didn't want to lose him again.

Daimon was in and out for the next few days, slowly waking more and more each day. He wasn't lucid enough to make any sense, but he was slowly getting there. At first, he only woke long enough to drink the blood-replenishing tea Evelina or Gloriana brewed. They took turns watching over him, and the other Riders visited him often.

Evelina met the rest of the crew during their visits—Aster, the only Undine of the group and soulbonded to Willow; Elias, one of the quietest Aegis she had ever met; and Ranick, another Aegis who was usually only around when Elias was.

She found herself struggling to leave Daimon's side. She just needed him to heal so she could go back to focusing on bonding with the Alpha Fleet and working with Gloriana.

She climbed out of bed that morning stiff and still tired. Gloriana had taken the night shift with Daimon and Evelina was to take the day. She heard voices echo down the hallway as she slipped into leather pants and a linen shirt.

"No, don't get up!" Gloriana nearly shouted, followed by the sound of a chair scraping across floorboards. "You may *feel* better, but you need to take it slow."

A frustrated grunt answered her.

Evelina peered around the end of the hall into the main room, finding Daimon propped up on several cushions and holding a steaming cup of tea. She sniffed the air, finding the minty scent of the replenishing brew.

"You're awake," Evelina said softly.

Daimon lifted his gaze to her, his eyes red with the heaviness of sleep. "This one won't let me get up yet." He jutted his chin out at Gloriana, who smiled.

She got up from her chair, stretching her back out. "He's all yours. I'm riding with Elias today."

Daimon's eyes dropped down to his tea as if it were the most interesting thing in the world as Gloriana left them alone. Evelina walked over and fiddled with jars on the wall, not knowing what to say now that Daimon was fully lucid and awake.

"Thank you," he whispered, his voice hoarse from hardly speaking the last few days. "Gloriana told me what you did when they brought me back to the cabin."

She swallowed thickly, hoping he couldn't hear her heart pounding. Even in the state he was in, she was still frustrated with him from their last conversation in the forest. But when she turned to face him and took his appearance in, it slowly dissolved.

His hair was messy, sticking in all directions. He hadn't worn a shirt in days, but it was different with him awake, with him staring at her the way he was. His eyes were open—vulnerable.

She took in the rigid lines of his abdomen, the bandage that covered his wound. She cleared her throat and walked over to the side of the table. "I need to check the wound—likely clean it, too."

He nodded his head and brought the cup to his mouth, taking a deep swig of the tea. She took the cup from him so he could lie down.

"How badly does it hurt on a scale of one to ten, ten being the worst?" She lifted the bandage and he hissed.

"Around a three," he said through a clenched jaw. She raised a brow. He sighed. "Maybe a five and a half."

She shook her head and huffed a short laugh. "You have to be honest with your healer." She pulled the bandage off and examined it, finding it healing nicely but in need of a debridement.

"I'll try my best to be," he whispered. His voice was so much deeper now. He had grown in more ways than one, his body toned and taller, his eyes harder and face unreadable.

She busied herself with heating water and prepping a bowl with crushed elonia. "This will sting, but not as badly as a few days ago." She dipped a clean cloth into the bowl.

He tilted his head, confused.

She gently pressed the cloth to his shoulder, starting at the top of the wound. "You probably don't remember. I did it when you first got here, and every twelve hours since," she explained. "You lost a lot of blood. It's natural for your mind to shut off when your body goes through trauma."

He hissed through his teeth and gripped the edge of the table as she dabbed the cloth against the wound. It was mostly healed now; just a faint pink cut was left of the once-gaping wound.

Once she was satisfied the wound was clean, she busied herself with brewing a cup of rhodiola for him. She could feel his eyes on her, the heat of his stare prickling the back of her neck.

When she turned back toward him, he inhaled deeply, and a faint smile tugged at his lips.

"To calm any lingering nerves," she explained, carefully handing the cup to him.

His fingers brushed against hers as he took it, and she could've sworn his cheeks burned red for a moment when they touched.

Something flickered in his eyes—a look of appreciation and something else she couldn't quite place.

"You're as brilliant of a healer as I knew you'd be," he said quietly.

She felt a crack in her heart, the tiniest sliver chipping away at the wall she had built around it.

The corners of her mouth twitched up. "And you're as stubborn of a soldier as I thought you'd be."

TWENTY-FIVE

EVELINA

EVELINA DIDN'T CRY OFTEN. SHE OFTEN BURIED HER emotions deep within her heart and focused on what needed to be done. It was something she had long since learned to do as a healer. A patient needed her to be strong for them. If they were scared and in pain, she needed to be their rock so they remained calm while she tended to their wounds. She would put on her healer face and focus on the task at hand.

But the night Daimon was finally strong enough to go back to his own cabin, no longer in need of a healer to watch over him, she cried for hours. All the memories of them together before the war slammed into her. She had missed him—so much that it hurt every corner of her soul. Seeing him look so much like his old self flung the floodgates wide open. She cried herself to sleep, the memory of his soft laugh ringing in her ears.

The following morning wasn't much better. Evelina's eyes were puffy from crying, her throat sore.

She needed to pull herself together before Daimon got here. He was due any minute for a morning check-in to ensure his wound was still healing properly.

To busy her hands and soothe her racing thoughts, she made three cups of rhodiola tea. She ladled water from the melted snow bucket and poured it into a small kettle. Gloriana had already started the fire, the rhythmic crackle of it helping ease the tension in Evelina's shoulders.

She'd meant to move over toward the herb shelf to do something productive, but she found herself staring into the fire, unable to look away. Her mind drifted to old memories, trying to reconcile the boy she once knew with the stone-faced soldier he had become.

It wasn't until she found herself sipping the last dregs of her tea that she realized Daimon should've been here by now. She grabbed a satchel filled with tinctures and bandages, her pulse fluttering faster. She pushed open a creaking shutter next to the hearth, finding the sun had risen higher than she thought.

He was late—Damion, the soldier who seemed to stick to a strict routine and value order. She pushed through the front door of the cabin, the morning air crisp on her face.

Brielle was lacing a tear in a pair of her riding leathers outside of Alpha Fleet's cabin. She looked up at Evelina as she approached, a soft smile on her face.

"Have you seen Daimon?" Evelina adjusted the strap on her shoulder, small jars clinking with the movement.

Brielle hiked her thumb over her shoulder, gesturing to the cabin behind her. "Hasn't come out of his room yet."

Evelina nodded, hesitating. She needed to check his wound. He likely needed extra sleep from the amount of healing his body had been doing, but it still made her breath hitch. She had to see for herself it wasn't something more than that.

"Come on," Brielle said, standing and brushing dirt from her legs. "Everyone else is up. Ranick and Elias are on morning patrol."

Even though it had been her goal all along, Evelina still paused a little too long before the door to the cabin. She had been closer to Daimon than ever here at the camp, but still. This was…closer.

She squeezed the strap on her satchel until her knuckles turned white. *He's a patient that just needs to be checked on*, Evelina chided herself. *There's nothing to be nervous about.*

Brielle grunted and Evelina startled, embarrassed. She took a deep breath, then followed her into the cabin.

It was cozier than it looked from the outside, the large and imposing Alpha Fleet cabin. The common room was decorated warmly with yellows and reds. While there were certainly aspects of any war room present—maps, strategy boards, weaponry— she was surprised to see it was far more like a home. Well-worn couches, books, games.

Aster was seated on a couch beside the front door, while Willow was sprawled out with her head in his lap. His focus was solely on a piece of parchment in his hands, while Willow was talking to Keir.

Willow and Keir's gazes swung to where Evelina had stopped in the doorway, while Aster didn't so much as glance up from his paper.

"Daimon was supposed to meet me for a check-in," Evelina explained, wondering if she had overstepped by coming in.

Keir's gaze traveled to a door opposite where Evelina was standing. "I'll wake him. He's had enough beauty sleep."

Evelina smiled awkwardly, wondering if she should wait for him back at her cabin. But the healer side of her was impatient to see he was fine, so she stayed rooted at the entry.

Willow popped up, earning a small grunt from Aster even as his eyes stayed on the page. She squished into Aster's side and patted the open spot beside her. "Come, sit while you wait."

Evelina swallowed, feeling entirely out of place. But Willow's smile was bright, showing off her high cheekbones and a small dimple in her right cheek.

"I can wait for him back at my cabin—"

"She's not going to stop asking until you sit," Brielle said with a laugh, settling herself in a wooden rocking chair stuffed beside the couch.

"She really won't," Aster added, earning a smack on the shoulder from Willow. At this, he finally looked away from his paper. He smirked at her and she narrowed her eyes. But a playful smile tugged at her lips as he tucked a strand of hair behind her ear.

Evelina took a small step back and the floorboards creaked, catching Willow's attention.

"Come on, Evelina." Willow patted the seat again. "We won't bite."

Aster snorted a laugh and Willow shot him a look. He held his hands up with a smile before resuming his reading.

Evelina crossed the room and sat beside Willow, placing her satchel in her lap.

"Tell us, how did you become such a brilliant healer?" Willow asked, her eyes bright with expectation.

Warmth spread across Evelina's cheeks. "Gloriana has been teaching me for years. I owe everything I know to her."

"Can't beat being a princess," Aster muttered absent-mindedly.

"It can, actually," she said pointedly, earning a surprised titter from the cabin. "Being a healer is my life's work."

Aster held up his hands. "Beg forgiveness, Your Highness."

His tone was hard to read, and a spell of tension hung in the air. Willow smacked his arm.

"By Eurydice, I just offended a Manor," he said, his eyes widening. "I swear I was just teasing."

Brielle cut in. "You'll have to excuse us. We speak a little too casually to each other in the camp."

Evelina's chest squeezed. Then just as quickly the apprehension she was feeling dissipated. She huffed out a laugh. "No, don't—I prefer it, actually. I hate the formalities."

A smile broke across Aster's face.

"Being formal is boring anyway," Willow added, waving her hand in the air. "It's much more interesting to cause a little chaos." She winked, her smile just as wide as Aster's.

"Don't think Keir or Daimon would appreciate that too much," Evelina teased.

Aster snorted a laugh and leaned over to Willow. "I like her."

They talked more, asking what it was like for Evelina at camp and telling stories of how they'd made it here, too. It was interesting hearing about the time when Daimon first left, when they were all just as new. Brielle wasn't even a soldier when she was chosen, and instead had opted to be an ironsmith at the start of the war. Whenever one of them seemed a little melancholy thinking about the home they'd left behind, another would crack a joke to cheer them up. Evelina found herself grinning so hard her cheeks began to ache. She could get used to this —esteemed soldiers who would rather have fun than be too serious.

They were just about to rope Brielle into sharing when the door across the room clicked open and Keir stepped out.

"I'd rather wake a sleeping wyvern than him," Keir grumbled. He shook his head and walked out of the cabin.

A sleepy-eyed, messy-haired, and *shirtless* Daimon stepped out of his room. He still had a bandage covering the wound, which likely wasn't needed anymore. His trousers were slung low on his hips, showing off the rigid lines of his abdomen and the deep V that bracketed his lower stomach, tapering off and disappearing beneath his waistline.

Evelina's mouth went dry as he stepped further into the room. He scratched his head and blinked a few times, as if not quite awake enough to focus on anything yet.

She hadn't seen him so...normal since being here. His features were softer, more boyish.

"Why do I need to be here again, Keir?" He groaned and ran a hand over his face.

Then he saw her.

"Evelina?" His voice was husky, rough from sleep.

Evelina nodded, her entire body sparking to life. Her gaze drifted back down to his chest, to the old scars that marred his skin.

"Evelina?" he repeated slowly as he took a small step toward her.

Her gaze flew up to his. The corners of his mouth were tugging upward. She realized she still hadn't answered him.

"I just need to check over your wound before you go out on a ride," she squeaked.

"Where do you want me?"

Her entire body flushed. She didn't know how to talk to him, let alone be *teased* by him. And based on the gleam in his eye, he *was* teasing her.

She cleared her throat and said, "Standing will be easiest so I can remove the bandage."

As soon as Evelina stood, Willow stretched back out on the couch and Aster abandoned his reading to run his hands through Willow's hair. Brielle swiped the parchment from Aster's free hand and leaned back in her chair to look it over.

There was something about being among this tight-knit group that made Evelina want to stop being so closed off around them—to get to know them more. While her stomach had been twisted with nerves a few minutes ago, it was beginning to relax bit by bit.

She walked over to Daimon, keeping her eyes on his.

"I'll just need to remove the bandage and then I can have a look, okay?" she whispered. She didn't know why her voice came out so quiet, but what she did know was that she could feel the heat radiating from his bare chest.

He nodded and watched her as she got to work. They didn't speak as she took the cloth off, and still nothing was said as she looked over the wound. She rifled through her satchel until she found the numbing salve she was looking for.

"This will help with any lingering pain." The moment her fingers touched his skin, she felt a rush of heat splash across her face again. Beneath the mostly healed wound, she could feel the hardness of his stomach, the warmth of his skin. She swallowed and focused on her task.

"Thank you," he whispered. Her gaze flicked up to his, and his midnight eyes brightened to a lighter shade of blue.

Aster, Willow, and Brielle talked behind them, their laughter filling the room.

"You have a good group of soldiers surrounding you." Evelina kept her voice low, as if sharing a secret.

"My family," he said softly, his attention drifting to the Riders behind them. "Years of training together, living under the same roof, and losing soldiers you've called friends for a decade will do that."

Evelina nodded, her gaze falling back to Daimon's abdomen to work on rubbing the numbing salve in. "You've built a good life here."

Her words didn't have any bite to them; they were soft—almost sad. He really *had* built a good life here, albeit a life without her. Her eyes stung as tears gathered, blurring her vision. She kept her gaze fixed on his wound, but she could've sworn she felt the ghost of his fingertips graze her cheek.

She finished the last of the salve quickly and handed him the jar when she was finished.

"Eve—"

"Apply once a day—preferably in the morning."

Her eyes finally met his and she found his cheeks tinted pink too. Something was beginning to settle between them—an understanding. Here, she could be the fleet's healer and he could be the soldier who needed her.

But she didn't want to be anything more than the Daimon and Eve they used to be—children who had died the day the war began. Seeing the life he'd lived here gave her relief as much as it gave her pain.

He was able to be happy without her, she realized. So why hadn't she been able to do the same?

"Have a safe flight," she said breathlessly, stepping away. She rushed past the Riders without a word, even as they called out.

Daimon had a life here without her—hadn't suffered the way she had. It only proved to her how one-sided her feelings had always been.

Resolved, she swallowed her emotions for him down for what she hoped was the final time.

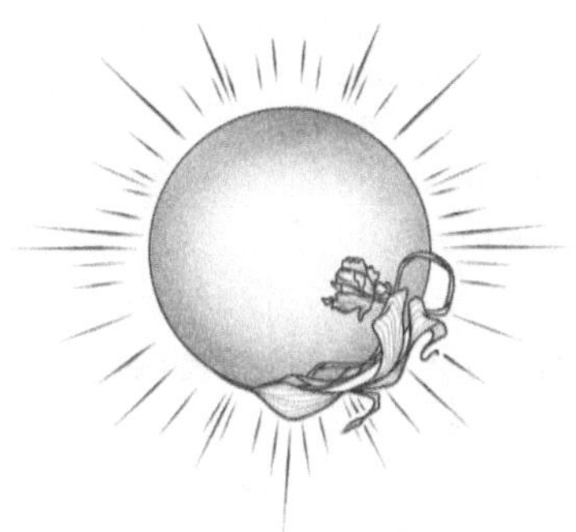

TWENTY-SIX

EVELINA

WITH THE ALPHA FLEET'S WOUNDS FINALLY HEALED, Evelina and Brielle finally decided to address the fluke of Essence with the arrow. They looped Gloriana in, spending the next few days trying to recreate the magic. Brielle filled Daimon in, and he lingered near their training and watched them at a distance.

Brielle held up a wooden rod and Gloriana coached her from the sidelines.

"Now!" Gloriana shouted. "Shield!"

The wooden rod was tossed at Evelina. She squinted and yanked on her Essence. The wood neared quickly but slammed into an invisible wall before it could hit her. It bounced off and clamored to the ground.

Gloriana cheered and clapped her hands. "I've never seen a lightwielder make a shield before."

Brielle's eyes gleamed with pride. "I know we've said that we should keep the healers further from battle, but we may not need to if Evelina can harness this power," she said, turning to Daimon. "With a little more training, she could protect herself in a fight, perhaps even the Rider she flies with. We could take her on patrols and practice in the sky."

Daimon looked at Evelina, weighing the possibility, then shook his head. "Keep training."

So they did. As Evelina's ability to deflect became more consistent, they brought in other Riders to stand beside her. Instead of throwing the wooden rod at her, they tested to see if she could deflect the rod from the person by her side. It took a little adjusting, but after a few more days, it started to click.

Brielle cast a glance at Daimon after another successful lesson—one of Evelina's best. She managed to stop a ferrum blade from striking a training dummy beside her, becoming regimented enough in her skill that she didn't need to rely on the emotional instinct of protecting herself or another fae.

Brielle put her hands on her hips and shouted to Daimon, who was watching from a few paces away. "You're holding her back, Commander! Imagine what she could do in the skies!"

They broke off, walking back toward the cabins and closer to Daimon. She assumed he would say no like he always did, that it was out of the question to risk another healer—a princess, at that.

"We could start with short patrols and see how it goes," he said slowly, surprising her. "And continue training whenever possible."

Her heart raced at the idea of going back to battle. It thrilled her as much as it terrified her. Still, she had to learn how to harness her gift. The more power she used, the faster it drained her. She would have to use it sparingly as she worked to hold the shield longer and longer.

"Evelina, you should ride with Daimon on patrols," Brielle suggested, leading their path back to Alpha Fleet's cabin, where the wyverns' wings were beating in anticipation of their Riders. Keir, Brielle, and Daimon usually took the night patrol after training. "If you can shield the Rider you're with, even temporarily, the commander would make the most sense."

"Brielle—"

"It's the wisest strategy."

Evelina knew it was. She looked at Daimon, her heart racing for a new reason. "I'll do it."

His brows flicked up in surprise, but he nodded his head. "Then why don't we start now?"

Zephyr landed behind him, along with Codax and Vero. Keir and Brielle mounted their beasts. Daimon gestured for Evelina to get on first. This time, when she grabbed the side rope and hoisted herself up, her movements were far smoother.

She beamed atop Zephyr, thankful she didn't embarrass herself. Daimon swung himself up gracefully, positioning himself behind her. Her cheeks warmed as his chest pressed snugly against her back, the saddle meant for one person rather than two.

"Wings up, Z," Daimon commanded.

They took the skies, soaring through the clouds for the rest of the day. They stayed silent, but for once, it was a comfortable silence. She couldn't help but feel every inch of where his body touched hers. She watched the trees blur beneath them, her eyes roaming the ground for rebels.

The next day, they did the same thing. And the next after that. She still never joined them in any active skirmishes or warnings, but they repeated the patrol pattern until the short patrols slowly turned into longer ones. Zephyr grew accustomed to Evelina, so it made sense for her to ride with Daimon each time. Soon, they were talking a little more each day.

Today was clear, hardly any clouds in the sky as they flew. Brielle flew on their right and Keir on their left as they always did.

Evelina's mind wandered, her eyes drifting across the forest below in search of rebels—or monsters. There were always rumors of a haunted wood along the edge of Zenovia. Trees that dark creatures hid inside until the sun set. Still, she hadn't seen anything peculiar during any of their flights.

"What are you thinking about?" Daimon asked softly.

She shivered at the thought. "The haunted wood."

He chuckled, his chest brushing against her back with the movement. "Why would you be thinking of old legends?" he asked with another laugh. "We've been here this long without seeing a single creature they speak of. No monsters to raid our camps or ambush our foot soldiers. If the stories were true, I'm sure we would've found out years ago when we first set camp here."

She shrugged, unconvinced.

"They're as rumored as the Talven fae still existing," he continued. "But at least the Talven are fact and not gossip."

She twisted around to face him, her brows furrowing. "The Talven haven't been seen by any living fae—who's to say they aren't gossip too?"

"But they *have* been seen, even if by stories passed down through generations, unlike the creatures of the wood."

Evelina narrowed her eyes. "What proof is that? The relic that fuels the falls in the palace?" she countered.

"The fragment of Queen Tallia's crown," he corrected.

Evelina huffed. "You mean the glacier that an *Undine* crystalized, welded into a solid piece of rock, and imbued their Essence into?"

He smiled and shrugged.

Evelina turned back around and muttered, "You're as bad as Gloriana. She used to tell me stories of the Talven when she was teaching me herbs."

She heard him hum, a soft sound that vibrated through his chest. "Have you spent a lot of time with her?" he asked.

"Gloriana taught me everything I know about healing," Evelina explained. "I'm surprised she hasn't demanded to fly with us yet."

Daimon laughed, his chest rumbling against her back. "She has. Multiple times." Evelina twisted around to face him. He raised his hands in surrender. "Keir and I want her to learn defensive tactics before she joins us on patrol," he said quickly.

"But it would be helpful for her to join so you two can watch each other's backs if we run into rebels."

She turned back around, mostly satisfied with the answer. *If* they encountered rebels was more like *when* they would encounter them. It was only a matter of time.

She tapped her fingers against the sharp scales beneath her. Zephyr shook her head, giving Evelina a look over her shoulder as they glided through the air.

"You know Z can tell how unsettled you are." Daimon's gruff voice cut through the wind. The wind was so cold that they often had to huddle together atop Zephyr to keep warm. It was impossible not to with the height's frigid temperature. "She isn't usually a fan of the tapping—has hung me upside down in the air when I do it too much."

"And yet she lets me do it," Evelina tossed back at him.

She could feel him smile against her shoulder.

Not for the first time, she reached her hand into the air and let the tips of her fingers graze through the vapors of a small cloud as they passed through. Her hands swirled the mist and left a trail in their wake as Zephyr flew by.

Evelina and Daimon had come to an understanding. They weren't becoming friends in the way they had once been, but she realized they were no longer strangers either. Sometimes they would chat, lightly teasing, sharing stories that never quite ventured into the time they shared before everything changed. And sometimes she needed silence, and he always seemed to know when. He would stay quiet, letting her get lost within the plains of her mind between comfort and chaos.

Daimon leaned forward, the movement causing his thighs to press into Evelina's hips. She straightened her spine, heat crawling up her neck as his chest pressed into her back. He was patting Zephyr, soothing her, and giving commands over his shoulder to his unit.

Evelina was having a hard time focusing on what he was saying until she noticed Zephyr's head snap to the left, her eyes searching the forest below. They were always ahead of the ground soldiers patrolling to warn them of danger, which meant there shouldn't be anything for Zephyr to be picking up.

Unless it wasn't their soldiers.

Movement on the ground snapped her to attention: small, dark figures scattering through the trees like ants.

"Rebels," she whispered.

"Brielle, take the lead while I report back to camp," Daimon ordered. "Evelina isn't ready yet."

Evelina's heart lurched. She was terrified—but eager, too. Now that she was here, she couldn't imagine going back to the cabin, forced to wonder what was happening while she was gone.

"No! You're the commander. You're staying. I'm staying."

Apprehension radiated off him and he went rigid behind her. Then, softly, he said, "Are you sure you're ready?"

She nodded firmly. "I'm consistent now." She meant it; she could feel her Essence steady in her chest, ready. "I know I can do this."

Daimon twisted to face his team, communicating using swift hand movements unique to them—a Rider language that had formed over many years of shouting fruitlessly over the wind or needing to communicate important messages from far distances.

He pointed at Zephyr, then held up two fingers and gestured over his shoulder. Brielle nodded once and tapped her fist across her chest twice, a sign of respect. She flanked right, splitting away from the group and going back in the direction from which they came.

It didn't take long for Evelina to catch on to some of their strategies when watching them train from the healer's cabin, one of the biggest being that they always did things in pairs. Typically, Ranick and Elias would warn the ground troops; Willow and Keir would work in tandem with fire and earth; while Daimon and Brielle would lead the pack as Aster watched their backs.

There were far more rebels than there were in the last fight she had experienced. Keir flew in closer to Daimon's side and they rose higher into the sky until they were covered by the clouds. It took nearly a half-hour for Brielle to return with the rest of the flight, minus Ranick and Elias, who often stayed close to give the ground soldiers coverage. Daimon flagged Brielle first, making a fist with his hand and then holding up three fingers—*Attack on my cue.*

He turned back around, leaning in once again until his face was beside Evelina's ear. "Be ready to cast your shield and hold steady until we can assess what we're up against," he whispered.

She nodded, feeling his breath warm against her cheek.

"Remember the plan?" he asked. Daimon made her recite the plan every single day before they took flight.

"Shield myself first before trying to shield you," she whispered back. It went against her nature, but it was just as Gloriana told her. She couldn't heal others if she was injured. She nodded again solemnly, confident.

She could see Daimon nod out of the corner of her eye, still peering over her shoulder. "Good, get ready."

Zephyr rumbled a low vibration, causing the other wyverns to draw closer toward them. They formed a V behind her, their faces set with an eerie calm—the look of a unit that had spent years having each other's backs. There wasn't a group of people that trusted each other more than these Riders did. They flew in perfect unison, ready to fly into battle.

Evelina was amazed at seeing the aerial unit in action. They were mesmerizing—lethal and precise.

With a tap against Zephyr, they dove out of the sky, the ground speeding closer and closer as Zephyr tucked her wings in close and nose-dived.

TWENTY-SEVEN

DAIMON

EVELINA WAS FOCUSED—SHARP. EVERY BIT OF A WARRIOR as the soldiers who traveled with them, even if she only considered herself a healer. Her high brows were pinched into concentration, her lips purple from the cold, blustering wind. Daimon was transfixed by her, especially as her Essence wrapped around his senses, warming the constant cold that clung to his body like a second skin.

"Conserve your magic," he growled.

She ignored him, the warmth of her magic flaring hotter around him. "You do your job, and I'll do mine," she shouted over her shoulder.

He grunted, unable to fight with her as they neared the rebels below. He tried his best to keep his distance, to avoid pressing his chest against her back just to reassure himself she was safe.

But the moment a rebel hurtled fire their way, he wrapped his arm around her waist and yanked her against him. He *knew* she still had the shield firmly in place. And yet he still cast a wall of shadows, their magic winding together for a brief moment. The mass of flame bounced off it, leaving them untouched.

Willow and Keir focused on getting the group separated,

Keir with his fire bursting through the middle of the circle they had formed. He would swoop down, send a blast of flames, and bank straight back up, only for Willow to swoop in behind him before they could reform, sending rocks, trees, roots—whatever she favored at the moment—to keep them split up.

Brielle, Daimon, and Aster circled the edges, pushing in toward whatever Keir and Willow concocted. It left the group unable to flee sideways or huddle close together.

A ball of flames shot into the sky from their right, headed toward Brielle's back. Daimon threw up a shield of shadows, deflecting it before Evelina could try to put hers up.

A flicker caught Evelina's attention from the corner of her left eye; another mass of fire was headed for *them* now.

Her shield snapped into place, sending the fire outward in all directions as it slammed into it. Daimon's head jolted to the left, his arms tightening around her.

She threw a smirk over her shoulder and said, "Told you I had it."

He huffed a laugh and steered Zephyr away from the cluster of rebels.

After several rounds, plucking out rebels to kill along the way, Ranick and Elias arrived with the ground unit. The two Aegis were lethal together, the final push of flames and mind influence building as the ground soldiers closed in around them.

"Daimon!" Evelina shouted, pointing to a cave in the distance. He watched as a line of rebels moved in and out of the cave, some running away from battle while others came out refreshed and ready to fight.

But a torrent of flames from the ground pulled his attention back to the fight. Zephyr rotated, flying sideways to avoid the fire. The ground unit worked with the aerial fleet, keeping the rebels distracted so the wyverns could swoop down. Several of the ground soldiers fell, and Codax took a nasty wound to the base of his neck, but they managed to whittle the rebels down until they were all gone.

Daimon was breathing heavily, and he could feel Evelina's shield flicker. She had never shielded more than herself for this long. He nodded to his fleet, motioning for them to lower to the ground. Evelina's shield receded, the chill returning to his skin.

"They were coming in and out of that cave," he shouted. "Brielle and Willow, take the first shift to patrol the skies. Set up a wider perimeter than usual; we don't want any lingering rebels catching us by surprise. Keir, Ranick, and Elias, investigate the cave."

Evelina slumped her shoulders, her back resting heavily against him.

"She doesn't look so good," Keir said, narrowing his eyes. "Best to get her back to camp."

Daimon glanced between Keir and Evelina, a tinge of distress working its way up his back. He knew she would be okay with Keir. He knew he had to stay and investigate the cave with his fleet.

But he didn't want to leave her.

Daimon nodded stiffly, dismounting and helping Evelina down. She nearly fell off Zephyr, her knees giving out when her feet hit the ground and her body collapsing against him. Daimon wrapped Evelina in his arms as Keir helped him lift her into Codax's saddle, securing her with the ropes. Keir didn't waste any time before taking back to the skies.

Daimon knew the moment they landed at camp, Gloriana would sprint over, her arms outstretched to help Evelina down— scoop her up and scold her for exerting herself too much. She would check her over for wounds, even though Daimon had already done so—already knew there wasn't a visible cut on her.

She was safe. He didn't have to worry. As commander, he had to stick with his fleet.

But as he watched Codax's wings turn into a black silhouette against the sky, all he could think was how it should have been him carrying her. Duty be damned.

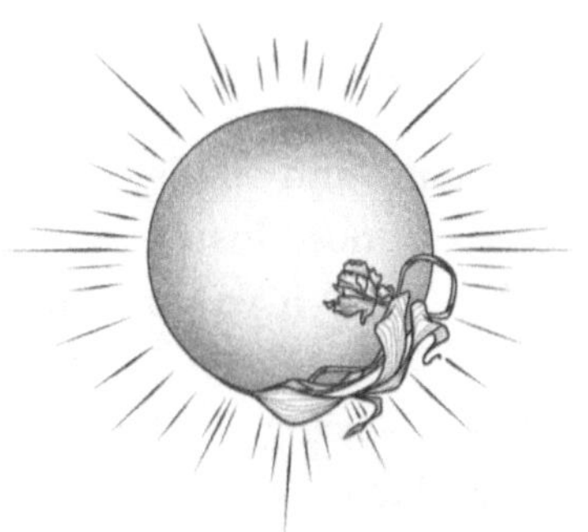

TWENTY-EIGHT

EVELINA

THE MOON HUNG BRIGHTLY IN THE NIGHT SKY. EVELINA'S body was exhausted, but she couldn't quiet her mind enough to find rest. All she could see were the faces of the rebels as they were killed, the faces of her own men as they fell too.

There was a small crack in the ceiling—a sliver she wouldn't yet mention was there, not when it gave her access to see the stars above. She considered going out to lay by the fire, but she couldn't seem to get up, warm and surprisingly cozy in her bedroll.

Besides, in here there was no one to see her smoke valeriana root and tell her to stop. She coughed through the haze, the room filled with smoke from the lavender and mugwort she'd been burning. The moment the smoke began to dissipate, she would light a small stick tipped with powder, letting it fill once more.

Gloriana checked on her every so often, even sat with her so they could pass the root back and forth. Evelina's skill in herbs didn't only revolve around healing; she also found ways to mix certain elements that would spark a small bundle enough to light the end on fire. And while the room was already filled with smoke, she added to it by burning rolled-up bundles of valeriana stems and filling her lungs with it. The effect of the root was almost instant, causing her limbs to loosen and her mind to relax. It was the only way she was able to stay afloat.

It was overwhelming—being in the midst of a battle and exhausting her Essence all at once.

She tried to focus on the good, on how she'd managed to save so many people during the attack. But instead of joy, she just felt…cold. Detached. Weightless and stuck in a state of decay. She didn't want to feel this way, but she didn't know how to pull herself out of it.

A knock tapped against her door. "Evelina?"

She held back a groan at the warm voice.

"Gloriana said you haven't been able to sleep." Daimon cleared his throat and added, "I warmed a kettle of broth for you."

"I'm good here, thank you," she said before he could ask if something was wrong. She didn't need him to come in and see her like this. It'd been years since she had him to talk to about these things, about her worries and pain.

"I would love to believe you," Daimon said from outside. His voice was serious, softer than how it was around the others. "But I can hear your self-deprecation from out here."

"You cannot," she mumbled.

He sighed. "You need to eat to replenish your strength."

As if she didn't know that.

"Aren't you supposed to be patrolling camp or something?" she called, still sprawled out across the damp bedroll.

"I just switched off with Brielle," he answered.

She raised the root back to her mouth, inhaling deeply and watching the smoke billow out of her mouth.

"I can smell the valeriana from here," he teased, his voice slightly muffled by the door separating them.

Her brows drew together at the lightness and familiarity in his tone, as if they hadn't missed a beat. The handle of the door shook and turned. He pushed it open, peeking his head into the room. "Gloriana asked me to bring your dinner up."

Evelina bit her lip, her heart skipping at the way his voice dipped to a deep and raspy tone while he whispered. She shrugged and dropped her head back, returning her gaze to the small crack she had been staring at above her, her body floating.

"Zephyr has been driving me insane to let her come see you," he said, his voice gentle.

Her chest warmed and buzzed with a flurry of emotions.

"Are you burning a whole *field* of lavender too?" He coughed, waving his hand to clear some of the smoke. He pulled the door open as far as it would go, the haze dissipating as it rushed into the hallway. As the smoke cleared, she could make out a bowl of steaming soup in his hand.

"You're letting all of my hard work out the door," she mumbled.

"Gloriana said you've been burning it all evening." He sighed, his eyes softening as he looked down at the soup in his hands. "I just want to make sure you're okay."

She chewed on her lip a moment, trying to sort through her mind and how to answer him. She wasn't okay—but she wasn't ready to admit it out loud. She was drained, exhausted, and couldn't shake the weight of feeling that she hadn't done enough. If her light affinity took so much from her, it left her useless to help others. She felt frustrated and weak, self-doubt eating away at her spirit.

"You may as well come sit," Evelina muttered to Daimon. She sat up, propping her back against the bedframe and bringing her knees to her chest.

Daimon hesitated, his eyes bouncing between Evelina and the small, empty space beside her. He held the bowl and a spoon out until she took them and then slowly lowered himself to the ground beside her instead, resting his elbows on his knees.

She quietly brought the bowl to her mouth and took a sip, the warmth filling her instantly. The broth tasted of fish, made more palatable by warming spices. Bugs hummed in the forest outside, filling the quiet cabin with noise, yet somehow, the silence between them was far louder than the creatures singing in the night.

The silence was the hardest part. It let her mind wander into the horrors of the battle. There wasn't even time for her to heal anyone; they were all dead by the time they hit the ground.

She dropped her eyes to the soup, fighting back tears.

"Evelina?" Daimon asked gently, his voice bringing her thoughts back to the room.

"Yeah?" she mumbled around a spoonful of broth, her taste buds dancing with the lemony, tangy aftertaste.

"It's okay to not be okay," Daimon said softly. "Do you need a dream?"

She let out a half-hearted laugh. It was something they did when they were children. Every time she was having a bad day, he would give her a good dream. Nocturna fae were the keepers of the dream realm, the protectors of the mind in its unconscious state. Daimon had shown a particular affinity for it at a young age, able to offer dreams for her to calm her mind or for them to share together.

"I can't remember the last time you asked that." Her voice was somber and soft.

He nodded his head slowly. "Dream with me," he whispered.

Evelina froze—it had been so long since he had said those words. She cleared her throat, pushing past the overwhelming rush of emotions and memories.

"What dream will you give me?" Saying the words felt odd, like singing a foreign melody she hadn't heard in years but to which she could still remember all the lines.

He smiled, his midnight eyes filled with a mixture of sadness and warmth. The dreams he used to give her varied from her growing wings and flying in a field of lilies to swimming with glowing creatures of the sea. But as much as she adored those dreams, she missed the company just as much.

"You'll find out," he said with a soft smile.

Without another thought, she leaned back onto the bedroll, closing her eyes.

"There once was a girl who spent more time awake in her dreams than she did in reality…" His words were laced with something so soothing that they would send her into a heavy sleep within seconds. He always started the story the same way, and she never heard what came next—his Essence always took her into her dream realm after a single sentence.

Evelina felt the world melt away, her mind easing into a familiar weightlessness. The last thing she used to think of before the blissful sleep was how thankful she was to have him. For the first time in a long time, she drifted off with the same thoughts swirling inside of her.

TWENTY-NINE

DAIMON

DAIMON'S SHADOWS DANCED BENEATH THE SURFACE, ready to wrap them in a cocoon of safety and never let Evelina go.

As peaceful as it was to be safely tucked away into a dream realm, Daimon preferred to watch Evelina sleep. It was the only time the little crease in her forehead was smoothed out and relaxed. That much hadn't changed, at least.

The only thing he had to offer her was a silly dream, a temporary fix for problems she would soon wake back up to face. It wasn't much, but it was all he had.

He waited a moment before he joined her. He smiled to himself, thinking about how she was probably growing impatient with each passing moment. They used to spend hours in her dream world, their safe haven, where they could avoid their problems.

Then he had an idea.

Daimon grinned and closed his eyes as he let his Essence curl around his mind, letting sleep pull him into darkness. He awoke in her dream, already knowing what to expect. It was a world he'd crafted just for her—a spot on the moon.

By the time he finally arrived, he found her sitting among

powdery dust and cracked craters. They were surrounded by a pitch-black sky and thousands upon thousands of stars.

"Beautiful, isn't it?" he asked, his eyes on her.

She whirled toward him, her forehead creasing in surprise. "You're joining?" she asked hesitantly.

He scratched the back of his head and nodded, feeling heat rise to his cheeks. "I know it's been a while since we've done this."

She smiled softly. His heart squeezed as he was reminded of the ways he used to be able to make her smile.

"I've always wondered what it would be like to sit on the moon," she mused aloud. "Do you think we could find a way to get here in the waking realm?"

Daimon walked over to her, sitting several paces away. He knew he was in dangerous territory already, letting his emotions get involved. But part of him hoped he could still, in some way, be a friend to her. She needed someone she could open up to. She stayed inside her mind far too often.

"Seems awfully lonely up here, don't you think?" he asked.

She sighed and reclined, watching stars shooting across the sky. "What's lonely about being alone?" The crease in her forehead returned. "Sometimes, I've never felt more alone than when I was surrounded by people."

He smiled softly. "You love being a healer, though. I've heard stories of the Manor princess who healed others with so much respect, it seemed as if *they* were royalty and not her."

She shrugged, dodging the compliment. "The soldiers are half-delirious when they come to me."

Her wall was up, even in the dream realm. He ached to know the side of her she didn't show people.

"I think it's obvious you prefer to be alone," he teased. "Do you remember when we were younger? You used to sneak off during parties and hide in the Mother Tree."

Evelina let out a soft laugh. "And somehow, you would always find me."

I promised I would always find you, didn't I? he thought to himself.

He looked down to where she was lying, her eyes now on him as he hovered over her. She didn't say anything for a minute, so neither did he. He just stared at her, his thoughts jumbled and confused.

Her gaze quickly slid back to the sky, her eyes lining with tears. He racked his brain for what he could do to help her. The dream realm was supposed to be her escape—a way to relieve the mounting pressure so she could eventually sort through it.

An upside to being a Nocturna fae meant that Daimon could use his shadows in the dream realm to conjure memories, another rarity that he mostly kept to himself. Except for Evelina, that is. He always used to tell her things he didn't tell others.

He lay down beside her and let his Essence build inside of him. When the memory he was looking for surfaced, he pulled it out and threw it above them. The memory stretched across the stars so they could watch it together.

While he could do this in his own dreams, it was strongest when both people from the memory were present. It allowed him to tug the view from each person and play it as if there were a third party watching.

Evelina let out a breath of air, a small gasp of excitement. "It's been forever since I've watched a memory like this."

"Now seems like a good time to watch one again," he said softly. Having such strong shadows was both a blessing and a curse. Memories that would fade for most were vibrant as the day they happened for him. He could pluck a memory from when he was an infant and watch it play out—but with the good always came the bad. Selfishly, he hoped this could become a routine for them again. He wanted to find every excuse he could just to watch that little crease on her forehead disappear.

"Which one did you pick?" she asked, the sadness leaving her voice as the image of leaves and branches played out before them.

"Shh, just watch."

He turned to catch her rolling her eyes, and something else too—a small hint of a smile tugging up her lips.

Thirty

Daimon

Twenty-Five Years Ago

"Evie, I know you're up there!" a young, bone-thin Daimon called from the base of the Mother Tree.

"You always know where she runs off to," Carwyn, Evelina's older sister, had quipped earlier in the evening to Daimon. He'd finally found a flask of ale to sneak back to Ren so they could see what it tasted like. But, as usual, Carwyn caught him, took the flask, and sent him to find her missing youngest sister. "Get her back before Mother notices she's missing again."

He did know where she always ran off to, which is why he was here at the heart of the palace in the Radix Room. It was thankfully empty while everyone was at the celebration. Tiny purple buds crunched beneath his boots, the dried herb sending a sweet botanical scent into the air.

He tried again. "You left buds from your lavender stems behind!"

"Go away, Daimon," she called out from within the depths of the tree.

He sighed, knowing that if she had lavender with her, then that wasn't a good sign. Limb by limb, he climbed through the

Mother Tree. Evelina was seated on a wooden swing hanging from one of the highest branches. It was held up by thick cords of ivy, and was wide enough for two people to sit on comfortably. She sat with a puffy dress hiked up to her knees, the hem streaked with dirt. Her bare feet were stained with mud, matching her soil-covered hands.

"Carwyn made me wear the dress," she huffed. "I told her I had to check on the lamiaceae in the herb garden before I got dressed, but she said there wasn't time for that."

"Let me guess…you checked on them anyway?" Daimon walked across the branch, placing one foot in front of the other until he could hop onto the swing with her.

"I took my flats off so they wouldn't get dirty, but the dress didn't fare as well as I would've hoped." She wiggled her feet out in front of her, causing pieces of dry soil to crumble off.

He hummed, holding back a smile. "Princesses don't usually wear dirty celebration gowns."

"Who cares?" She shrugged, not bothered in the least. "Mother said I've shown a lot of potential with mixing herbs, so they can't be too upset."

This time, he didn't hold back his grin. She never seemed to care what others thought, just marched to the beat of her own offbeat drum.

"Carwyn wants me to take you back to the party," he admitted.

She grinned and moved her legs out and back in, spurring the swing into action. "How about you skip it and stay up here instead?"

He considered it a moment, knowing that he wasn't part of a strong family and could get away with such a thing.

In the Valon Empire, wealth was irrelevant. Most everyone's needs were met through trade or freely given by the crown.

Still, there was a hierarchy. A pure bloodline with strong magic gained certain fae favor in the realm. A powerful bloodline meant people either respected you or feared you. It was a position of power that was earned by generations of noble fae lineage, not something that could be bought, stolen, or manipulated.

He was the youngest to have such control over his shadows in generations, but he was still young—and that's all most fae saw. The only reason Daimon even got to stay near the castle was because of Maliena's position. Even though he was not her real son, they gave him the same permissions they gave to Annora, a true council head's child.

But he couldn't say no to Evelina. "Ren and I already got caught trying to steal ale, so I should probably hide out here for a while."

"You shouldn't let them boss you around." She unbound her braid one strand at a time as she spoke. "They're only a few years older than us."

He watched her fingers work, running through the pieces of light brown hair and unraveling them strand by strand.

"They can still control their Essence more than I can." He sighed.

"For now." She wiggled her brows, causing him to laugh. The lavender she carried around with her sat between them. She picked up a couple stems, examining them closely.

"What was it this time?" he asked gently.

"Carwyn said I was a bad princess." She squinted at the lavender. Her voice was filled with annoyance—at herself or at her siblings, he wasn't sure. It could be any number of things, and he wished he could read her thoughts just to figure it out.

"You aren't."

She brought a small stick with sulfur at the end against the wooden swing and a flame roared to life. He smiled, remembering when she learned how to mix a large bag of it and nearly blew the entire herbal storage room to bits.

"Are you sure lighting that in a tree is a good idea, Evie?" he asked, pondering how he would explain to the queen that he let her daughter burn down the most sacred tree in all of the empire.

"I'll be careful," she mumbled, not really paying him any attention.

But he didn't push it. She only lit lavender when her anxiety got so bad that she needed to calm her heart. She never explicitly told him that was why she did it, but he could feel the rapid thrum of her pulse when she was stressed. And right now it was beating so quickly that he knew she needed it.

Evelina lit the end of the lavender and they both watched in silence as the flame ate away the buds. The fire quickly worked its way down the stem, letting off a sweet and smoky aroma. After a moment, she blew it out, letting the smoke drift around them.

"How many times have you done this already tonight?" He kept his voice quiet, trying to gauge her response. Her answer would tell him all he needed to know about her level of stress.

One burning meant she was just a little overwhelmed and needed to cool off. A couple burnings around the room meant that she desperately needed to clear her thoughts and the energy around her. More than that meant something terrible had happened, and he wasn't sure how to bring her back from that.

"I already walked the perimeter with a few stalks," she mumbled.

A few stalks. He could work with that.

"Did you crack one of the windows?" he asked, nodding to one of the many panes lining the far wall of the room.

"Of course I did." Evelina rolled her eyes. "How else would the negative energy leave?"

She was talking, and that was a good sign too. He could see her visibly relax, but, more than that, he could feel it. Her anxiety thrummed to a dull ache instead of igniting into a roaring panic.

She sighed. "Being around people can be overwhelming.

Herbs make sense to me. They require certain things, and I know the outcome I'm going to get and what each item will produce after the right amount of care. But people are fickle. Confusing."

He nodded his head, though he didn't fully understand. The only person he cared about understanding was right next to him.

"Just let me know when you feel like you need a break and I'll cover for you." His voice was tender and soft. They were young, but he knew that he wanted to help her in any way he could. Her siblings sometimes forgot about her—with how quiet and stoic she was, it was easy for her to get lost in the fray.

"Can you just stay with me?" She turned to him, chewing on her lip, her voice filled with hesitancy. "We can just sit and not talk if you want."

"Whatever you need." He smiled, and so did she.

THIRTY-ONE

DAIMON

THE MEMORY FADED AWAY AS IT ENDED, THE STARS COMING back into view.

Being here with Evelina almost made it feel like old times, when there wasn't a war and Daimon was still the Nox boy she could lean on. He didn't know if they'd ever get back to being so carefree with each other. He was curious if she felt the same, if she too missed what they had once had; the ease of a friendship between two people who trusted each other completely.

Daimon turned his head to ask Evelina if she liked the memory he chose, but the moment he saw her, he froze.

Tears streamed down her face. Her cry was so silent he hadn't even noticed it.

Without thinking, he laced his fingers through hers. He half expected her to pull away, still unsure where they stood. But she held on. His thumb itched to rub her hand, but he forced himself to stay still—too afraid to move and have her retreat.

"There's no crying in dreams," he said softly.

In all honesty, he didn't know what to do with her tears. She was one who rarely let a tear fall, her emotions staying bundled up in her mind instead.

She sniffed and let the tears keep falling. "Sometimes, tears are freeing."

His brows jumped in surprise at her response. Even when her older brothers would play tricks on her and everyone would laugh at her, she wouldn't cry as a child. Not even when she would fall down while running in the glade when they were hardly old enough to walk.

Seeing her emotions displayed so clearly on her face had his own buried hurt coming to the surface. She made him want to face it head-on, this strong and brave woman who faced the most painful feelings with full force. It made him want to mend old, broken wounds, because with her by his side, it wasn't as painful.

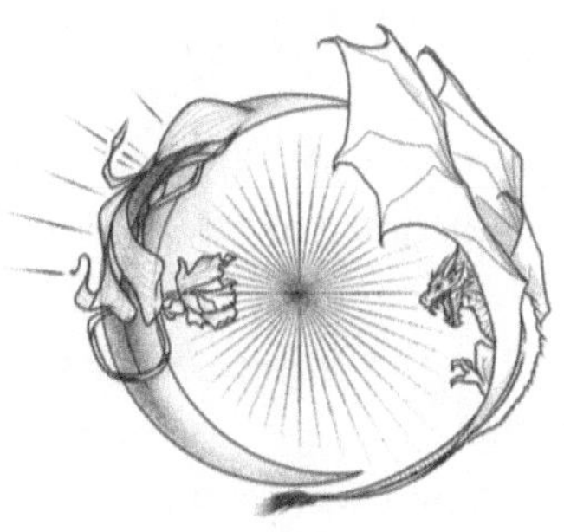

THIRTY-TWO

EVELINA

SOMETHING COLD AND WET SPLATTERED ONTO EVELINA'S forehead, jolting her out of her peaceful sleep. She blinked open her eyes as another droplet of water hit her. Through her blurry vision, she found a steady drip of water coming from the crack in the roof.

Sighing, she stretched her arms over her head. Birds chirped, replacing the creatures of the night and their song. The sun hadn't fully risen, and the sky glowed a soft lavender. From the sounds of it, the rest of the camp hadn't awoken yet.

She slipped on a fresh leather top and pants, wondering if she'd be able to ride with Zephyr today. And, of course, Zephyr's Rider...the same Rider making her head a confused mess this morning.

At some point, Evelina had drifted out of her own dream realm into the first uninterrupted night of sleep she'd had in ages, maybe even since the early days of the war. Spending time like that with Daimon again brought back a flood of memories —and all the buried feelings that went with them. The repressed hurt and betrayal she kept locked in a box deep within her mind, one she tried to ignore. Even the anger she allowed herself to feel was only a fraction of the rage that stayed hidden too.

What if, deep down, he was still the boy she longed for?

A seed of hope blossomed inside her at the possibility. He might look and act older, might have been the commander of the most lethal legion in the empire…but she had seen glimpses of the boy she once knew.

For now, all she wanted was to tell him she missed him. She wasn't sure if she was ready to forgive him for staying away yet, but it would help if he finally explained why.

She could give him a chance to explain, which was more than what she was willing to do in the past. She *needed* to know why he left before she could open herself any further to him. No more dancing around the topic without fully confronting it. She needed answers.

Her mind set, she left the cabin with her back straight and her gaze set on the dimly lit forest.

Daimon

Daimon set out on his morning patrol with Keir and Brielle. He'd slipped out of Evelina's room as soon as the dream ended. He needed room to breathe—to think and separate himself from the intoxication he felt when she was near.

They were almost like their old selves last night. He hadn't planned on sharing a dream with her—it was something far more intimate than two sort-of-friends should've done.

But recently, they had begun to ease into a familiar rhythm. It had started happening slowly—ever since the day he was injured in battle. As if more was starting to heal between them just as she mended his wound.

They were edging back toward becoming friends again, the safest option. But more and more he wondered if keeping the truth from her was the right thing to do.

It wasn't lost on him that he was already putting her in more danger than he'd ever intended. Encountering rebels on patrols had become a more frequent occurrence, with no end in sight. Nothing came of the cave they had seen them running in and out—another dead end.

Daimon needed to be focused to keep everyone safe. Getting distracted by his feelings for Evelina was a luxury he couldn't afford.

Keir, Brielle, and Daimon finished their patrol, landing their wyverns in front of their cavern. Evelina was standing at the side of the fleet's cabin, her arms folded over her chest. Her hair whipped around her face from the wyverns' landing. Leaves scattered and small trees bent in the rushing wind.

She locked eyes with Daimon and his pulse quickened. He slid off Zephyr and strode toward Evelina, Zephyr's golden eyes watching them curiously as she shifted behind him. Keir and Brielle quickly peeled off, sensing their need for space.

The closer he got, the more nervous he felt. Something looked off about her; she was fidgeting, switching between messing with her hair and the hem of her shirt.

"You're up early," he said evenly.

She swallowed and took a deep breath. "We should talk."

His eyes bounced between hers. "About?" he asked hesitantly.

With a small step toward him, she appeared to steel her spine. "You *promised* you would come back home," she whispered. "And when you finally did, you didn't try to explain why. You've had countless opportunities since we've been here."

His chest tightened. This was exactly the kind of misstep he couldn't afford to make right now. He knew he made a mistake as soon as he woke up, offering a piece of his heart when he could never give it to her in its entirety.

"Why did you stay away?" she continued, her eyes filling with tears. She angrily swiped them away as they fell. "Why wouldn't you come back to visit or at least write to me?"

Daimon clenched his jaw, his mouth pressed into a thin line. It was an impossible question. How could she understand the truth? That he stayed away because he had the blood of a dark god running through his veins. That his birthright was to become the Lord of Shadows, a game piece manipulated by the gods.

That his fate was the kind that could only bring ruin.

"Please, just say something," she whispered.

"Evelina." He swallowed. "I—"

"Pack a bag," Keir shouted from behind them.

"—can't," he finished weakly, his eyes dropping to her frown. He turned around.

Keir had a piece of parchment in his hand. A hawk was sitting on his shoulder, a small tin attached to its foot. "There's been word from the palace!" he yelled, walking closer to them. His mouth was set in a deep frown. "We're to report back for a briefing on the recent attacks."

Keir glanced up at Evelina, a brief glint of uncertainty in his eye, and Daimon knew it then. Something was wrong. Keir clenched his jaw and crumpled the paper in his hand. Whatever it was, he didn't look inclined to share.

"Gloriana needs to stay in case a healer is needed with the ground troops," he said without slowing down. "We leave in an hour."

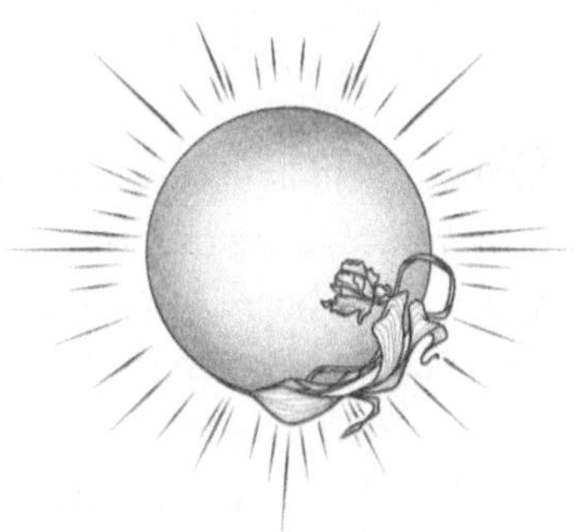

Thirty-Three

Evelina

Daimon took off with Zephyr just as Evelina walked out of her cabin. She only caught sight of Zephyr's tail as they disappeared on the horizon. Evelina walked over to where Brielle was sitting, lacing her boots.

"I'm not riding with Daimon back?"

Brielle looked up at Evelina and then at the sky. "Daimon, Ranick, and Elias are taking point in case we encounter any danger." She finished her laces and stood. "You can ride with me. Keir, Willow, and Aster will fly with us. Besides, I think Vero likes you."

Evelina could hear wings flapping behind the cabin and the small chatter of the wyverns preparing for a flight. "The entire fleet is going?"

Brielle nodded and led Evelina to the back of the cabin. "We shouldn't be away for long. They want us to patrol villages near the palace while we're there."

Evelina nodded vaguely, a sense of unease in her stomach.

The ride back to the palace was quiet. Even with the sky clear and open, Daimon, Ranick, and Elias were far enough ahead that she couldn't catch a single glimpse of them. They landed near the palace after the sun had set, leaving the wyverns next to an open cavern and making the short trip on foot.

After the few weeks she'd been gone, the forest felt…different. The trees that normally stood tall were drooping slightly, their leaves browning on the edges when they should've been a vibrant green. She studied them as they neared the palace, her mind distracted up until the doors closed behind her.

All her siblings were waiting just inside the entrance. Ren looked as if he had just arrived from the coast, still in dirty navy leathers. His usually bright smile wasn't on his face. Lyria ran to Evelina, pulling her into a tight hug. Carwyn stood behind Lyria with her hands folded behind her back, her face blank.

"What's going on?" Evelina asked.

Ren and Lyria looked on the verge of breaking down into tears—Lyria had just started to cry—but Carwyn was calm.

"Daimon and Keir have begun briefing the council on your latest fights," she said evenly. "I wanted to see you before joining them."

Something bad was coming, Evelina could feel it. The air was too tense. She braced herself.

"Mother has taken ill."

Lyria's cries fully let loose, and Ren pulled her into a hug.

Everything clicked into place for Evelina—the odd summoning back to the palace with no real explanation, the uneasy feeling in her chest, and the usually green and lively trees looking as if they were dying.

Her vision blurred as the words sunk in.

"When?" she squeaked out.

"Just two nights ago," Carwyn said with a frown. "It happened so quickly, like her body couldn't withstand the strain of darkness bearing down on the land. It started as a cough shortly after you left. She was better yesterday for a time… But then she started sleeping more and more, and now she's unable to leave the bed."

Her words felt clinical—cold. Evelina supposed she wanted

to keep it together as the next in line for the throne. Even now, in their mother's absence, it would be left to Carwyn to pick up the torch in her stead.

Carwyn turned to Lyria. "Why don't you take her to see Mother?"

Lyria nodded, her tears slowing, and reached out to grab Evelina's hand. They left their siblings at the entrance, a quiet tension in their wake as Lyria guided them through the corridor. She was squeezing Evelina's hand so hard she had lost feeling in it. But it was also the only thing holding her together.

Everything was too bright—too much of the same. Nothing had changed in the weeks she was gone, down to the paintings on the walls and the warmth that enveloped the halls. But somehow, it felt different, more empty and too shiny.

Lyria gave her hand a squeeze. "I'll wait outside while you visit," she whispered.

Even with Evelina's emotions threatening to bring her to her knees, she didn't miss the way Lyria spoke. There was something broken and hollow in the way she said it, so much so that Evelina quickened her step, eager to prove that her mother was just as she'd left her. That everyone was wrong, and when she opened the bedroom door, her mother would be fine.

They stopped in front of her door and Lyria hesitated. She hugged Evelina swiftly. "Evie, you should prepare yourself."

Evelina's focus blurred, her mind turning fuzzy. She didn't know what to do. She reached for the handle, her hand frozen and unable to move once she touched it. Lyria placed her hand over Evelina's and pushed the door open with her, bringing her face-to-face with a pain she wasn't certain she could deal with right now.

"I'll be here if you need me." Lyria's voice wobbled. She left Evelina in the doorway, holding herself together much better than Evelina would have guessed. Evelina had always felt like she was an older sister to Lyria, but in this moment, Lyria was being strong for her in a way only older sisters could.

She took a deep breath and tentatively stepped into the dimly lit room. A few candles flickered on the walls, but the shades were drawn and Evelina could hardly see her mother in the bed. She crossed the room, passing the chair she used to sprawl out on and complain to her mother about Carwyn getting on her nerves. On her left, she passed the small wooden vanity with an intricately carved frame that she would sit at while her mother brushed her hair.

It wasn't until she got to the foot of the bed that her resolve began to falter once more. The blankets were perfectly fluffed, not a wrinkle in sight. Her mother's eyes were closed, her mouth relaxed as she slept. She looked peaceful—not exactly the image Evelina had in her mind when Lyria told her to prepare herself.

Evelina turned, not wanting to wake her.

"Evelina, darling, is that you?" Her mother's voice was hoarse, crackling and ending on a cough.

Evelina slowly rotated to face her mother, too scared to move any closer than where she still stood at the foot of the bed. "Mother," she said softly.

Her mother's eyes were hardly open. The queen lifted her head off the pillow, only to let it fall back as if she didn't have the strength to hold it up. "Come closer," she rasped. "I need to know it's really you."

Evelina started to shake, willing her feet to move but unable to make them comply. "It's me, Mother."

Queen Embry held out a hand to Evelina, her fingers shaking as she reached for her. Finally, Evelina forced herself forward. She sat at her mother's side on the edge of the bed. Her mother lifted both of her hands, cupping her cheeks.

Evelina leaned forward so her mother didn't have to reach as far. She felt her face, tracing her nose and her ears. Her eyes were fixed slightly left of Evelina, over her shoulder.

"Ah," she whispered with a smile. "There's my girl."

Her arms dropped back by her side and Evelina immediately grabbed one of them. She studied her mother's face, still noting the way her gaze didn't focus directly on her. Dread slithered into her stomach as she realized what was happening.

"You can't see me?" Evelina breathed.

Her mother's smile faded. "One does not always see with their eyes."

Evelina shook her head, the frustration and anger of the past few days starting to claw at her chest. She'd felt hollow since the cavern, like a piece of her died there. But it was hitting her now—the unfairness of it all. Of seeing the strongest woman she had ever known fading before her eyes.

"Carwyn said you were sick." Anger stirred in her chest, an accusation sprouting from misdirected anger. "You're the queen. You can't be *sick*."

Queen Embry let out a long sigh, the sound crackling like she had water in her lungs. "The land is weak, Evelina."

The image of the browning leaves and drooping trees flashed into her mind. She didn't want to believe—*couldn't* believe it.

"It can't be," she gasped. "There has to be a way to heal you before it's too late."

She jumped up, prepared to run to the infirmary and bury herself in mixing as many tonics as she could think of. But her mother squeezed her hand—a small twitch of her fingers.

"The crown I wear is heavy. My body will not weather it for much longer." Acceptance filled her voice. "Darkness has invaded too much of our world. The land needs a stronger ruler to bear the weight of this crown."

"Then abdicate," Evelina demanded. "Before it kills you."

Her mother coughed, the sound wet and raspy. "It's too late for that. If I abdicated now, I wouldn't survive it anyway. This way I can hold the darkness off a little longer…and sort my affairs."

Evelina stared at her mother in horror, the reality that there was nothing to be done sinking in. Her mother was preparing for her death, not for a solution—not for salvation.

"Immortality is not all it's made out to be, my dear," she

whispered. "I will not grieve an early return to my true home in Caelum."

Just when Evelina thought her heart couldn't break any further, an irreparable crack splintered down the middle of it. Tears slid down her face as she looked at her mother, the brave queen who had always been the picture of strength.

Her own land, which she loved so dearly, was slowly draining the life out of her.

"What can I do?" Evelina asked, though she knew it was a futile question.

Her mother patted her hand. "You can sit with me awhile."

But something had to be done. There had to be a way to fix this.

"I can't let you die," Evelina whispered. "Perhaps the Keeper knows, or we could go to the temple and pray for a council with Eurydice."

Her mother shook her head. "There is only one possible answer now."

Evelina sat up straight, her heart quickening. "What is it?"

She would do anything for her mother, weather any storm or fight any opponent to get her what she needed. She was a *healer*, for goddesses' sake. If anyone could find a remedy to prolong her life long enough for them to find a real solution, it would be Evelina.

"Carwyn is already ruling in my stead, preparing herself to take the crown."

"That doesn't help you," Evelina snapped. She took a deep breath, forcing herself to stay calm. "That doesn't save you," she tried again, softer this time.

Queen Embry frowned. "There is no saving me. Even if the land was saved, it has already taken too much of a toll on my body. My Essence is close to being entirely drained, feeding into the land to keep it alive."

Another bone-rattling cough abruptly shuddered through her chest, cutting her words off. She pointed to the small bedside table with a shaky finger. Evelina fumbled for the glass sitting there, bringing it to her mother's mouth and holding her head up so she could drink. As her mother caught her breath, Evelina glanced out the window, noting the way dark clouds had gathered in the once-clear sky.

"This is Moros's doing," Evelina hissed.

He was leading the rebellion, raising an army that had invited the darkness into their land. She had lost so much in the past twenty years. Her father, her best friend, a countless number of her people. And now she was supposed to sit by and watch him take the one person who was supposed to lead them through it all.

It was all his fault. And yet she'd always felt entirely hopeless to stop him.

Queen Embry drifted to sleep, no longer able to stay awake. Evelina held her mother's hand, her grief turning quickly to a silent rage.

When she left this room, there would be only one thing on her mind.

Vengeance.

THIRTY-FOUR

DAIMON

QUEEN EMBRY WAS DYING. THE HEAVINESS OF THAT reality hadn't fully sunken in yet. Not as Carwyn led the strategy meeting with Senna at her side. Not as Daimon had to brief *her* instead of her mother. He liked Carwyn well enough, but he had served Queen Embry for years.

And then there was Evelina.

He swallowed, his throat tight thinking about what she must have been going through.

"Our victories have been short-lived with how often the rebels have been trying to push past the border," Senna said. He was on Carwyn's right, standing beside her comfortably.

Daimon watched the naval commander with interest. He and Daimon might both have been commanders, but they couldn't have been more different. Senna was revered with a pristine bloodline, while Daimon had clawed his way to the top.

"There's been more skirmishes on the coast. We should consider shifting some of the ships closer to the border to strengthen our presence there."

Carwyn nodded and looked at Keir. "Thoughts, Commander?"

The door to the strategy room creaked open as Evelina

stepped in. Daimon straightened, only catching a glimpse of her face before looking away. She had been crying. Her eyes were puffy and her cheeks were red.

"Evie?" Carwyn said with a touch of surprise in her voice.

Evelina walked up to the table. He could feel her eyes on him, but he fixed his gaze on the wood in front of him.

"I'd like to join the meeting tonight," she whispered.

Blessed Divine, even her voice sounded like she was crying. He gripped the table to stop himself from reaching for her. He didn't know how to act around her at the camp, let alone in front of the entire council.

The air was tense. No one had expected Evelina to be here tonight, not after just learning about her mother's illness a few hours ago.

Keir cleared his throat and continued. "It'll stretch us thin on the coastline toward the palace, which could leave us weak," he said. "But, if we shift Beta Fleet Five to cover the empty waters, it may be enough to make it work. We could use as much extra patrol on the border as possible."

The rest of the council stood around the strategy table, studying the board as Keir and Senna moved pieces around.

"We can move additional Undine to the weak points as well." Seretha, the Undine council head, reached forward, pushing a wooden block carved into a wave to where Keir had stationed the beta fleet. "And here. It will lessen what we have in Syreni, but if there are fleets watching the seas from above, the loss shouldn't be too heavy."

Carwyn nodded, pleased with the idea. "You've more than proven your capabilities as a leader," she said to Senna. "We can only hope every move we make brings us closer to victory. We'll meet tomorrow to continue. I'd like to go see my mother, see if she has any council to provide."

Daimon rose, keeping his attention on *anything* but Evelina. If he looked at her, he didn't know what he would do. Would he grab her hand and take her away from the palace so she could breathe? More likely, he would say the wrong thing and make even more of a mess after their last conversation… So instead, he avoided her gaze.

Evelina stayed behind to speak with Senna, and Daimon slipped out of the room before he made a fool of himself. His head was a disaster, stuck between his instinct and his mind. He wanted to hold her and comfort her as badly as he needed to breathe—but to truly protect her, he knew he had to keep his distance.

He left the strategy room feeling exhausted. The walk through the palace was eerily quiet, his footsteps echoing through the warmly lit corridor.

A second pair of quick, light footsteps sounded from behind him. His breathing quickened as he recognized the gait.

"Daimon." Her voice sounded as tired as he felt.

He slowly turned around and clenched his jaw. "I'm sorry about your mother," he whispered, but he kept his eyes on his hands as he said it. For a moment, he thought he could feel her heart still.

She let out a shaky breath and said, "Me too."

He pressed his fingernails into his palm until it hurt, desperate to focus on something other than her broken voice. He wanted to hug her, to tell her everything was going to be okay.

Daimon took a step toward her. "If there's anything I can do—"

"You could be honest for once," she said sharply, taking him by surprise. "Why are you avoiding me?"

His gaze lifted to hers. There was a fire behind her eyes he hadn't seen in a long time, an anger he'd been long expecting but had never arrived. Now it was clear to see. She was hurting. He knew there was a reason for it, and he also knew he couldn't fix it—or give her the answers she wanted. He would only cause her more pain.

He shook his head and started to leave.

"I'm trying to understand." Her voice stilled him. "How the same man who gave me a dream last night is the one who can't look me in the eye today."

He paused, half-turned as he said, "Maybe you're starting to see me for who I really am—who I've always been."

THIRTY-FIVE

EVELINA

EVELINA TOSSED AND TURNED, THINKING ABOUT HER conversation with Daimon, about *why* in goddesses' name he went from glimpses of the boy she knew to the cold-faced commander again. Once she finally fell asleep, her dreams were plagued with images of her mother dying, over and over again.

She needed to calm her nerves. Mixing tonics and grinding herbs usually helped soothe the worries that ran rampant in her mind.

She pushed open the wood door to the infirmary, the hinges squeaking as the door swung open.

"Up so early?" one of the healers asked as she entered.

"Lots to do," she muttered. Evelina noted the way the healer was just finishing up from the night before. She recognized her as someone she'd worked with a few times at one of the refugee camps. "Late night, Alaina?"

Alaina smiled, her hair ashen and eyes soft. "The Aegis never cease to amaze me," she said with a sigh. "Training accident last night. One of the trainees took a firebolt straight to the chest."

"They always seem to find trouble, don't they?" Evelina said softly. "Good luck."

Alaina gave a polite smile and wished Evelina a good day as she slipped out of the room.

Evelina walked over to the shelves of jars, taking stock to ensure they were ready for the day. The stock was far lower than it should've been, likely spread thin with the increasing number of attacks lately. The refugee camps were surely overflowing by now.

She found one jar completely empty. She sniffed inside it, the scent of sandalwood and leather wafting into her nose.

All it took was a single whiff and Evelina could identify what plant it was and what it could be used for.

"Princess Evelina?" Willow's light voice filled the room.

Evelina turned around, surprised to see her. They hadn't spoken much since Daimon's injury, but even from the brief encounters she had with her, she had taken a liking to the Woodland Rider.

"Is your wound bothering you?" Evelina asked. "I can mix up a quick salve for you."

Willow shook her head quickly. "No, nothing like that. I'm headed out with a beta fleet Rider to patrol around Baile the rest of the day. I was told to see if a healer was available to come pick up the herbs. But I didn't expect it to be you... I'm sorry I asked."

Evelina's eyes flickered to the diminished stock on the shelves. Evelina loved Baile, a quaint town brimming with joyful villagers who mostly grew herbs for the healers in the palace. And she could see Ian, the elderly human gardener who held a soft place in her heart.

"No, I'll go. It'll be nice to get some fresh air." Evelina grabbed a spare supply satchel and slung it over her shoulder.

"I'm sorry to hear about your mother," Willow said softly from the door.

Evelina paused, her heart twisting. Fresh air was exactly what she needed.

It would be a quick flight to Baile, likely no more than an hour. Evelina admired the trees beneath them and basked in the morning sun as it turned into a warm afternoon light, contemplating how much her life had changed since the war—how much the entire empire had changed.

Before the war, she and her siblings spent so much time outside of the palace. They would go out into the other territories—Drogheda, Syreni, Viridian—and spend whole days out in the glade from sunup to sundown, only going back to the palace to bathe and sleep.

Evelina hardly remembered what that kind of life was like before the rebels started to pop up. The realm used to be a well-greased ecosystem between fae and humans.

She could practically hear Aderyn, her old instructor, who made them recite texts back to her. The texts ranged from learning the creatures of the forests to learning about older rulers' accounts to studying how the empire ran so smoothly for so long. Evelina's siblings would memorize things quickly, but she always needed a little more repetition.

Woodland would use their Essence to foster growth in the land, while the humans would tend to the produce by growing, harvesting, and tilling the land the Woodlands recharged. The Nocturna would keep all fae and human dreams safe from creatures that fed off dreams and nightmares, while the Aegis guarded the land from the monsters of the waking realm. The Undine were harder to understand, their world a kingdom of their own beneath the water.

But for years now, it seemed like their days were mostly spent within solid walls and a roof blocking the sun from their view. There were so many others less fortunate than her—the ones with straw roofs and clay walls, vulnerable to the growing darkness. How could she stay chained to her perfectly manicured palace when the empire was suffering?

"We'll touch down for a short period of time," Willow shouted, and then, to the wyvern of the beta Rider flying with them, "Khaline, find us a place to land."

Children played in the town square, fae and human alike. People gave Evelina and Willow a pleasant wave or a quick smile as they passed over. Baile was bustling with shop owners trading and selling goods. Several stalls had been set up as a makeshift market. Those not selling or buying sat on wooden porches, rocked in chairs, or stood and talked.

They landed in an open field on the outskirts of town and walked in. Evelina trailed behind while Willow and the beta Rider discussed fleet matters. As they made it into town, the Riders peeled off to speak with the townspeople, checking to see if any rebels had been sighted recently, a standard survey for each town they patrolled.

Evelina spent the afternoon drinking ale with the townspeople and buying goods from their shops, including enough sandalwood to refill the entire jar back in the infirmary. She bought an apple from a stall by the square center and wandered over to a small bench to have her modest lunch.

There were plenty of people milling about, but her attention was mostly pulled by three small girls tossing a ball nearby. The ball soared over one of their heads, landing at Evelina's feet.

"Pass it to me!" one begged.

"No, me!" the other jumped in.

She laughed and tossed it to the one that hadn't asked for it, the other two groaning. As she watched the girls' vibrant smiles, so full of life, a small weight lifted off her chest.

While the Riders walked back to the field to feed their wyverns, Evelina settled into a tavern, a small space with a few wobbly chairs and uneven tables. The villagers sipped on watered-down ale and laughed with one another, quickly looping Evelina in as they shared about their lives.

Evelina leaned forward, elbows on the table, entranced by the female who had lived for centuries. She wove tales in such a way that Evelina found herself holding her breath.

"The wyverns are beasts of intellect and stealth," the female said, her eyes crinkling in the corners. "But the dragons?" She laughed and shook her head. "They're brute force, fire-breathing predators."

Evelina's eyes widened. "Dragons…"

Dragons didn't exist. No one had ever seen one for themselves; it was always someone's cousin's friend who had heard someone else telling a story that they *might* have seen one.

"Saw it with my own two eyes." The storyteller pointed to the eye that was shut, a deep scar running through it. "Until it decided it wanted to make a meal out of me and nearly gutted me."

Evelina gasped, while the others at the table laughed, clearly having heard this story time and time again.

But the female waved her off. "That was eons ago. They tend to stay secluded now that they're nearly extinct."

"So secluded that no one has *ever* seen one but you, Emma," a red-faced, bearded man said with a hearty laugh.

Evelina brimmed with questions to ask the female. She wanted to know everything about dragons and how they differed from wyverns. But the conversation quickly derailed to the next topic, and she settled back into listening.

Soon, Evelina got up to pay for her drink, the silver coins clinking on the metal plate by the bar. She smiled at the barkeeper as she walked to the door. "Thanks for the—"

A crash sounded.

There was a flurry of motion through the closed shutter, though it was too old and cracked to fully see through. A scream pierced the air.

Evelina darted for the door, her heart in her throat as she braced herself for what lay on the other side.

"Princess Evelina, you can't!" the storyweaver shouted from behind her.

But it was too late—she was already out the door.

She spun in a circle, frantic as she took in the view around her. Soldiers glimmered in the growing fires as they lit the straw roofs ablaze, storming the village. Smoke filled the air. Though she tried, she couldn't find Willow in the haze.

The rebels shouldn't have been able to get this far, not without being detected. They had made it to Nox Grove, but only a few, and without being able to make any stand. How there could be this many, fully equipped for an ambush? Something was different. Darker.

Evelina heard the roar of Khaline from above, but the smoke was still too thick. Even with two Riders, they would need reinforcements. Quick. The stationed Valon soldiers were clearly outnumbered and unprepared for such an onslaught in this small village.

She could see the outlines of figures running through the smoke, flumes of fire roaring to life, while some held weapons that glowed with the shimmer of a curse. There were dozens of them.

A man screamed from her right, snapping her attention to him. She watched as he writhed on the ground, clutching his neck. She ran to him, dropping down at his side, and slung her satchel off, doing a quick check of the supplies with her. It was more than enough for an accident or two, but nothing compared to what she'd need now. Only a couple of bandages, a few pinches of feverfew, and a tin with skin-mending salve. The supplies she had bought were for specific maladies and brews, not immediate trauma.

Screams echoed around her, and her focus was torn between the man before her and the rebels attacking.

"Please." His words were garbled as blood trickled from the corner of his mouth. "My wife and daughter are in our house behind the paint shop."

She hushed him, his face pale and eyes fluttering.

"I'll find them," she gasped. "But I need you to move your hand so I can take a look."

He nodded and lowered his hand. Blood began to pour from the cut on his neck. She lunged forward, pressing two bandages against it to stop the bleeding.

Another scream, and Evelina turned to see a rebel smiling at her from the front of the tavern, clutching a bloody mass in his hand. Her eyes followed the pool of blood. The barkeep she had just paid had fallen on her side and now faced Evelina, a hole where her heart should be.

Evelina's hands froze.

The rebel didn't look human *or* fae. His face was cracked with lines of black, as if his veins had turned to obsidian and glowed beneath his skin. He looked like a monster, a nightmare that she couldn't wake from.

She frantically looked back down at the wounded man, feeling his pulse weaken beneath her fingers. She couldn't just leave him.

When she looked back up, the rebel was running toward her, his eyes bloodthirsty and eager. But before he could get any closer, an axe was driven into his chest. His eyes widened as he fell to his knees.

The storyweaver from earlier swung the axe again, ending the rebel's life and saving Evelina's. Other villagers had banded together, carrying scythes, axes, and other farming tools.

She saw the massive belly of a wyvern swoop low to the ground. The smoke had settled like a blanket over the square, making it impossible for the Rider to tell who was friend or foe.

The man in front of her wheezed, his breath coming out in short spurts. She needed to get him out of here. Now. She scooped what remained of the skin-mending salve and lathered it onto his neck. He was still bleeding, but the flow slowed tremendously.

She looked up again, desperately searching for a place to hide him. The smoke started to dissipate enough for her to see.

The villagers weren't winning their charge. These rebels were lethal. Ruthless.

She had heard the stories of how they fought with strange tactics, but these had *shadows*, a sickening darkness pulsing from them. Not typical Nox-wielded shadows, but ones black as night and crackling with sparks of light. They had a stench that clung to them, something she could only describe as decay. They came in unrelenting waves at the villagers, ripping them to shreds before Evelina's eyes.

It was her first time coming face to face with this level of destruction from ground level. Never had she heard of the rebels using shadows like these.

The Aegis patrolling the area sent funnels of fire toward the attackers. There were at least fifteen soldiers she could count through the haze, their movements swift and coordinated. But there were three times the number of rebels, starting a new fire almost as soon as another was put out.

Khaline landed in the middle of the square, her wings clearing more of the smoke and sending the acrid scent of burning flesh away.

Evelina could see the rebels clearly now. They all had the same face as the rebel the storyweaver killed. Weblike black cracks spread across every inch of their exposed skin. She opened her mouth to flag Willow down, but a scream pierced the air from beside her, just to the right of the tavern.

She scrambled to her feet and rounded the corner of the building, where she found three small children huddled against the siding. They were the same little girls who had been playing in the square earlier.

A rebel raised his splintered, black-veined hands, aiming right for the children.

Evelina broke into a sprint toward them, watching in horror as the oldest child—no more than ten years old—stepped in front of the smaller two, a look of sheer determination on her face. Her short, cropped hair was plastered to her head.

Evelina raced for them, fear spurring her faster, but she was still too slow to reach the dark-ridden being in time. The rebel snickered, a sickly crackling of a laugh, as the little girl stood tall, her fists balled tightly, arms out wide in an attempt to shield the other children.

"At least you'll die brave," the rebel soldier quipped, his voice garbled and warped.

Evelina screamed.

THIRTY-SIX

DAIMON

DAIMON ALWAYS HAD THE FEELING OF A KNIFE TWISTING IN his stomach when something bad was coming. He'd felt it the night before the attack on the outskirts of Drogheda, pacing his room until Aster had told him to calm down.

So many terrible things were happening during this war that it was impossible to try and decipher why his gut was telling him something bad was about to happen now. There weren't many Nocturna that had an affinity for shadows as strong as his, but he was fairly certain the shadows were the ones warning him of danger.

These thoughts often kept him awake at night, unable to fall asleep with the number of fae that expected so much from him. But he would smile and pretend he wasn't scared shitless for the sake of his aerial legion. He had to lead, and a commander couldn't be afraid. They needed him to be strong for them.

Daimon let out a long breath and fought to remain present at the war table. They had been in here all day. The council had left hours ago, but Keir, Carwyn, and Senna continued to strategize.

Small, whittled pieces of wood had been carved out in different shapes and placed all over the painted map. Some were soldiers to indicate where they stationed guards, while others were tiny wyverns that were laid down where they planned to have an aerial patrol.

"My men on the eastern front noticed a change in the rebels. The last few encounters, they've seemed…different somehow," Senna mused. "There was a heaviness in their presence, a darkness that's growing."

Daimon glanced at Keir. They had felt it too.

"We've noticed them using more cursed weapons lately," Daimon added. "Almost every rebel had one during the attack on Drogheda's edge."

Carwyn hummed. "As I've said before, we need a weapon. Something to combat this dark magic."

Keir cleared his throat, cutting his eyes to Daimon. Daimon had specifically asked him to keep Evelina's shield quiet for a bit. He didn't want to put extra pressure on her with everything going on, and mostly, he was worried about the implications. What danger it might put her in.

Carwyn looked between the two of them and raised a brow. "Is there something I'm missing?" she asked.

Daimon's nostrils flared. Although he didn't want to share it, at this point it'd be negligent as a commander. "Evelina has been able to shield on occasion, a small one that stops weapons from harming her. She learned by accident, but has been able to train it to protect others as well."

Carwyn tilted her head to the side. "A shield," she said slowly.

"But it isn't worth the risk taking a healer, who isn't trained in battle, to the ground," he quickly amended, hoping to close the conversation. Carwyn's eyes narrowed. "Too much expenditure wears her out. We wouldn't want to leave her in the middle of a battle with emptied Essence."

"It isn't an option," said Senna firmly, agreeing. "She would be putting more than herself at risk if she were to run empty during a battle."

Carwyn nodded her head, clearly taking it all in.

"But we could send more healers as we begin to transition the naval units closer to the border," Keir jumped in. "It would be wise to have more, perhaps some that take to wielding a sword quickly. Even learning a few defensive stances would give them the upper hand."

Senna hummed his agreement.

The door burst open, followed by a loud smack as it flung into the wall. Brielle ran in, breathless. Heads swiveled in her direction.

"Commander." Brielle's deep voice sliced through the war room.

The feeling tugging at Daimon intensified. Judging by the look on her face, it wasn't good. It felt as if all of the air had been sucked out of the room at her words. No one dared speak, didn't dare to breathe as they waited.

Then her eyes locked with Daimon's, and he knew. He knew deep down that he needed to prepare himself for whatever she was about to say next.

"Baile was just hit." Her voice shook. Keir, Daimon, and Senna instantly started for the door, but Brielle's hands trembled as she quickly added, "It's over now."

"*Another* attack?" Keir demanded. He looked at Daimon, eyes wide. "Were any Riders patrolling there today?"

"Two were stationed near Baile this evening," answered Daimon shortly. "Willow and a beta Rider." His eyes flicked quickly back up to Brielle, barely grinding out, "Tell me what the fuck is going on."

Brielle's mouth opened and then closed.

Keir's nostrils flared with impatience. "Spit it out, Brielle."

Brielle wasn't a delicate fae—she was a warrior. One of the strongest Daimon had ever seen. She never turned away from a battle, never faltered to throw herself into danger. And yet here she was, barely able to hold herself together.

"They're all dead," she whispered.

THIRTY-SEVEN

EVELINA

AT LEAST YOU'LL DIE BRAVE.

Time slowed to a stop as Evelina's scream rang in her ears. She'd heard soldiers talking about what it felt like to almost die. They told stories of seeing their favorite memories flashing across their minds, while some thought about a regret they wished they could change.

Evelina saw Carwyn telling her she would be better suited as a healer. She saw the two Nox from the attack on the grove whom she had been too late to save. She saw her mother dying before her with no solution to prevent it.

At least you'll die brave.

The words clanged through her mind. Evelina wasn't just brave.

At least you'll die brave.

She was strong.

At least you'll die brave.

She didn't want to die.

And as the cry of terror left her throat, a burst of light exploded from her body. A deep, thrumming power came to life, and she grasped onto it desperately. She wouldn't let them hurt those children—her people.

Evelina didn't know what it was, this primal magic inside of her. But she latched onto it, pulled it from the depths of her soul where it was buried. Perhaps it was a gift given to her by Eurydice herself.

Evelina didn't question it. She used it. And threw every ounce of her fury at the dark creature that stood before her.

She felt her body being hurled backward with the force of the power leaving her body. She slammed into the ground and her vision faded into darkness.

THIRTY-EIGHT

DAIMON

DAIMON GRIPPED THE EDGE OF THE TABLE IN FRONT OF him. "Brielle, a beta fleet is stationed halfway from here to Baile—take them with you."

She nodded sharply and quickly left the room.

"Reinforcements should arrive within half an hour." Keir moved a wooden piece to Baile and then shifted around other pieces near the palace. "Two units will position near the palace to ensure they don't plan to use the same tactic they did with Drogheda and the grove. We don't want a repeat of them using one attack to distract from another."

Carwyn's face was as cold as ice, her shoulders set and eyes roaming the board—an expression that seemed odd for her, even with the little time Daimon had spent around her. Senna shifted closer to her, worry etching his brow.

"I'll take Zephyr and meet Brielle there." Daimon turned, his legs restless.

"No," Keir said. "You're needed here. Brielle is an excellent Rider."

Daimon rolled his neck, his nostrils flaring as he said, "We ride in pairs."

As if Keir didn't already know this. They had flown together for years. But Keir wasn't his third in the flight here; he was the Aegis council head. They stared at each other, the silence tense as they both refused to back down.

Daimon led over ten aerial units, but he was no commander over an entire race.

Senna looked between the two. "Brielle will have a beta fleet —she isn't alone. We need you both here to strategize and protect the palace if need be."

Keir nodded his thanks and turned back to Daimon. "If things escalate in Baile, then we'll *both* go."

Daimon couldn't argue with that. He itched to fly alongside Brielle, to know that he was the one who had his second's back. But another attack this close to the palace meant everyone was on high alert.

Willow burst into the room, her chest heaving, a hand on her abdomen.

Carwyn gasped. "Willow. What happened?"

It took a moment to catch her breath. She was covered in soot and her hair was plastered with mud.

"Are you hurt?" Daimon demanded.

She shook her head, but her eyes shone with fear. "When they attacked, there was smoke everywhere, fires being set to houses, and people screaming. It was chaos." Her eyes were distant. "I couldn't get a good view from the skies. The smoke was too thick."

Something else was wrong. He knew his Riders, and Willow was always calm after a battle. Something had shaken her.

"They wielded shadows in a way I've never seen," she continued in a whisper, wrapping her arms around herself. "Funnels of darkness that crackled with streaks of lightning."

Daimon's heart squeezed. Vidaris had to be helping them, growing her power in the Vale from the slaughter. Anger surged through him, hot as molten lava.

"They've never used shadows like that," Keir growled.

"There's more," Willow said quietly. She swallowed, her

throat bobbing. "The rebels didn't make it out alive. Not because of me and the other Rider, and not because of the foot soldiers patrolling the area." Her voice trembled. "The story that was told by multiple witnesses was that *Evelina* somehow killed them—*all* of them—at once."

Daimon gripped the edge of the table, his vision swaying. He forced his shadows to stay beneath his command; they were desperate to break free and take control.

"Why would Evelina have been in Baile?" He could barely hide the edge of venom filling his words.

Willow's gaze shifted to him, her eyes filled with guilt. "I invited her on the patrol," she whispered.

Daimon felt like he had been hit by a boulder.

"Then where is she?" Carwyn demanded.

"Lost, Princess Carwyn." Willow's shoulders shook. "The villagers saw the light erupt from her. Many said they could feel the warmth of her Essence shielding them. But she—" Her voice broke and she tried again. "She disappeared along with the rebels. They were torn to pieces, exploding and disintegrating into ash."

No one could speak. Daimon couldn't voice the question he desperately needed to ask. It seemed Carwyn couldn't either. Evelina had never been able to shield to that magnitude before.

"Are you saying you believe Evelina is dead?" Senna finally asked. His usually level voice held a tinge of disbelief, and perhaps even anger.

Willow closed her eyes, and a single tear rolled down her face. "Whatever magic she unlocked, it must've been too much for her body," she said quietly. "We found no trace of her in the village, nor at its perimeter. No rebels survived to escape or take her." Her voice grew desperate, clearly disturbed by her findings. "I saw how fatigued she was when she shielded last. I can't imagine she could have run far if she had survived."

Carwyn exhaled a shaky breath. "Her light has never been strong enough for something like this. It—it isn't possible."

"I saw it myself," said Willow, awe overwhelming her guilt. "It was like the sun itself burned away the shadows."

Keir cleared his throat, rising from his seat. "We must gather the rest of the council." He called to one of the palace guards by the door. "Bring the rest of the Manor siblings to the throne room."

Daimon could feel his lungs burning with each breath he took. He wanted to find a host of rebels and tear them apart limb by limb, while another piece of him wanted to succumb to the grief building inside of him.

"We can alert the council together," Senna said, rising with Keir. "Though what of the queen?"

Carwyn wiped away a tear. "We wait to tell her. Her body weakens every day. This news could destroy her."

Senna nodded solemnly and left, Keir following close behind. Carwyn finally broke her composure, shoulders slumping as the tears fell. She took a deep breath and walked out of the room.

Daimon prayed to the moon goddess as the others filed out of the war room.

She couldn't be gone, not truly—no matter what Willow saw or heard. There was still a chance, as unlikely as it seemed. He refused to lose her, to imagine a world in which her light betrayed her in such a way.

And if it had, if she'd been stolen from him and taken to the gates of the afterlife, he'd raze the whole of Caelum down to bring her back.

Thirty-Nine

Evelina

Evelina awoke to the sound of a baby crying. Her head buzzed and she blinked her eyes, her vision blurry. Her arms trembled as she tried to push herself off the hard ground, but they gave out and she collapsed face-first into dirt.

She rolled onto her side to try and figure out what had happened. Her vision slowly cleared as she searched for danger. Her brows pinched together when she realized she'd landed far enough away from the small village that nobody could likely see her, hidden beneath the bushes and tall grass near the forest's edge.

Her muscles tensed, and a brief moment of terror coursed through her body as she remembered the little faces she had so desperately wanted to save. The rebel soldiers she had hoped she could stop, though she knew she was outmatched.

But she didn't feel helpless before she blacked out. She felt strong—powerful.

Slowly, she tested her strength and braced herself on her elbows. She waited a breath to see if her arms would hold, and when they did, she peeled herself off the ground. Every muscle in her body ached. Each movement was a painful strain on her body.

She leaned against a pine tree, her head spinning. After the stars cleared from her vision, she was able to see the village better.

It was a sight she'd never seen. A small crowd had formed on the outskirts of the village, escaping the smoke still burning off the buildings. The villagers looked safe—the children she thought dead alive and well before her eyes. They were being held by a plush female with auburn hair and a deeply tanned male who was broad enough to hold all of them in his arms.

She strained her ears to listen.

"The rebel soldiers are all gone," an Aegis warrior announced.

Everyone paused to listen, a palpable relief pulsing in the air.

"The princess saved us—saved *all* of us!" the little girl cried.

Evelina's breath picked up.

She couldn't have killed those soldiers… It wasn't possible.

Despite them being horrible, terrifying beings, she felt a wave of guilt. Her vow was to protect as a healer, to never do harm to another. Now she had killed—*murdered*—not just one but countless others.

They were infested with a darkness she didn't understand, so ruthless that they would've destroyed the entire village, the children, the storyteller—all of them. And yet she still felt the sour pang of guilt.

The child's mother shushed her, the resemblance between her and her children unmistakable. "She'll be remembered, Briar. The brave Manor, savior of Baile."

"Evelina is dead?" a familiar voice demanded. It was Willow, her eyes wide.

"Here," Evelina rasped, her throat scratchy and sore. She could barely hear it herself.

The little girl—Briar—pointed toward the village center, where piles of ashes trailed into the road. "A blinding light exploded from her and she turned those scary creatures into nothing more than ash." Her voice was young but strong.

Unafraid. "But the light didn't hurt us. It wrapped around us and kept us safe."

"And Evelina?" Willow demanded, her voice cracking. She cleared her throat. "She didn't make it?"

Briar shook her head, her eyes dropping to the ground. "When the light spread, she disappeared with the rebels too."

"I saw it too," a man behind Willow called out. "They all disappeared into thin air, like they had been consumed in the rising sun."

"It can't be…" Willow muttered.

An Aegis soldier laid a hand on her shoulder. "We've already checked for survivors. We would've at least found her body by now, but it seems…" His eyes trailed to the ash around them.

Willow gave a curt nod and stalked over to Khaline. She jutted her chin out to the beta Rider who rode with them. "I'll get word to the palace. Oversee the aid and report any findings to me after."

No. They couldn't leave her here, couldn't tell her family she was dead.

"I'm here." Evelina's voice broke. She was too weak, helpless as a stranded bird.

Surely she hadn't done as the little girl had said? Her light had never hurt a single soul, not even a bee—let alone reduce *all* the rebels to nothing more than ash in the wind. She could shield herself and one other person at best.

But her memory was fuzzy. She remembered Briar's bravery in protecting her siblings and how much she wished she could protect them. It was an instinctual feeling, just like when the arrow had flung by her on patrol. But this was bigger—almost unfathomable—and she couldn't wrap her mind around the possibility that she had really done it.

She needed to get to the palace, to tell them what had happened. She shook her head and winced, the movement causing pain to splinter behind her eyes. Whatever she had done, it had drained her completely.

The Aegis would patrol beyond the village soon to check for any lingering rebels, and she needed them to hurry. Because she was alive—had survived and prevented whatever massacre the rebels had intended on Baile—and Willow was on her way to the palace to tell everyone that she was dead.

FORTY

DAIMON

IT WAS AN AGONIZING WALK TO THE THRONE ROOM, EACH step like striding over hot coals. Daimon stalked in with Willow beside him. Carwyn was standing at the back of the room, where a large, imposing tree rose from the floor and bent across the ceiling. The two thrones made of its woven branches and roots were empty. Senna and Keir sat at the rectangular oak table, already discussing strategy. Daimon took his seat next to Keir.

Eventually the council filed in, along with Annora, and sat at the table.

He tried to avoid looking at Annora, who came in with her parents. Annora was Evelina's closest friend. Seeing Annora's grief so clearly displayed on her face would make it feel more real. Would make him remember the way her eyes would brighten when he caught glimpses of her in the healer's cabin. Would bring the painful memories of how curious and wild she was—too untamed and bright for this war-stricken world.

It would be hard to find a person that Evelina hadn't touched in some way. Even now he felt taunted by each painting that reminded him of her, each person in this room who loved and admired her in their own way. This was her home; it was as if her ghost already filled the palace.

Daimon cleared his throat, emotion so thick that he felt trapped. Stifled. As if the walls were closing in on him.

He should've come back sooner. Should've returned years ago and told her the truth. She had grown to become as brave as any Rider, and more beautiful than the stars. Even with it being so long since he had last seen her, he knew the moment his eyes landed on her during that meeting.

His thoughts spiraled into memories of her, into all the things he couldn't help but notice the last few weeks. She still had the little crinkle between her brows, and her eyes… Blessed Divine, her eyes. Bright, curious, and the perfect mix of green and brown. That perfect hue he might never get to see again.

He never should've stayed away as long as he had. He should've pushed his shame aside and told her what happened with Nyx the day it happened.

He should've *been here* for her.

Carwyn stood with her back rigid. Her face remained as cold as stone. The only evidence of pain were the tears still falling down her cheeks. It wasn't until the doors to the throne room opened and the rest of her siblings filtered in that she started to shake.

Seretha slowly rose to her feet.

"What's going on?" Ren demanded. His eyes flicked to Daimon briefly.

"Baile was attacked by the rebels," Carwyn said slowly.

Shock rippled through the room. Ren stepped forward. Daimon could practically see the wheels turning in his mind— he knew there was something Carwyn wasn't saying.

"Blessed Divine," Lyria gasped. "Another attack?"

Seretha stepped forward. "The tides are changing. Safety behind the borders is no longer guaranteed to us."

"That is not all," said Carwyn. Her voice broke and she closed her eyes for a brief moment. "Word has come that Evelina was there at the time of the attack."

Daimon watched as Maliena laid a hand across Annora's

chest, as if stilling her from running out. Annora's eyes were already full of tears, anticipating the worst.

"Evelina?" echoed Neve hollowly, looking to Daimon. "Was she harmed?"

Carwyn braced herself, then said, "She did not make it out, but she saved the village."

A wave of disbelief rolled through the room, then a cascade of emotions. Lyria fell to her knees, her gentle face scrunched in despair. Ren quickly dropped beside her, holding her in his arms. Maliena was staring at Daimon with an inscrutable look as Neve turned all his attention to Annora, stunned and rigid at his side. Seretha hissed with a contempt so terrible the guards trembled by the door.

"May Eurydice smite the rebels who did this," Seretha cursed. "May she lay waste to every one of them."

Keir and Senna raised their fists to their chests as they bowed their heads in respect to this wish.

Carwyn's tearful eyes blazed. She clenched her fists. "May it be done," she rasped, her voice raw, "in honor of my sister."

The words struck Daimon in his heart. His shadows writhed just beneath the surface of his soul, begging to be let out, to taste the sweetness of death as they rained darkness onto the rebels. He had no mercy left to give.

Daimon cleared his throat, clinging desperately to any shred of strength that remained in him as he said, "We should still search—"

The doors to the throne room burst open, nearly torn from their hinges. His shadows felt the light surging close. His entire body froze—terrified that his hope was a figment of his imagination.

The sight of her bright hazel eyes nearly knocked him over. Their gazes met, and he briefly wondered if he had died and passed into Caelum. Or perhaps he was hallucinating, seeing what he so desperately wanted to see.

Lyria's gasp echoed through the room as everyone else froze in place.

"I'm here," the figure said breathlessly.

FORTY-ONE

DAIMON

THE THRONE ROOM WAS DEATHLY SILENT. EVERYONE WAS frozen in time, their breaths held as Evelina's chest rose and fell rapidly.

Daimon's head was spinning. He didn't even notice Brielle standing behind her until Evelina took a small step forward. Her skin was pale and smeared with dirt. She fell to her knees, her body trembling.

"You're alive," he whispered in disbelief, his throat hoarse.

His words set the room into motion.

Everyone jumped to their feet. Carwyn seemed spellbound, as if struggling to decide who they all needed more right now: the leader, or the sister. Lyria raced to Evelina and met her on the floor, knee-to-knee as they hugged. He watched the way Evelina's mouth tilted downward and her hands shook as she embraced her sister. Lyria's delicate arms held Evelina with a protectiveness only a sister could possess.

Ren ran over next, helping Evelina back to her feet and hugging her fiercely.

No one spoke as the siblings embraced. They had risen from their seats but were not yet moving, as if waiting for things to fall apart at any second. It wasn't until they were all mostly calm that anyone dared disrupt the fragile moment.

"While we are all certainly glad to see you well, Princess Evelina," said Seretha, drawing out the words, "we would all still like to know how you have made it back to us."

"As you can see, I didn't die during the attack," Evelina said softly, her voice hoarse. Ren was close to her side, looking ready to catch her at any moment. "I was blasted back from the town's square—by my light or the force of the shadows against it, I'm not sure. My Essence was drained, so much so that no one could hear me calling for help. Until Brielle came across me."

"Vero spotted her from the sky. We rode back as fast as we could," Brielle said, her gaze on Daimon.

He nodded to her, clenching his jaw to keep his emotions at bay.

"So, you observed the shadows the rebels wielded?" Keir jumped in, turning to Evelina. He earned a warning look from Carwyn, but still, everyone looked at her, needing to know.

Evelina nodded, her shoulders trembling slightly. But her eyes were distant. Worn. "They weren't just shadows, they were..." She struggled to find the words. "Streaked with crackling light. They felt like death, like I was breathing in acid just being near them."

Maliena stepped forward, her eyes wide. "What else, child?"

"Their skin was almost transparent, their veins solid black and spreading across their entire body."

"How could they harness this darkness?" Keir mused. "They're a mostly human force, with very few ties to Essence. Even the fae on their side shouldn't have this kind of power."

"Furies," Seretha said sharply, stunning the room to silence. "The rebels have Furies now."

Daimon stilled. It couldn't be.

"Furies?" echoed Lyria with uncertainty, holding Evelina tighter.

"The ancient texts talk of curses being used to inhabit a body—in this case, humans," Carwyn explained. "They're curses straight from the depths of the Vale, possessing a willing host and poisoning their souls. The Furies are the worst kind of curse, a kind of demon—something that could severely tip the scales in this war."

"How could they have found a way to call on these curses?" Senna asked, his eyes wary.

Carwyn's mouth pressed into a thin line. "The gods are at play."

Her words sucked the air out of the room, an icy chill sweeping in. Daimon could feel the subtle shift from those around him, the fear.

"The dark gods are answering their prayers," she continued. "Fueling their magic and warping it, creating Furies out of possessed humans."

Rage simmered beneath Daimon's skin. He knew Moros was willing to do anything to gain power, but this didn't just damn his soul—it damned every human who willingly let a Fury in.

"Then how do we kill them?" said Keir bluntly. "Surely there's a way."

"In legend, Furies are strong, nearly impossible to kill," Carwyn said. She turned to Evelina, her brows furrowing. "What happened with your light today?"

Everyone stayed silent as Evelina recounted everything she could remember, from the children who stared bravely into the face of death to the untapped power she felt deep within her and the light that exploded from her body.

"The magic just…came to me. I called and it answered. The only thing I could focus on was how I wanted to stop them from harming the villagers, to save the children that were about to be killed. It was like my shield had been magnified by a thousand."

"So your magic is a weapon?" Keir asked, his eyes focused on Evelina in a way that made Daimon itch to stand between them.

Maliena shook her head. "I don't believe it's that simple," she said. "It's a protective form of magic, but it seems to manifest in an offensive way if needed in the moment. Since the threat was large, it chose to fight back."

"Perhaps their reliance on shadows has also made them more vulnerable to the light," added Neve thoughtfully, well-versed in the shadows. "Her light's aim might have only been protection, but if their shadows were vulnerable to it, they would've collapsed on their own. It would certainly explain the ash."

Keir took a step forward, eyes brightening. "Carwyn could have been onto something when she said we needed a secret weapon." He tipped his head to Evelina. "She could be our edge."

A sinking feeling weighed in Daimon's stomach. His fingers curled into a tight fist, letting his nails bite into his flesh.

Those were the last words he wanted to hear.

He wanted Evelina as far away from this as possible. But it was Keir's job as the Aegis council head to strategize and plan in this way. To always be calculating what the next move could be.

How could Daimon blame him? Something was finally turning the tides in this war, in the most dramatic of ways. All those rebels decimated in one single act of light.

Daimon wished he could see it the same way.

Whispers buzzed around the room, surrounding him from all angles.

"This evening has been overwhelming for everyone." Carwyn's voice quieted the whispers. "We will discuss this further in the days to come. For now, I think we are allowed an evening to rest. Evelina especially."

The group split in a loud rumble of diverging conversations. Annora broke from her parents' side, rushing to Evelina.

Evelina laughed as tears welled in her eyes, pulling her friend in close. Annora was as much a sister to her as all the others were. Lyria hugged Evelina again from her other side. Daimon watched every muscle she moved, noted the way her arms shook and her skin had paled. He narrowed his gaze, a warrior assessing someone who was experiencing shock. He'd seen it in battle time and time again. Her laugh with Ren was too on edge, too high-pitched.

"Commander Daimon." Carwyn snapped him back to attention. "Escort Evelina to the infirmary. Ensure she gets there— *safely.*"

Daimon nodded, turning. Ren, having heard the order, directed Evelina toward him. She walked slowly over to his side and they left the room, her eyelids fluttering. She looked exhausted. This close, he could finally see what she had endured. Her eyes were swollen and her hair was tangled into knots. Her riding pants were singed on the bottom hem, as if they had been held against a flame, and her shirt was covered in soot.

She swayed sideways and stumbled a step. Her knees buckled again; only this time, she kept falling. He lunged forward, catching her by the waist. She was leaning heavily enough that the majority of her weight was against him. She couldn't walk like this.

He scooped her up and cradled her against his chest. She felt so small in his arms, her skin cold. She laid her head against his chest and her eyelids fluttered closed. Every twitch of her body had his eyes flickering down, his hand sliding over and tightening around her waist. Her entire body trembled now.

He pushed open the door to the infirmary and strode in. Though the healer there seemed taken aback by Evelina in his arms, she got quickly to work, directing him to set her down on a cot before running to the other side of the room to grab supplies.

As carefully as he could, he sat her down on the edge of the cot. He didn't let go until he knew she could sit there without falling over.

She looked up at him and he instantly shifted, prepared to catch her. Still, neither one of them spoke. Evelina paused, taking him in. Then she flung her arms around his waist. Slowly, he wrapped his arms around her loosely.

He hadn't held her in *years.* Even the times they rode

together on Zephyr weren't like this. They were close out of necessity, but this… She was *choosing* this.

He could feel her melt into him, his arms winding around her waist and pulling her so close that she could rest her cheek against his chest. His heart was beating wildly, moving so rapidly he was certain she could feel it tapping against her face.

His senses were overwhelmed. His arms encased her in a safe place. He could smell the traces of lilies that clung to her like a second skin. He knew he should pull away, but he couldn't seem to make himself move. No words passed between them, but he could feel the ice melting away entirely as she clung to him.

She was safe. And he would keep it that way for as long as he could.

This was where they had always belonged. Now that he knew this, he would never let go.

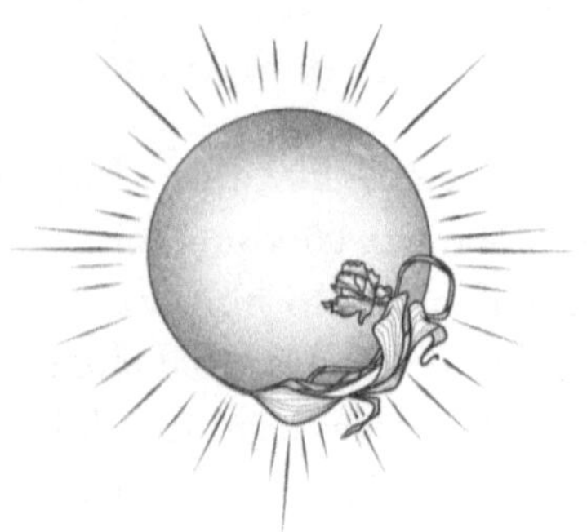

FORTY-TWO

EVELINA

IT WAS EARLY IN THE MORNING WHEN EVELINA AWOKE. SHE blinked through her blurry vision and looked around. There was a brief moment when she thought she had fallen asleep after a night of restocking shelves in the infirmary—as she so often did before leaving for the border.

But then she remembered that *she* was the patient. Had been fussed over by Alaina and Lorene all night after Daimon walked her here.

Flashes of the day before—of killing rebels with her magic and watching villagers nearly die by their hands—crossed through her mind. She still couldn't believe her Essence had protected so many.

"Eve?" a soft voice called, followed by the scraping of a chair against the floorboards. "How are you feeling?"

Her body ached from head to toe. It felt like a blanket made of heavy stones had been laid over her, making it difficult to move. She swallowed, her throat scratchy and raw. A familiar face leaned over her, framed by stray pieces of ashen hair.

"Gloriana?" she whispered. She tried to push herself up. "I thought you were still on the border." Her arms buckled and she slipped back down, groaning as her muscles screamed in protest.

"You mustn't get up yet," Gloriana said quickly, bracing a hand beneath her shoulders. "Word came of what happened in Baile and Aster brought me back. I would see to it myself that you recovered when the news came."

Evelina smiled weakly. "Thank you."

Her eyes were too heavy, as if just trying to get up had exhausted her. She drifted off into sleep again. By the time she awoke, the sun had risen. She was feeling stronger—exhausted, but a little more clearheaded. She took a deep breath and slowly sat up. Her arms held her this time, but her head swam the moment she was upright. She swayed heavily back toward the cot, just catching herself.

"Evelina!" Maliena gasped and shuffled over to her. "I'll go get Gloriana. She just left to rest for a little—"

"No," Evelina said breathlessly. "Let her sleep."

Maliena steadied her and helped support her back as she positioned herself to sit on the edge of the cot. "But—"

"I promise I'll tell you if I think you need to go get her. Let her rest."

Maliena hesitated, but nodded her head. "Annora just stepped out. She should be back soon."

Evelina was thankful for a few moments of quiet. She wanted to soak it in while she could. So much had happened since yesterday. Her mother was dying, *she* almost died, and Daimon…

She could still see his face when she showed up in the throne room. His commander mask had fully dropped. It showed her more than just a glimpse of his emotions; it bared every raw inch of it.

It made her realize he had always been her shadow boy, through and through. Even now, as much as he wanted to hide it.

"Do you know why he left?" she asked suddenly. "You and Neve were like parents to him. I was too young to ask you at the time."

Maliena paused, her lips parting. She blinked a few times and said, "He never told me. You knew him better than most, if I remember correctly."

Evelina's brows drew together as she thought about it. "Not as well as I hoped, I suppose."

Maliena nodded sympathetically, clasping her hands together. "When he was young, he always kept to himself. Until he met you, that is." She smiled softly. "I confess to never quite knowing what was in his mind."

"Did you know his parents? Or where he came from?" Daimon had never told her, an abyss he never seemed ready to discuss.

Maliena's eyes grew distant. "His mother was troubled before she died, but she loved him very much."

"Troubled?" Evelina echoed.

Maliena shook her head, as if clearing her mind of painful memories. "They were outcasts. And the day he was born, his mother paid dearly for it."

Evelina winced. She knew Daimon had lost his mother young, but not so quickly—and so tragically.

"And his father?" she asked cautiously, feeling as if she were finally getting to the heart of things.

Maliena paused, her brows knitted together tightly. "He—"

Annora strode into the room, breaking the tension. She carried a tray with a steaming bowl of broth and freshly baked bread. Her shoulders slumped in relief when she saw Evelina. "Good, you're awake."

Maliena patted Evelina's knee and stood, switching places with Annora. Evelina watched her leave as she ate, still curious.

There were only so many reasons a fae would be outcasted. Crimes against the fae—killing, maiming, torture. Refusing to adopt the customs—or, worse, following human customs instead. But the first was rare and the second wasn't worth the kind of tragedy that had struck Daimon's life.

She had heard of a much more common tale, though—one that had culminated in this very war.

Dark god worshippers. The very fae who set the scene for Moros's rebellion and facilitated corrupted Essence into the rebels' hands.

If Daimon's mother had been one, it would explain why her people had turned against her and her child. And if his father was still alive…he could be one of the very rebels Daimon fought.

Her heart lurched at the thought. No wonder he couldn't look a Manor princess in the eye, not after everything the rebels had taken from her—and after everything she planned to give them back.

Perhaps he'd known they were on opposing sides all along: shadow and light. And she was only just now catching on.

FORTY-THREE

EVELINA

SOMETIMES, YOU HAVE AN IDEA ABOUT WHAT YOUR FUTURE will be, and then fate steps in to ruin your carefully laid plans. Evelina never saw herself as someone in the spotlight, never considered herself to be a leader like Carwyn or a skilled warrior like Ren. She didn't even consider herself to be an easy-to-love personality like Lyria.

Her mother was one of the only ones who saw her; who chose her as a formidable healer to be stationed on the border.

But her mother wasn't here.

Now that her light had presented in such an undeniable way, Evelina had been made the center of attention. The people who had overlooked her presence for years were now arguing about what to do with her.

She stood outside of the throne room, her body still weak. Her strength was just starting to return after sleeping the entire previous day and late into the night.

"We need to make an offensive push into the Zenovia Mountains." Carwyn's voice was steady, already sounding like a queen. "I've already sent Daimon, Brielle, Aster, and Gloriana back to the border to prepare."

Evelina gripped the fabric of her dress between her hands. He was already gone.

"Once Evelina has recovered, she'll fly back with the rest of the unit as both healer and warrior—"

She shoved open the doors to the throne room, and the council's heads all swiveled to face her. As she stepped into the room, she fought to keep her chin up, to not look as nervous as she felt.

"Am I to be a warrior now?" Evelina asked the council, her eyes on Carwyn. Her lip wobbled as her confidence faded. "I thought I was to be a weapon, used as someone else saw fit."

In the corner of her eye, she could see Seretha watching her with curiosity.

"Your newfound magic could help tip the scales back in our favor," Carwyn said slowly.

"Do I have a say in this?" Evelina asked.

Carwyn held her gaze, her eyes revealing nothing. She didn't respond, which was answer enough.

"Then I want to hear the plan."

Carwyn cleared her throat. "We may not know of a light affinity working in this way, but it has to be a sign from Eurydice, a blessing that she's brought to us so we can end this war once and for all."

"You would be joining us as we advance past the mountains," Keir explained. "With Furies in the mix, we're going to need you with us up in the air."

"When would we leave?" Evelina asked.

"As soon as you've regained your strength," Keir replied.

She could already feel her strength returning. But it was too soon. She couldn't leave her mother in the state she was in. She grew more fragile by the day.

"You'll be with Daimon at all times," added Keir. "It'll be just like the patrols as usual. Only this time, you'll be our biggest weapon—and the focus of all of our defense."

"So he's to be my guard?" Evelina swallowed, uncertainty eating at her. Things were happening so quickly.

"Consider it a mutual defense. You protect our commander, and the commander protects you," Keir said with a shrug.

Evelina thought of Daimon's skill in battle, of Zephyr's imposing power. "I don't think he needs it," she said, almost under her breath.

Keir gave her a reproachful look. "You know why we ride in pairs, Princess Evelina? Because even the strongest of warriors need backup."

Evelina closed her eyes, the wind hitting her face as Codax flew through the sky.

She had said her goodbyes to Lyria and Carwyn the day after she learned she had to go back to the border. Annora hugged her so long she thought she might never let go. And she made Ren promise to stay safe as they prepared to head back to the coast.

Every other moment had been spent with her mother, telling her about her newfound magic and needing to leave for the border. Evelina held onto the memory of her—of holding her hand and hugging her more times than she could count. She didn't want to consider the possibility of it being the last time she ever saw her.

The camp was quiet when they returned that night. Gloriana ran out to meet her, eager to see how she was feeling after the flight. Evelina told her about the plan for her to join the Alpha Fleet as more than a healer. About how they wanted her to be their shield—more, if need be.

Gloriana gasped. "But you've hardly used this magic."

Evelina nodded, her body tired and numb. She couldn't help but wonder if what happened in Baile was a one-time burst of magic, or even an uncontrollable side she wouldn't be able to use long enough to keep others safe. But she had to try.

"Both a shield and a weapon—it's exactly what we need to have the upper hand," she said quietly.

They walked back to the cabin, a heaviness weighing on her shoulders. She felt like she couldn't breathe, like the world was caving in on her. It was as if the last few days were a fever dream and she was finally waking up.

Everything was catching up to her. Her mother was dying, and she couldn't be with her because she suddenly had a pivotal role to play in this war. She was scared, uncertain—her power was a fluke at best, and now everybody would be relying on her to somehow create a miracle again.

"I need some time to think," she said abruptly, stopping at the threshold of their cabin.

"I'm here if you need me," Gloriana said softly.

Evelina drifted, walking until the camp was obstructed from view by the forest and she had room to breathe. She followed a stream, stopping once she heard the rushing of a waterfall. Her heart thrummed, a shred of relief forming in her heart.

She was world-weary and tired, but she was still a healer. And if she had learned anything these past twenty years, it was that there was nothing a good bath couldn't fix.

Forty-Four

Daimon

The moment Daimon landed from his patrol and saw the rest of his fleet's wyverns, he searched the camp for Evelina. He'd almost lost her. He didn't know what he would say when he found her, but he just needed to see her. To convince himself that she was still alive—still breathing.

He knocked on the door to her cabin, shifting from one foot to another. Gloriana yawned as she opened the door. She blinked, her eyes still bleary with sleep.

"I'm sorry to wake you," he said quickly, "but I need to speak with Evelina."

The corner of Gloriana's mouth twitched up and she pointed over his shoulder. "She went to clear her head. Last I saw, she was walking in that direction."

"Thank you." He followed her direction, walking along the outer edge of camp. There were light footprints along a small stream. He followed them until he heard the rushing of a waterfall and was reminded of the last time he was here. It was the night Nyx last visited him, when Evelina had just arrived at camp and they had still hardly said a word to each other.

He found her silhouetted by the moonlight. She stood with her back to him on the muddy shore. Rocks were formed high around the pond behind her, encircling the area like a cave with no roof. A waterfall poured across from where he stood, flowing over the boulders and into the pond below.

It was private and secluded. The waterfall masked his steps as he approached.

He stumbled when he realized she was removing her gown. Underneath, she wore only a thin cotton gown that reached midthigh. She pulled the hem up, and his eyes stuck as it raised higher and higher. It wasn't until it reached the curve of her hip that he forced himself to speak.

"Eve," he choked out.

She whirled around, dropping the hem as she faced him. Her hand flew to her chest.

"Daimon," she said, like a breath she didn't mean to let escape.

He swallowed, nerves fluttering in his stomach. "I thought I lost you," he whispered.

He walked closer until he was standing with her on the bank, his boots sinking into the mud where the water pooled nearby. Her eyes bounced between his. She took a small step toward him so they stood within arm's length of each other.

A look of understanding washed over her face.

"There was a moment I thought no one was going to find me," she said softly.

"Had you not been found, I would've never stopped looking."

Goosebumps pebbled her exposed skin. The night air was brisk and she was far less clothed than a princess ought to be in the presence of a male—or, even worse, of the man tasked with keeping her safe in the days to come.

"I'm safe now," she whispered, her cheeks flushing.

His eyebrows pulled together and pain flashed through his eyes. He took a deep breath and held her gaze.

"And I'm sorry for how our last conversation went before we went to the palace," he admitted. "And…at the palace."

Her gaze fell, a sadness overwhelming her. "I don't want your apologies anymore, Daimon. I need more than that."

"I'm sorry, I just—" He winced, hearing his own words. He seemed to be doing everything wrong. She wanted answers that he wasn't prepared to give. Even when she called him out at the palace for avoiding her and keeping something from her, he still held firm to his secret.

To keep her safe. Always. Above all else.

"Nothing has changed, has it?" Her eyes shifted with anger and she took a step back, wrapping her arms around herself. "You still can't be honest with me." Hurt swirled beneath the anger in her gaze. "Why can't you just tell me the truth? Why did you promise you would return, only to stay away for decades?"

"Evelina, I—" His voice broke. "I didn't want to hurt you."

The way her mouth tilted into a frown made him want to wipe it away. If only he could reach out and trace a finger over the curve of her lips until they turned back up.

"But I *did* get hurt." Tears gathered in her eyes. It was like he was being slowly tortured to death with each tear that fell. "It took me months—maybe even years—to move on. Even now, the wound still feels as fresh as the day you left it on my heart. What could possibly hurt me more than that?"

The mask he wore cracked and pain flashed across his features. For a moment, he just stared at her, blinking.

Then he looked away.

"Don't do that. Don't shut me out," she pleaded.

"There are things that are better left unsaid," he whispered, his jaw clenched.

"You decided for me." Her voice rose and echoed off the rocks around them. "You can't do that, Daimon. You *left* me. Cut yourself off from me and never returned."

He stepped forward, needing to be closer. But she receded a step, refusing to relent. Twenty years of frustration and anger came bubbling to the surface.

"You're hiding something, Daimon," she continued, holding his gaze. "After the Baile attack, I spoke with Maliena." Her eyes were wide. Determined. "She told me about your mother, about how she was an outcast like your father. And I realized even if you never knew your father, he might have found you—and he might have made you feel like an outcast yourself."

He swallowed and his head began to pound. She was so close to the truth, so much closer than she realized. Pressure was mounting against his chest, against his entire body, like a dam about to break.

"Just be honest with me," she pleaded, sensing she was close. "Why shut yourself off from me—from the world—and not come back home? If it's something with your father, we can figure it out. Even if he worships the dark gods—"

"My father doesn't worship the dark gods," he burst out. "He *is* a dark god."

Evelina's chest rose and fell rapidly, her eyes widening.

"My father is Nyx," he said firmly, feeling instant relief, like the weight of the Zenovia Mountains had just been taken off his shoulders.

He had finally said it. And there was no going back.

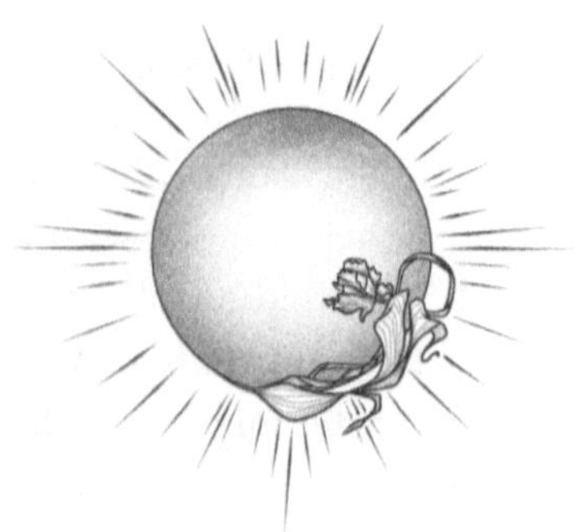

FORTY-FIVE

EVELINA

MY FATHER IS NYX, THE GOD OF FEAR AND DREAMS.

Evelina froze. The words slammed into her over and over again.

"My mother was fae," Daimon continued. "*She* was the one that worshiped a dark god, devotedly and without fail."

The blood drained from her face.

"How long have you known?" she whispered.

He ran his hand roughly through his hair. "Nyx came to me the day I was supposed to return back to you. He showed me memories—" His voice broke and he took a steadying breath. "Memories of my mother being burned alive just after my birth. It was at the hand of the villagers in her own town—people that had known her since she was a child."

Evelina swallowed thickly. Her mind raced as the words sunk in. *Daimon* was the son of a dark god. The shadow boy with midnight eyes who comforted her when she was plagued with sadness. The soldier who left her behind. The commander who shared a dream with her when she was overwhelmed.

"A midwife was supposed to come in after my Essence released, but she came too soon," he continued, looking at the ground. "She saw the way my Essence cut off, the way it didn't seek out anyone other than my mother. Maliena ran out the back of our cottage with me in her arms. She's hidden the truth all this time."

He wouldn't look at her. There was so much pain in his eyes that she felt his sadness mingle with her anger. He'd dealt with this alone for nearly his entire life.

"Maliena knew?" she asked softly.

He nodded his head and looked up at her. "If anyone learns who I am, whose blood runs in my veins, they would treat me just as they did my mother. What future would you have with a forsaken god's bastard?"

She held his gaze, her body unnaturally still as she took his words in. Worshiping the dark gods was punishable by exile to the wildlands—untamed forests with creatures straight from the Vale.

"I refuse to doom you to the same fate," he vowed.

She reached forward and took his face in her hands. "That is still *my* decision to make."

"But it's more than that," he added quietly. "Nyx wants me to rule over the Shadow Realm as Vidaris's right hand." He gently pulled her hands away from his face, putting space between them. It felt like an entire mountain separated them.

"It's my birthright. Whether I will it or not, one day the gods will ensure I take up the helm and fulfill my duties." He shook his head and laughed bitterly. "Only one born of both worlds can sit on the throne of darkness in the Shadow Realm. It's written in the stars for me."

Her breath caught. She fought against the tears threatening to spill—blessed Divine, she was tired of crying. Her body was exhausted, but buzzing with energy at the same time.

"You don't have to carry this alone anymore—you never should have done it alone. All this time we could've..." She trailed off, unable to keep the frustration from her voice. "Nyx doesn't know what our future holds. No one does."

His gaze landed on her tears and his face fell, the mask of the commander crumbling again. She stared into the eyes of the boy she once knew, his vulnerability seeping through his normal facade at her words.

"But it doesn't make it a risk I'm willing to take." He held her gaze, his midnight eyes blazing with determination. "I want to keep you safe. To prevent you from the possibility of losing me all over again."

Evelina growled in frustration. She placed her palms against his chest and pushed him back a step.

"You didn't have to decide this alone!" she shouted, her temper flaring. She pushed him again, and this time, her hands curled around the collar of his shirt as she seethed. "This is *my* choice. *I'm* willing to chance it. We've seen so much death, Daimon. So much pain and loss. Our days could be numbered as it is, and you want to spend it being in fear?"

His eyes traveled down to her mouth, her hands still gripped in his shirt. She didn't know if she was pulling him closer or pushing him away.

He'd had countless chances to tell her this, yet he hadn't. Despite the grief she felt for what he'd gone through all alone, she was still furious with him.

"I always thought you never came back because you grew tired of me," she admitted. "You led me to believe that. You had the chance to tell me the truth and you chose not to."

"My heart will never tire of you," he said immediately, his voice a low hum.

Her nostrils flared as he stared down at her. She squeezed the fabric bunched in her hands tighter and pulled him a little closer.

She didn't know where her pain ended and his began.

She needed him to fight for her, to show her that he wouldn't abandon her again. As much as she wanted to fall into his arms, she couldn't forget the years he'd stayed away. He'd built walls around himself so high that she didn't know how they would ever truly come down. But she needed to see him try.

"Then don't give up so easily," she begged. "Don't let me go this time."

Forty-Six

Daimon

"Easy?" Daimon shook his head, wishing Evelina could see the years he'd spent throwing himself—mind and body—into being a soldier just to hold himself back from returning to her. From letting his selfishness win and ruining her life just to love her.

"I've held myself back for years," he whispered. She deserved the truth—the full truth of how tightly his chains were bound. "From accepting Nyx's fate, from ever allowing what happened to my mother to happen to another, and *especially* from making you love someone as unworthy as me."

He wrapped a hand around her waist and brought the other up to slide into her hair. She leaned in closer to him, their noses nearly touching. They were tucked away on the edge of the pond and hidden between the trees, an escape from the war and pain that plagued their lives.

"You have always been worthy, Dai," she whispered.

There was a time he craved to hear those words—hoped that if she believed in him, then he could believe in himself too. But it was more than that. The wound of feeling like he didn't belong ran deeper than even her words could heal.

Growing up, he had always known something was...off

about him. Maliena and Neve were great to him, but he knew he was not their real child, and he knew the depths of his shadows were something to hide rather than celebrate. It wasn't until Nyx found him that he understood why he should feel so ashamed of them—that his very existence had turned his mother to ashes. His past so dark he could not bear to look at it, and his future promised to even more darkness.

But he had become a wyvern Rider, had bonded with a creature sent by Eurydice herself. He had lived a life where he could pretend he belonged. He had fought faithfully for the empire and resisted the call to be the Lord of Shadows. Maybe Eurydice had favored him for his resilience and faith.

The only reason he had done any of that was because of one person and one person only.

Evelina. The woman right in front of him.

He felt a sense of belonging with her in his life, felt understood.

He had always been afraid of what his future held. If he were honest with himself, he had always been terrified by the possibility of losing Evelina. So he pushed her away and lost her anyway.

But when he looked into her bright hazel eyes, he wasn't afraid anymore. He'd always thought he had to do this alone, but now he could see just how wrong he had been.

A wave of emotions rolled through him: relief that she didn't hate him for being the son of a dark god; gratitude that this perfect female could see past the stains on his hands; and a passion he had kept suppressed for so long surging free.

Fate had held him back his entire life, chains binding him, until he realized he was the one imprisoning himself.

Well, fuck fate, and fuck his father.

For this woman clothed in moonlight standing before him, he was at her mercy.

"No one can be worthy of you," he murmured. "But I'll damn well try."

His lips crashed into hers.

He was floating. Dreaming. Because it was impossible that this was real.

Her hands wrapped around his shoulders and she pressed her body against his. She kissed him as if she wanted him to feel her years of anger and grief. Like she wanted him to feel the repressed frustrations of twenty years without hearing a word from him.

Every kiss she gave, he met with his own grief of the years he spent hating himself over things he couldn't control. But beneath the pain, there was undeniable longing. He drank the taste of her lips, drawing her closer and closer.

She pulled away from him first, her chest heaving. Slowly, she backed away.

His brows pulled together and he opened his mouth. Confusion marred his features as he watched her step closer to the pool of water.

"Join me?" she whispered.

Daimon froze. His eyes bounced to the water behind her, then back to her.

"Please," she added, lifting the hem of her thin gown until it grazed the tops of her thighs.

His eyes lowered and studied every inch of her. Evelina's fingers curled around the fabric and she took it off entirely. His entire body warmed.

She turned and stepped into the water. He sucked in a sharp breath and quickly stepped out of his pants and shed his shirt. He followed her into the water, his heart racing.

She kept swimming until she was treading water in the center of the pond. When she faced him again, he had already stepped waist-deep into the water. He waded toward her, his gaze heated. The water felt cool against his bare skin.

They moved in spellbound silence. She swam to the small waterfall on the other side of the pond. She was closer to the bank there, giving her space to stand. As she slowly stood, the waterfall crashed in front of her. She stayed with her back facing him, but turned her head to the side to look over her shoulder.

"Don't make me wait, Commander."

He moved toward her until his chest was against her back. With steady fingers, he tucked her wet hair behind her ear and slowly traced its pointed outline. She shuddered beneath his touch, leaning back until her entire body was pressed against his.

Evelina was his everything. She knew his sins and yet she still found it in her heart to forgive him.

Deep down, he knew he would lie awake tonight, thinking through what would happen next. But right now, all he could think about was the woman in his arms. Because she was right; their days were numbered.

No one knew what tomorrow held. Fear had ruled his life for too long. Shame had kept him quiet. Compliant. But his grand scheme of always keeping his bloodline to himself had gone to shit.

All at the hands of one very demanding female.

Without a word, she turned back to the waterfall and walked through it, straight to the other side.

There was so much water that it was like a wall had been placed between them, a curtain so thick he couldn't see her anymore. But he would follow her anywhere. He took a deep breath and stepped through.

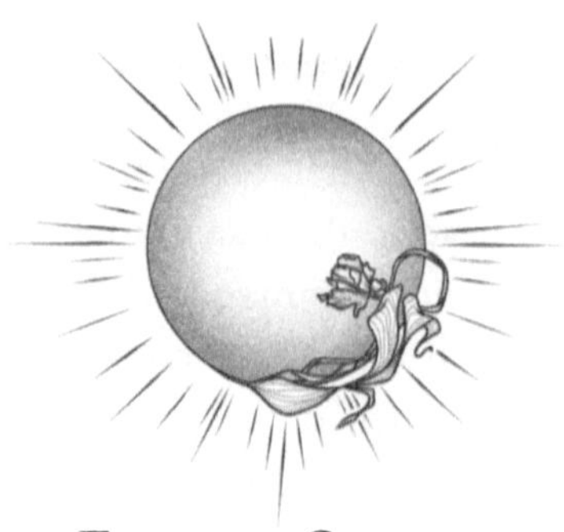

FORTY-SEVEN

EVELINA

EVELINA HAD NEVER TRULY BELIEVED SHE WOULD EVER marry for love, the main reason being that the only male she saw herself marrying wasn't an option in the eyes of the kingdom, and then he never came back home.

But now she had his explanation—something she never would've imagined being the reason he'd stayed away. For years, she had resented him for leaving to become a Rider in the first place—and then staying away during the war—but he did it to protect her. It was all for her.

She had always thought that he'd left because he didn't feel as deeply for her as she did for him. They were just children when he left. But she had been wrong—so very wrong.

Daimon slowly stepped forward and the sheet of water behind him parted like a curtain. Behind the waterfall was a smooth boulder. It was large enough that when Daimon followed her in, they were already pressed closely together.

He brought his hand to her face and cupped her cheek.

"I'm sorry, Eve," he whispered. He lowered his forehead and pressed it against hers, their breath falling into rhythmic unison. "I'm sorry I didn't tell you."

She let out a shaky breath. "I'm not happy you lied to me. But…I understand why."

He dropped his hand from her chin, tracing his fingers down the curve of her neck, over her shoulder, and didn't stop until he reached her waist. He leaned down, pressing his other hand behind the crook of her knee.

Without hesitation, she wrapped her leg around his waist. He responded in tandem, sliding his hand across the back of her thigh, digging the tips of his fingers into her soft skin.

"I need you, Daimon," she said quietly.

Wrapping her other leg around his waist, his hands steadied her on the backs of her thighs. He took a small step forward, pressing her back against the cold stone. She sucked in a quick breath from the icy sting of it, jutting her hips out at the sudden contact—which drove her straight against him.

Daimon groaned and closed his eyes briefly. His fingers squeezed tighter as he stood deathly still. She brought her hands to his shoulders and reached around until they were tangled into his hair. He leaned down and pressed his lips against hers.

Evelina's world shifted beneath that kiss.

It was different from earlier. This was deeper, less frantic. He kissed her like she was his world.

As the water rushed behind them and covered the glow of the moon, she felt safe—cherished. She basked in the feeling of his mouth, the kiss deepening as he pressed his hips forward.

He broke the kiss, cupping her cheek with one hand while his other still gripped her thigh. She squeezed her legs tighter around him, craving more.

"If you want to stop, we will—no questions asked," he rasped. "I only want what you want, Eve."

She huffed a laugh and pulled him closer, his nose almost touching hers. "I've never wanted anything more."

His lips met hers again and he kissed her until all her nerves melted away. She breathed him in, quickening the kiss as she begged for more, her hips rocking against him. It didn't take long for him to oblige her silent request.

When he finally pushed into her, her head fell back against the stone behind her. He leaned in and kissed down her neck as he slowly eased out and back in. She gripped his hair, guiding his head to her breasts.

His lips closed around her nipple, sucking and drawing a cry from her lips. She felt as if lightning had struck her, and all she could do was squeeze her legs tighter around his waist as his pace quickened.

She needed more—needed to be closer.

"Remarkable," he praised.

In the darkness of their haven, she could still feel the scars that riddled his chest. Some small and some the size of her hand. Years of fighting had left its mark on him, but she only found him more captivating. He wouldn't be Daimon without them.

His hand slid around her neck and into her hair. He threaded his fingers into the wet strands, pulling her head back. He swept soft kisses along her jawline, slowly dragging his lips back down to her neck and collarbone.

This time, when he pushed into her, he didn't hold back. He gripped her hair with one hand and her hip with the other, driving his hips forward until her breath caught and stars streaked her vision.

As she cried out, he followed her over the ledge and they flew together.

Between the rock and the waterfall, she could pretend there was no war. Could convince herself that she was just a woman, and he was just a man, and nothing stood between them. No inexplicable powers and royal duties. No soldiers relying on their commander. No ownership other than to each other.

She could be his. If only for one night—for one fleeting moment—she could be his.

FORTY-EIGHT

DAIMON

HER FACE WAS GAZING UP AT THE DARK SKY AS SHE FLOATED on her back, her hair gliding around her. Daimon was floating beside her, but he wasn't looking at the stars. He couldn't stop watching her, couldn't stop replaying every delicious feel of her against him.

"What is it like talking with a god?"

"Overwhelming." He answered so quietly that the sounds of the rushing water nearly covered his words. "Like my entire body was itching from the presence of his power."

Evelina was patient as he talked, listening as he told her of what it felt like to speak with a god, of the power and darkness that surrounded him. He told her about every visit with Nyx, about other memories he had played of his mother. She was quiet through it all, letting him get it out. He explained how his magic hummed when Nyx was around, even when they got deeper into the Zenovia Mountains. How he didn't have the magic of a god—not exactly. It was still difficult for him to understand himself. Nyx hadn't exactly sat him down and explained everything, and he wasn't given any kind of guidebook.

"My Essence is far stronger than the average fae—especially after my trial—like my magic has been given a boost."

Evelina stopped floating and faced him. "So that's why your magic felt different when you shielded me from the rebels' fire?"

"Exactly." He smiled softly and stopped floating too.

She was quiet, her face scrunched in thought.

He waded toward her, getting an idea.

Evelina leaned forward and said, "What are you—"

Her words abruptly stopped and she looked down into the water, a flurry of fish rushing past her, all headed in the same direction.

"Nature recognizes the ancient bloodline within me," Daimon said with a soft smile as he watched the fish. "I've learned to close my connection to the world around me so they don't do this at the wrong time, but when I open that connection…" He held his arms out beside him and Evelina gasped.

All the fish in the pond began swimming in a circular motion around him, moving in perfect unison, a pattern of endless motion.

"But you're not Undine," Evelina said in disbelief. "Fish shouldn't respond to a Nox."

"A god's blood runs through my veins," he said. "Sometimes the trees will bend in my direction, or the grass will reach out to touch me as I walk through it. It's so small sometimes that it's hardly noticeable unless you're looking for it."

He dropped his arms, tampering with the connection he felt to the living things around him. The fish immediately broke their pattern and swam out in all directions as if nothing had happened.

"Incredible," Evelina breathed, watching the fish recede into the depths of the water. A smile tugged at his lips, watching her with wide and excited eyes. She was more beautiful every day he saw her, but when she was brimming with curiosity, she took his breath away. "*You're* incredible," she repeated.

He could feel his cheeks heat beneath her praise. The oddly warm sensation spread across his chest.

She swam to the pond's edge, rinsing her hair beneath the flowing stream. He watched her for a moment, in awe of the woman before him, until his breath hitched. Her arms were trembling with fatigue.

It was a miracle she was awake at all with how spent she likely was. He kicked himself for doing this now. She needed to rest, to let her magic continue to replenish.

A tree with conelike fruit hung over the water. Evelina reached up, plucking one from a low branch and holding it in her shaking hand.

"You know we have bathing oils back at camp," he said with a soft smile.

"Woodland." She shrugged, squeezing the fruit until a thick substance seeped out. She barely seemed to notice her fatigue, her eyes clear.

Heat stirred through Daimon's chest. Even on the war front, she was as beautiful as the day he had met her and every day since. He swam over to her, his feet hitting the soft bottom of the pond when he reached her.

"Let me help you," he whispered, his voice nearly swallowed by the sound of the waterfall.

Her eyes locked with his and it nearly took his breath away. She nodded once and held the sudsing plant out for him. With a soft smile, he took it from her, his fingers grazing across her palm.

He watched in wonder as she closed her eyes and turned, tilting her head back for him. This woman who had protected herself so fiercely, who had never allowed anyone in these past few years, was letting him do this.

There was no other feeling in the world that could compare to what Evelina Manor made Daimon feel. And as he lathered the soap in his hands, he found his fingers trembling.

They didn't talk about gods or war. There was something new, something peaceful, that rested between them in the quiet.

She leaned her head back further, the motion bringing the curve of her breasts above the water. His heart beat wildly. The water was crystal clear, molded to her skin as the moonlight made her body glow.

Gently, he worked the suds into her hair. Her eyes stayed closed, her lashes fluttering as he ran his fingers through her hair. The scent of lilies filled the space around him, the smell so sweet and intoxicating that he lost all thoughts in his mind.

"I must be dreaming," he whispered.

The words fell out of his mouth, as if he had no control over the things he said and his heart was saying it for him. Her eyes slowly opened, lids heavy as she watched him with her head still tilted back.

"I'm tired of dreaming without you," Evelina said softly.

She gazed up at him, their bodies facing each other. Her breath was coming out rapidly, her chest expanding and grazing the top of his abdomen with every inhale, her eyes as bright as the moon above them. He could lose himself beneath the twilight.

"I'll dream with you always," he said, whispering his promise onto her skin. "Forevermore."

FORTY-NINE

EVELINA

EVELINA DIDN'T SLEEP THE FEW SHORT HOURS THEY HAD before sunrise. She lay in her cabin, wondering if Daimon was able to sleep. She wished more than anything that she could lie with him, but that would lead to questions from the others. She was happy in their bubble together, just the two of them.

Her legs were sore, but her body was far more relaxed than it had been in years. Still, she hadn't been able to sleep, her body buzzing after last night's confessions. As the sun finally lit the sky, she slipped into mostly clean leathers and left the cabin before Gloriana woke up. She found Keir sitting by the camp's center, stoking the fire with a stick.

"You know you could just use your fire instead?" she asked as she walked up to him. Keir shrugged, his eyes not leaving the flames. "You okay?" She sat down on the ground beside him.

"Yes." He sighed and shook his head. "No. Do you ever get tired of fighting in this war?"

At this point, everyone had to be tired of it. It was impossible not to. Still, it was a surprise coming from the Aegis council head. War was bred into their souls. It spoke volumes that he seemed just as tired as everyone else.

"I look forward to the day we get to go back home for

good," she admitted. "If anyone can lead us to victory, it's you and Daimon."

He poked at the fire again, sending a flurry of embers into the air. "You know, I was worried about you two working together at first with the history you have."

She turned to him, her brows jumping up. "He told you?"

Keir smiled, still stoking the fire. "We've done a lot of patrols together throughout the years." He glanced at her, his eyes sad. "I always told him what an idiot he was for not returning to you."

"He could use a little push sometimes," she said with a small smile.

Keir grimaced, offering a commiserating look.

She realized how thankful she was for Keir—for all of the Riders—in this moment. For the most ruthless warriors in the realm who supported Daimon above all else, not because he was their commander, but because they respected him.

"Most Riders could," he admitted. "We're hard to love."

Evelina released a long breath. "You're soldiers. You spend so much time being strong for others that you forget to be strong for yourself."

Keir huffed a laugh. "You sound like Senna," he muttered.

She stood and brushed her palms against her thighs, rubbing the dirt off. "I wouldn't want to do this with anyone else," she assured gently. "They rely on you, you know. None of you would exist without the other."

He nodded, closing his eyes for a brief moment, as if clearing out a passing pain. "And us, you." His weathered face softened. "You're a part of our fleet too."

Tears welled in her eyes as she felt a sense of belonging in the last place she expected to feel it.

Evelina was lost in the memories of last night as she took stock of the shelves. She replayed every kiss—every touch.

She sat on the floor, her legs crossed as she weighed rennew powder in a small bronze scale. Once it tipped two ticks down, she marked the weight on her parchment and beside it added, *Low stock.*

The wooden floorboards behind her creaked and she whirled around. Daimon was leaning against the doorframe, the door open to let the cool breeze in. His arms were crossed loosely over his chest and his eyes were brighter than she had ever seen them, a soft blue instead of the usual blazing midnight.

"Don't stop on my account." He pushed off the frame and slowly walked toward her, his gaze roaming her body. "I could watch you all day."

"You could watch me count and tally jars all day?" she teased.

He smirked and stopped once he reached her. She looked up at him from where he stood and her heart began to beat a little faster. In all her time in the camp, she hadn't allowed herself to really admire him, to drink in the curve of his lips, the short beard that lined his jaw. He crouched down until he was eye level with her and reached forward to tuck a strand of loose hair behind her ear.

His hand paused against her face as he said, "I could never tire of watching you, Eve." She swallowed and her cheeks flared red. He smoothed his thumb over the blush. "So beautiful when you blush for me."

Before she could answer—or swat his hand away—he stood again and offered his hand to her.

"I want to take you somewhere," he said softly.

She raised a brow but slipped her hand into his. He helped her up, a gleam of excitement in his eyes. His normally guarded expression was gone—he almost looked like the boy he used to be, carefree and ready to take on the world.

"Where are we going?" she asked.

He smiled and slipped his hand into hers. "Somewhere I've never taken anyone."

Zephyr was waiting outside the cabin, watching them expectantly as they approached her. They were going to fly.

Evelina stopped and tugged at his hand. "Shouldn't we be training or something?"

He rubbed his thumb over the back of her hand. "We won't be gone long," he promised.

She nodded and followed him to Zephyr. She grabbed the rope hanging off the saddle and hoisted herself up. It had become easier to mount her in the times they had patrolled together.

Daimon swung himself up next and seated himself behind her. The saddle pushed them close together, her back pressed firmly against his chest. But she'd be lying if she said she wasn't leaning against him regardless.

Zephyr stretched her wings and pushed off the ground. They were above the clouds in seconds, her wings stretched out wide as she sped through the air.

Evelina leaned her head back against Daimon's shoulder. He rested his cheek against her and wrapped his arms tightly around her waist.

As Zephyr leveled out in the sky, Evelina thought about all the years she had missed with Daimon. They could've been doing this since he became a Rider, had he chosen to tell her the truth. Still, he made his decision, and they would both have to live with that. She could hate him for leaving her in the dark for so long, or she could take advantage of the time she had with him. There'd been so much loss during the war, and had there not been, she might've chosen to stay angry with him. But she'd seen death, experienced how quickly things could change. All it took was one stray ferrum arrow—one exposed move—for a life to be taken.

No one was invincible—not even immortals.

So instead of holding onto her anger, she let it drift behind them in the wind.

They flew over the clouds blocking the forest beneath them. She couldn't tell if they were headed west or east, but Zephyr seemed to know the way. Daimon pressed a soft kiss against the curve in her neck and she shuddered. He smiled against her skin.

"You are far too good for me, Evelina Manor," he whispered, his voice nearly lost among the howling wind.

She turned her head and buried her face in his neck. The scent of cedar and frost enveloped her. She couldn't help but breathe it in. He smelled like a forest on a crisp winter morning —as if fresh snow had just blanketed the ground.

Now she understood why the Riders loved to fly so much. There was a calmness in being so high up—a sense of freedom that came along with the possibilities that lay ahead. She could spend hours with him up here, far away from the war and the worries on the ground.

Zephyr tilted her nose down and started their descent, though Evelina would've been happy to fly the rest of the day.

Once the clouds cleared and she could see the ground, she saw they were above a lake. The sun splashed rays of light onto the water's surface, making it sparkle and glisten with each ripple. Zephyr flew them closer, her wings churning rolling waves. She landed on the muddy shore, her talons sinking into the wet soil.

Daimon slid off first and turned around to help Evelina down. Once on the ground, she turned to admire the beauty around them. A patch of willow trees surrounded this end of the lake. They swayed with the breeze, their branches dancing to the sound of the wind. Small white butterflies hovered around the trees, floating through the cascading leaves. In the midst of so much heartache and war, Evelina had forgotten how beautiful her land could be.

"It's beautiful," she whispered. She turned to him, finding his eyes on her.

"Yes, it is."

He grabbed her hand and led her toward the willows. There was a small, worn path that was etched into the grass. It disappeared behind the tree closest to them, the long branches of the willow hung like a curtain to what lay beyond it.

Daimon gently pulled back its branches, rustling it enough that several butterflies flew off. Evelina stepped through the tree and he let the curtain of leaves fall behind them. The branches were so thick that they were shaded from the sun.

"What is this place?" she asked, her voice filled with awe.

He continued to lead them down the small path, through more branches and trees. "A place I come to when my thoughts are too loud and the world is too heavy." It was like they had been transported to another world, a place without their past and their sins. "But this isn't what I brought you here to see," he added.

Even if it had been the reason they came, it would've been more than enough. Just being here with him was all she needed.

Through the trees, she could see an outline of rocks glistening in the sun—the opening to a cave, she realized.

A wide stream fed into the cave, the water so clear that she could see the bottom of it; teal stones speckled with white, purple crystals practically glowing, and every color in between.

But they didn't stop at the colorful stream. Instead, Daimon led them into the cave. The walls were damp and the ceiling barely high enough for Daimon to stand up fully in.

The deeper into the cave they walked, the darker it got. The sounds of the forest quieted behind them, leaving only the ripple of the water bouncing off the cave walls.

Somehow, it felt more secluded than being alone above the clouds.

"Just a little further," he whispered.

They had walked far enough that there was no longer light from the opening to see the path before them. She could barely see the outline of his body, let alone where they were going. He kept her close, his hand never leaving hers.

He slowed to a stop and sat down, tugging her hand to get her to do the same. Once she was seated, he released her hand.

It was pitch-black. Without his hand, it almost felt like she was alone. She only knew he was still there from the sound of his soft breaths.

"This is what I wanted to show you," he whispered so softly she had to strain to hear him. He brought his hands together, a loud clap echoing off the walls.

"What are you—"

Her breath caught.

Thousands of tiny blue lights snapped on and glowed so brightly that she could see him sitting beside her now. The lights lined every inch of rock and reflected off the water around them.

It felt like she was *in* the stars.

"What is this?" she breathed.

"Small insects that glow in the dark," he explained. Their light began to fade and he clapped again, causing their light to brighten once more. "They live in dark, quiet places."

She watched as their glow slowly dimmed, in awe of the tiny creatures. "I've never heard of a creature like this," she whispered. "How did you find it?"

"During training with the fleet, we would take solo trips exploring with our wyvern." He clapped again once the lights winked out completely. "Z found the lake and refused to explore anywhere else after. She kept bringing me here regardless of where I wanted her to go." He chuckled to himself, lost in the memory. "Finally, I started to explore more and more, until I found this place."

There were so many sides to Daimon that Evelina hadn't seen in her time at camp. A softer side that he didn't let others see.

"You're not who I imagined you to be, Commander," she said softly.

He turned to her, his eyes gleaming in the blue glow of the cave creatures. "And who did you imagine me to be?"

She reached forward and pressed her palm against his cheek. He melted into her touch as she said, "I thought I had lost the boy I once knew. I'm starting to see he didn't go anywhere."

The light above them dimmed and they were plunged into darkness again. This time, he didn't clap. They sat in silence together, letting the darkness surround them.

"You're not the girl I used to know," he finally said. He wasn't whispering anymore, his voice loud enough to cause a handful of the creatures to glow. She could see the curve of his lips, the upward tilt of his smile. "You know who you are—what you do and don't want to be. Either way, I'm just as in love with you today as I was back then."

Her breath froze in her lungs.

In that moment, she knew she had never stopped loving him. Even through the years of anger and pain that he had left in his absence—through the ache of losing him and never understanding why.

She never imagined he felt the same way. That the love she kept hidden in her heart for him mirrored the love he had for her.

"I don't want to lose you again," she said suddenly, loud enough that more of the creatures flared brighter. "If we make it through this wretched war, I don't want you to disappear again."

He leaned forward and rested his forehead against hers. "You're still a princess, Eve."

She gripped the collar of his shirt and shook her head. She knew the feelings she had for him ran deeper than love. It was more than that—her soul sang when his was near.

"I'm the *last* heir that would be chosen for the crown." She leaned away from him. "If this were Carwyn, perhaps it would be hard to convince our mother and the council to allow her to be with a fae of her choosing, but we all know I'm not Carwyn. I'm not even Ren or Lyria."

He sighed and took her hand in his. "You really believe we could convince the council and the queen to let us be together?" he asked quietly, his eyes fixed on where his fingers were laced with hers.

"I do," she swore. "When this is over."

He looked up, bringing his gaze to hers. "When this is over," he said with a sad smile.

Deep down, she knew this was the least of their concerns. Even if the council approved, Daimon's fate would still hang over their heads until the day the dark gods decided to claim him.

But in this cave, with the blue light fluttering, she couldn't feel the weight of the outside world anymore. No Nyx, no Vidaris, no Moros or rebels. It was just them, together, beneath the false stars.

Fifty

Daimon

The moment Daimon stepped back into his cabin, a smile still on his face, he found Keir waiting for him.

"Word came from Beta Fleet Ten," he said. "Rebels were spotted returning through the cavern where we saw them last. We've decided to launch an offensive and clear them out of the mountain range. We leave at dawn."

Daimon had always known their brief bubble wouldn't last. There was still a war to fight. And with Evelina's light power, they could finally push the enemy out past the border.

The rest of the night was a blur, hardly giving him time to see Evelina as the army prepared for the attack and she trained with Gloriana and Brielle to shield.

He had so much more to lose now. Evelina had shown her skill on patrols before, but the rebels they encountered were still battles they won fairly easily.

This time would be different; it would be war in a way Evelina had never seen.

"Today we fly into battle." Daimon stared into the faces of his Alpha Fleet, along with hundreds of ground soldiers. Keir stood beside him, his presence calming Daimon's nerves. "The Alpha Fleet will fly ahead, leaving the betas to remain stationed around the empire. Soldiers stationed with the naval fleet on the coast are being diverted to us, so the betas will be covering the gaps of coverage in that area and beyond."

Keir nodded and cleared his throat. "We'll track the cave we saw them at and delve deeper into the mountains from there. If we spot their army from the skies, we'll send two riders back to prepare the ground troops for what's to come."

Daimon saw Evelina hug Gloriana out of the corner of his eye. He fought to keep his gaze fixed forward, but it drifted back toward her as Keir spoke.

"Be ready for anything. May Eurydice's light guide us all back home."

The soldiers prepared to leave.

This was it. Their chance to secure a stronger foothold on the border.

Daimon pulled Evelina closer as Zephyr flew above the clouds. The fleet was spread out, giving them time to be alone. He dragged his mouth along the curve of her neck, cold chills pebbling her skin with each kiss he pressed against her. He would savor every moment with her he possibly could.

They couldn't see the mountains beneath them, but Daimon could feel them. The pull in his chest was tugging him toward them, as it had every time they'd swept along the mountains.

He spread his hand out on her waist, holding her tight and breathing her in. The scent of lilies that clung to her chased away the feeling in his chest. He could breathe a little easier, think a little clearer.

Zephyr slowed, and a pang of worry shot down their bond. He patted her neck, her scales prickly and tense.

"What's out there?" he whispered to her.

They had flown so high above the clouds that the forest below was entirely obscured. It made for good coverage from any unwanted eyes on the ground, but also left them unable to see what was happening.

"Daimon, something's wrong," Brielle shouted from his right, breaking through the clouds along with the rest of the fleet.

He twisted around, bringing one arm tighter around Evelina's waist. The wyverns were *all* restless. They were shaking their heads and nipping at one another, their wings beating rapidly as they tried to slow down and hover in the same spot. Zephyr snapped her jaws, gaining the beasts' attention.

"We need to get below the clouds," he commanded. He turned to Keir on his left and added, "Brielle, fan out but keep formation. Keir, I want you further back and low. Willow and Aster, keep close and stay side by side. Ranick and Elias, flank us on the sides."

Daimon faced forward, his heart racing. The hairs on his neck stood on end and his blood thrummed with adrenaline. He could feel a slimy darkness beneath them, something that wasn't natural—wasn't of this world.

"Do you feel that?" Evelina whispered.

Daimon nodded and pulled her closer. "Tell me the plan again."

Evelina swallowed and recited her shielding plan as she always did. His heart slowed a fraction as she repeated what she was supposed to do if they saw rebels, and *especially* if they saw Furies.

Making such a strong attack against the rebels meant he needed to focus on being the commander. He couldn't let his judgment be clouded, or he would be putting her—and his entire unit—in danger.

With a nudge on Zephyr's bond, she descended. For a moment, they soared through the clouds. A white haze was all he could see, the coverage so thick that the rest of his unit disappeared around him.

Zephyr broke into clear skies first, and for a moment, it looked like the usual mountainous forest. The tops of the mountains were snowcapped as they always were, an eternal winter at their height. Further down, trees and small, open clearings peppered the mountainside. Small valleys ran between the steep slopes, with creek beds and flowing rivers running through.

Everything seemed normal—a mountain range they'd swept through countless times. Peaceful, even.

He heard them before he saw them. The faint clinking of metal along with the unnatural sounds of screeching creatures. A sickening smell hit him next, one that reeked of death and burning flesh.

Like a vein being corrupted, the rebels filled and flowed through one of the valleys, storming along the bank of a river. They were like a thousand ants swarming their nest.

Evelina gasped, and within seconds, the familiar warmth of her shield wrapped around him. It pressed against his skin, pulling him into a comforting embrace that cleared his head.

"Where did they all come from?" she gasped.

Daimon didn't answer; at this point, it didn't matter. This was it. He could feel it deep in his bones. And instead of his body screaming for him to get away, it was singing, as if welcoming him home.

"We work as a team," he called out over his shoulder. "Stay together and watch each other's backs. You are all prepared for this."

He couldn't see them, but he knew the Valon ground troops would be spread out on the other side of the mountain range, awaiting any incoming rebels to cut them off before they could pass. But the rebels weren't *all* heading for the mountains. One of the veins of soldiers splintered off, heading in the direction of Drogheda.

"Keir," he shouted, gaining the Aegis's attention.

Keir's gaze flickered to the troops headed for Drogheda, then back to Daimon. The moment they locked eyes, he knew they were thinking the same thing.

"We divert the westernmost troops to converge just before the edge of Drogheda," Daimon commanded. He nodded to Ranick and Elias next. "Do not engage with any rebels. Fly straight to the western edge and cover the soldiers as they shift positions. Beta Fleet Seven should be along the water's edge just before Drogheda. They can take over from there."

They each nodded once and tapped their fists in unison across their chest twice, as they always did, before breaking away.

Daimon veered Zephyr around, facing his fleet. They were formed into a V, with Daimon at the point. "You were chosen as the elite aerial unit because you've proven you can handle yourselves when push comes to shove. We need to do as much damage as we can to help the ground soldiers. We give no mercy. We take no prisoners. For the Valon Empire and those the rebels have slain, we will not lose here today."

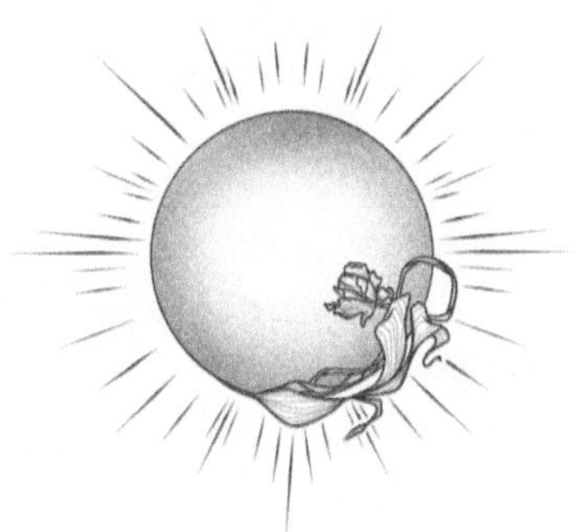

Fifty-One

Evelina

Evelina willed her breathing to calm. She had to be strong, to be brave and focus on protecting those around her. But if she were being honest, she was terrified. Hundreds—if not *a thousand*—rebels were nestled into a small valley in the mountains.

"Back above the clouds," Daimon barked. Zephyr shot into the sky, pulling them back above the clouds and cutting off their view below. Moros was making his final push.

"Daimon, there's no way we can stop them. There's too many." Evelina hated that her voice shook. She twisted her face to his, finding his brows drawn and jaw clenched.

His gaze dropped to hers. The look in his eyes made her stomach sink.

She knew that look. It was the look of a warrior.

"We can't turn back now," he whispered. "We have to advance." He dropped his forehead to hers, and for a heartbeat, nothing around them mattered. "If something goes wrong, Zephyr is going to take you away."

Evelina opened her mouth to protest, but Daimon kept going. "You are the princess, Eve. You are *mine*. And I won't let you die here today."

He didn't give her a chance to respond, quickly strategizing with his unit as they flew above the clouds. Evelina tried to pay attention—she knew she *needed* to pay attention—but the words went right through her.

The sounds of the rebels drew closer with every beat of Zephyr's wings.

You're going to make it out of this. Daimon is going to make it out of this. Everyone is going to make it out of this, she repeated over and over in her head.

She could do this. She could protect everyone from the rebels' darkness and keep them safe.

"We have two advantages here," Daimon said, facing his team behind him. "The element of surprise is on our side. We need to attack the *second* we drop from the clouds. I doubt it'll take them long to realize what's happening, but it should give us enough leeway to gain the upper hand."

"And the other advantage?" Brielle asked.

Daimon turned back to Evelina, a somber smile on his face as he said, "The chance for a miracle."

The screaming beasts and clanging metal were right below them now. The wyverns were unsettled, huffing through their nostrils as their Riders tried to keep them calm.

"Wings up, Z," Daimon whispered.

Murmurs of Riders repeating the same to their wyverns sounded from behind them.

Evelina closed her eyes and dug deep within herself as she prayed to Eurydice that she could stay strong long enough. She tugged on her Essence, pulling until the shield covered more than just her and Daimon. She pushed further until it draped over the entire fleet.

Evelina felt weightless as they dropped out of the sky. Daimon gripped her with one hand and commanded his shadows with the others. The moment the clouds cleared from around them, everything changed.

They soared above thousands of rebels, the mass so large they were having to squeeze their way through the valley. Their movements were unnaturally quick, gliding on shadows at twice the speed any human should be capable of.

Brielle and Keir flanked Zephyr, fire blazing in their palms as they raced toward the ground. Evelina didn't have to turn around to know that Willow and Aster were directly behind them, flying in a formation of five instead of broken into a trio and a pair.

The wyverns barreled down.

Willow moved first, compelling the roots below the rebels' feet to wind around them. They burst from the ground and grabbed ankles, wrists, necks—anything to get them on the ground. The moment they fell, more roots wrapped around them, tying them up.

A burst of shadows shot from the ground. There were too many Furies to see where it came from, but it was heading toward Willow. Evelina gritted her teeth and pushed her Essence toward Willow, enveloping her in a shimmering shield of light. The shadows bounced off, dissipating as they touched the shield. Willow's eyes snapped to Evelina, and she smiled. The grin was predatory, a Rider ready for war.

"Now!" Daimon shouted at Brielle and Keir.

Instantly, they released their fire, raining flames onto the ground below to keep them from advancing. Evelina could see the Furies more clearly now; the black veins that lined their bodies like a web of darkness intertwining with their souls.

"Eve." Daimon pointed to the mass of Furies glowing beneath Aegis flame.

Evelina shuddered and clung to her Essence. Sweat was already collecting on her forehead as she reached deep within herself and tugged on her magic. She pushed the shield of light through the fire and onto the Furies. The light blazed through a large section, turning them to ash.

Keir and Willow broke off, while Brielle and Aster stayed with Daimon.

They repeated the same pattern, Willow using the nature around them while Keir held them back with his fire, and Evelina followed behind with a sweeping wave of light. Even as they took out large portions of soldiers at once, it still felt as if they were attempting to put out a forest fire with one bucket of water.

She tracked the rebels, noting how each time the fleet took out a mass of Furies, a new group was already there to take their place.

"Daimon," Evelina breathed.

His eyes snapped to hers and he frantically looked her over for any signs of harm.

"Look," she insisted sharply. She pointed below, a little ways away from the center of their attack, where more rebels were flowing in. Only…the way they were moving was unusual, like they were rabid animals being held back rather than marching in natural unison. "They're all Furies," she said breathlessly. "How they got such power… Vidaris must have offered her full powers to Moros."

Suddenly, Zephyr shuddered beneath them, shaking her head and veering chaotically. She reared back, leaving Daimon and Evelina to clutch her neck to keep from falling off.

"Z?" Daimon yelled. Evelina could hear his panic rising.

Yelling rose from their left and she looked to see the other wyverns reacting in the same way. It was as if something was in their heads, a frequency only they could hear. Whatever it was, none of them would respond to their Riders.

"I can't feel her," Daimon shouted. "It's like she's cut off from me." Evelina's heart raced as Daimon struggled to get Zephyr steady. "We need to get her higher," he snapped. "The Furies must be doing something."

He was able to direct Zephyr enough to fly higher away from the disorienting influence. Brielle and Keir followed behind, their beasts flying in a choppy pattern.

Aster and Willow didn't make it up to meet them, stuck just above the tree line, their wyverns struggling to rise.

"No one gets left behind!" Daimon shouted, directing his fleet back to retrieve them.

Brielle at their side, they swooped back down into the negative force as they focused all their attention onto Aster and Willow below. If they could swoop beneath their wyverns, they could create enough updraft to perhaps help them escape. Keir dashed lower, using his blasts of fire to clear the space below them. Evelina focused her shield onto him, though the tether was difficult to maneuver against whatever power was manipulating the wyverns.

"Get out of here!" Willow screamed as they lowered, tugging at Khaline's reins. "You'll get stuck too!"

Zephyr roared against the power embattling her mind, screeching as Brielle and Vero pushed up on Khaline. They were nearly there when an arrow the size of a wyvern's head shot straight up and into Khaline's sternum.

The beast roared in pain and slipped from Vero's grip.

Willow howled a bloodcurdling scream as they tumbled through the air. Aster dipped in altitude, frantic at hearing his soulbonded screaming for her wyvern.

Brielle managed to dart to the side and get Vero's claws around Khaline as she dropped, taking on some of their weight, just as another arrow launched into the sky, narrowly flying past the two wyverns. With the wyvern's flight restricted, they were an open target, prey ripe for the predator.

Evelina searched for the source of the arrows, watching as another shot into the sky. Vero thrashed, fighting against invisible chains. She felt Daimon start to move Zephyr toward the archer on the ground. But Keir was closer.

"Fucking bastard," Keir shouted. He broke apart, racing Codax toward the Furies below. Codax was strong, nearly as large as Vero. But he was flying slower than he should've been, barely breaking through whatever control the Furies had on them.

"Keir, stop!" Daimon called after him.

But he was already gone. No one could stop an Aegis blinded by rage.

Evelina briefly closed her eyes, willing her focus to stay strong as she clung to her light, trying to travel after Keir as he flew further away. When she reopened them, she found him positioned between Brielle and the Furies beneath as he headed for the archer.

Another arrow shot from the ground, clipping Vero's wing this time. The beast screamed as Brielle frantically tried to pull up.

Evelina's eyes widened as Zephyr reared back with a sympathetic roar, shock causing her hold on her shield to slip. She could feel Daimon desperately trying to steer Zephyr toward his fellow Rider, but the dark magic disturbing her was too strong.

It only took a second. In the blink of an eye, a torrent of shadows filled with crackling light barreled toward Keir, wrapping around his neck. Next, the chains made of shadows reached for Codax, wrapping around his legs and the base of his wings. It pulled him down with a forceful yank. Wyvern and Rider went crashing into the ground, rebels swarming them within seconds. Codax didn't have time to attempt to get up before the Furies battered him with dark magic, piercing his scales as if they were made of flimsy armor. Zephyr screeched, crying out for her friend.

Keir made a garbled cry, hanging in midair as the shadows around his neck held him in place, slowly draining the life from him. His eyes were on Codax's lifeless body, his arms and legs flailing as he reached desperately for him.

Evelina panicked, reaching inside herself for her Essence. But it was too late. Before her magic could reach him, the shadows tightened around his throat, snapping his neck.

Evelina screamed as his body dropped to the ground beside his wyvern, landing with a sickening crunch atop the rebels below.

FIFTY-TWO

DAIMON

DAIMON COULDN'T MOVE HIS GAZE AWAY FROM KEIR'S lifeless body. He was sprawled on his back with his eyes open, staring blankly at the sky above—directly at Daimon.

He wasn't quick enough to save him. Rage and pain twisted together, rolling through his entire body in punishing waves.

Keir was dead. Codax was dead. Wyvern and Rider lost together in battle.

Daimon was supposed to lead as commander, to keep his fleet safe. But he didn't.

The world around him quieted, his vision blurring and his ears rushing as if he were beneath the sea.

"Daimon!" Evelina shouted. "*Daimon!*"

The sounds of battle filled his head once more. His eyes snapped to Evelina. A tear slipped down her cheek.

A flurry of motion beneath them made him tear his gaze away from her. Elias and Ranick were joining the fray, their wide eyes set on where Codax and Keir lay, their bodies nearly covered entirely by swarming Furies.

Daimon took one long, final glance back to where the rebels swarmed his comrade's body completely.

There wasn't time to grieve.

Willow and Aster were still stuck, and Brielle had no choice but to steer Vero and Khaline sharply to the left, making a break for a clearing close by as Zephyr's updraft pushed Aster and Ryug back into the sky.

Descending into the tree line, Brielle split from the two, staying near as she watched them lower. Daimon couldn't see them anymore, but he could hear trees cracking and breaking beneath the pressure of the wyverns landing heavily.

He sent a prayer to Eurydice that Khaline would survive. For now, they still had a battle to fight. While they were guiding Willow and Aster to safety, the Valon ground soldiers had arrived. A mixture of Woodland and Nox, from the looks of it. The Woodland were encasing the rebels with chunks of soil and rock, but they were breaking through it as if it were dust. The Nox were trying to use their shadows to stop them, but the Furies' magic was darker. Stronger.

Daimon shouted commands at his remaining fleet, calling out for them to follow. Their wyverns didn't hesitate, briefly emboldened by their rage at the loss of Keir and Codax, quickly falling in line alongside Zephyr. Brielle flanked Daimon's right in her usual position, but Elias now rested on his left instead of Keir. Ranick watched their back.

Daimon knew they would be hurting. He needed to be strong for them. To lead them.

There wasn't time for emotions, not as a new wave of rebel soldiers came barreling in.

"Shit," Daimon breathed. "Elias and Ranick, close in from the left side while Brielle and I take the right. We take out as many as we can to help the ground troops."

Elias and Ranick shifted toward the left side of the valley.

Daimon reached around, grabbing Evelina's chin until she was face to face with him. "You can do this, Eve. Focus on the edges of the ground soldiers' formation and take breaks before you burn out. Only shield yourself for now, conserve your energy."

She nodded once, her eyes clouding with tears. "It only dropped for a second. But—"

His chest tightened. "You can't save them all," he whispered. What happened to Keir wasn't her fault. If anything, it was his. He was the commander. "But you're already saving more than if we didn't have you here." He leaned forward, giving her a soft, quick kiss on the lips. He released her chin and she took a deep breath as they dove into the fray.

Ranick and Elias were creating a wall of fire along the back edges of the ground soldiers, but from the looks of it, it wasn't enough to stop the rebels' darkness from slipping through.

That's when Daimon felt the weight of their cursed weapons dampening his magic. Evelina's shield wavered, the heat of its presence against his skin faltering.

A mass of Furies collided with a group of Valon fae beneath them, their darkness hurtling in all directions around them. Daimon was still struggling to control Zephyr, who was quicky losing control again. Daimon could feel the warmth of Evelina's magic flare, her eyes set on the soldiers beneath. "Eve, not yet—"

Within seconds, the Furies attacking their soldiers were gone—mere dust flying in the wind as her light tore them apart from the inside out.

"You have to conserve it," Daimon called out over the sounds of battle.

Her shield dropped almost instantly and she took a steadying breath. Her breathing was heavy; he had a feeling she only listened because she was spent.

A roar came from the river, where Ranick and Elias were holding off the new wave of rebels. Daimon's head snapped toward them. They were overwhelmed, their wyverns screeching.

The enemy was relentless. No matter how many they took out, more came streaming into the valley.

They had to get to their source.

It was a dangerous idea, even with Evelina's light power. But the longer Daimon watched the stream of Furies flow toward the heart of the fae lands, the more he realized this might be the battle where they could lose it all. If Vidaris's magic was feeding the rebels' strength… They had to stop them.

"Give up offense! Follow the river," Daimon shouted. "If we get to the source, we might have a chance at winning this!"

Fifty-Three

Daimon

Daimon was losing his fleet one by one—his family. Willow and Aster were stuck on the outskirts of the battle with a wounded wyvern, while Keir... He couldn't think about Keir right now.

Daimon shoved down the emotion clawing at his throat. They needed to find a way to stop more Furies from joining the fray. The Valon soldiers were holding strong, but if more rebels kept coming, they wouldn't last forever.

They had already seen their entry point in the last battle, the cavern that came up empty. He had wondered how they'd left no trace, but if Vidaris was possessing them with inhuman powers, anything was possible.

From the skies, the nest they all oozed out from had been shaded in shadows, too dangerous to consider storming alone. And with the wyverns so affected by the power emanating from it, they wouldn't be able to fly close.

This was no regular army. An endless stream of shadows was being formed somehow from within the cavern. The only way to end this was to close it off.

"We have to stop them at their source," Daimon said sharply over the wind. "The wyverns are too shaken by the Furies' shadows. So"—he swallowed thickly, trying to hide his concern— "we'll go in without them."

Silence reigned for a brief moment as the fleet processed his words. Riders without their wyverns were like a sword with no hilt. Only the most desperate of situations would call for such an action.

Then the group slowly signaled their agreement. Ranick tapped his fist over his chest, Elias gave a grim smile, and Brielle nodded with a determined gleam in her eye.

"For Keir," Brielle vowed.

Evelina squeezed Daimon's hand where it was still clasped around her waist. "Tell us what to do and we'll do it."

Daimon's eyes flickered in the direction of the cavern. All they had to do was follow the riverbank up to it.

It would be a simple task, if not for the power of the shadows strengthening around his Essence and the growing tide of Furies blocking their path.

Nonetheless, he set his jaw and raised his chin. "We descend and send our wyverns back into the sky to where they aren't affected by the darkness so they can patrol the other side. Then we go on foot and make our way to the central cave. If we can collapse it, we should be able to stop new rebels from coming out."

The fleet shouted, "Yes, Commander!"

Their wyverns landed them in a small opening, the Riders hopping off before they even fully touched the ground. Daimon patted Zephyr on the neck, giving her one last fleeting look as she led the others back into the sky.

Bodies blurred past at a blinding speed. Daimon kept Evelina close enough that he could still feel her. If he could touch her, his eyes could be elsewhere. He needed to know she was safe so he could breathe—so he could think enough to get them out of this alive.

Ranick, Elias, and Brielle surrounded Daimon and Evelina in a tight-knit circle. They moved through the chaos as swiftly as they could. Daimon only diverted his attention to send a shadow toward any soldier in need, as the others did with their fire. He could still feel the chains of dark magic tampering with his magic, keeping it at half-strength.

He was so proud of how brave Evelina was being; he could feel her shielding the group in a staccato rhythm. Instead of a constant shield, she flung it up to cover them—or someone nearby—when it was absolutely needed. She was being smart, as tactical as any soldier.

The arrows wreaking havoc on the ground stilled and disintegrated in the golden haze around them, though they still kept what little control they had on their Essence at the ready in case Evelina's shield slipped.

A Fury stepped into their path, a crazed look in his eye. Blood from fatal wounds along his neck seeped into his tunic.

He looked more beast than man.

The Fury's lips didn't form words, just mangled sounds as he screamed. He charged them so quickly that Daimon barely had time to react. Just as Daimon's shadows reached out for the Fury, he disappeared. His flesh tore apart into a million pieces, his face cracking and splintering until there was nothing left.

Evelina.

He gritted his teeth, having no choice but to continue. But still, he leaned in close enough for Evelina to hear as he said, "You're doing incredible. Stay strong and listen to your Essence. If it's telling you to take a break, then take a break."

She didn't respond, her eyes wildly searching the area they were running through for anyone who needed help.

The path before them was carnage, a body to jump over every few steps. The rebels were gaining on their ground soldiers. It wasn't until they were deeper into the fighting that Daimon realized why it was such a bloodbath.

The shadows weren't only affecting the wyverns. They were corrupting the soldiers too.

He watched in horror as his own soldiers started to turn

against one another, their flames or shadows aimed at their brothers. Soldiers who had been fighting together for years—some longer—were killing *each other*—as if they hadn't shared ale, watch rotations, or broth around a fire.

"They're using our own men against us," Brielle gasped.

His stomach sank, dread filling him.

"Their eyes!" Ranick shouted, breathless as they kept their pace. The soldiers' eyes were pitch-black, inky veins starting to spread from their eyes and onto the rest of their faces.

Evelina slammed to a halt, causing the others to follow suit. Daimon turned to her, panic gripping him as he saw her face as pale as a ghost.

"Eve?" he asked, examining her from head to toe.

She slowly turned to him, her eyes wide and voice wobbling as she said, "Moros is here."

Daimon glanced at Brielle, who mirrored his confusion and apprehension.

Evelina held a finger out, pointing toward the mouth of the river. Toward the cavern. "I can feel him," she whispered, holding her hand over her chest. "The darkness surrounding him is so strong—so *wrong* and twisted."

Moros was here. It all suddenly made sense. He was the only ungodly force in this world who could channel such a corrupted power.

But if he was here…it meant he saw this as a final battle too. Why else risk his own mortal body at the frontline?

His power was awful, but it was also desperate. Maybe it was Eve's light shielding his mind to have clarity, but Daimon could finally see past the shadows.

Moros was *afraid*.

Daimon squared his shoulders, making a decision in a split second and praying to Eurydice it was the right choice.

"We stick to the plan," he said quickly to the group. "There's no turning back now."

Any sane person would have retreated. Their own men were

turning on them, and who was to say they wouldn't also turn on one another?

But the Alpha Fleet was the most feared unit for a reason. They each held a fist over their chest and tapped twice, their faces grim with determination.

"Our focus still needs to be on blocking the exit of the cavern," he continued as they blocked attacks, pressing further up the river. "But if we have the opportunity to bring Moros down with it, we need to take it." He turned to Evelina; the fleet encircled them both, guarding them while Daimon made their plan. "How long do you think you can hold a shield over all of us?"

Evelina's eyes blazed; light rimmed her irises like twin suns.

"Long enough to kill the bastard that killed my dad."

FIFTY-FOUR

DAIMON

FURIES CHARGED THEM FROM BEHIND, WHILE A NEW DROVE came from the direction of the cavern. They had no choice but to forge ahead. They were surrounded, a flock of birds closing in on a single worm.

"Ranick, Elias, create a path for us!" Daimon shouted. "Brielle, focus your fire on keeping them off our back. I'll watch the sides."

He didn't have to tell Evelina what needed to be done—she was already scorching the dark rebels that were getting too close into ash.

Aegis fire met cursed rebels as the fleet blazed a path toward the cave. Clumps of soil, rock, and debris flew from the energy of the magic clashing. Evelina's shield pulsed against his skin, the heat of her magic so hot that his skin crawled. It was chaos, the rebels growing frustrated that their magic and weapons were bouncing off the invisible shield Evelina had wrapped around them.

The Furies were growing in number behind them, pushing them closer and closer to the cave. They were nearly there now, Ranick and Elias fighting to clear a path ahead while Brielle fended them off as much as she could from the back.

But Daimon could feel the tamper on his magic, his shadows barely holding off the enemy coming from the sides. He threw up wall after wall, blocking the Furies from closing in. One slipped past his shadows, heading straight for them. Daimon's eyes widened as he felt Evelina's magic flare, seemingly unaffected by the cursed magic.

The rebel that slipped past had the look of victory gleaming in her eye, but the moment she reached Evelina's shield, she began to scream. The black veins glowing beneath her skin writhed, as if trying to escape the light. It only lasted a moment before her flesh dissolved into ash.

The tree coverage thinned as the cavern opened up ahead. They reached their destination—the nest of the Furies.

Furies flew out of the cavern, their movements animalistic and unnatural. They were pouring from the exit in droves, far more of them than the Alpha Fleet could manage alone. Not to mention the writhing darkness pulsing from the cave's mouth.

Daimon grabbed Evelina's hand as rebels surrounded them. The fleet stood back-to-back, doing what they could to keep the enemy at bay. Brielle, Ranick, and Elias all used as much fire as they could, but it wasn't enough. The Furies were pressing closer, fingers brushing against Evelina's shield and disintegrating on contact. Her hand was cold and clammy in Daimon's. She couldn't hold it forever.

"Hold steady, Eve," he gritted out.

He wasn't going to let them die.

The tamper on his Essence was still there, but he reached for it anyway, sending a prayer to Nyx to let his status as bastard of a god mean something for once in his life. Evelina's shield flickered and a Fury shot at Ranick, grabbing him by the throat. Her shield roared to life again, searing the rebel from the inside out.

Beneath the hold on Daimon's magic, he felt a darkness, a primal magic so ancient that he was always too afraid to let it out.

He didn't have a choice now.

He held his breath, and a wall of shadows cocooned his friends—his family—in a web of black, blocking the Furies from their view. Warmth grew between Daimon and Evelina's connected hands. As Daimon yanked on his magic, the warmth where his skin touched hers blazed. He felt the familiar tingle of her shield press against him. A surge of energy burst through his body, an energy that was purity incarnate. It was Evelina—her Essence, intertwining with his. He felt her magic flowing through him, and he felt his magic flowing through her. In this moment, they were one. Their magic, their minds—they were light and they were darkness. The sun and the moon. And together, they would take the Furies down.

When he exhaled, the wall of shadows blasted back, a pulsing, shimmering light mingling with it. As their combined magic was unleashed, it sent the rebels, trees, rocks—everything close to them—flying in all directions.

Even the darkness over the cave had paused, momentarily receding.

The boulders above them shook from the force of their magic, threatening to crumble and fall.

"Into the cave!" Daimon shouted.

They ran into the cavern as the rocks loosened and rained down onto the ground below. Daimon held Evelina's hand as tight as he could, pulling her along with him. The mouth of the cave collapsed, sealing them off from the outside.

Daimon's chest heaved, straining his eyes to see through the thick dust flying around the dark cave. Slithers of light beamed in from the outside, illuminating the area around them. His body was buzzing, like he had been struck by lightning, after calling on more magic than he ever had. He braced himself, his muscles tensing in preparation for another fight within the cave.

But the only sound was his heaving breath and Brielle coughing. Water dripped from above. His chest constricted; it was suffocatingly humid.

The cave was completely empty. Quiet.

"Where is everyone?" Elias whispered.

Something was wrong.

"Evelina," Daimon said slowly. "Can you still sense Moros?"

Evelina squinted, the warmth of her shield now gone. "I can still sense him, but he feels like he's…everywhere."

Ranick grunted in frustration. "Then what are we supposed—"

"Nice of you to join us," a voice interrupted. A deep laugh bounced off the walls, echoes scattering everywhere.

They spun around, searching for the voice.

"Come out, Moros," Daimon snapped.

Another laugh. "If you insist."

A whoosh of icy air blasted from a small tunnel in the back of the cave. Daimon felt as if the air was being sucked out of his lungs. The fleet collapsed in coughs, struggling for air.

"I can't shield," Evelina choked. "I'm trying, but it isn't working."

"Of course it won't work, Evelina, darling." Moros was close now, his voice no longer an empty echo. "Lovely to see you again."

He materialized from the depths of the middle tunnel, shadows enveloping him. The cold air slowed, giving them their breath back. Daimon stepped in front of Evelina, shielding her with his body.

"Traitor," Brielle hissed.

Moros laughed. "Brielle, lovely as always."

Brielle bared her teeth. Moros took a step closer, and Daimon's shadows roared to life, wrapping around his wrists and arms. Moros's gaze shot to Daimon. He smiled. Daimon growled, warning him.

"Stop this madness," Evelina demanded. "You could end this war—all this death—right now. You're sacrificing your own souls for nothing."

"*Nothing?*" Moros sneered. "Do you think we've enjoyed being the 'weaker' race? Fae have been slaughtering humans for years. Humans are nothing to them—an irritating bug on the land that they smash. Our use of Furies and cursed weapons are our *salvation* from the way the crown has ruled for generations."

This time, it was Evelina who growled. The noise was so intense that it took Daimon by surprise. "My mother has done her best after being betrayed by *you*."

Moros smiled. "And yet, she didn't do enough, it seems. We finally grew tired of being a plaything for bored immortals who place themselves on the same level as the gods. Things changed when the gods answered *our* prayers."

Moros took a step back, now positioned closer to the opening of the cavern. "And Evelina?" He chuckled. "I'm so very sorry for the loss of your mother. Maybe the next queen will be willing to see what she couldn't."

Daimon's lip curled, pure hatred boiling inside him. He stepped forward just as Moros flung a hand out, shadows flecked with crackles of light barreling toward them.

"No!" Evelina bellowed as she lurched forward. She jumped in front of Daimon, screaming as the warmth of her shield exploded from her body. Brielle lunged after her, dutifully protecting her side even as the shadows raced toward them.

The shadows slammed into an invisible barrier. Moros's dark magic pushed harder against her shield. Evelina screamed, blood dripping from her nose.

Ranick and Elias were only a few steps behind, sending streams of fire at Moros, but the moment the flame reached him, it flared around him, bouncing off. Moros turned toward the Aegis like they were nothing more than a fly irritating him.

Evelina screamed and her light flared bright, fighting against Moros's dark shadows. Her magic pushed against him, forcing him back a step. This time, it wasn't a shield she pushed; it was rays of light aimed at him like arrows. She sent them hurtling toward him, one of them catching his arm and slicing through the muscle.

He screamed out in pain, his eyes widening. She sent

another wave of light at him and he stumbled back another step. His eyes grew wide with panic, his chest heaving. He twisted around and sent a slamming wave of shadows out of the cave.

Daimon didn't see what happened until it was too late. All he could see were the shadows flying off and past them as Moros's magic flew out in all directions, Evelina's shield firmly in place around Daimon and Brielle.

But not Ranick and Elias.

They were dead the moment the shadows swept over them, their bodies dropping lifeless to the ground. The force of Moros's magic blasted the rocks away from the mouth of the cave, opening it up to the outside world.

Before Evelina could go on the offense once more, Moros fled the cave, leaving silence in his wake.

The second the shadows stopped pressing against her shield, she slipped out of Daimon's grasp and sprinted to the Aegis' side. Daimon ran past her, searching outside for any signs of Moros. But there were none. He was gone.

Everything was quiet…too quiet. No sounds of fighting, no battle happening outside. He turned to find Brielle pressing her finger just beneath Ranick's jaw.

"No pulse." Her usually stable voice cracked. She twisted to where Elias had fallen, his body unnaturally still, and did the same to him, shaking her head solemnly.

Daimon fought back the tears that threatened to spill down his face. Evelina had collapsed a distance away, sobbing. He crouched down and cradled her face between his hands, forcing her eyes away from their bodies.

"Eve, we need to go." Her breathing was shallow and sobs racked her body. "*Evelina,*" he snapped. "Look at me." It took a few moments, but she finally brought her gaze to him. "We have to leave, *now,*" he repeated. "Before they decide to come back."

Her eyes were vacant. "He said my mother was dead."

He fought against the nausea, the bile climbing the back of

his throat. If he fell apart, he could be risking her life. That was the only thing keeping him moving. Focused.

He tugged on his bond with Zephyr, nearly gasping in relief when he found it was still there.

Zephyr landed moments later, followed by Aster, Willow, and Ranick and Elias's wyverns. Daimon was relieved to see Willow's wyvern alive, her wing patched with mud and leaves, a small reprieve from the unbearable grief.

"A mass of shadows swept over the valley, killing rebels and Valon soldiers alike," Aster said breathlessly. "What happened—"

His eyes landed on Ranick and Elias.

Willow was frozen atop Khaline, her mouth agape in horror.

Aster slid off his beast and ran to Daimon. He took in the scene before him: a sobbing Evelina, a hauntingly quiet Brielle, and their fallen comrades beside them.

"Help me tie them to the wyverns," Daimon said. "We're going home."

Aster blinked before nodding his head. They silently gathered their friends to take them home and give them a proper burial. One where the stench of darkness wasn't surrounding them, and they could pass into Caelum, finally free from this needless war.

FIFTY-FIVE

DAIMON

THEY FLEW OVER THE REMAINS OF THE BATTLEFIELD. THE ground soldiers who had not been infected by the shadows were stopping to check on the wounded. Evelina was silent on the ride back to the palace. Daimon wrapped both of his arms around her waist and tucked her in close. He traced circles over her abdomen, lost in his mind as much as she was in hers.

Every death settled like a heavy weight against Daimon's chest. They'd lost half their flight, the skies feeling far too empty without Ranick, Elias, and Keir. They had trained as a unit for years. To suddenly have their closest friends ripped away from them, to have to fly so soon, was like a knife to the gut. Willow had almost lost Khaline, too, the wyvern's wing still stiff and her flight slow.

But the empire had not just lost soldiers today.

The Valon flags they passed on the way to the palace were all already flying half-mast, confirmation that Moros's words were true.

The queen—Evelina's mother—had passed on to Caelum.

Daimon sat in the throne room, seated at a table that connected to others to form a square. Lyria had quickly come running down the hall when they arrived, pulling Evelina away. He couldn't stop thinking about the look on Lyria's face, the devastation. How it only made Evelina close further in on herself.

It felt like a knife was driving into his chest as he watched her walk away. He wanted so desperately to go with her, but he was still a commander. He had to report on the catastrophic battle, unable to stay by her side.

The council had already been seated around the table when Daimon arrived, along with Senna and Carwyn. There was an empty seat where Keir was supposed to sit. Maliena was on one side of Daimon, Neve on the other. It made him feel a little less alone, but the shock of losing Keir lingered. He felt as if he should be unraveling right now, or screaming until his throat turned raw. But he felt nothing. His body was numb, his mind fuzzy, his vision blurred. It didn't feel real that Keir was gone— that Ranick and Elias would never fly with him again.

Daimon recounted the battle for the council, telling them about Keir, Ranick, and Elias. He fought to keep his voice even. He told them of the way their own troops were turned against them, fighting as if possessed.

"These soldiers are strong-willed—fierce," Daimon continued. "The rebels' power is out of control, turning the strongest of warriors against their own."

Maliena gasped and Carwyn clenched her jaw.

"How is that possible?" Neve demanded.

"Moros has learned to harness the darkness Vidaris has offered him." Daimon seethed, his temper barely contained. He pushed to his feet, unable to sit still. "We should make another push—perhaps by sea this time."

He looked to Senna, awaiting the naval commander's approval. But Senna's face was uncommonly distant, lingering on Keir's empty seat.

"No," Carwyn jumped in. She slowly stood, her hands braced on the table. "We need a plan. To recover. My mother's passing was not the only development here."

Daimon paused. He looked around the room, at the heaviness on each face. "What do you mean?"

"The western fleet aided the diverted troops." It was Senna who finally spoke, seated at Carwyn's right side. "They staved off further attack into Drogheda, but the losses were numerous."

All eyes turned to Carwyn. But she was quiet, only releasing a shaky breath.

"Ren was among the losses," Senna added quietly, his voice filled with regret.

Daimon's heart froze in his chest. Evelina hadn't just lost her mother, but her brother, too.

"A lux will be held for them tomorrow, and for all who sacrificed themselves for the empire." Carwyn recovered herself, steadying her voice. "Things will be moving quickly. We must prepare for the crown to transfer to the next queen."

She meant herself. He knew Carwyn was strong, but he was surprised she was moving forward so quickly after all she had lost. He supposed she didn't really have a choice. She had an empire to lead.

"And our next offense?" Daimon asked.

"For now"—Maliena placed a hand on his arm—"it'd be best to focus all our attention on the transfer of the crown. All we can hope is the land will be better protected with a new surge of Essence."

A somber rumble of agreement spread across the table. The meeting dissolved, everyone dispersing with a weighted silence.

"Daimon, please stay a moment," Carwyn said, scrutinizing a roll of parchment on the table. Once the room was emptied, she looked up at him. "I think we should double our efforts at the border. I want you at the helm, leading those stationed there. Not just the Alpha Fleet, but the ground soldiers and three additional beta fleets."

He didn't know what to say—what to think or feel. He just felt numb. He didn't want to simply go back to the border and keep playing this endless game of defense. He wanted to find Moros and make him pay.

"We should be going after Moros," Daimon hissed. "We'll never win if we don't stop him."

"If we rush our forces back out, we'll face another slaughter," Carwyn said slowly. "We need to go back in prepared next time."

Rage flared inside of him, heating his chest. Moros killed Ranick and Elias. He stoked a rebellion that ended in Keir's death—in *countless* others dying.

How does one prepare against darkness? There would always be a level of unpreparedness; now was as good a time as any.

"I'll give your fleet time to mourn the losses of today's battle, but I'll want you back on the southern border in a few days," Carwyn said with a sharp finality in her voice.

A few *days*. Daimon could be given a lifetime to mourn and it wouldn't be enough. Not for Ranick, who was the first Rider to teach Daimon how to saddle Zephyr. Not for Elias, a steady and calm presence, ready to follow Daimon into battle without fail. And certainly not for Keir, the Aegis council head he had looked up to since he was a wide-eyed, thirteen-year-old chosen to become a Rider. The commander who believed in him when no one else did and made him a part of Alpha Fleet. Keir had been with him through it all.

"Evelina will need a few days as well before she goes back," Carwyn added.

The words settled like a weight on his chest. Selfishly, he wanted her with him, no matter where that was. They both had experienced unbearable loss, and he wouldn't lose anyone else.

"She will have a choice to do as she wishes, but a Manor

never backs away from their duties," Carwyn continued. "Once she's on the border, she can do as she pleases." She gave him a pointed look.

His heart thumped in his chest. Once the lux was over and the crown passed, he could focus on taking down Moros. On making him feel every ounce of pain Daimon had felt in the past two decades. He would do it with Evelina by his side, light and shadows working together to defeat darkness.

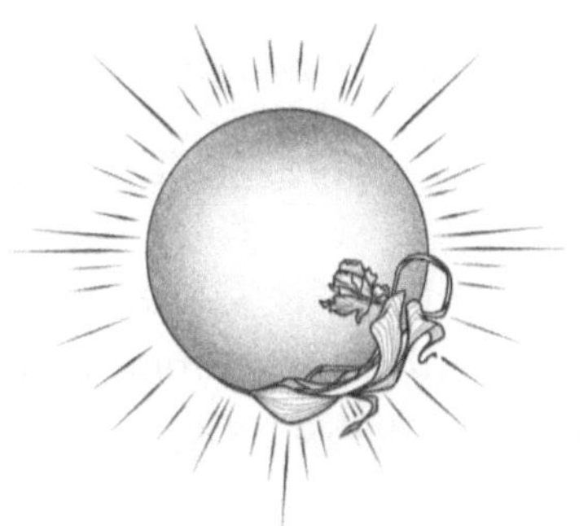

FIFTY-SIX

EVELINA

LYRIA HELD EVELINA AS SHE CRIED. THEY WERE LYING IN Evelina's room, though the bed seemed foreign to her. She missed her rickety cot in the healer's cabin. She missed seeing the Riders pouring in and out of their cabin at all times of the day and night, when Ranick and Elias would take off on a patrol together, or Keir would sit with her by the fire.

Her chest ached so badly she didn't know if it had stopped beating altogether. She should've done more during the battle, should've found a way to keep Keir safe—should've found a way to push harder to stop Moros before he could kill Ranick and Elias.

She couldn't stop the sobs that poured from her. It wasn't just them she was grieving; it was her mother and brother too. She couldn't even remember the last conversation she had with Ren, the last time she hugged him or told him she loved him.

A soft knock rapped against the door, nearly drowned by Evelina's heaving cries. Her eyes were swollen shut, her throat raw. The light patter of steps moved closer to her and Lyria.

The weight of the bed dipped as someone came to lie down with them.

"I'm sorry, Evie," Carwyn's gentle voice soothed. "You're not alone."

An arm draped over her waist and squeezed her, sandwiching Evelina as Lyria snuggled in close from the other side. Evelina didn't know what she would do without her sisters; they were her lifeline in this.

"Mother is with Father now," Carwyn added softly. "The light of Caelum is upon them."

Lyria hummed her agreement and sniffled. "We still have each other."

Carwyn nodded, her face somber. But there was something in her eyes, a hesitation. "Evie," she whispered. "Are you up to discussing a few things?"

Lyria frowned. "Carwyn, we should probably wait—"

Evelina shook her head and pushed up, resting her back against her headboard. She sniffled, wiping her nose with her sleeve. "Whatever it is, I want to know."

Carwyn and Lyria both sat up, settling themselves beside her. Carwyn blew out a long breath, and Evelina noticed the deep circles that had formed beneath her eyes. With the news of her mother dying, Evelina hadn't had time to consider what this meant for the realm—for Carwyn.

"You're preparing to take the crown," Evelina said. Her voice was raspy, broken. "I'm sorry. You need us to be here for you—"

Carwyn waved her hand. "Nonsense. We *all* are here for each other." She looked down at her hands. "But yes, preparations have already begun for the crown to be transferred. Though it happens by the will of the Divine, it should be any day now. I'll be ruling in the interim until it officially passes and the coronation can be held."

Evelina nodded her head. The realm needed a strong leader right now; they needed Carwyn.

"That's not all," Carwyn continued. "In the wake of so much shaking the foundation of the empire, the people need stability. They don't just need a queen; they need a king."

Lyria and Evelina exchanged a glance. Her sister's eyes were wide, just as shocked as Evelina.

"And they'll be getting one at the lux," Carwyn said finally.

Evelina's mouth popped open.

"Who?" Lyria demanded.

Carwyn smiled sadly. "Senna."

Evelina nodded slowly, absorbing the news. It wasn't a total surprise; Senna had always been the obvious pick for Carwyn's consort. He was more than worthy—he would be a great partner at her side—but it was another thing entirely to marry him. Manors *never* married their consorts. Carwyn was forsaking the tradition of bonding human and fae rulers, a tradition that had kept peace between the races for centuries.

He would be the first fae king in all of Valon's history.

"But he's fae," Lyria gasped.

"He is," Carwyn said slowly. "Which is what the people need. If there are any humans left on this side of the mountains, they're all in hiding. We must show our strength, our unity to what remains of this empire."

Evelina's head spun. She knew Senna wasn't in love with Carwyn—just as Carwyn was not in love with him. It was a political match and nothing more, a notion that made Evelina desperately sad for them.

"Manors don't marry for love," Carwyn added, sensing Evelina's thoughts. "Do not pity something I will gladly do for our people."

Lyria sniffled and Evelina reached for her hand.

They were all Manors, but it had always been Carwyn who had carried the responsibility of the name. She was the only reason Lyria was still so innocent and Evelina was able to reunite with Daimon—none of it would've been possible if they had been forced to carry the same responsibilities as Carwyn.

Evelina admired her sister…but also was sad for her. She was handling this in stride, caring for her sisters and her empire during their mother's declining health. The empire needed stability; and that stability was Carwyn.

Evelina sat beneath the shelves in the infirmary. She inhaled deeply, smelling the herbs behind her, the scent a mixture of floral and spice. She needed a moment to breathe, to sit in a place she felt more like herself. The room was quiet, all other healers asleep for the evening or off tending to patients.

Her knees were tucked into her chest, her arms wrapped around them. She wanted to shut herself in here for a week, or flee to the garden. To lose herself with her hands in damp soil and grinding herbs.

She let out a deep, shaky breath as the door to the infirmary creaked open. She pressed herself against the shelves, wanting to be alone to grieve.

But as the male turned toward her, she relaxed.

"Senna," she said quietly.

He jumped, placing a hand over his chest as his gaze fell to where she was sitting. "Blessed Divine, what are you doing down there?"

She raised a brow. "What are *you* doing in the infirmary?"

He sighed and walked over to her, dropping down to the floor beside her. "Looking for something to help me sleep," he mumbled.

She nodded her head and pointed to shelves across the room. "Second row from the top, far left. It's the jar with little yellow flowers and dried green wisps."

Senna was quiet a moment, making no moves to get up. "You okay?" he finally said.

Evelina dropped her chin to her knees and whispered, "No."

Thankfully, he didn't press, nor did he try to say how sorry he was. This was something she always appreciated about him; that he didn't always feel the need to fill the silence.

They sat together for a little while, a comfortable quiet resting between them. Her thoughts drifted to her mother's smile, to memories of Ren playing pranks on her when they were children.

This was the problem with silence, though. Too soon it was filled with memories that filled her with pain to remember.

"Carwyn told me," she said gently. "That she's announcing your match at the lux tomorrow."

Senna huffed a joyless laugh. "Something to look forward to, I suppose."

"Do you really want to marry Carwyn?"

The unsaid question hung in the air. *Don't you want to marry for love?*

"I think that chance has already passed me by." His voice cracked. "I've already lost the one my soul was made for."

Shock thrummed through Evelina. In all the years she had known Senna, he was always considered a strong match as Carwyn's consort.

She twisted toward him. "I never knew you found your soulbonded."

"We were soldiers together for a long time," he explained. A sad smile spread across his face. He huffed a laugh and shook his head. "It was a lot harder when he became a Rider. The war took something from all of us," he continued softly. "I would do anything to get Keir back, and if becoming the next king helps me honor our people and his memory, I will do it without hesitation."

Keir. The Rider he was in love with.

The memory of sitting beside a fire with Keir just before the battle surfaced in Evelina's mind. Of Keir mentioning how she sounded *just like Senna*. She didn't think anything of it then— they *had* served together as soldiers for years, after all.

But neither one of them bore the mark of the soulbonded.

"Keir was an incredible man," Evelina whispered. Her heart ached and she watched a tear roll down Senna's cheek. The image of Keir's lifeless body flashed through her mind.

"I didn't tell him I loved him the last time we saw each other." His voice cracked. "The last thing I said was something unimportant and useless."

Tears welled in Evelina's eyes. "Senna—"

"We never know how limited our time is, nor do we know what fate has in store." His gaze met hers, undeniable heartbreak shining in his eyes. "If you find someone you love, spend every day as if it were your last."

FIFTY-SEVEN

DAIMON

A SHEET OF RAIN FELL LIKE A CURTAIN OUTSIDE, THE WHIR of rainfall covering the sound of crashing waves from the beach nearby. Daimon was hollow inside, breaking piece by piece as he grieved in silence. His anger slowly melted away in the dampness of the cave, leaving nothing but remorse and grief in its wake. Now that he wasn't giving reports or being the commander, there was nothing to stop the memories of his friends dying in front of him.

He saw Keir and Codax as they plummeted to their deaths. Ranick and Elias as they were killed by Moros. So many of the soldiers who had followed him into battle and ended up never leaving that dark-infested valley. Soldiers who would never come home to their families.

Tears streamed down his face. He swatted them away, his breathing uneven.

The empire had lost so much…

Every bone in Daimon's body screamed for him to find Evelina.

Zephyr huffed, her eyes following him back and forth as he paced.

"Zeph—"

His mouth froze as a rain-soaked Evelina appeared across from him. She was shivering, her arms crossed over her chest, hugging herself tightly. His eyes fell to her white satin gown, which was molded to every curve of her body, translucent from the water. His mind immediately went to their night beneath the waterfall together, when their friends were still alive. When they had hope of winning the war without losing those closest to them.

"I can't stay long," she whispered, her teeth chattering. "But I—" Her voice broke.

Zephyr nuzzled her side, and Evelina wrapped her arms around the wyvern. Daimon's heart squeezed at seeing his two favorite girls so closely connected. The wyvern finally pulled away and moved past Evelina to the mouth of the cave. Despite the heaviness weighing down on Daimon's chest, he smiled as his beast sat outside in the rain.

Her tail swished behind her as her body blocked the opening. She chomped at the air, jumping and catching droplets in her mouth. She loved the rain—always had. But he knew it was more than that. He knew she was keeping watch while he and Evelina talked.

A sob tore free from Evelina. Daimon ran to her. He pulled her against his chest and held her close. She was freezing, her skin as cold as ice. He wrapped one hand around her waist, the other cradling her head.

For a moment, he just held her. No words could ease the pain of what they had both lost that day—but he could hold her.

"Ren is gone," she said, breaking the silence. "Lyria said Mother just passed last night."

Daimon pulled her closer against his chest, as if he could shield her from her heartbreak.

Evelina had lost her father when she was younger, but she hadn't been through war before—hasn't seen firsthand what brutal death looked like. Daimon may have been hurting, but he wouldn't break, not when he needed to be there for her.

"I'm sorry, Eve," he whispered, his heart thundering in his chest. "Tell me what I can do. Tell me what you need."

He wanted to grab her hand and let Zephyr fly them to a remote island. To find an untamed place for them to make their own. No war, no Furies or death or heartbreak.

She leaned back, her hands sliding up his chest. "I need *you*," she whispered. "I need to feel something other than this pain." She eased the collar of his shirt apart, slowly opening its buttons one by one until she reached the bottom. Her eyes fell to where her hands rested on his lower abdomen.

He needed her so badly it hurt. She was the only remedy for his heartache.

His muscles clenched beneath her touch. He trailed his hand from her hair to her jawline, stopping with a finger beneath her chin. He lifted her face to his, kissing her as if it were the last kiss they would ever share.

She pushed his shirt off and pulled away from him abruptly. Her eyes were fixed to his hip. He opened his mouth to ask if she was okay when she suddenly reached forward. She traced the ink etched onto his skin, running a single finger over the sword.

"My Rider mark," he explained softly. "We get them the same time as our wyvern when we bond fully. The same sword is on her side."

Evelina nodded. "Beautiful," she murmured. She looked up at him, eyes wide and filled with pain.

He leaned in, holding her as if she were going to disappear. She stepped away from him and slowly removed her gown. His gaze never left her.

When he lowered her to the ground, he held her gently. And when he looked into her eyes, he felt the tightness in his chest ease. She didn't seem to be able to look away from him either, their kisses desperate and needy.

Even as he undressed them, he held her gaze. If she needed this, he would gladly give it to her. He took his time, his hips working at a slow and tortuous pace. He kissed down her body, relishing every feel of her skin against his. He kissed the curve above her hip, then the swell of her breast, mapping her body with his mouth.

They held each other after, her head on his chest.

They were quiet, their breathing shallow and cheeks flushed. Evelina pushed her damp hair out of her eyes for the third time, the strands refusing to stay in place. Daimon stood and walked around her, sitting behind her. He gently pulled back the pieces of hair that had already fallen into her eyes and began to weave the strands over one another.

"What are you doing?" she asked, twisting around.

He reached out and angled her face forward to stop her from turning toward him. "Braiding your hair." His fingers quickly wove three separate strands together, careful to keep it tight.

"Where did you learn to do this?" she asked softly.

A memory washed over him of learning how to tightly secure his hair when he first became a Rider.

"Do you remember how long my hair was when I first became a soldier?"

She nodded. "Nearly past your shoulders."

"Far too long for a soldier," he said softly. "When I bonded with Zephyr, Willow taught me how to keep it secured with a braid. It's impossible to learn to ride a wyvern with your hair in your eyes. It was hard enough as is."

"Why not just cut it?"

His fingers stopped their weaving. "I wasn't ready to give my old life up just yet," he whispered.

He slowly resumed braiding her hair, then turned to re-braiding just to prolong the moment. He murmured tales of being a young boy without a family to suddenly having more love than he could ever dream of when he became a Rider. The Riders were his family. *Keir* was his family.

Evelina's head was tilted back, eyes closed as he talked about a past he never thought he'd share with anyone. His mouth couldn't stop moving, couldn't stop opening up to her as she silently listened.

He got to the end of the braid and tore a small string off the hem of his shirt to tie it off. Then he pushed the braid over her right shoulder and rubbed her back.

"Carwyn wants us back on the border soon," he said softly.

"I asked her to let me go back," she confessed softly. Daimon blinked, surprised. "I always felt so useless in the palace, even if they allowed me to be a healer. But I think there's a reason my light came alive in the mountains with you all. It needed to see real darkness first."

"The darkness is what I'm worried about," he whispered. "I'm worried I won't be able to protect you."

Evelina twisted around to face him. "I would go anywhere with you."

They stayed together in the cave the rest of the night, until the sun began to peek over the horizon and Evelina had to go get ready for the lux. He wanted to go with her, to stay by her side the entire time.

But they weren't on the border. She was back to being a princess, and he was back to being a commander in crisis.

FIFTY-EIGHT

DAIMON

A LUX WASN'T FOR THE DEAD. AND IF DAIMON WERE honest, he wished they weren't for the living either. Each race of fae had its own way of celebrating the loss of life, but he could do without all of them.

When a Woodland died, a ceremony was always held somewhere in the glade. There were flowers and songs, dancing and drinking—but it was still a lux. The Nox gathered in the grove and dreamed together, bringing memories of the fae they lost to life.

He did always feel partial to how the Undine celebrated. They would have a day of silence and remembrance, staying quiet in the depths of the Andronicus among luminescent coral that glowed at night.

The Aegis held a pyre, letting it burn a day for each year the fae was alive. It often ended in them brawling, fighting each other to escape the grief of death. It was how he knew Keir would've wanted things done for him—Ranick and Elias, too.

But no matter the tradition, a lux was supposed to represent someone passing into the light of Caelum, their souls living in harmony alongside the Goddess of the Moon, Eurydice.

Humans had their own kind of lux—a funeral. He had only

seen one human funeral, and he had watched it while hiding behind the bushes with Ren beside him, eager to get a glimpse of a human tradition.

This lux was far more different than any he had ever been to. They were holding a mass ceremony, honoring the lives of those lost in battle. There were fae from each race gathered in one place with pieces of their traditions patched together.

His eyes searched for Evelina—as they always did—the moment he arrived with his aerial unit, or what remained of it. The reminder turned his veins to ice, his insides twisting. Daimon would rather be anywhere but here, his chest far too tight.

He didn't want to grieve around people he didn't know. He wanted to build a pyre for Ranick, Elias, and Keir. A private lux with only Evelina, Brielle, Willow, and Aster present. He would honor Elias and Ranick the best he could while surrounded by strangers. The pyre for Keir was empty, with no body left to burn.

But it seemed *everyone* that could make it to the lux in time came for it. Eager to honor the warriors who lost their lives, including the prince of the empire and the queen. There were flurries of bright clothing and bare skin, a show of celebration to honor those who were buried deep in the dirt.

A flash of honey-brown hair caught his eye, disappearing behind dozens of nameless faces. Her hair was still braided from the night before, though slightly messier. His heart raced, touched that she had left it just how he braided it. Wondering if she too wasn't ready to let the night go.

Evelina

The lux was outside of Eurydice's temple—a deep, painful reminder of the last time Evelina had been here for Annora and Aldric's bonding ceremony. It felt like a knife twisting in her stomach.

There had been a brief happiness that night, seeing her closest friend bind her soul to her love in such a sacred tradition. But then she left for the border, and everything changed. Maybe that's why Eurydice had looked at her the way she did while inhabiting the Sacred's body—a warning of what was to come.

Now Evelina was back, in a once-happy place, feeling like her heart was going to stop at any moment from the amount of pain she felt.

Fate had a way of being cruel like that.

She took a deep breath, her hands beginning to shake.

A burst of laughter came from in front of her—a Woodland dancing and drinking juniper fizz. Evelina tore her gaze away from the smiling fae; the bright disposition of those celebrating the lux was blinding.

She was considering finding a place to hide when she finally caught a glimpse of Annora. She looked mostly the same, still beautiful with her raven hair and bright gray eyes. But Evelina gasped as Annora turned toward her, a hand resting on her swollen belly.

Evelina felt a pang in her chest at all she had missed.

Their gazes met, and the pain eased slightly. Annora walked over to her, Aldric close behind.

"I'm so glad you made it back," Annora whispered. She pulled away, swiping a tear from her cheek.

"You're pregnant," Evelina blurted.

Annora smiled softly. "There was no hiding the scars on our palms after we found out we were having a child." She looked up at Aldric and he placed an arm around her shoulder. Annora turned back to Evelina, her eyes misty with gathering tears. "I'm so sorry for what you've lost," she whispered.

Evelina couldn't stop her own tears from falling. "If I had been with Ren, maybe—"

Annora shook her head and placed a hand on Evelina's shoulder. "You have no control over who lives and who dies, as much as you'd like to, Evie."

Evelina's tears rolled down her cheeks, one after the other. She was supposed to be the shield, the protector. But she was beginning to learn she couldn't save everyone.

"My mother should be here." Evelina's voice cracked, raw from screaming into her pillow for nearly an hour that morning. "They should *all* be here."

Even after seeing Daimon in the cave, she still felt like screaming until her voice gave out. Being with him only dulled her pain, the ache flaring the moment she had returned to her room.

"We'll see them again one day," Annora whispered.

They pushed through the crowd—through the dancing and the drinking—but they kept getting stopped by those who wanted to share their condolences.

"They're all basking in the light of Eurydice now," a Nox said with a smile, his face genuinely happy. "May we all make it there someday."

Evelina gave the Nox a tight smile and looked for a way to escape as the fae kept talking, telling stories of a time he spent an evening drinking with Ren in a tavern. Thankfully, Annora cut into the conversation and kept them moving.

A deep calm fell over Evelina, wrapping around her senses and easing the tension in her chest. The moment she realized what was causing it, she felt a warm hand press against the small of her back.

"Are you okay?" Daimon's deep voice washed over her as he whispered into her ear.

She shook her head and looked up at him. "Are you?"

His mouth pressed into a deep frown. He leaned closer to her. "No," he said quietly.

Even though they weren't okay, they both seemed to understand that they might be someday—and that it hurt a little less when they were together.

Evelina slipped her hand into his, needing to hold on to some semblance of steadiness.

Gasps rang out from all around her as people started to point behind her. From the corner of her eye, she saw Annora turn. Her hand flung to cover her mouth.

Evelina turned too, freezing once she saw what had caused the commotion.

A ring of white fire was glowing over Carwyn's head.

FIFTY-NINE

EVELINA

SOFT MURMURS BROKE THROUGH THE CROWD AS THE Sacred stepped forward. Evelina hadn't seen her yet; it was as if she had emerged from beneath the shadows. The Sacred positioned herself in front of the ceremonial pyre, which burned for the entirety of the lux. Her voice vibrated with authority as she announced, "The Eternal Crown has chosen Carwyn."

Everyone stilled.

"It hasn't even been two days," Annora whispered in disbelief.

"The realm is at war, Annora," Aldric whispered in reply. "It must sense the need for new Essence to bind to."

The Sacred disappeared into the crowd like a ghost in the wind. The murmurs grew louder and louder.

"We knew this day was coming," Carwyn said firmly. "I have prepared for this with the council. We will ensure this transition happens as smoothly as possible."

The chattering crowd quieted. She was already so good at commanding a crowd, so strong even in her grief. And she was right. She had been leading since their mother fell ill, already preparing for this moment. Evelina had always envied Carwyn's fortitude, but now she was only grateful.

"As of now, there will be no consort in a realm at war with humans." She took a deep breath, her eyes landing on Senna. He nodded his head once, encouraging her to go on. "Senna has been blessed by the late queen to be the first fae ruler to be married to a Manor."

Gasps rippled through the crowd.

Carwyn raised her hand and added, "Senna is a strong leader, as you all know, gifted at keeping our seas safe. We've all lost so much. Let this be our hope toward a new future."

"Breaking the tradition isn't patching the problem up," a lithe Woodland in the crowd gasped. "It's severing it entirely."

Carwyn shook her head, her voice gentle but firm as she said, "There is no human ruler to contest against Moros. Their houses are empty, their belongings left behind as nearly all of them have joined the rebels. The humans have chosen a path of darkness, one we will not follow. Eurydice—and two fae rulers united against them—will guide us to victory."

Whispers settled into silence.

"Senna." Carwyn looked at him, motioning for him to come forward. The crowd parted for him as he walked to her. He stopped by her side and gave her a quick nod.

They were loyal to their realm, and nobody could deny that two great leaders stood before them now.

"Senna will be crowned king in a way only a fae can be." She held up a knife and he stuck his hand out. She cut into his palm, slicing deeply.

He held up his hand, hovering it above Carwyn. "I vow to protect this realm, to put it before all else and serve as king for as long as I live. To be tied to the Eternal Crown just as the Manors have been. I make this unbreakable oath to bind me to my word, so shall my blood be spilled tenfold as it is today should I break it."

He squeezed his fist, letting his blood drop onto the fiery crown. The crown flared brighter.

A rumble of thunder clapped. Evelina looked up, finding

dark clouds gathering in the sky above. A flash of lightning struck the ground by Carwyn's feet, followed by a heavy *crack*. Screams and horrified gasps broke out through the crowd.

The crown of white fire above Carwyn's head turned black.

Evelina took a step forward and Daimon grabbed her elbow. Carwyn's eyes were wide with fear, reaching her arms out as if she couldn't see. Her limbs stiffened and then relaxed entirely. She dropped to the ground, her body landing in a heap. Senna gasped and crouched down, disappearing with the crowd blocking Evelina's view.

Evelina twisted out of Daimon's grasp and ran to her sister, pushing the crowd aside. By the time she made it to Carwyn, people had already started backing away from her, whispering cries of a cursed omen. Evelina skidded to a halt, finding her sister's normally olive skin pale and lifeless. She leaned down, ready to scoop her up and take her away to figure out what was going on.

"What happened?" she begged Senna. "Why is she like this?"

"A false queen," a voice murmured from the crowd, striking dread into Evelina's heart.

Senna ignored their words, trying to lift Carwyn by her shoulders. He motioned for Evelina to help when, without warning, she doubled over, gasping.

"Eve?" Daimon rushed to her side, rubbing her back to soothe her.

"Something's not—"

A blinding pain shot through her, causing her back to arch and her vision to blur. She screamed, falling into Daimon's arms before hitting the ground. She heard her name being screamed by so many people, but she couldn't make her mouth move to respond.

Another shock of pain shot through her, making her body go rigid and her vision go black entirely. Once the next wave hit, she felt like she was floating, no longer confined to a body held down by gravity.

SIXTY

EVELINA

"*OPEN YOUR EYES, MY DARLING.*" A DELICATE VOICE FILLED Evelina's empty mind.

Her eyes snapped open. She wasn't at the lux anymore, no longer in Daimon's arms.

She gasped, her lungs filling with air as she took in her new surroundings. The night sky twinkled above her, illuminating the hill on which she stood. Tall grass danced in a small breeze, tickling her ankles.

She stood on a hill that overlooked acres and acres of land below. It felt as if she could see the entire empire from this spot, perched like a bird on the tallest tree. She could see the peaks of the Zenovia Mountains in the distance, the moon mirrored onto the Andronicus Sea at its farthest edge.

How did I get here? she mused.

"Evelina."

She spun around, coming face to face with the last person she expected to see.

Her mother smiled at her, her skin glowing, a soft smile on her mouth. "I must say, I'm surprised to see you here."

Her mother stood before her, clothed in moonlight, wearing a shimmering, pale blue dress that flowed down to the grass and sparkled with her every movement. She was the picture of perfect health, her skin vibrant and no longer sweaty and pale. Her hair had a shiny luster, her eyes bright as she smiled at Evelina.

Evelina had a million questions. But she didn't say anything, because she really didn't care to get any answers at this point. All she needed to know was that her mother was back to being herself. She threw her arms around Embry, basking in the gentle touch of her mother.

Embry was quiet, stroking Evelina's hair as they held each other. With every passing breath came the realization of where she had just been. Evelina pulled back abruptly, her thoughts catching up with her.

"I was at the lux," Evelina said softly, noting her mother's smile dimming. "Carwyn had just been chosen by the crown."

She spun around, looking harder at her surroundings in an attempt to find something she recognized. The hill was foreign —even the stars above weren't constellations she recognized.

"Evelina," her mother said softly.

Evelina twisted around again, her breath quickening.

Her mother reached out and placed a steady hand on her trembling shoulder. "Evelina, look at me."

"Are we dead?" Evelina blurted out. "Is this Caelum?"

She remembered being at the lux when the pain hit. There wasn't time to find out what had caused the pain—it all had happened so fast. And now she was here…with her mother.

Embry sighed and placed her other hand on Evelina's shoulder, forcing her to face her again. "You're not dead and this isn't Caelum," Embry said firmly. "Breathe."

Evelina's pulse still raced, but she took a steadying inhale with her mother.

Embry smiled and cupped Evelina's cheeks. "Let me explain." She dropped her hands and tilted her face toward the stars. Evelina glanced up, too, still wondering why she didn't recognize the night sky.

"The constellations are all backwards here. It's like we're on the other side of the stars and we're looking at it upside down. You're among the very few that have been brought here, a place where no one can travel unless chosen." Embry looked away from the sky, bringing her gaze to Evelina's. "This is the Celestial Plane, the dwellings of the Divine."

Evelina sucked in a sharp breath, her eyes bouncing between the unfamiliar sky and her mother. "Why am I here?"

Embry tucked a stray piece of hair behind Evelina's ear, her touch light and warm. "You are not the only one who was brought here."

A gasp came from behind Evelina, causing her to jump. She spun around and found Carwyn lying on the ground. Panic gripped her chest, pressing down like a boulder.

Carwyn's eyes found the two of them standing beside her. She scrambled to her feet, her mouth hanging open in disbelief.

"Mother?" Her gaze flickered over to Evelina. "Evie?" She didn't run to her mother like Evelina had. Instead, she flinched back from her. Shame swirled in her gaze. "What's happening?" she asked.

Evelina didn't know how to answer—she wasn't even sure herself.

"Carwyn," their mother said gently. "You have been brought to the Celestial Plane."

The fiery crown had disappeared from above Carwyn's head. Darkness seemed to cling to her; a shadow followed her every move. Evelina's eyes dropped to the ground, unable to stand the look of pain in Carwyn's eyes, a look she didn't understand. She gasped, finding the grass beneath Carwyn's feet had decayed.

Her sister took a step forward. The moment her foot touched the ground again, that patch of grass died too.

"Carwyn," Evelina said, lifting her gaze. "The grass."

They both looked down. Carwyn backed up, another patch of grass dying, then another and another as she backed up further.

"No." Her voice was panicked, nothing like the strong and confident ruler she had been at the lux.

"What's happening?" Evelina turned to their mother, desperate for an answer.

Embry's eyes were sad as she watched Carwyn. "I think only Carwyn can answer that question."

Carwyn covered her mouth with her hand, muffling the sobs attempting to break free.

"Carwyn… What have you done?" Evelina whispered.

"I thought Eurydice had given up on us," Carwyn said in a pleading voice, as if seeking understanding. "We'd been losing for so long—and then when mother got sick, it all but confirmed Eurydice had turned her back on us." She slowly lifted her gaze to Evelina's, her voice growing quiet. "I turned to the dark gods for help."

Evelina froze. It felt as if a bucket of ice water had been poured over her.

Carwyn *always* had stronger faith in Eurydice than anyone she had ever known. It was Carwyn who said Eurydice would guide them to victory only moments ago at the lux.

"I was having horrible nightmares every night about mother dying before she got sick." Her gaze flickered over to Embry. "And then when she *did* fall ill, it felt like my nightmares were becoming reality. None of the healers could save her, and when the Sacred said it was because the land was dying, I had to do something. I couldn't sit back and do *nothing.*

"So I asked the dark gods for help. I prayed to them to save Mother, and they listened. The price was a small portion of my Essence—nothing compared to saving our mother. And for a few hours…she got better. I thought it had worked." She swallowed, her eyes dropping to the ground. "But then she got worse. Right up until the very end."

Evelina could shake her sister for being so foolish, though she knew her intentions came from a good place. "You didn't specify how long Mother would get better for, did you?" she asked slowly.

Carwyn shook her head, her shoulders dropping.

The dark gods were unpredictable. Cunning and selfish. They knew exactly how to take advantage of even the most brilliant minds in their most desperate moments.

"But it was a mistake," Carwyn rushed to explain. "I can still be queen."

Their mother pulled her in close, wrapping her in a hug.

A gentle and unfamiliar voice drifted on the wind. "This is not a mistake that can be reversed."

Evelina spun around to face the voice, her eyes widening. The hilltop was filled with six stone chairs, simply carved with ivy crawling up the sides. They weren't there a moment ago, and yet they looked as if they'd been there for ages.

But it wasn't the chairs that caused Evelina's mouth to hang open. It was the beings sitting in them, their presence so overwhelming that she knew they weren't fae. They each had their own gravitational pull, like an invisible force tugging her toward them.

Evelina didn't want to believe what her eyes were seeing. She had seen countless depictions of the lesser-known gods and goddesses, had heard stories of Azmara's beauty and the crown of ice atop Zillah's head.

But she *couldn't* be standing before them. And yet her gaze locked with split-color eyes, one of midnight and one of bright green. His hair was the same color as Daimon's, his face strikingly similar with his strong jawline and full lips that were smiling at her.

Nyx, God of Fear and Dreams. Daimon's father.

"Welcome to the Celestial Plane." The same gentle voice from a few moments ago greeted her. Finally, Evelina tore her eyes away from Nyx to look at the woman seated to his left. "I am Azmara, Goddess of Growth and Nature."

Evelina felt as if she had been punched in the stomach.

Azmara was almost blindingly beautiful. Her strawberry-blonde hair cascaded down to her waist in loose waves. She wore a sheer white dress that gathered over one shoulder, leaving the other shoulder bare.

Evelina turned to her mother and Carwyn, finding only Carwyn stood with her now.

"Your mother will return shortly; she isn't needed here for this," the man on Azmara's side said. "Xenos, God of the Seas."

Evelina shuddered. Another one of the dark gods. His hair was the trademark white of all the Undine, his eyes as blue as the deepest parts of the sea. But his skin was almost translucent, covered in patches of green, shimmery scales. His lips were a pale blue, his teeth razor-sharp and gleaming like pearls.

Evelina didn't know what to do, so she bowed deeply as they introduced themselves. Out of the corner of her eye, she saw Carwyn doing the same.

The next god didn't need an introduction, his smile feline. He looked at Evelina as if she were a mouse caught in his claws. "Nyx." He inclined his head toward her. "God of Fear and Dreams."

Evelina held her breath, waiting for him to say something more. But he just smiled, his gaze unsettling. She quickly bowed.

"Zillah, Goddess of Chaos and War."

Evelina had recognized her instantly, her depiction in the texts shockingly accurate. She wore a crown of ice atop long, dark hair that was perfectly straight.

"Astoria, Goddess of Hope," the next said softly. She was quiet, her eyes matching the gentleness of her smile.

Evelina felt the tension inside of her melt away as she looked into Astoria's gaze. She felt as if all her hopes and dreams could actually happen, like she could run away with Daimon, keep her empire safe and her siblings happy all at once.

Astoria tilted her head. "Interesting."

Evelina winced, remembering the tales of Astoria's mind-reading.

Astoria laughed, the sound like birds singing in the early morning. She inclined her head as Evelina quickly bowed.

"And I'm Celeste, Goddess of Wisdom," the sixth and final god said. Her ebony skin gleamed beneath the moon, a light green dress shimmering as it caught strands of light. "It's coming time for you to wake back up, daughter of Embry."

Carwyn bowed deeply, stepping forward.

"The other daughter," said Celeste sharply.

Evelina's brows pulled together. "But Carwyn—"

"Will not be returning," Xenos interjected. His eyes were curious as he watched Evelina. "She has made her choice to be bound to darkness, and the Eternal Crown will not tie itself to that."

"No," Evelina gasped.

Xenos's gaze swung to Carwyn, an eager hunger in his eyes. Evelina trembled, taking a step closer to Carwyn. When she turned to her sister, she found her face resigned in shadow.

"You gave your soul to the dark gods in exchange for the healing of your mother." He laughed, his voice deceptively light, like honey. "I have come to claim your soul."

"No!" Evelina screamed, lurching forward.

Xenos barely looked in her direction as water rose from the ground, pulled from the soil and the grass. He turned the water into ice, creating a barrier around Carwyn. Evelina tried to run around it, but another wall formed. Then another and another, until Carwyn was entirely encased. Evelina pounded on the cage of ice, screaming.

She tried to breathe through the panic. She wouldn't lose her sister—she'd already lost too much. She had to do *something*.

Carwyn looked up, her eyes filled with tears. Evelina watched in horror as Carwyn slowly froze until she was nothing more than a statue.

Evelina slid to her knees, screaming until her throat became raw.

"Evelina, darling," her mother said from beside her.

She jumped, and her screams turned into cries as she reached out for her mother. Embry looked different this time—slightly see-through, as if she were fading.

"The time has come for you to bear the weight of the Eternal Crown," Embry continued. "My spirit can only rest once it's complete. The crown is already imbuing itself into your Essence."

Evelina never wanted to be queen—she never even had a *chance* to become queen. Carwyn was the one always prepped to wear the crown, and even before Evelina, Ren and Lyria would have been next in line.

If she became queen…she would lose Daimon.

There were already so many reasons they couldn't be together; their fates were always pulling them in opposite directions. If anyone ever found out he was the son of Nyx, he would be outcasted into the wildlands. There would be riots if it was discovered the princess—the *queen*—was in love with the offspring of a dark god.

But becoming the queen meant taking a king, someone who had already been bound to her by blood and by oath. She would have no choice but to marry Senna. Even if she wanted to try with Daimon, the choice had already been made. Senna had sworn himself to the *crown*, no matter who wore it.

She glanced back at Carwyn, frozen in time. "And if I don't want it?"

"You have the right to abdicate after the transfer is complete," Azmara said from beside them. "But if it wanted another, it would have chosen them. The repercussions of rejecting it are not light."

Evelina swallowed. "Repercussions?"

"Once it passes on to you, it imbues itself within your Essence," Azmara explained. "You are one with the crown. To give it up is to also give up your magic. You would remain fae if you so choose to reject it, but your magic cannot be untangled from it. It would stay with the crown and pass on to the next, leaving you powerless."

"So, what will it be, daughter of Embry?" Astoria pressed.

Evelina took a step back, shaking her head. "It was always supposed to be Carwyn."

She glanced at her mother, who was almost fully invisible now. Evelina reached out for her, desperate to feel her one last time. But her hand went through her, her body no longer solid.

Embry nodded. "I will love you regardless." She smiled softly and said, "I will be with you always."

Evelina's stomach sank. With a quick breath, she twisted back to the gods and goddesses. She nodded and took a deep breath as she met Astoria's gaze, determination filling her.

"I agree to bear the weight of the Eternal Crown."

"Your empire will need you in the days to come." Astoria's voice was fading, sounding farther away, as if Evelina had cotton in her ears. "Your gift of light is a mark befitting a queen. Hold those words close to your heart."

Evelina's vision darkened, and she felt the pull to return to her body. It was like her soul was tethered, but not quite settled, and now her body was calling her home.

Evelina knew her future was about to change. She could feel it deep in her bones. The change wasn't subtle; it wasn't a slight shift of the wind or something so slow she couldn't notice it until after it happened.

The change was quick. Sharp.

The swift swipe of a blade, cutting down all her dreams.

SIXTY-ONE

DAIMON

SENNA HAD CONTROLLED THE CROWD ENOUGH TO GET them to migrate away from where Evelina and Carwyn were lying—impressive, considering the faerie wine crates had nearly been emptied by this point.

But Daimon couldn't pull himself together enough to wrangle the crowd. Evelina didn't *look* as if anything were wrong. Her face was peaceful, no crinkle on her forehead in sight. And he would know if something were wrong; he had no doubt that he would feel it in the depths of his bones.

Still, none of those things helped him calm down. He was seconds away from ripping someone's throat out if they tried to speak to him. All his energy was centered on her, on praying to Eurydice that she would wake up perfectly fine.

"We should call for a healer," he growled to Ellerry, his patience thinning.

The Keeper had pushed through the crowd the moment Evelina fell. Ellerry waved her hand in the air. She knew something and she wasn't saying it.

"It won't be long now," Ellerry said quietly. "Patience, Commander."

He closed his eyes, panic filling his chest as he thought of her and only her.

His body swayed, his head growing light.

For a moment, he could see her. It was like a frosted glass had been placed between them, making her outline hazy. But it was her. He would recognize her anywhere.

She was standing on an empty hill, an odd pattern of stars above her head, flowing grass beneath her feet. She was crying softly.

"Eve?" Daimon whispered, taking a step forward. "Tell me you're okay."

She wouldn't look at him, unmoving, as if she hadn't heard him. Her eyes were sad.

"I'm sorry, Daimon," she whispered desperately, like a rush of wind twisting around him and cascading over his skin. He shivered at the way her voice sounded saying his name, at the way her lips formed the word in a way no one else's could.

But it didn't feel like she was saying it *to* him.

"Why?" he asked. "What's wrong?"

This time, she turned toward him, as if hearing him for the first time.

"Daimon," she breathed. Her eyes glistened with unshed tears. "Everything has changed."

He shook his head, not understanding.

"The crown is going to me."

Shock rolled through him. "How do you know?"

"We're in the Celestial Plane." She gestured to the space around them. "Carwyn is gone and now the crown has gone to me instead." The tears broke free, slipping down her cheeks. "*I will be the next queen of Valon.*"

Even as the words left her mouth, they didn't feel real.

Daimon wasn't just losing her on the border—a daily routine to which he had grown accustomed—he was losing *every* piece of her. It would never again be as simple as stealing her away for a ride through the clouds or sneaking off to the waterfall. He would never feel her lips against his, because she was bound to marry another. Would Senna get her smiles? Her laughter?

His stomach roiled with nausea.

Would he get to keep her love?

But he always knew, in a way, this would be their fate. She was exactly what the kingdom needed: a queen who would never put her needs first. A queen who would love her people so fiercely she would protect them until her dying breath.

Daimon didn't know what words he could say in this moment—didn't know what could properly convey the weight of his grief, or of his love. So instead, he said, "Dream with me, my queen."

She stepped forward, and he bent down, pressing his forehead to hers.

"Always," she whispered.

He closed his eyes and breathed her in. His shock dissipated and began to turn into something darker—more painful. Despair filled his chest, his lungs.

He opened his eyes and found hers already open, watching him.

"I don't want to go back and face this. Not without you." Her voice broke.

His heart twisted. He wanted to take her pain away.

"In another life, maybe," he whispered.

She pulled away from him, her eyes flaring with anger and desperation. "No," she gasped out. "*This* life. You're the other half of my soul, Daimon. You fill every empty space of my heart." Her eyes widened when she realized what she said.

The other half of my soul.

"Evelina—"

"You are," she said, louder this time. "You *are* mine—my soulbonded."

He swallowed as tears welled in his eyes. There would never be another he loved as much as he loved her.

She'd always been so much more than his first love. What they had was deeper than that, something he never thought he was worthy enough to have. Especially not with her. There was no doubt in his mind that his soul was made to love hers. He had always known she was the other half of his soul, the answer buried inside of him, waiting for him to accept it.

But he had never imagined Evelina loving him the same way back. How could the dark blood that ran in his veins be fit for a Woodland princess—a queen? She'd be binding her soul to his own, which was bound to Vidaris by fate. He would be dooming her soul to be as tainted as his, corrupting the goodness inside of her. Not only that, but the pain for both of them to be separated while bonded when he was inevitably forced to become the Lord of Shadows… They had both already lost so much, had endured so much pain.

"You're going to be queen," he said gently. "And Senna is going to be king. Being soulbonded won't change the oath he's already made to the crown."

"I need you, Daimon. My soul is already yours to have." She shook her head. "Our physical bodies may not be here, but I want to declare it here, beneath the stars of Eurydice, that I am yours."

"My soul was never mine to give," he added. "We've run out of time, Eve. Even if we wanted to do a bonding ceremony, the next equinox is months away."

She reached forward and cupped his cheeks. "Then we do it here." Her eyes lifted to the stars above. "We're in the realm of the gods—we don't need an equinox."

He wanted this—blessed Divine, did he want to bind his soul to hers forever. But he knew it would be better to walk away. To let her live the burdens of their fate free of him—a soul always fading into shadow.

Still, as his gaze met hers, he found himself asking, "How do you know?"

She shook her head. "Do you have any doubts we were made for each other? That our souls are two halves of a whole?"

He looked into her eyes, seeing this beautifully courageous woman refusing to back down. She was so much braver than he was; the least he could do was jump with her.

Besides, he couldn't lie. Not to her. If he were a better man, he would tell her they weren't made for each other, wouldn't be selfish enough to bind her soul to his.

But he wasn't a better man.

He wrapped his arms around her waist, and her hands slid around to the back of his neck.

"I can feel you." He laid a hand over her heart. "Your pain is my pain; your joy is my joy. You were made for me, Evelina Manor—and I for you."

She buried her face against his chest and he pulled her in close.

"Bond with me," she whispered.

He leaned back and watched her closely. His heart raced. The word *unworthy* echoed through his head.

"You're sure?" he asked slowly.

The corners of her mouth turned upward. "I've never been more sure in my life."

His fears quieted with her words—she always had a way of doing that.

She crouched down and picked up a jagged rock from beneath their feet. There was no Sacred, no temple or special dagger. It was just them and the stars of the Divine.

"Just repeat after me," Evelina began. Her voice gained an ethereal quality, as if Eurydice was echoing within her. "*I'm certain my soul mirrors yours.*"

He hadn't been to many bonding ceremonies, but the

Manors had been to hundreds. His hands shook as he looked down at her. He didn't know how he got so lucky as to be the one she deemed the other half of her soul.

"And I'm certain that mine mirrors yours," he answered.

A gentle breeze swept around them. It picked up leaves and twirled around their feet in a circle. He felt warmth press against his chest, the same warmth he felt when Eurydice was present in the Sacred—as if she were here with them.

"*I'm certain that my soul is the same as yours, cleaved in two the moment they were conceived,*" she continued. "*I understand that this declaration can only be made once, and if wrong, it will forever separate us from our true mates by falsely choosing another. I make this decision confidently.*"

He took a deep breath and the breeze strengthened.

"And I'm certain my soul is the other half of yours," he whispered. "Forever to be separated from my true mate if we're wrong. I make this decision confidently."

Evelina held the rock to her palm and made a small cut. She handed it to Daimon for him to do the same. The rock was cold as it bit into his skin.

She held her palm in front of her and made a fist, squeezing until blood fell on the grass beneath. She motioned for him to do the same and he mirrored her movement.

He remembered this part of the ceremony. If the blood sought the other's out and became one, then their souls would be sealed together, marking that of a true bond. But if they ran parallel to each other, then they weren't a match, and they had forever sundered their souls from their true mates.

The wind around them settled suddenly. Time stopped as their blood dropped to the ground below. It stained the bright green grass a deep maroon and glistened in the moonlight.

Daimon's stomach twisted as the blood began to move. He looked up at Evelina, unable to watch. Her gaze was fixed on the ground, a calm smile on her face. She gasped and he looked.

Their blood was inches apart, but quickly closing the

distance. The separate streams trailed toward each other and collided.

A rush of adrenaline coursed through his body the moment they became one. He could feel his soul being stitched together with hers, like a thread that was loosened finally being pulled tight.

He cradled her face in his hands and dropped his forehead to hers.

"It worked," she murmured, her voice returning to normal. "We have to accept the bond to seal it."

He pressed a kiss to the top of her head. "I accept this bond with every fiber of my being."

She reached up and gripped his wrists, clinging to him as she said, "And I accept this bond without any doubt in my heart."

A gentle breeze swept around them again. The moon's light flared brighter, as if Eurydice was blessing their bond.

Evelina held her palm out; a new stark-white scar had formed where she'd cut it with the rock. He held his out beside hers, finding the same scar on his hand.

There were still things he wanted to say—promises he wanted to make—but he could feel something dragging him out of this place, pulling him away.

Evelina suddenly disappeared from his arms, as if she hadn't been there at all. He stumbled forward, reaching out for someone who wasn't there. Storm clouds rolled over the moon, the gentle breeze turning frigid and harsh.

"*Everything is about to change, son of Nyx,*" a raspy voice taunted in his mind.

He spun around, his heart racing. "Who's there?"

"*Your soul is mine to give, son of Nyx. And anything bound to it is bound to me.*"

He twisted and turned, searching, his heart racing.

"*Time is running out. The day will soon come that you will take your place by my side.*"

His mouth went dry. "Vidaris?" he whispered.

His body felt as if it had been struck by lightning. His eyes flew open and he took a step back, stumbling as the ground gave out beneath him.

Daimon jolted awake. He was back at the lux, everyone's focus on Evelina and Carwyn. Everyone except Ellerry. The Keeper was watching him closely.

He looked down at his palms, finding both smooth and without blemish. There wasn't the scar of the soulbonded. Had he dreamt it all?

Daimon glanced over at Brielle, who was shaking her head in warning. She opened her mouth—likely to tell Daimon to relax—when Evelina gasped, pulling everyone's attention.

"Evie," Lyria gasped.

Slowly, her eyes fluttered open. The group huddled over her and pressed in tighter. Daimon reached for her, grabbing her hand. Evelina's skin grew hot, almost too warm to touch. Her eyes were open, but they weren't focused on anything, just gazing up at the night sky.

Suddenly, she moved, rolling onto her side to face Carwyn. She pushed herself to her knees and pulled Carwyn to her chest, slowly rocking back and forth.

"Evie?" Lyria dropped to her side, placing a hand on her shoulder.

Evelina jumped at the contact. Senna lowered to her other side, grabbing Carwyn's hand. Daimon watched as Evelina's eyes followed his touch, wishing he could protect her from the pain.

"Evelina, what happened?" Senna pressed. "Why isn't Carwyn waking up?"

Evelina shook her head, her voice cracking as she said, "She's gone."

"What do you mean she's *gone?*" Lyria asked quietly.

Evelina gently set Carwyn down. She tucked a strand of Carwyn's hair behind her ear and leaned forward, gently kissing her forehead. Daimon helped her to her feet.

"Carwyn's soul will not be returning to this plane," Evelina said. Her voice wobbled, but she took a deep breath. "She's with our mother now."

Gasps rippled, followed by murmurs from the crowd. Lyria broke into tears, her hand flying to her mouth.

Daimon hadn't dreamt of being in the Celestial Plane with Evelina. She was about to become queen. His hands shook and he tucked them into his pockets.

Ellerry placed a hand on Evelina's back. Evelina twisted around, her panic palpable. Ellerry gave her a solemn nod as Evelina's forehead pinched, gathering the strength to speak to the crowd. Daimon wished he could stop her from saying the words that would change them forever. Instead, he took a step back, realizing this was a moment she could only face alone.

Evelina took a deep breath and said, "I am to be queen."

A blazing crown of white flames ignited above her—the Eternal Crown that had been forged by the gods and goddesses themselves, gifted to the fae to be passed down from generation to generation. It hovered just above her head, formed into sharp points all the way around.

All eyes were set on her, on the crown she now wore.

Ellerry leaned over and whispered in her ear. Evelina nodded, reaching up, her fingers skimming the bottom of the floating crown.

"The Eternal Crown has chosen its successor," Ellerry shouted. "Long live Queen Evelina Manor!"

Evelina's eyes found Daimon. When their gazes met, he could hardly breathe, his lungs fighting to work. Gone were the hazel irises he loved, and in their place were halos of fire matching that of the crown. Her brows drew together sharply, causing the crease between them to deepen. He longed to smooth it out, to stroke his thumb over it until her worries melted away.

He slowly lowered himself to the ground, kneeling before her. Among a sea of people, there was only them.

"My queen," Daimon murmured.

Slowly, the crowd followed him and began to bow. One by one, they dropped to their knees, shouting their wishes for Queen Evelina's long reign. Once the entire crowd had bowed, the full weight of what was happening came crashing down on Daimon.

"The Valon Empire has been forged by blood and strength," Evelina addressed the crowd, her voice steady and sure. "We are not weak, and neither is our land."

The ground rumbled beneath their feet, the vibration slowly growing stronger until glasses of wine toppled off of crates and crashed to pieces against the rocky soil. Flowers bent toward the crown, trees swaying as if reaching out for Evelina.

It was as if life were being breathed back into the forest, rippling out into the empire at large. A new queen brought a rush of fresh Essence, especially with a fae as strong as Evelina. Her light was intertwining with the land, dispelling the darkness that had been slowly sucking the life from it.

The land welcomed her, and so did its people.

Sixty-Two

Daimon

There was always a part of Daimon that knew he would lose Evelina. Even with their souls bound, their bond didn't connect to the physical world—to their physical bodies. His hand, smooth of the scar, was proof that their love couldn't exist in this realm.

She would be queen, bound to wed another, and he would go to the border just as he always had.

The crowd surrounded her, offering praise and whispers of blessings. Senna stepped to her side, helping her back to the palace. Daimon watched them disappear into the crowd, while he faded into the background.

A council meeting was called, but he stayed away, sending Brielle in his—and Keir's—stead. He couldn't bear to face Evelina.

Within a few short hours, they declared the wedding would be happening tomorrow, a ceremony to go along with the coronation. Brielle told him the news as if she were afraid he'd keel over at any moment. Maybe she was right to worry.

He left and found Zephyr. Without a word, he jumped onto her back and flew into the night sky. His throat burned like acid as he swallowed down the pain that consumed him.

He ran through the last several hours in his head, reviewing how everything had changed so quickly.

Fate had decided for him after all.

A pain that wasn't his shot through their bond. He knew his wyvern was mourning the loss of Evelina just as he was.

"There's a wedding happening today," he murmured.

Zephyr growled, and the itchy sensation that came with her annoyance filled him.

There was always a part of him that knew he would lose Evelina.

"It's too hard to go back, Z." His voice broke.

Zephyr cried out, her flight slowing. She turned her head to look back at him, a burst of agony shooting Daimon straight in the chest. Her golden eyes drifted to the palace disappearing in the distance behind them.

"It'll only make it harder on both of us to have to say goodbye."

This time, he felt anger from Zephyr. But he wasn't ready to say goodbye to Evelina yet. He wanted to pretend she was still his for at least a few more hours.

Zephyr shook her head and growled. She thought he was being stupid.

"She's getting *married*, Z."

But how could he leave her without a word? He was her protector when she needed it, her dream away from the world when there were storms she couldn't weather. There were years he wasn't there for her. He couldn't do that to her again. If she needed him to support her rise as queen, he would do it. No matter how painful it was for him.

"I can't leave without seeing her," he whispered to Zephyr, realizing he had to turn around.

He needed to find her before the sun rose, to give him enough time before the wedding and coronation.

Zephyr dipped her left wing instantly, spinning them back toward the palace, when a gust of wind pushed them back.

A blur of darkness flashed in the corner of his eye. He twisted around, feeling Zephyr slow the moment he saw it. Anger seared down their bond, hot and fiery like a heated iron rod poking at his chest.

She reared back and hovered in the air. Her wings beat steadily.

There was only one person who preferred their meetings to happen in the sky.

"Interesting how things have played out." Nyx lowered from above, descending until he floated level before Daimon. "Who could've guessed the devout and perfect Carwyn would turn to the dark gods?"

Daimon's nostrils flared. "You've known this entire time she wouldn't be crowned queen."

Nyx waved him off, unbothered. "It isn't a matter we should involve ourselves with." He folded his hands behind his back, his smile unwavering. "The Eternal Crown may have passed to a different heir, but *your* birthright still awaits you."

Daimon thought back to his encounter with Vidaris in the Celestial Plane. *The day will soon come that you will take your place by my side.*

"This war isn't over," Daimon seethed. "I'll never offer more power to her."

"Power to her?" Nyx hovered closer, confusion marring his face. "I don't think you understand what this means," he said slowly. "Yes, if you rule the Shadow Realm, Vidaris will be free to use her powers elsewhere. But *you* will gain power too."

Daimon would never get Nyx to understand why he wanted no part in ruling the shadows. Nyx was a god, not bound by emotions, love, or duties of the heart.

"I understand perfectly," Daimon growled. It was *Nyx* who didn't understand. "I don't want the Shadow Realm."

Nyx's lips curled sharply, like a cat staring at its dinner. "Even if it meant you could end this war?" He tilted his head. "Not even to save your precious kingdom?"

The air between them tensed.

"Being a servant of Vidaris won't make any power I gain worth its price," Daimon hissed.

Lightning crackled in the air, causing the hair on Daimon's arms to rise. Shadows gathered around Nyx, slithering up his ankles in two strands like twining snakes. They gathered at his waist and crossed over his chest, flickering against his neck.

Nyx had always been so calm, so confident and unbothered during their meetings. One could almost forget that he was a god.

But now Daimon was reminded of who he truly was. The God of Fear and Dreams, the god who crafted the first Nocturna, the one from whom they derived their shadows. Their shadows were watered-down and dampened compared to Nyx's. His were unbridled, wild, untamed.

"Do not underestimate the gods." His voice was different—darker. It was a low hum that rumbled like thunder. "Zenovia is the last big battlefront left. *Think* about it. If you ruled the Shadow Realm within the mountains, *you* would have full control over the border."

Daimon's blood turned to ice.

"If you take up this helm, you could end this war."

His thoughts raced with the possibility of being able to change the tides of the war on his own. It was too good to be true, too obvious—right in front of him the entire time.

"I'm not falling for your tricks."

"Not to mention the Shadow Realm is rumored to be the resting place of Nightfall," Nyx added, ignoring Daimon. He was taunting him, dangling the things he wanted most in front of him.

"That blade is a myth."

"Is it?" Nyx smiled. "What if you could find it and not only close the border, but kill Moros once and for all?"

Daimon stilled. Nightfall was a blade of the gods, a story

told around a fire about the mighty weapon strong enough to pierce any darkness.

"Think it through," Nyx said lightly, the shadows dispersing. His light and easy tone had returned, offering no sign of the power he had just displayed. "Though time *is* running out."

A threat lingered behind the words. If Moros and his forces made it far enough into the border before it could be fortified, it would be too late.

All Nyx cared about was using Daimon to get him closer to stealing the Vale from Vidaris. He didn't care about Daimon— nor did he care about saving this realm.

But Daimon cared. More than he ever had.

There wasn't any room for Daimon to *think it through*. He could save them all.

Nyx smiled, pleased. "I warned you about this day." He drifted upward, now looking down at Daimon from where he hovered. "It would've been easier on you to cut these ties long ago."

Daimon didn't want to think about the ties he was about to cut. The family he was leaving behind.

"How do I accept?" he asked, his voice rough.

Nyx's smile turned feral. "You go to the Zenovia Mountains and pray to Vidaris. She will lead you. If you accept her deal, you will become the Lord of the Shadows, made to usher lost souls into the Vale and keep watch over the Shadow Realm. Your shadows will be at their greatest strength, though you will be bound away forever from the realms of light."

Daimon swallowed. He would be giving his soul to shadow, ferrying the fae punished to an afterlife away from the light of Caelum to their eternal torment in the Vale. He had spent his whole life hiding his shadows, terrified of what it meant to have such a power—but it all came to this.

"But be wary of crossing into the Vale," Nyx warned. "You may rule the Shadow Realm, but to cross into the Vale is to give yourself over fully to Vidaris. Darkness would consume you."

The god disappeared into the clouds with no final parting, leaving Daimon to make the choice alone.

There was so much more he wanted than to be bound to that wretched realm. He wanted more for his life, more than what his father planned for him.

But he would do it. For the realm—for Evelina—he would give himself over to Vidaris and rule the Shadow Realm.

Fate was cruel that way.

It showed him the possibility of having his deepest desires—and then ripped it away.

SIXTY-THREE

DAIMON

THEY HIT THE GROUND HEAVILY, FAR LESS SMOOTHLY THAN they normally did. Zephyr shook her head out, a nervous tic he had only witnessed a handful of times. She shuffled her wings, restless, and then tucked them in close.

Waves crested and broke, washing up along the shore beside them. They were near Zephyr's cave, close enough that he could see its familiar shape even in the darkness.

But he froze when he saw the figure beyond the cave.

Evelina was standing on the shore of the Andronicus. She was wringing her hands together, fidgeting with the rings on her fingers. The crown had faded, no longer visible on her head. The flame had dimmed from her eyes.

Daimon unmounted, casting a fleeting glance at Zephyr. Her golden eyes shined with sadness as she laid her head down to rest in the sand.

The moment his boots hit land felt like a final nail in his coffin. He walked over to Evelina slowly, dragging out the inevitable.

When he stood in front of her, he wrapped his arms around her. Her arms instantly snaked around his waist, her head on his chest. He tucked her in close, stroking her hair with one hand while the other held her against him.

Evelina's heart pounded so fiercely that he could feel it tapping against him, so at odds with the beats of his own. His was beating just as quickly, but they weren't tapping in unison. Not anymore. Every time her heart paused, his beat.

He pulled back, stepping away. There was so much that he wanted to say to her. But with one look at her face, the words faded from his lips.

She looked down, her finger lightly tracing her palm. His hand itched, as if her finger was touching him instead. He squeezed his hand into a fist to stop himself from reaching out for her. When her gaze lifted to his, he braced himself.

"I—I've made my choice, Daimon."

I will follow you anywhere, Eve.

"We can't do this. We never could, and I think we both know it," she whispered, looking down at her hand once more. She continued to rub the smooth skin where the scar should've been.

I will love you through the depths of despair, to the ends of our land, and into every blissful moment you offer me.

"I love you. But I love my people more."

He held her gaze, drinking in the curves of her face, the hazel eyes, the soft lips, one last time. He couldn't seem to speak the words trapped in his heart.

You are where I want my days to begin and end.

"I need you to go. Go be happy without me, and make a life for yourself. Because maybe you were right the first time for leaving. Maybe it's too hard being close when we can't ever be together..." Her voice faltered, her eyes pleading with him. "Daimon? Please say something."

Every word was a dagger in his chest.

He swallowed, the words leaving his lips like a leaf blowing away in the wind. "I'll go."

The answer is always yes, to whatever you ask of me.

Daimon stepped forward, unable to stop himself from this final goodbye. He leaned down, pressing his lips to hers and searing the memory of it into his mind. She melted into him, greedily chasing every kiss he gave.

He pulled back, willing his heart to keep beating despite the pain wedged into it.

Their gazes locked, and his legs threatened to give out.

"Goodbye, Evelina," he whispered.

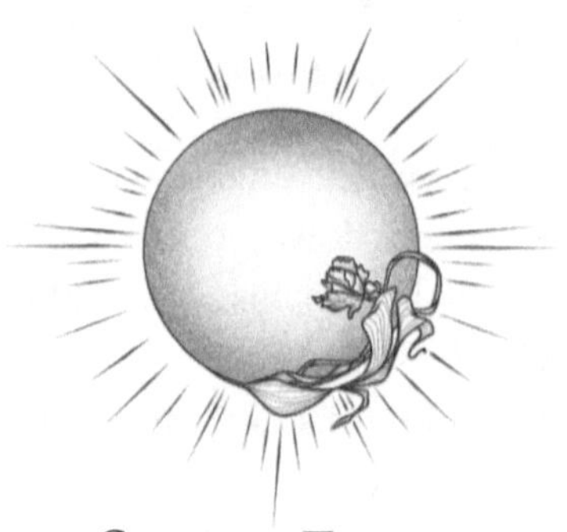

SIXTY-FOUR

EVELINA

EVELINA LOOKED AT HERSELF IN A LONG, GOLDEN-FRAMED mirror. Her stomach flipped as her gaze traveled down the dress Lyria had brought to her this morning.

It was the most stunning gown she'd ever seen, composed of delicate gold and white fabric. Tiny crystal beads were woven into it, filling the bottom hem and trailing up to the waist like ivy. The top was supported by thin straps, just enough to keep the dress in place.

But the back was what made Evelina's breath catch. It scooped low, stopping near the base of her spine. The hem of the dress fanned out, a train so long that it would take up half the aisle when she walked down it.

It was the kind of dress she'd imagined marrying Daimon in.

But he had his duty. She had hers.

Every moment with Daimon felt like she was flying against the sun, knowing that she would one day get too close. Her happiness wasn't her priority anymore. Her people were.

She didn't know how to rule, not when it was always meant to be Carwyn. But she would do this for her. Would do this for her mother. For Ren, Keir, Elias, and Ranick. For all the soldiers she couldn't save and those who had given their lives for the empire.

Then there was Senna. Someone she had considered a friend from a young age, someone who was already marrying out of duty to his people. He was sacrificing for their empire just as she was, all the while grieving the Rider he, too, had lost.

She turned away from the mirror and faced Lyria. Her sister gazed at her, eyes hopeful and misty. She wore a pale pink dress that gathered at her waist and spread out widely around her, embellished with embroidered pink flowers sewn from head to toe.

"Evie, Mother would be so proud of you," she said softly. "Carwyn and Ren, too."

Evelina swallowed down the emotions clinging to her throat. The image of Carwyn's face frozen in Xenos's ice flashed through her mind, remembering the way the pain stayed frozen in her eyes too.

She threw her arms around Lyria, hugging her tightly. "I wish they were here."

"Me too," Lyria said. She pulled back and wiped a few stray tears away. Her eyes were sad, and Evelina knew the day would be far more bitter than sweet for the both of them.

"I always imagined Ren walking me down the aisle on the day I got married," Evelina admitted.

Lyria walked over to the door, picking up a small basket. "I will be with you the whole way," she whispered. "It's time."

They walked arm in arm to the throne room. Evelina could already hear the light music that played, and the chatter of hundreds of people who had spilled into the corridors. They passed Aegis guards stationed in the hallways along the way, which would have been odd before the war but was now commonplace.

Once outside of the throne room, Evelina began to panic. She turned to Lyria, eyes wide as she realized what she was about to do.

"I can't do this," Evelina whispered.

Lyria grabbed her shoulders lightly. "If you want to run, then I'll hold your dress and we'll run," she said. Evelina's brows jumped up. "If you want to storm in there and find a way to do this without having to marry Senna, I'll open the door. If you want to cry, I have a shoulder and a cloth to dab your eyes with."

Evelina's eyes filled with tears.

"But, for what it's worth," Lyria said softly as she squeezed her shoulders, "you're going to make a marvelous queen. You're kind and gentle, but you're also one of the bravest people I know. You don't balk in the face of peril or uncertainty—you take it head-on. *That* is the kind of queen this realm needs right now."

The music shifted behind the door, a lullaby for a bride. Evelina reached for Lyria's hand and took a deep breath. Lyria was the only family she had left now. She didn't know how she would get through this day without her.

"You'll be with me the whole way?" she whispered.

Lyria smiled and pulled her into a hug. "Every single step."

Evelina pulled away. She nodded at the two Aegis stationed outside the throne room and took another steadying breath as they opened the doors.

The room was packed wall-to-wall with people. Paper butterflies tied to strings hung from the ceiling, and the aisle had been lined with a sea of lavender and white flowers.

Ellerry waited at the end of the aisle with Senna at the bottom of the steps that led to the twisted-branch thrones. Senna wore a perfectly fitted white jacket and pants, covered with gold thread sewn into swirls. A perfect match to her gown.

The council sat on either side of the thrones. Maliena gave her a gentle, somber smile.

Lyria squeezed her arm and they stepped forward together.

Evelina smiled at those standing as she passed them. They wore flowing gowns and tailored jackets, jewels around their necks and flowers in their hair.

The music swelled as she stopped just before Senna and Ellerry. Lyria gave her a quick kiss on the cheek and moved into the crowd.

Senna reached for her hands, his touch light and warm. He smiled at her. Seeing how calm he was kept her focused. The music slowed to a pause and, within the silence that followed, a thick layer of anticipation suspended in the air.

"People of Valon," Ellerry began. "Today, we bind together not only two fae, but a queen and her king." She held a short rope in her hand, her face reserved and unreadable as it usually was. She placed the rope over Evelina's arm first, then looped it under and around Senna's, tying them together. "Repeat together after me: We bind this marriage in loyalty, honor, and respect for one another."

"We bind this marriage in loyalty, honor, and respect for one another," Senna and Evelina repeated in unison.

People cheered and clapped as the rope was laced another time around their wrists.

"In the way of the Woodland, we leave the rope securely tied for the remainder of the ceremony as a reminder of two being bound as one," Ellerry continued. "An eternal knot is one of unwavering strength. It holds against any weight, secures the weakest of objects, not to be separated by weather or force."

Evelina looked up at Senna at the same time he turned his head to look at her.

"We not only celebrate this day; we also mourn the loss of the late Queen Embry. But we honor her by carrying on her legacy to strive for a better tomorrow."

Evelina swallowed, blinking back tears.

"We bring forth a new crown, as is the tradition of each new ruler, one forged on the morning of their coronation." Ellerry motioned for the crowns to be brought forward. They rested on a velvet maroon pillow in the hands of one of the Aegis guards. "Not a single crown, but two. One for Queen Evelina and one for King Senna. They each bear a symbol of our kind: a golden vine for the Woodland, forged from the fire of an Aegis, cooled in the water of an Undine, and made by the hand of a Nocturna."

Evelina swallowed as Lyria retrieved the crowns and brought them forward, stopping between them and the crowd. Evelina's crown was ringed with tall points, the bottom lined with a single golden vine, while Senna's was composed of three thick vines woven together.

"As each ruler before you, you will kneel before your people, pledging your lives to serve and honor them."

Evelina swept aside her gown, kneeling on the stairs. Senna did the same, helping her with her dress and settling beside her.

Ellerry reached over them, grabbing Senna's crown off the pillow first. "Senna, do you promise to uphold the duty as King of the Valon Empire, to rule in the light of Eurydice, to bring peace when able, and protect when needed?"

Senna nodded and said, "I will."

Ellerry lowered the crown onto his head. Senna was always calm, but in this moment, Evelina saw his jaw tighten and his brows draw together just slightly.

The first and only sign of his hesitation. She was glad she wasn't alone in that.

Then Ellerry leaned forward again, picking up Evelina's crown. She heard the tapping of Lyria's shoes against the wooden floor as she returned to her seat by the council.

"And do you, Evelina Manor, bringer of light, promise to uphold the duty as Queen of the Valon Empire, to rule in the light of Eurydice, to bring peace when able, and protect when needed?"

Evelina's breath caught. Her heart pounded in her chest as she answered, "I will."

The crown was lowered onto her head. It was lighter than she expected.

"Then may you both be blessed by Eurydice." Ellerry

motioned for them to stand, their backs still to the crowd. "And long may you reign as queen and king."

Evelina and Senna were now married, bound together forever as husband and wife. They promised to protect the empire just as they promised to protect each other.

People cheered, throwing flowers into the air. Together, they walked hand in hand up the stairs. They paused in front of the thrones and turned around.

Everyone was smiling, cheering, clapping. Evelina's eyes searched for Daimon, but the familiar pull she felt when he was near was absent. She couldn't blame him for not coming.

Evelina turned to her sister, who was wiping a tear from her cheek. Annora was nestled against her and they stood together, hand in hand. She looked around the room, seeing Brielle towering above the crowd, a sad smile on her face. Evelina's heart squeezed when she saw Willow and Aster beside her. She caught a glimpse of Gloriana, whom she hadn't seen since they were at camp together. The healer waved, her eyes filled with pride.

Senna's eyes were turned to Evelina, waiting for her move. Slowly, Evelina lowered herself onto the throne, and he followed.

They sat together, side by side, as Queen and King of the Valon Empire.

SIXTY-FIVE

DAIMON

THE WAVES OF THE ANDRONICUS CRASHED AGAINST THE shore. Daimon stood at its edge, hands in his pockets, as he watched a bird fly over the cresting waves. If the ceremony was to start at first light, it was likely almost over.

Evelina would know what he had done when he didn't report on the border as commander. Zephyr would return to the palace without him, and Evelina would know.

But it would be too late by then. He would already be bound to the Shadow Realm.

He turned around, facing Zephyr. She was still resting her head on the ground, looking up at him with her large golden eyes.

"Up for one last ride, Z?" he said softly.

Zephyr whined, a small and broken cry. She lifted her head and her gaze shifted to the sky. She whined again and heavily laid her head back on the ground.

He walked over to her, his heart squeezing with every step. "Come on, don't be like that."

She lifted her head, nudging his hand with her nose. He felt a rush of emotions through their bond: sadness, fear, and... pride.

"You're proud of me?" he whispered.

She nudged his hand again and this time stretched her wings out, rising to her feet.

He reached for the rope attached to her saddle, pausing when he gripped it. With a final look, he glanced back out at the sea. Then at the cave that had given him and Evelina so much respite from the world, the final place he'd seen her. Lastly, he looked toward the palace, unable to see it through the tall trees of the forest.

He took a deep breath and swung onto Zephyr's back.

For the final time, he said, "Wings up, Z."

The air was cool as they flew over the sea. He didn't know how he would say goodbye to Zephyr, but he knew she couldn't come with him. Not where he was going.

A pinch of guilt tugged at his stomach for not saying goodbye to the people he was leaving behind. Brielle, Aster, Willow. Brielle would lead them well, and would likely find talented beta fleet members to replace the lost members of their fleet. They would recover without him.

He wondered what they would think of him; if they would think he had abandoned his post or perhaps died fighting. If they would curse his name, thinking he was a coward, or drink ale beside a fire, reminiscing, sharing stories of their time together.

Neither of those options made him feel better.

But this was a path he had to take alone.

Zephyr soared through the sky, alternating between flying high above the clouds and dropping low, skimming the waves of the Andronicus. He knew she was stalling, extending the ride by flying side to side rather than straight there. But he let her, wishing more than anything the ride could last longer too.

Zephyr lowered to the ground as they arrived at the camp. He stayed atop her, looking at his old cabin, now empty and quiet.

Then he looked to the healer's cabin, seeing the ghost of

Evelina through the closed shutter. How many times had he walked through the center of this camp, just to catch a glimpse of her?

He remembered when he was injured, lying on the hard cot, the scent of lilies wrapping around him. Of the way she slowly opened herself back up to him, forgiving him when he didn't deserve to be forgiven.

The pain he felt in that moment was almost more than he could bear. But he would. He would bear it all for her. For Brielle, Willow, and Aster. For those who could no longer fight, the members of his fleet he would never meet again in Caelum. For the empire he would likely never step foot in again—an empire he was never worthy of inhabiting to begin with.

For all his years of fighting his fate, it amounted to this loneliness. As much as he tried to deny it, he was his father's child.

Daimon slipped off Zephyr, his chest tight as his feet landed on the dirt. He walked around to face her, dragging his palm along her scales.

"I need you to watch over Evelina for me," he whispered. "Even if you keep your distance, just check in on her. Okay?"

Zephyr whined.

"Please." His voice broke. "You know why I have to do this. I need to protect them, just like you needed to protect me."

He leaned forward, resting his forehead against hers. Her scales were still cold from the flight. She closed her eyes, a deep rumble coming from her chest.

"May we meet again."

Warmth shot down their bond, filling him.

He took a step back, his heart nearly tearing out of his chest. Zephyr stepped forward, her eyes wide with panic.

"You have to stay here, Z," he said gently. "I'll be okay."

Tears gathered in his eyes. Losing her was losing part of his soul—a soul that was already tattered and bruised, splintered and broken. Zephyr had been his only family when he had lost everything else—Evelina and the life he knew before. Saying goodbye to Zephyr made it feel real, like he truly would never see this camp again. His fleet. Evelina.

To save the realm, he had to lose it all.

It took everything inside of him to turn his back and walk away. A pain so intertwined with his own seared through their bond. His vision went black and he stumbled a step. He could feel her calling out to him, yanking desperately on their connection to get him to turn around.

She cried out, her whine soft and broken. He couldn't turn around, couldn't bear to look back. He walked out of the camp, and then deeper into the forest, until the day turned to night. There wasn't a specific direction he walked in, no entrance to seek out. But as midnight's darkness fell like a blanket over the sky, he sent a prayer of shadows to Vidaris. He could feel a tugging in his chest, pulling him where he needed to go.

His soul screamed to turn back, but he kept walking. Because if he didn't, he couldn't close the border. He couldn't give the empire a leg up in the war. And he couldn't give Evelina the one thing he had left to offer.

His love had no place to go, his body no recourse. All that was left to give was his very soul.

It was the Zenovia Mountains as they always had been, but something shifted. Like a curtain had been raised and he stepped into an in-between place, tucked into a plane that rested between the mountains and the Vale.

Daimon knew the role he was agreeing to step into. It was a position his father had groomed him for since he first met him in the sky. It was the future he had fought against that fate forced him into. It was a knife to the heart he knew he would never recover from, the wounds of fate everlasting.

As he stared into the eyes of death herself, he briefly thought about running away with Evelina. In another reality, he took her hand and led her into the unknown. The two of them would've braved untamed forests alone, seeking refuge in a house they built together, living off the land and in blissful happiness.

But that wasn't their reality.

Daimon never thought he would be the man to have a happy ending, and now he knew how right he had been. This darkness was always meant to take him.

He was in the goddess's domain now, her strength palpable. Her power had likely doubled since the last attack; there were so many deaths, so many souls fed straight to the Vale.

Screams wailed in the forest ahead of him, an off-tune chorus that grated against his ears. Shadows wound through the trees, followed by vague outlines of what looked to be people, before they disappeared.

He had never seen something like this in all his time in the mountains. All of this was closed off from the living, but Vidaris was lifting the veil for him now.

A chill ran down his spine. He was at the edge of the Shadow Realm.

"Are you ready to bind the deal?" Vidaris's sultry voice was thick with bloodlust, a companion to the greed in her eyes. "My brother Nyx did a wonderful job with you." She was encased in shadows crackling with energy and streaks of light—the same as the Furies.

Daimon raised his chin, grinding his teeth together as he held her gaze.

"I'm ready."

Her eyes flashed with delight, her hair floating around her in dark, wispy tendrils.

In the back of his mind, Daimon knew all along that fate would push him to this point—of having to decide if he would truly become Vidaris's puppet. A sword that felled the ghosts haunting the Shadow Realm, torturing souls and delivering them to her.

"I've been waiting for the one who could finally fulfill the role of Shadow Lord. A creature both god and fae, a foot in each world. It's time for you to bind your blood with mine and mine with yours," Vidaris said with a sharp curve of her lips. "Everything you are, everything you create, and anything that belongs to you will belong to me. This power you will be given is not a gift, but a trade for your life and all you own."

Vidaris held up her hand, her nails elongated into long sharp points. With a quick swipe, she sliced her finger across her palm. Black blood pooled up from the cut as she held it out to Daimon.

"A fate sealed with blood and bound by promise. Do you agree to serve your remaining days with me, son of Nyx, wielder of shadows and dreams, as my commander of darkness?" Vidaris asked, hunger in her dark eyes.

It was what Daimon had always avoided. But he could already feel his shadows pressing out across the realms of the living and dead, stronger than ever. Nyx was right; he could block the mountains with this power.

He nodded his head, holding his chin high.

She reached forward and snatched his wrist, pulling it toward her. With another quick swipe, she slashed her nails down his palm. He hissed at the sudden sting of it. She pressed her palm to his, their blood mixing.

A searing pain started in his hand, scorching a path up his arm and throughout the rest of his body. He could feel the oath searching every inch of his soul for his Essence, corrupting it, changing it, and turning it into something new entirely.

There was no going back.

PART THREE:

MERCILESS

SIXTY-SIX

EVELINA

SIXTY YEARS LATER

THE THRONE WAS COLD BENEATH EVELINA. HARD. No matter how she shifted, there was no comfort to be found in this seat—for sixty years, it had felt so rigid. Though she couldn't erase the pain of the life she had left behind, she tried her best to look forward. To plant a new seed of hope and wait for the day it would blossom inside her—watered by the promise of change.

Evelina felt it the moment Daimon gave his soul to Vidaris. It was a sharp pain that had started in her heart and radiated throughout her chest.

It still hadn't dulled—she wondered if it ever would.

Zephyr had arrived shortly thereafter without Daimon. She stayed close to the palace and hovered above whenever Evelina would step into the gardens.

But she couldn't bring herself to look up, to see the wyvern's saddle empty. Couldn't bring herself to accept Daimon's choice, as much as she imagined he struggled to accept hers.

It was too painful to think about.

She convinced everyone that he had died—if he had still been alive, Zephyr would've been with him. The Riders were the hardest to convince. But he was their commander, their family. Of course they wouldn't give up until they knew for certain.

But Evelina knew. Daimon didn't tell her he was going to become the Lord of Shadows, but she knew from the feeling in her chest, from the secrets he had shared with her. She could feel the loss of him across their soulbond—as if there were a string binding them together, and it had been abruptly cut in half.

Over time, she began to understand why, as the border naturally healed itself of conflict—he must have found a way to use his powers to block the border. He had saved the empire, and nobody could know. Her heart broke as she watched the faces of what was left of the Alpha Fleet grow solemn throughout the years. But Daimon had made his decision, and she would trust him. Protect him. No matter how much it killed her.

She prayed to the moon goddess that her people would have a reprieve from death, but things were far from over.

Years, then decades passed with few fae deaths as they slowly reclaimed what was once theirs. Evelina and Senna garnered more peace, securing more and more land beyond the mountains. Moros had become a ghost, retreating and hiding for the last twenty years, when suddenly, in a last-ditch effort, the unthinkable happened.

Moros used his hate and corrupted Essence to cast a curse along the Zenovia Mountains. No human should have been able to cast such a powerful curse, but Moros found a way. Surely, selling his soul to Vidaris and feeding her chaos, pain, and destruction in return.

There was no physical barrier to be seen, no shudder of darkness or warning that it had happened. Instead, fae became lost on the other side of the border, and those on the edge of the mountains were torn to pieces beneath the weight of the curse. They became lost souls, roaming the Shadow Realm.

At first, they didn't know what happened. Those on the border simply stopped returning for reports. Evelina and Senna had sent scouts to the mountains, only for them to return with word that everyone had disappeared.

It wasn't until they attempted to cross the border that they learned what had happened.

Every fae who attempted the crossing died instantly, suffering the same fate as their fallen comrades. People Evelina had known for years died as the land was split in two, fae on one side, humans on the other. The Valon Empire became two kingdoms—Crea and Penyth.

There were things she'd never forget.

Beautiful, innocent Lyria's dull, distant eyes as she was lowered into the grave beside her mother and siblings. Lyria had changed after losing the majority of her family, joining the front as a healer in Evelina's footsteps, right on the border. At first, Evelina was proud—before she realized her sister would never come back, caught in the shadows of Moros's curse as it spread through the mountains.

Aldric's gentle eyes glinting out from under thick pools of crimson blood—not only his. He was found under a pile of fae bodies. The look of devastation on Annora's face that never fully went away, even when she smiled. The way their child, Avery, seemed to know before it happened, tugging at Evelina's hem the day before and asking when her dad would be home.

"Soon," she had said, not knowing she was lying.

Wave after wave of loss, scouts uncovering new massacres every day as they trailed the wreckage along the mountains. Bodies piled so high that mass graves had to be dug. What had once been their new stronghold at the border became a graveyard.

Evelina slowly cracked beneath the weight of all the pain.

She honored them the only way she knew how. There was an empty fallow field behind the palace. She prepped its soil for two seasons, rebalancing the land until it was ready for new growth. At first, she planted a seed every time a loss was reported. But soon it was uncountable, leaving her to plant handfuls at a time, staining her nails with soil.

It grew into the largest garden in the entire realm. She didn't think she could take any more loss, her heart squeezing every time she looked out into the Remembrance Garden.

The curse separated her people, leaving behind the hope of reuniting fae and humans. With the border permanently sealed, there was peace, but no justice.

It was as if the war just paused, suspended in the air, hanging like an ax over Evelina's head. The wyverns, who were supposed to return to their rest at the end of the war, instead stayed by their Riders, as if they could smell impending doom. As much as her people yearned for this to be the end, it couldn't be over.

The need to make Moros pay for what he had done lived in Evelina's heart, even as her kingdom moved on—desperate for peace. She threw all her focus into finding him, into working with the Riders to hunt him down. They used the aerial fleets to search for him, flying as close to the border as they could, before the pull of the curse threatened to snatch their souls from their bodies.

After so long searching, many assumed Moros had died in his last cruel sacrifice to the shadows, and they moved forward. With so much to mourn, the fae instead rejoiced. For all the lives lost, the lands were healthy again; they had, in their minds, won the war.

Where before Evelina felt the decaying land over her body with endless sores and aches, she now felt lighter, less burdened. But there was a cold deep within she could never shake. No matter what people thought, she was certain Moros was still out there.

The curse left the darkness in Crea to fester, leaving Penyth closer to peace than they ever thought they would be. Flowers grew where bodies were buried; the scent of rotting flesh turned to fresh, dewy air.

Any remaining humans trickled out of the cities and hid

deep within the forest—or perhaps found some last portal magic to escape over to the newly formed Crea. Like them, Evelina yearned for a time everyone else was eager to leave behind. She could not rejoice in the separation of her people and everything they could not recover.

In her bones, the pain was gone. But in her heart, it only kept growing.

They had lost so much to Moros's games of power, and Vidaris's hand in aiding him. The many soldiers, civilians, fleets —her mother and siblings, friends and colleagues. Droves upon droves of bodies even an immortal could not fathom.

And Daimon. He had done so much to save them, forever bound to the Shadow Realm—an eternity for what only came to be twenty years of relative peace.

Sixty years flew by without a change to Evelina's golden complexion or in her heart. She blinked and summer froze into winter. She woke up one morning and realized winter had melted away into spring.

Daimon was her first and only love, but it was Senna who had been by her side. And as she saw little, lonely Avery grow up, Evelina held on to a secret wish.

One day, her heart couldn't contain it any longer. Snowy days melted into warm, sun-filled ones. Her sense of hope was slowly returning, even as her pain stayed nestled in the deep corners of her heart. The morning she decided to tell Senna she was ready to start a family, she found him sitting beneath the Mother Tree, flipping through pages of a novel. The room was quiet save for the handful of Woodland tending to the shelves.

"Senna," she whispered, her longing clear in her voice as she sat beside him.

He gave her his gentle attention as he always did, his warm brown eyes absorbing every layer of intention between them. "Yes, my queen?"

"I wish to have a child." She took a deep breath. "With you," she added, tears in her eyes. "My king. The one who has been by my side a thousand moons and more."

They both wanted a family, wanted to find a seed of hope in the darkness that surrounded them. Their friendship was strong. Immovable. And a part of them wondered if they could ever be more.

For a short time, they tried to be more. There was a love that she had never experienced between them. It was gentle, soft. The kind of love that made her feel warm and safe. It was what she dreamed of a marriage being. But beyond comfort and solace, they would always long for the love left behind. For the Riders their hearts still sang for.

But for all they had lost, it was enough. And in time, they found that they had already been blessed by Eurydice.

Finally, there was something to live for beyond duty or honor. For the first time since the shadows took Daimon, she felt that seed of hope begin to take root—and blossom.

SIXTY-SEVEN

DAIMON

THE DAYS BLED TOGETHER IN A HAZE OF CHAOS AND PAIN. Daimon's routine consisted of ushering souls through the Shadow Realm and into the Vale when Vidaris was ready for them. He had yet to step foot in the Vale—as his father had carefully instructed him to avoid it—but there was a connection between him and Vidaris nonetheless. The power inside of him tugged at his gut, pulling day and night to unite with the darkness of the Vale.

He couldn't get away from her. She was everywhere. She might have been caged within the Vale, but her darkness filled every inch of this wretched place. His tower of nightmares was a never-ending pit of decay, and he feared the day he stopped seeing it that way.

He had spent over sixty years trapped within the confines of the Shadow Realm, stuck within the empty walls of the obsidian palace. He was a king who ruled an empty court. To some, the king of the dead.

A tug at his chest had his feet pulling him out of his castle and into the forest. His connection to the Goddess of Vengeance gave him safe passage through the mountains, a place no breathing being could safely travel through without the goddess's permission.

These lands were an in-between, a foot in the living realm while the other was firmly planted in the Shadow Realm below. To feed the constantly rotating wheel of life and death, a being of both worlds was tasked with shoveling the lost souls into the layers of the Vale.

Daimon still didn't know much about what it was like in the Vale—though that was likely where his soul was headed one day. All he did was bring the lost souls to where the veil was at its thinnest, an icy black pit that rested at a cavern's edge through a wide tunnel. It was nestled next to the castle he slept in, leaving him with unfortunately easy access to it at all times.

A scream tore through the trees.

It took him weeks to get used to the sounds that came from the Wailing Woods, a thicket of twisted, rotting trees that surrounded the castle for several miles. Now he was numb to the constant stream of cries and pleas for help. Creatures from the Vale could slip into the Shadow Realm, torturing the souls that plagued these lands as their own personal toys.

It filled his days with a never-ending stream of helplessness, of snatching souls that were trapped there and bringing them to Vidaris. She liked for them to wait in the Shadow Realm, to feel decades of pain there while anticipating how much worse the Vale would be.

He didn't have a choice now. His shadows were wilder—more bloodthirsty. They would seek out the lost souls, eager to bring them pain and drag them to their fate.

It was all he did, day in and day out.

Except one thing.

Daimon had resigned to his fate the moment he prayed to Vidaris. But he still sought revenge against Moros—if anything, his bloodlust only grew. There was one night out of the year he could freely roam without Vidaris's watchful eye. It was the one night Eurydice's light would pierce the Shadow Realm, confining Vidaris to her domain. He learned a long time ago that there was no disobeying Vidaris on any night besides this one, with the scars on his soul to prove it.

But tonight was the Harvest Moon. Young fae would be taking their trials to gain immortality, sending a wave of pure Essence into the air. It chased away the shadows, if only for one night. The moment the moon became visible in the sky, he would lie down, letting his dreams carry him around the realm —and search.

He didn't let his thoughts wander to Evelina. Never to her. He couldn't bear to get a glimpse of her now, knowing he could never hope to be near her again.

Instead, he focused on looking for a way out, possibly even a way to sniff out Moros. Daimon could still feel the dull thrum of his weakened shadows. No matter how weak they might have gotten, it was still dark magic—and Daimon wanted revenge.

He needed a way to end Moros once and for all. More than that, he needed a weapon if he ever hoped to make a stand against Vidaris and escape from the Shadow Realm. There was only one weapon capable of that kind of power—the power to kill a god.

The sword of legend—Nightfall.

Daimon spent endless Harvest Moons seeking out his escape and his revenge. He split his time between the dream realm, searching for Moros, and the waking realm, searching for Night-fall. After searching for the blade for over fifty years, he had started to believe its existence was indeed a rumor.

But just when he began to doubt Nightfall existed at all, he felt it call to him from the farthest corner of the Shadow Realm, hidden beneath a tree.

The blade was bone-white, forged from a dragon's tooth, with the point dipped in blood so dark it was black—blood of a god was what the legend had always said. But he couldn't be sure. The hilt was solid black, its guards curled in like his shadows curled on the ends. The pommel was set with what looked to be a clear jewel to the average eye, rumored to be a fractured star plucked out of the sky and formed into an oval encased in a gold plate.

Daimon walked through the castle, eager to enter his dreams and search for Moros. He was still strong enough to hide beneath his darkness, making it far more difficult for Daimon to find him than he would've thought possible.

His boots clicked against the polished black floors and echoed off the matching black walls. The castle was completely empty, his and his alone. His tower of nightmares.

He lit a few candles in the corridors, if only to have a little less darkness surrounding him. It was constantly cold here—no warm summer mornings or breezy spring nights. An eternal harsh winter that always left him hollow.

His room was dark and damp when he got to it, but he didn't bother lighting any candles. There was only a bed and a small stand beside it, even though the room was massive. He didn't need anything else. No point in decorations or comfort.

It would never be home for him.

He lay down in bed, closing his eyes and slipping into the dream realm. Moros had enough power to veil himself from Daimon's dreamwalking, but it didn't stop him from searching.

His shadows took him to a cliffside on the coast of the mountains. It overlooked the Andronicus. The sea thrashed against a harsh wind, the Harvest Moon shining brightly down onto it. He wandered along the cliffside, letting his magic seep from him while he walked. His shadows hummed in anticipation. They tugged him further down the cliff, bringing him to a rocky shoreline.

He felt it then.

There was a darkness here, a heaviness that felt like death and decay. He walked closer to where the cliff now looked over him, finding a split in the rocks into which the sea fed.

He had no choice but to step in the water, the world around

him hazy through his dreamwalking. The water didn't ripple as he moved through it, his body floating as if he were a ghost.

Once inside, he knew why it felt different.

After sixty years of searching, he had finally found where Moros was hiding.

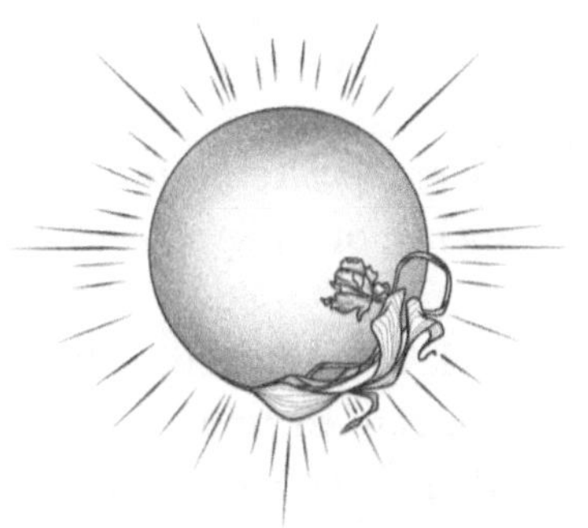

Sixty-Eight

Evelina

Evelina wrapped a protective hand around her swollen belly. "She's kicking!"

Senna spun around, eyes wide. He sprinted over to Evelina and placed his hands on her stomach. His face fell. "It always stops by the time I get here."

"Just give her a second," Evelina said with a laugh.

"How are you so confident it's a *her*?" He raised a brow.

"Because a mother knows." Evelina smiled.

The baby kicked swiftly against her stomach. It felt like an Aegis soldier practicing their swings against her insides.

Senna's eyes widened and he gasped. A smile spread across his face as she kicked again.

"Told you to just be patient," Evelina whispered. "Gloriana says she'll be here any day now, so she's getting restless."

He kissed her forehead and tucked her blankets tightly over her. "With the Harvest Moon tonight, we are surely blessed," he whispered. "It's no coincidence our heir will be born so close to the most sacred night of the year."

She smiled and gave him a peck on the cheek as she always did before he returned to his own chambers.

It took her well into the night to finally fall asleep. The baby was always in the worst position, pressing on her bladder, kicking against her organs, or begging for her to get up and eat something.

Evelina was happier, more hopeful. But her thoughts were still plagued with the desire to find Moros. She wanted a safe kingdom for her child and her people. She wanted to break the curse and reunite the Valon Empire. But she had to find Moros first. He had cast the curse, had stoked the rebellion into a fully-fledged war, leading them deeper into darkness. The war never felt truly over, not with the cold darkness she could still feel lurking deep within the land.

She opened her eyes, confused to find herself on a sandy shore instead of her bed. She was alone. Cliffs surrounded her on the right, the wild seas of the Andronicus on her left.

A cold breeze swept across her skin.

Her hand fell to her stomach, finding her belly as round as it was in the waking realm. It felt like each step she took was unusually slow, like wading through mud. Her breathing quickened and she began to panic. She had never been so lucid in her sleep—she was Woodland, not Nocturna. She had no magic when it came to dreams.

She spun in a circle, trying to get her bearings. It still *felt* like she was dreaming, only she didn't know how she came to be so aware. Up ahead, moonlight shined down on an opening in the cliffside. Its entrance wasn't on the sand, but in the sea. Her feet were drawn to it, moving before she could stop herself. The hair on the back of her neck stood on end and her heart pounded. Her magic flared in answer, her shield snapping into place as if it sensed danger ahead.

There was a darkness in that cave that she hadn't felt in a long time. Her palm burned and she hissed, looking down, seeing the mark of the soulbonded that she only found in her sleep. It flared pale white, radiating a soft glow.

She took a step back and slammed into something solid.

Something *moving.* She spun around, coming face to face with the stranger.

But it was no stranger—it was someone she never thought she would see again.

This really was a dream.

He wasn't the same as the last time she had seen him. Instead of wearing his Rider leathers, he was in all black. His eyes were dark, his nostrils flaring. And his face... He was staring at Evelina as if she were a ghost. His chest heaved.

"Daimon?" she gasped. She took a step toward him, pulled in as though by a gravitational force, and his gaze dropped down to her stomach. His eyes widened.

"Eve," he whispered. She drew in a sharp breath.

"*Daimon?*" she said again, wondering if perhaps this was a nightmare, her pain coming to haunt her. "You're here." She could see his body began to tremble, just as hers did. "You're in my dream?" she whispered, still in disbelief.

He nodded slowly. His eyes fell to her stomach again.

"Are you—" Her voice broke. She didn't know how to ask it. *Are you okay? Are you still...you?*

"Your light found a way to bring you here," he said quietly. He lifted his hand, palm outward. "And my shadows can only roam freely beneath the Harvest Moon."

She stilled, her questions abating. The Harvest Moon. When Eurydice's light shined on every corner of the realm.

Silence stretched between them. She wrapped a hand around her stomach and rubbed circles over it out of habit. She wanted to run to him, to pull him in close and be reminded of what it felt like to be in his arms.

But she didn't run to him. She could barely remember to breathe.

There was an emptiness in his eyes that hadn't been there before. Even as he eyed her stomach, they were distant.

She followed his gaze, an apology in her eyes. "I—"

"You have every right to move on." His voice was flat—

neutral. He took a step back, redirecting his focus. "Your light brought you here for a reason, just as my shadows did. There's a darkness here that needs to be destroyed." His eyes lacked their old warmth, instead full of bloodlust.

Evelina's heart was torn, half of her needing to figure out what he meant by that, and the other half desperate to speak with him about how she *hadn't* moved on. Not fully. A piece of her would always belong to him, the man who became the Lord of Shadows to save an empire that wrote him off as a deserter.

"Senna and I did try to move on. For a time, we did," she finally said, her voice soft.

Daimon clenched his jaw, and a flicker of pain flashed through his eyes.

If this was the only time she was going to see him, she would give him the truth. One last time.

"But our hearts already belonged to another," she continued. "We both lost our Rider during the war." She took a small step forward and his eyes widened.

"Senna—"

"And Keir," she finished quietly. "He didn't talk about it much, just as I couldn't bring myself to talk about you."

She could see his mind racing, trying to piece together his old friend's hidden feelings.

"Keir was always a private person," he gritted out, his voice thick with pain.

Evelina felt her own pain stab at her chest, the loss of Keir as fresh as the day he died. She never imagined her life turning out this way all those years ago. Being married to Senna, being queen. Losing Daimon…

Daimon cleared his throat. "Thank you for telling me."

She wanted to tell him so much more.

"I never thought I'd see you again," she whispered.

Daimon's bottom lip trembled and he looked away. Unable to stop herself, she walked to him and closed the space separating them. He looked down at her, his eyes suddenly giving way to emotions so clear that it startled her.

"It's really good to see you," he whispered.

She threw her arms around him—as best she could with her pregnancy at full-term. He bent down and buried his face in her neck.

They stayed like that for several breaths, holding each other and listening to the bugs sing.

She couldn't believe he was here, that he was *real*. That he felt just as he did in the waking realm, smelled just as she remembered. It was like experiencing euphoria and heartbreak at the same time. Like holding on to the sun, only to know she'd lose it when the night came. She didn't want to let go.

Daimon moved first, slowly peeling himself away from her and taking a step back.

"Daimon—"

He vanished. Evelina whirled around, finding herself entirely alone.

SIXTY-NINE

DAIMON

DAIMON AWOKE IN HIS EMPTY CASTLE. HIS HANDS WERE shaking and a tear had trailed down his face in his sleep.

Evelina was there. She was *there*.

He shook his head and pulled himself off his bed.

The Harvest Moon still hung high in the sky, but he wouldn't have long to get the dagger ready. He could feel the traitorous human king's shadows leaking from the cave like smoke from a fire. Vidaris had hidden Moros right under Daimon's nose, or at least let him weasel his way to the edge of the Shadow Realm, straddling the line between Penyth and Daimon's domain.

He needed to get to Moros and end this once and for all.

There was even more to fight for now, Evelina carrying a child of her own. He couldn't think of it now—the child wasn't *theirs*.

He stalked out of the castle and into the Wailing Woods to retrieve Nightfall. He knelt beneath a tall pine tree and began to dig. He pulled the damp soil apart until he felt a lump of cloth. It was caked in dirt, but still wound tightly around the dagger. He unrolled it and released a breath when he found the blade still inside.

It was warm when he wrapped his hand around the hilt. His magic sang in answer to its silent call. His shadows flared, whispering in his ear, begging him to use the blade on anyone who stepped into his path.

He took a deep breath, squeezing his eyes shut tightly. Reluctantly, his shadows withdrew into the depths of his soul.

It took him a moment to regain his bearings and open his eyes again. Slowly, he got to his feet and looked down at the weapon. The dragon bone gleamed in the moonlight; the tip of it sparkled where the black blood of an unknown being had melded into it.

Now all he needed was to take care of this final loose strand, and then maybe he could find a way out of this joyless place.

Daimon traveled on shadows and darkness to the edge of the Shadow Realm. He wished he could see Evelina, wished he was still dreaming. But he couldn't do this in his dreams, couldn't risk waking up or not getting to Moros.

He needed to draw Moros out of the cave. There were too many small holes and places to escape. He needed them out in the open. With nowhere to hide. He also had to be careful not to risk Vidaris somehow finding out, needed to draw Moros out and get him out of the Shadow Realm without Daimon himself stepping too far outside of it.

Daimon wrapped his shadows around himself until he was hidden. He slid into the cave, sticking close to the walls. If anyone looked his way, he could pass as a shadow cast by the gleam of moonlight.

He felt a heavy darkness at the mouth of the cave, and the deeper he ventured, the heavier it weighed on him.

It didn't surprise him when he found a small host of Furies with Moros.

Their *king* had gone into hiding, and so had they.

Daimon left his shadows concealing most of his features, but released them enough to get Moros's attention.

"Who are you?" Moros spat. "Show yourself."

He looked...*old.*

His skin was wrinkled and leathery, with deep circles beneath his eyes. He looked more like a decaying corpse than a living being. Daimon could still feel his dark magic, could feel how much stronger it was than the body that held it.

By all accounts, he should have been dead in human regard, already over a hundred years old. The toll this amount of magic was taking on his body might just kill him before Daimon got the chance.

Moros surrounded himself in darkness, wrapping himself in a shield of safety. Shadows billowed off the old king, spewing from his flesh and encasing him in a magic that reeked like a decaying body.

Daimon set his shadows loose on the cave, sending sharp rocks falling from the ceiling and tumbling down onto the rebels below. He backed away, slowly forcing them out of the cave as rocks fell. Moros shielded himself from being struck, as did the Furies. He couldn't kill them in here, but he could get them to come out.

Daimon taunted them, striking their bodies so they would follow.

Moros's face reddened with rage.

Daimon smiled. His plan was working.

Moros and his followers had been drawn out of his hiding place and were nearly to the edge now.

A screech filled the air. Daimon froze. He knew that sound. It was a wyvern. He had heard it a thousand times over the years, had fought with the beast's Rider just as long. The Alpha Fleet was here.

Moros heard the sound too, as did the Furies with him. He screamed in anger and turned around to retreat, but Daimon was behind them. Now, the Furies would have no choice but to run across the border into the fae lands, away from the safety of the curse that would trap souls inside.

Moros ran, slow in his old age.

Vero's wing crested over the cliffside first. His massive body came next, so fast there was nothing Daimon could do to stop it. Two more wyverns flanked Brielle and Vero—Aster and Willow atop them.

The three wyverns flew over him, their eyes fixed on Moros.

Daimon clothed himself deeper into his shadows, making it impossible for anyone to see him in the darkness.

Willow and Aster descended first, swooping down and using their magic together. Willow pulled any kind of nature she could from the forest's edge—large branches, clumps of soil filled with sharp rocks—while Aster called on the sea, surrounding the rebels with a torrent of water to try and drown them.

Brielle set Willow's projectiles on fire, and Aster made openings in the water for the fiery weapons to soar through.

Daimon couldn't see through the chaos, but he could feel his magic flare in answer. He took care of the five Furies with a single spear made of shadows. They rushed toward him and he sent the spear sideways. It tore through their throats one by one.

He ran after Moros. He got close enough that he caught Vero's eye. The beast turned its head and growled. Brielle looked over her shoulder, but he was still invisible to her.

A wave of sickening heat slammed into him; the familiar pulse of darkness that lived inside of him sang in answer. Moros was about to attack.

Alpha Fleet split their attention between Moros and the rebels, but they couldn't attack Moros. Not yet.

Daimon knew it wouldn't work—not with Moros's dark magic still coursing through him. They wouldn't be able to kill his body without severing his connection to the dark magic. It had to be both. Death to his magic as well as to his body.

They didn't know that. Didn't know just how deep his ties to Vidaris ran—but Daimon did. His shadows peeked a curious eye out near Vidaris, recognizing the likeness. Moros's darkness did the same.

Soldiers erupted from the forest, with Senna leading the charge. They outnumbered the rebels ten to one. Senna's group closed in on them quickly and the rebels started to panic.

Daimon crept closer, fighting against the pull in his chest that was yanking him back toward the Shadow Realm. He had to be careful, could only go so far outside of it. He kept his eye on Moros as he slowly withdrew his dagger, close enough to—

The ground beneath Daimon's feet trembled so hard he almost tripped. A sound pierced the air, like the high-pitched screech of a wyvern, but heavier. Deeper. Something he didn't think could leave the Shadow Realm.

Moonlight was blocked out as the massive creature flew overhead. It was shrouded in shadows, the edges of its wings blurry and hard to see in the night. But it was unmistakable.

A dragon had joined the fight. And it was answering to Moros.

SEVENTY

DAIMON

THE SOUND OF THE DRAGON ROARING MADE DAIMON SKID to a halt. The creature should not have been answering to Moros, and yet it was.

Another roar sounded and Daimon snapped into focus, his feet moving as he ran for Moros. This creature was three times the size of the wyverns—even Vero, who was the largest Daimon had ever seen. Not only that, but it breathed fire. No wyvern could do that.

Seeing the fleet made his chest tighten. On instinct, he searched for Zephyr, calling on their bond so they could join their unit. But the connection that tied him to his wyvern was empty—broken. Like the rope was there, but severed in the middle.

Senna was still on the ground with their army, slowly picking apart the remaining rebels. They had a vast quantity of soldiers with them, while Moros's numbers had dwindled to less than fifty.

Moros and the dragon shot into the sky, disappearing into the clouds. Vero took off after them, and Brielle shouted his name in panic. Aster and Willow immediately followed and they all disappeared within the clouds.

From the corner of his eye, Daimon saw the blur of light. His shadows stirred inside of him in response.

Evelina.

He could feel her magic, even though he couldn't see her. She was still here, safely tucked away in the dream realm.

The dragon roared, followed by the high-pierced shriek of a wyvern.

Daimon couldn't see a damned thing from the ground. He growled in frustration. He couldn't kill Moros if he was in the sky.

He watched as time suspended. The sky was dark—still.

A wyvern screamed in pain.

Light flashed through the clouds, a blazing stream of fire. It all happened so fast. The fire showed the outline of a wyvern in its crossfire, but the wyvern banked right just in time.

It went dark again, the fire dying out.

Daimon's heart pounded in his chest, his frustration growing.

In a flash, the dragon's fire illuminated the sky. Daimon watched the outline of its jaws close around the neck of a wyvern.

"No!" Daimon screamed at the same time a burst of light shot from beside him, barreling through the sky, aimed directly at the dragon clothed in shadows. For a moment, he saw the shimmering outline of Evelina, her cheeks streaked with tears.

He watched as her magic enveloped the creature and it thrashed, trying to hide from her. The dragon pulled back, retreating into the night sky, Moros with it.

Daimon strained to see where the dragon went, calculating how to track it down.

But then Moros was momentarily forgotten as a wyvern dropped through the clouds. It tumbled through the sky, belly up and wings folding around itself.

It was Vero.

Daimon watched in horror as he free-fell at a blinding speed.

The wyvern crashed into the ground, sand flying in all directions with the impact.

Daimon sprinted toward the wounded creature, his flesh prickling as if the Shadow Realm were attempting to peel it back, to hold him within it. But he kept going, knowing he was teetering on the edge of being too far outside of it. There was still a cloud of sand in the air, making it nearly impossible to see what was happening.

Silence followed as the shaking ceased.

Daimon coughed, using his shadows to clear the air. He froze once the sand settled.

Vero hadn't brought his wings in by mistake. He had fallen with Brielle tucked into his talons, his large, leathery wings cocooning her.

She rolled out of his talons, coughing and clutching her stomach.

"Vero." Brielle's voice shook. "Get up, V."

Vero didn't move.

Everything was still as Brielle approached her wyvern. She reached out a shaky palm and pressed it against Vero's scales. A sob broke from her chest and she fell to her knees. She clutched Vero's side, tears streaming down her face.

"No," Daimon breathed.

Brielle clawed at her chest, screaming, as if her heart had been torn out of her body.

Daimon kept his shadows wrapped tightly around him, but watching Brielle sob against her wyvern made him release them slowly.

A dark shadow passed over them and his head snapped up. He watched the dragon fly to the ground and land on the beach, unbothered, while Moros screamed. They landed on the edge of the border, the creature being pulled to the Shadow Realm just as Daimon was.

He needed to get to them before it was too late.

Daimon took off, back toward the border, his heart

clenching as Brielle's cries faded behind him. She hadn't seen him. It was easier that way.

The dragon screamed, shrinking away from something only it could see. It shook Moros off its back and took off into the night sky.

Wyverns were fiercely loyal, always putting their Rider first.

But dragons bowed to no master.

The beast left Moros. It had likely bent to the strength of his dark magic, but Moros never had any business calling on a creature of such esteem.

Daimon watched him double over with his hands bracing his knees.

"Moros," he hissed. He stood tall, his magic poised and ready to strike.

Moros whipped around, his chest heaving. When he saw Daimon, his face twisted into anger. Daimon drew Nightfall and smiled. He knew he had him—that this was all about to be over. He stalked toward him, his shadows shooting out to wrap around Moros so he couldn't move.

Moros's eyes widened when he saw the dagger. He struggled against the shadows, hissing as Daimon approached.

Daimon stopped in front of him and leaned in close. "You've harnessed a power that no human should." His voice was low. Dark. "You've led a rebellion that turned into a war that ended countless lives."

He could hear footsteps behind him. He glanced over his shoulder and found Senna running toward them, the rest of the group further down on the beach.

Moros opened his mouth, but Daimon didn't give him a chance to speak.

"You'll never hurt someone I love again."

He drove the dagger into his chest.

For Keir.

The knife sunk deeper and Moros's eyes widened.

For his fleet.

Daimon yanked the blade out and slashed it across Moros's face.

For Queen Embry, Carwyn, Ren, and Lyria.

Daimon felt his shadows flare with hunger at the taste of the blood they so often craved. He let them feast, drawing more and more pain out from behind Moros's eyes.

Senna stopped beside him, his chest heaving, as Moros dropped to the ground.

For the thousands of others who have died on both sides.

Darkness reached for Daimon, wrapping around him as Senna turned to him. His eyes widened.

"You're alive," Senna whispered. His gaze fell to Moros. "You did it."

Daimon slowly stepped back, the pull in his chest forcing him back as the sun began to crest the horizon.

"Daimon, you're *alive*," Senna repeated in disbelief. He lowered his blade. "You killed Moros."

"No," Daimon said quickly. "I didn't. No one can know I was here."

Senna's brows furrowed. "You'll return to a hero's homecoming. Evelina will—"

"You have to be the one." Daimon drew to the ground, dipping his hand to Moros's chest and coating it in his blood. Then he reached up and smeared it along Senna's blade. "You're the one who slayed him. Do this for me."

Senna shook his head, growing frustrated. "I cannot lie about such a thing."

"You must, for Evelina." Daimon wrapped himself in his shadows once more, securing the walls he was supposed to keep built. "Tell her that her happiness is all I've ever cared about."

No one could know Daimon was still alive. He was still bound to the Shadow Realm, and he couldn't risk anyone looking for him—especially his fleet. He knew them well enough to know they would try, but he also knew their efforts would be futile. He wouldn't be the reason anyone else lost their life. He still belonged to the shadows; deep down, he always knew that he would. No matter how hard he fought for redemption, there would always be a stain of darkness within him.

Valon soldiers were sprinting toward them. Daimon slowly backed away, over the border and into the Shadow Realm. The soldiers had their magic at the ready, but it dulled once they reached Senna and they saw the body and the blood on his sword. Before he could say a word, they praised Senna's name as the rebel slayer.

A shimmering light caught Daimon's eye, a flash of hazel eyes blinking up at him. He could hardly see her, but he could feel Evelina there.

"The sun is nearly up now," he said softly.

Her lips moved, but no sound came out.

He shook his head, and just before disappearing back into the darkness to which he was bound, grief rumbling in his throat, he said, "This time, Eve, I need you to wake up."

SEVENTY-ONE

EVELINA

EVELINA'S EYES SNAPPED OPEN.

She was staring up at soft green leaves, the sky beginning to lighten above. Everything that had happened in the dream replayed through her mind: the dragon enveloped in shadows running from her light; Vero dying and saving Brielle as they hit the ground; Daimon thrusting a dagger through Moros's chest.

Daimon had seen her, had told her to wake up. She tried to tell him she wasn't going, that she wanted to bring him back with her. But he couldn't hear her.

Her pulse raced. Was it just a dream? A nightmare?

"Evelina," Annora whispered.

She blinked, her mind still foggy.

"Moros is dead," Iris said slowly, snapping Evelina's attention to her surroundings. She turned to the Aegis council head, the woman's sharp cheekbones and piercing green eyes standing out in the dark forest. Dream orbs glowed around her, the twisted trees of Nox Grove curling over her.

She realized she wasn't alone. Annora helped Evelina to her feet and the entire council stared down at the dark orb in Annora's other hand.

"It's over," Seretha whispered.

The council watched Evelina closely. Evelina shook her head, trying to piece together what was happening.

"What are you all doing here?" Evelina breathed, putting a hand over her racing heart.

"Annora had a feeling you would be waking soon," Iris answered. "We moved you to Nox Grove."

Annora placed a hand over Evelina's. "I was tending to the grove when your dream orb…changed. When I looked closer, I saw Moros." She took a deep breath. "We were able to pinpoint where the dream was happening and sent reinforcements to where he was hiding."

Evelina's breath quickened. That was just a dream—a nightmare. "How are they there already?"

She had *just* awoken; they couldn't be at the coast already.

"You've been asleep half the night," Annora said softly. "They left hours ago."

It wasn't a dream. Everything she saw—Daimon, Moros, Senna… It was all real.

Suddenly, there was a flash of light. Then a loud *crack* followed, sounding as if it had split the ground open. The ground beneath their feet shook. Evelina reached out for Annora, and they clung to each other until the shaking subsided.

"What was that?" Annora breathed.

The council looked between themselves, a moment of fear passing through the grove.

"The temple." Seretha pointed to where the light came from. Evelina could see the tip of the temple poking through the trees.

They all rushed toward the temple, but Evelina froze after taking a few steps. She placed her hand on a tree to steady herself. She screamed as a tidal wave of pain tore through her. It felt as if her entire stomach was cramping, twisting tightly together and then releasing. Her hand flew to her stomach.

"You're in labor." Annora's voice trembled. "The baby is coming."

The pressure subsided and Evelina's eyes widened. "But

Senna isn't here. I can't—" Another wave shot through her body, and this time, it almost brought her to her knees.

Maliena appeared at her side, lifting her. "Get Gloriana to meet us at the temple," she said to Annora.

Evelina didn't have time to celebrate the death of Moros or to investigate what had happened to the temple. Her baby wasn't waiting any longer.

She cried out in pain.

A rush of liquid hit the ground at Evelina's feet.

"The baby is coming," Maliena said. "Now."

It wasn't until the next day that the baby arrived.

There were whispers of the child born the morning after the temple was struck. They'd arrived just after the flash of light and the quaking of the ground, finding new markings on the temple wall. Ellerry spent the entire night deciphering it, while the council waited at the palace. The temple priestesses all gathered, praying to Eurydice to bless the birth.

Senna made it back just before the baby came. Evelina reached for him, pulling his forehead against hers. He did as Gloriana instructed when the head began to crown. Evelina didn't know if the pain would ever end. But when she was finally holding her little girl in her arms, the memory of the pain melted away. She cried and laughed, her body drained from her labor.

"Queen Evelina," Gloriana said softly. "The council is arriving for the blessing."

There was no resting, even after just giving birth. A child's Essence would drift out of its body not long after it took its first breath. They would all rest later, but first, they had to bless the child's magic.

Gloriana stood and walked to the gate of the temple to meet them.

Evelina looked down at her little girl, at her perfect eyes as she stared up at her. She was so small, so fragile and innocent.

"Have you thought of a name?" Senna asked quietly when it was just the two of them.

Evelina smiled. "You know the tradition is to wait until after the ceremony."

The morning sun was warm and cast soft hues of purple across the sky. Shadows briefly flew across the grass. Evelina looked up, seeing wyverns flying above. But their Riders were no longer with them. They were all flying south together, back to where they came from with the threat of Moros gone.

It felt like a part of Evelina left with them; as if a piece of her soul was carried away on their wings. She watched as her old life disappeared into the clouds. She wasn't a healer in the war anymore, nor was she a princess who met her soldier beneath a waterfall for stolen kisses, making promises neither of them would keep.

Evelina smiled softly, her heart squeezing in her chest as happiness and sadness warred inside of her. Moros was dead. The war was officially over, and now her child was in the world, tucked within her father's arms. She had never felt so much joy and so much agony at the same time.

She wished Daimon was here.

Every new beginning felt like losing him all over again. But this time, she wasn't alone.

From the corner of her eye, she could see the council gather beside her and Senna. But she kept her eyes on her child and so did he.

She expected it—the council was always present when the Essence was blessed for a new heir. The Sacred came out of the temple, clothed in her usual robes. Still, Evelina glanced nervously at them, feeling exposed even as she lay in the grass fully covered.

"Hey," Senna said gently. "It's just you and me."

She tore her gaze from the council to focus on him. A gentle breeze picked up around them and the Sacred drifted closer as Senna handed the child back to her.

As soon as the sun peeked over the horizon, Evelina felt a surge of Essence buzz around her. She gasped as a small light emerged from the baby's chest. It hovered in the air between Senna and Evelina.

"Light for the Woodland mother and father," the Sacred said from in front of them. "May it return to which it came."

Slowly, the light separated into two. Evelina watched in fascination as one of the orbs floated toward her and the other to Senna. She felt the light wash over her as it passed through her chest, warming her body and making her whole. Senna shivered beside her and placed a hand over his chest.

The Sacred stepped closer and laid a single white rose at Evelina's feet. "You have chosen to have your child on the sacred grounds of Eurydice's temple," she declared. "Your child will be blessed for it."

A tear slipped down Evelina's cheek and she smiled down at the baby. "What do you think about Leda?" she said softly to Senna.

He reached for the baby's hand and watched as her tiny fingers curled around his finger. "Leda is perfect."

Evelina laughed, holding Leda tighter. "She is perfect."

"I believe I've deciphered the writing on the walls!" Ellerry sang as she skipped out of the temple. Her bright eyes widened, landing on the child. "Oh! A baby! We can wait until later to—"

"No," Evelina cut in. "What have you learned?"

Ellerry paused. Even the Sacred was waiting with wide eyes.

"Her mark is in her gift of light,
Her throne of wood and early morn'
Yet a savior she will never be—
Lest she's earned her crown of thorns."

The words settled heavily against Evelina's chest. Something tapped against her memory. *Her mark is in her gift of light.*

She'd heard that before.

"What does it mean?" Iris asked.

Everyone looked at Ellerry, who smiled. "A prophecy, of course."

A prophecy on the night of Moros's death, the night before Evelina's child was born. There were no coincidences.

The council immediately started to discuss potential meanings, but Evelina's focus quickly drifted away. It was too much—exhaustion was catching up. And she had had enough of fate for a lifetime.

The baby was sleeping peacefully in her arms. She felt her eyelids grow heavy.

"You need to sleep, Evelina," Senna said softly, reaching for the baby. "I'll watch her, but you should rest." He helped her to her feet.

The council fell silent as she stood. They all bowed, dropping to one knee before the new heir.

"What should we call her?" Ellerry asked.

Evelina looked at Senna, and he smiled.

"Leda," Evelina said. "Leda Manor."

PART FOUR:

SHATTERED HEARTS

SEVENTY-TWO

EVELINA

TWO-HUNDRED YEARS LATER

THEY LIVED NEARLY TWO HUNDRED HAPPY YEARS together as a family. The empire still faced small skirmishes from the last of the dark god worshippers, but their strength was greatly weakened as Vidaris's power receded in the years of peace.

Perhaps that was what led Evelina to get so comfortable—to not consider the risk when Senna asked for a chance to go to sea again with his old shipmates. He was a hero to the people, the slayer of Moros—and the greatest enemy of the last of the rebel fae, who had nothing left to lose. His ship was overrun by a rogue group of rebels, nearly killing everyone aboard. Only one survivor was left to bring back the news of the ferrum blade that was driven through Senna's heart.

Evelina had no words to experience the grief and guilt she felt. She should've been there. He was alone when he died, with her and their daughter a sea apart. Senna was her closest friend, someone who understood the pain she felt and the burden of ruling the realm.

Then he was gone—stolen in the dead of night while she

400

slept safely in the palace with Leda. It was almost too much to bear. How much more loss could she have weathered?

A queen without a king, a mother without her child's father. She had to learn how to be on her own again, for the sake of her daughter and her kingdom. In the hurt that followed her loss, Evelina set a law banning worship of the dark gods. The council readily agreed, as did the people of the realm. The twisted magic of those who worshiped the dark gods would never be welcome in her land again, not after the death and destruction it had caused during the war.

The centuries floated by like leaves drifting to the ground. Her once-broken empire had become prosperous, filled with people still learning to heal all these years later. She made sure she could be there for Leda without fail; the job of being a mother to her beautiful child always came before the crown. Evelina's heart was so full every time she looked at Leda and the woman she'd become throughout the years. Her thoughts were filled with ways to make the kingdom better, to keep Penyth fair and good.

But there were nights that were darker than the others—the stars covered by clouds—and she would find herself remembering a time when she wasn't so alone. She would replay the fading memories, holding on to them for as long as she could. Though she was certain she was already forgetting little details.

One night every year, she felt the ice around her heart thaw. In her dreams, she could see glimpses of Daimon on the Harvest Moon—flashes, like a tether still connected them. She felt him reaching out to her from the Shadow Realm, on the one night Vidaris was bound to the Vale. Evelina reached back to him, her light at its strongest. But still, the tether never held for long.

At first, she was lucky if she saw him at all. But over time, the connection seemed to grow. Now she could see him each year through a shrouded haze, though the connection was not yet strong enough for her to hear his voice when his lips moved.

The moment she saw him, she would awake in her bed,

covered in sweat and breathing heavily. She always tried to hold on to her dreams, to stay asleep beneath the Harvest Moon and talk to Daimon. It never lasted long enough for her to even hug him—to see if she could feel him.

It was the only night she allowed herself to sit in the grief that she kept stored away the rest of the year. But the loneliness she felt never faded.

She still wore a smile every day despite it.

But, as always, she wasn't entirely alone. She and Annora were closer than ever after the heartbreak they had experienced. Annora was the only one who understood what Evelina had lost, why Evelina hadn't moved on or taken another king. They told everyone it was because of losing Senna, and, in a way, it was. But it was more than that. She had never moved on from her first love. She and Annora had not just lost partners, but the very halves of their souls.

Annora's daughter, Avery, had grown alongside Leda. The two were polar opposites, but they worked well together. Leda was fierce—like an Aegis. She seemed determined to honor Senna in all that she did.

Much of the council remained the same, otherwise. Seretha married an Undine named Warrick who had spent time with Ren on the warfront. They had just had their first child—a little girl named Adeline—and Iris and Cyprian were due to have their first any day.

Evelina now spent most of her days in endless council meetings, sneaking in time in the garden or to watch over Leda's training. On rare days, she made it out toward Astern, visiting the refugee camp and making her rounds through what had become a small community. She would dress in her old healer's garb, not wanting to draw attention. A part of her yearned to only be a healer again, not the queen sneaking out of the palace.

There were only a handful of humans left now. Most had fled to the other side of the mountains even before the curse separated the land. But a few remained, lingering in the refugee camps. Their place in Penyth was difficult, earning little sympathy after Moros's rebellion.

After her visits, she would stop by a small gallery on the outskirts of Astern, resting between the town and the refugee camp. A small bell chimed on the door as Evelina entered the old shop. The floorboards were uneven oak splattered with paint. There was a small counter on her right by the window, along with a sign reading *Landscapes & Topography: Hand-painted Portraits of Penyth.*

Splashes of gold and emerald speckled the floor, while a wide range of portraits filled every inch of the walls. Some of them were set in simple wooden frames, but others had been mounted with frames of solid gold, intricately designed.

For years, Evelina had visited this shop in hopes of finding a painting that depicted a particular location. Every time she went in, she prayed to Eurydice this was the time she finally found it. Though the owner, Clara, tried to refuse her money, she still bought something each time she came.

"Queen Evelina," a light voice gasped. "An honor."

Evelina blinked away the haze in her mind and fell into an easy smile on instinct. She nodded. "Morning, Clara. Any new pieces today?"

Clara beamed at the question. Her strawberry-colored hair was braided behind her back, and the light freckles covering her face had darkened with the summer sun.

"A few just arrived—haven't even unpacked them in the back yet." Clara gestured for Evelina to follow as she pushed open an aqua-colored door, revealing a dimly lit room full of paintings covered in cloth, leaning against a wall. "Forgive the mess, Queen Evelina. Stay here as long as you'd like and just give a shout if you need any help. My courier will be unloading some new pieces in the next few minutes, so don't mind him."

"Thank you, Clara," Evelina said as she stepped into the room.

Clara smiled brightly and closed the door behind her.

Evelina reached out to remove the cloth from the first one. It was a beautiful depiction of the Mother Tree, artistically drawn with black lines.

The door banged open, the noise jolting her.

A man came in with a crate full of wrapped paintings, sweat rolling down his temples. He didn't notice Evelina at first, the paintings covering most of his face as he walked to the center of the room.

"Is that the last of it?" she asked softly.

He jumped, the crate tumbling forward. Evelina rushed toward him and caught the paintings before they spilled onto the floor.

"That would've set me back a few months." The man laughed—still holding the other end—and peered around the side. "Thanks, miss—"

His words died in his throat as he took Evelina in. She smiled, watching as the realization washed over his face.

The man quickly rebalanced the crate and set it on the floor. He dusted his hands off on his tweed pants. He was fairly young, and couldn't have been older than twenty-five or thirty. He was handsome, with a slender frame, dark hair, and...round ears. Evelina's eyes widened.

He was tall for a human, and if his hair were a tad longer to cover his ears, she could've easily mistaken him for fae.

He cleared his throat, his demeanor changing instantly. "Queen Evelina," he said with a quick bow, keeping his eyes fixed on the ground. He spun on his heel, nearly tripping over his own feet.

"Wait," she called out. She didn't know why she said it. "Do you live here?"

His back was still to her and he didn't seem too keen on turning around. Hesitantly, he angled himself toward her. "In the refugee camp," he said softly. His hands trembled.

Evelina had been here countless times and had never seen him. But as she looked down at the paintings, she recognized the style; she had seen it more and more over the past few years. All of them were signed with the same looping cursive letters, *R.R.*

She hummed, and an awkward silence filled the space between them. "Do you know the painter?"

"A seller I deliver for, Queen Evelina." He tucked his hands behind his back, but not before she saw streaks of paint covering them. His brows were pulled together, and he swallowed thickly.

"May I?" she asked gently.

Without waiting for an answer, she crouched down to the crate and began looking through it. There was more black-lined art, all with harsh streaks across the canvas and no color. She could feel his eyes on her, but she continued to silently look through each painting.

This man looked so much like a young human gardener she once knew. His smile was more hesitant, but he had the same nose as Ian, the same eyes.

The memory of the humans leaving this side of the mountains haunted her. Of all the things that happened leading up to the moment the rebellion formed and the things the crown could've done differently to avoid it.

She couldn't blame the humans entirely—not even Moros himself. Everyone involved played a part in the empire crumbling.

This man seemed…scared of her. Like he couldn't wait to get away. It broke her heart.

"I'll take them all," she said without looking up.

The man inhaled sharply. "You'll *what?*" he breathed. He took a step back and shook his head.

"Of course, if you don't wish to, then you could just take the money and sell elsewhere." She smiled.

After looking between the paintings and Evelina at least four times, he finally regained his composure enough to speak again. "I don't need charity," he said harshly.

But his eyes told a different story. They didn't match his

sharp tone because they were filled with tears. Evelina's heart broke at seeing him so affected by selling a crate of paintings.

He spun around toward the door and angrily wiped away a tear, taking several deep breaths. When he turned back toward her, he wasn't looking at her with as much anger. He stuck his hand out to help her stand up.

"Lawrence." He cleared his throat. "My name is Lawrence."

"Nice to meet you, Lawrence," said Evelina softly. "I'm Evelina."

He stood incredibly still. She wasn't sure what possessed her to treat him as a friend rather than a subject. Perhaps she felt guilty for all he had lost in her reign.

He nodded his head sharply. "I'll deliver the paintings to the palace later this week."

SEVENTY-THREE

DAIMON

THE SOUND OF WINGS BEATING AGAINST THE SKY accompanied the cries of agony. Wings soared over the tree line. Daimon only caught a glimpse of its spiked tail, so large that it could clear ten trees in one fell swoop.

Dragons. One of the deadliest creatures of the Shadow Realm.

Daimon's chest ached as he thought about Zephyr—his companion and just as much a friend as any other fae. Even after all this time, the pain of losing her still felt like an open wound that hadn't closed. He didn't see dragons often, only a handful of times since the night Moros died.

A shrill cry pulled his thoughts back to his current task. He followed the tug on his chest leading him through the woods, toward the soul he was about to pluck out of the Wailing Woods.

"Please!" a woman pleaded. "Please, help me."

She was like every other soul here; she looked and sounded like any living fae, but the moment she reached out to grip his arm, it went straight through him.

Her eyes widened and she screamed again. "What's happening to me?"

He tried to be sympathetic—he really did. But listening to the same question for over two centuries made it hard to find pity. Especially knowing that they weren't entirely innocent, otherwise they would be in the peaceful fields of Caelum.

Instead of trying to explain what was happening—like he tried doing the first ten years after Moros died, before he finally gave up—he called on his shadows. They were just going to scream either way.

The shadows wound around the woman, binding her hands together and snaking up her arms. Daimon turned his back as she continued shrieking at the top of her lungs, pleading for him to let her go. But it was too late for her now; her fate was already sealed. He was about to deliver her to the Goddess of Vengeance.

As they walked through the woods, he no longer battled against his guilt or searched for an escape. Instead, he wondered, *What layer of the Vale will this one go to?*

There had always been stories about the layers of the Vale, how the somewhat tainted souls were right on top—still miserable, but less…tortured—while several layers down were for murderers and thieves, a place of pure agony.

She begged him to stop the entire journey to the Vale's entrance, but the words drifted through him as easily as her hand had. Even as his shadows brought her to the end of the cavern, he ignored her cries.

As he watched the invisible wind suck her into the darkness, he felt the great void in his soul. The one that had once been his, and, in a life he could barely remember, Evelina's too.

SEVENTY-FOUR

EVELINA

EVELINA VISITED CLARA EVERY WEEK AFTER THAT, BUYING several of the portraits Lawrence had delivered and hanging them in an art room in the palace.

One of Clara's workers delivered the paintings, a Woodland with a soft smile and hair that brushed his shoulders. It didn't surprise Evelina that Lawrence arranged for someone else to deliver them, not with how afraid he looked in her presence.

The bell on top of the shop door dinged as Evelina entered.

"He's in the back," Clara called out from behind the counter.

Evelina nodded her thanks, walking on the paint-splattered floors all the way to the back storage room. She rifled through the paintings, waiting.

Lawrence walked in with a crate. "You know, you could always commission a painting."

Evelina looked up, her brow furrowing.

"Instead of digging through the backroom every time," he said, almost teasing. "You can just ask for what you want, and I'm sure the painter would be open to your suggestions."

Her heart thrummed. She had, of course, considered it before, but it felt intimate—like she was revealing too much of herself by asking for it.

"There's a waterfall near the border," she said without looking up. "A place I used to visit during the war."

Lawrence hummed. "The painter usually doesn't go that far, but if you describe it for me, I can pass it along."

She smiled as she described the waterfall that flowed into a small pond. She remembered every detail she could: how it was nestled behind the old war camp, the rocks that rose high around it, the trees that hung over the edges with the conelike fruits used for cleansing hair.

Lawrence nodded his head and promised to pass the message along to the painter. She had an inkling that the *painter* was actually him—based on his paint-streaked hands and the way his eyes lit up discussing the art.

But if he signed his paintings as someone else, she wouldn't press it.

Still, she had come to enjoy spending time with him. He was someone she could be friends with, and that was something she very much missed. Even if he was still a little shy around the fae queen, she could sense him warming up.

That is, until he didn't show up the next week—or the week after that.

"Said he needed a break," was all Clara said.

Evelina grew restless when the weeks turned into a month. She even searched the refugee camp nearby on her next visit, worried something had happened to him. When she asked around for Lawrence, people shrugged, saying they hadn't seen him.

She started to get more and more worried until one morning, her maid, Lila, came into her room holding something wrapped in thick parchment.

"This was left for you," Lila said brightly. "A note is attached to the back of it." She smiled and slipped out of the room.

Evelina stood, still in her night robes, and walked over to the rectangular package. She flipped it over, grabbing the note.

. . .

Dear Queen Evelina,
    I hope it is the way you imagined it to be.
Sincerely,
R.R.

She gasped and dropped the note. Carefully, she ripped the parchment off.

Tears gathered in her eyes. It was *just* as she had remembered it. The painter had even chosen to depict it at night, with a crescent moon in the sky and little stars dotting the upper portion.

It was the same place she had learned about Daimon's bloodline and his reason for leaving when they were younger. The place she had finally let her guard down and let him in.

She smiled. It was perfect.

Evelina changed into a simple pale blue gown, glancing at the painting every few seconds. She couldn't look away.

Even as she floated to the throne room to meet Leda, Annora, and Ellerry, she thought about it. They discussed the upcoming Harvest Moon trial happening in a couple of months, but her mind drifted back to the painting that sat in her room. The trial was the same every year, though Leda seemed intent on making it more perfect than the last.

As they wrapped up the meeting, Annora turned to Evelina. "Isn't that good news, Eve? Iris had her firstborn this morning. A boy."

Evelina recovered quickly and smiled. "He came late."

"Seems he'll be stubborn," Leda muttered. "They named him Graylen. Odd name."

Annora smiled from across the table. "A strong name."

"He'll need to be strong with a mother like Iris," Evelina said with a small laugh.

They closed the meeting, slowly peeling off. Evelina stayed

behind a little longer, still deep in her thoughts.

"Queen Evelina," Lila said breathlessly, bursting into the throne room. "A human was found at the entrance of the palace, passed out. I think he's the same one who delivered your painting earlier. He's been taken to the infirmary."

Evelina shot to her feet. Her heart raced as Lila walked with her to the old infirmary. It was far less busy since the war ended, but still had its uses. She often had weekly tea there with Gloriana.

"I just called for Gloriana," Lila said as they approached the room.

"No need." Evelina pushed the door open. "I'll call on her if I need her assistance."

Lila bowed her head and Evelina thanked her, closing the door behind her.

Lawrence was lying on a cot, his brows drawn together and tears brimming in his bruised eyes. His bottom lip was swollen and cut, and he was clutching his side.

"What happened?" she gasped.

He flinched, as if the sound of her voice was too loud, even though she was speaking softly. "It'll heal." His throat was scratchy and his words came out as more of a groan. "I just need a moment."

He clearly needed *more* than a moment to rest.

"This needs to be taken care of," she said firmly, her voice in full healer mode. "A bandage to stop the bleeding, possibly even a few stitches."

Evelina didn't give him time to answer. She made quick work of rummaging around the shelves and grabbing a handful of different vials. They clinked together as she dumped them onto the worktable. She slid over a small granite bowl and measured out a teaspoon of feverfew, half a tablespoon of goldenseal, and a full tablespoon of withania. She ground them together until they were a powder, feeling an ache deep in her bones. She had almost forgotten how much she loved to do this.

"Still with me?" She glanced over her shoulder.

He nodded, silently watching her. "How do you know how to do this?"

"I learned when I was younger," she answered with a shrug. She turned around to dump the powder into a tub of linndula root—more of a slime than a root—and mixed it into the cleansing salve. "I'll need you to roll onto your side." She walked over with her hands full of supplies. "And I'm afraid we'll need to get you a new shirt."

He shot her a look, his cheeks reddening.

"I'll be quick," she promised. "I just need to make sure the salve sits undisturbed for a few minutes before we cover it."

Lawrence nodded and carefully peeled off his shirt. He hissed as he stretched his arms over his head, but was able to get it off and roll onto his side.

Evelina was swift—clinical. Her hands moved as if she still did this every day. Just looking at him, she could tell he had a fever, which meant she needed to work quickly.

"This might sting at first, but it should lessen the pain and help break your fever." She smeared a spoonful onto the gash on his side as an odd sense of nostalgia washed over her. The last time she'd done this…

The memory of Alpha Fleet slammed into her so hard she had to take several deep breaths. Of doing this for Daimon after thinking she had lost him during a battle with the rebels.

Lawrence looked up at her, his eyes vulnerable and open. "Thank you," he whispered. "For helping me."

She frowned, wishing more than anything that he didn't have to live in such fear.

"Did this happen while you were delivering the painting?" she whispered.

He remained silent, which was answer enough. She continued rubbing in the salve and he flinched as she touched the open wound.

"Tell me something," she said. When his eyes flared with

fear, she explained, "To distract you from what we're doing." She had used this with countless soldiers and refugees, finding that if they focused on something else, it would help with the pain. She didn't expect much, but to her surprise, Lawrence sat up. He winced as she stitched up his wound.

"I don't have anything to share, really. My parents died when I was fifteen." His gaze fell. "I've been alone ever since."

"Mine died long ago," Evelina whispered. "The pain of losing someone you love never truly lessens."

He nodded slowly. "My father's father and his father before him all lived in the refugee camp. In a small green cottage."

"It overlooks the glade," she said, her eyes lighting up in recognition. "With the two rocking chairs on its porch."

He smiled, nodding. He continued telling her about how Clara had spotted a painting he had sold to someone in the refugee camp. When she learned he was human, she didn't seem to care.

"And you decided to sell your paintings," Evelina said, a smile on her face. "I'm glad."

Lawrence's eyes widened, startling and sitting up, but she pressed him gently down.

"I know you're R.R. I promise not to tell."

His eyes softened, his body relaxing. "I almost told Clara no when she first asked. She lets me use the back of the shop so I don't have to be seen. We pretend I'm just the courier in case anybody…"

He didn't have to say it. There were plenty of fae who would shun his work if they knew it was created by a human. Some might even burn it.

"I'm sorry for the way fae have treated you," she said honestly.

"I've never been one to have friends." He shrugged, trying to look unbothered. But she could see the pain in his eyes. The loneliness.

It was the kind of loneliness no one should have to experience. She hated the way the realm was still divided, the way the curse left a permanent reminder of the land being broken into two.

"Well, now you have a one." She smiled and so did he.

Slowly, Lawrence came to the palace more and more. He and Evelina spent months together in the gallery room and he would bring a painting or two each time.

The room was empty save for the paintings on the walls and a lounge chaise in the center. She would come and sit in here, staring at the paintings of the realm's landscapes for hours.

Lawrence stood with his back to her, looking at the section of R.R. paintings she had hung up.

"I painted this one in a meadow by the southern coast," he said quietly.

"I love your landscapes," said Evelina. "But have you ever considered portraits?"

He paused, considering. She was almost certain he was going to deny her, but then he said, "For a friend, I'm open to suggestions."

Evelina beamed. "Then be my official royal portraitist."

At this, he looked at her, his eyes wide. "Is that even a real position?"

She laughed. "No, but that's the benefit of being queen." Her smile faded when she realized he didn't believe her.

"I...can't," he said. "The fae would never accept—"

"I accept you, Lawrence. The realm will one day do the same," she said gently. His eyes softened, a hopeful look in them. "So, what do you say?"

He nodded, his gaze determined. "It would be my honor."

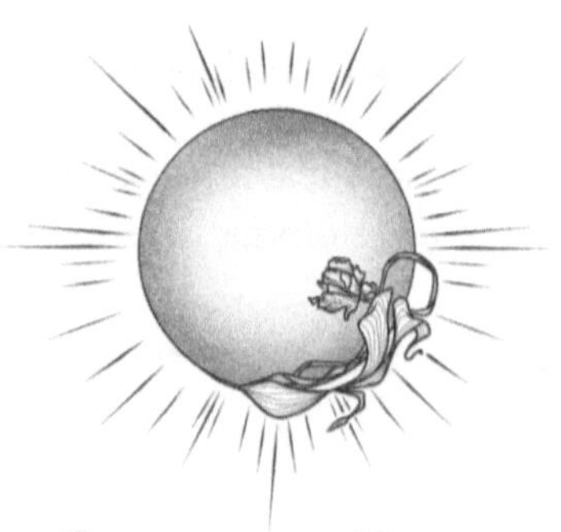

Seventy-Five

Evelina

The entire palace was quiet, even though the sun was high in the sky. It would typically be bustling with life by now. But that was how each celebration before the trial went: a twenty-four-hour long party, resulting in fae sleeping the entire next day, only to wake up just in time to either take the trial or anxiously await the return of someone they knew taking it.

It was the reason Evelina was able to escape to the Radix Room tonight. She brought the painting standing guard at the entrance a crystalized rock she had found in Astern. Only those who brought a gift to her would be let into the room with the Mother Tree. Evelina had been doing it for so long that she knew just the kind of trinkets the painting would like.

"This is from beside the Syreni castle," she whispered, holding it out.

The woman in the painting opened an eye and peeked out. The painting shifted as the woman leaned forward and plucked the rock from Evelina's hand. She settled back into place and clutched the rock to her chest.

Slowly, the door to the Radix Room appeared behind thick, moving vines. Evelina pushed it open, breathing in the smell of the thousands of books stacked on the shelves.

The Radix Room was warm and quiet, the beauty of the Mother Tree on full display. It allowed her to feel more connected with the land, with the roots that ran to the farthest corners of the kingdom. There was a time when the roots stretched to the other end of the continent, but after the curse, she wasn't able to feel anything beyond the Zenovia Mountains anymore.

Still, the room was bursting with magic, giving her the evening to herself. Ellerry was out prepping for the trial, along with Annora and the other Nox that helped. It made the Radix Room the emptiest place to be. Tonight, she wanted to be alone.

Evelina quickly scaled the Mother Tree, eager to rest and recharge her Essence. Once she reached the small bench that hung in the branches, she smiled.

She shivered as she settled on the bench, laying down on her back and closing her eyes. The room felt brighter than usual with the Harvest Moon streaming in through the tall windows.

She fell asleep, hoping she would see a glimpse of Daimon in her dreams, if only for a second.

Evelina blinked open her eyes, still in the Radix Room, though now it was dark. She leapt onto one of the thick branches, twisting around.

A soft, warm glow flickered on the ground through the leaves.

She descended, curious. When her feet hit the ground, she gasped. The Radix Room had shifted. The Mother Tree was the same, but the library was now smaller—more intimate.

Instead of a plain wall of books, a fireplace crackled with flames by the back window. Evelina hesitantly walked over to the pile of blankets and pillows resting in front of it. Books still lined the shelves, their leather scent wrapping around her senses.

It felt like a dream.

But she couldn't be dreaming. The last time she was this aware in her dreams—

A flash of light lit up the room, followed by a crackle of thunder.

She walked over to the window, watching as rain poured from the clouds. The pattering sounds of drops tapping against the glass covered her jagged breaths. Her legs began to tremble as her mind finally caught up to what was happening.

Her palm burned and she hissed, looking down at it. Her soulbond scar was glowing white.

"Eve?" a deep voice rumbled, as dark as the thunder outside.

She spun around, a flash of lightning brightening the room and illuminating the man in front of her.

"Daimon," she breathed. He smiled, his eyes wide and as surprised as she felt. "I can hear you—I can *see* you." She gasped, her feet frozen in place.

The candlelight illuminated his skin, making him glow.

His face was just like she remembered it, his eyes still the midnight blue she wanted to get lost in, his lips still curled up at the edges. His hair was still dark and falling into his eyes, but it was shorter than it had been; it didn't curl at the nape of his neck anymore.

She could even smell the familiar scent of frost and cedar lingering around him, something she never thought she would get to smell again, wishing she could bottle it up and bring it home with her. He wore a black cotton shirt that buttoned down the middle, and black trousers that clung to his thighs.

It was him; it was well and truly him. So different from the glimpses she had caught of him during Harvest Moons past. It didn't make sense why he was suddenly so clear.

But she didn't care why—all she cared about was that he was *here.*

Her feet were still frozen in place, her body failing to catch up with her thoughts as she stared at him, her mouth agape. Her hands trembled as she took a small step toward him. She found him doing the same, both afraid that it was too good to be true.

"Have I been blessed by the Divine enough that it's you?" he whispered. "Or are you just a mirage haunting my memories?"

Slowly, he walked toward her and stopped an arm's length away.

"It's me." She swallowed.

He lifted his hands toward her—fingers trembling. He paused just before he touched her, as if afraid she wouldn't be real. Or, perhaps, afraid she *was* real.

His hands slid onto her face, cupping her cheeks.

They both drew in a sharp breath. She could *feel* his skin against hers. He was colder than she last remembered, but it was still him. Still her Daimon.

His eyes glistened as they stared at each other in quiet disbelief.

"It feels so real," Evelina breathed. "You can't be real."

"If it can't be real," he murmured, "then dream with me, Eve."

She buried her nose in the side of his neck, breathing him in.

"Evelina," he sighed against her, peppering the top of her head with kisses.

She looked up at him, her eyes wide and filled with tears.

He dropped his forehead to hers. Her pulse began to race and panic clawed its way up her throat. She had done it so long without him—had learned to be okay sitting in her constant pain. So much so that she had forgotten what it felt like to not feel it.

But now he was here, even if only in her dreams. She could still touch him, still hear his voice. It cracked her chest wide open, breaking down the walls she had built and exposing her bleeding heart.

"I'm scared we're going to wake up." Her voice broke. "You're *here*. How can I go back to my life without you?"

He sighed and shook his head. "I'll always be with you, Eve." He placed his hand over her heart. "Always."

She shuddered beneath his touch. She had forgotten what it felt like to be loved in this way, to be loved so completely and without restraint. There was so much she didn't realize had faded from her memories through the years: the feel of his skin against hers, the smell of cedar and frost that clung to him, and even the way he looked at her—with unbridled love.

A slow smile spread across his face as he lowered his mouth to meet hers. He pressed a gentle kiss against her lips and her legs nearly gave out.

He wrapped his arms around her waist, holding her so close she could hardly breathe. He walked them across the room, murmuring praise into her ear the entire way.

She felt something solid press against her back. Finally, she collected herself enough to pull back and look at him. His eyes were desperate—the sight of it matched the painful ache she felt in her heart.

She realized she was against the Mother Tree, the bark snagging her dress. The fire blazed behind Daimon, though his face was cast in shadow, dark enough that she could hardly see him. Her hands slid over his shoulders, pulling him closer.

"I think I've forgotten what it feels like to be held by you." She stared at him, desperate to drink him in.

They were both different now. She had become the queen of Penyth, and he was the king of the dead. They weren't the same as they were during the war. She was no longer a healer convinced she could save everyone, and he wasn't a soldier spending his days flying with his wyvern.

She was younger then, more fragile. They both had lost a piece of themselves when she became queen and he surrendered himself to Vidaris. But they did it to save their realm.

She didn't want to be reminded of that night, of that pain. She just wanted him.

"How are we here?" she whispered against his lips. She leaned back and cupped his cheeks, her eyes bouncing between his.

Year-round, she played the role of the perfect queen. But tonight, she allowed herself to be a woman again, to feel need and desire—to want what she wanted without needing to think of the kingdom.

"Show me that this is real," she pleaded.

His mouth pressed against hers, causing heat to pool low in her stomach. She met every slow, torturous kiss until it became something more—something needy. She kissed him faster, as if he was going to slip through her fingers at any moment.

His hand slid to her thigh and he began to bunch the fabric of her gown. She reached down to help him pull it off, wanting him to move faster, but Daimon broke off the kiss, grabbing both her hands. He pinned them above her head, her wrists digging into the bark. She leaned forward to kiss him again, but he held her firmly against the tree.

"Stay still and leave your hands there," he said as he held her gaze.

Her breath caught.

He released his grip on her wrists and continued to slowly peel off her dress, taking his time as he pulled it over her hips, her waist. He didn't stop kissing her until he had to, and the moment the dress was off entirely, he brought his lips to hers again.

He stepped back and watched her with a primal gleam in his eyes. She squirmed beneath his gaze as she stood naked before him.

"As beautiful as the day I last saw you," he whispered.

She started to lower her arms from where she still held them above her head, but the moment she moved, something wrapped around her wrists.

"I asked you to stay still," he growled.

Her body filled with warmth and her eyes widened.

Shadows coiled around her body, slithering up her thighs and over her hips. They were cool against her skin, light and teasing. She whimpered as one grazed her nipple.

The shadows continued their ascent up her body and paused at her neck. Her breath quickened as a shadowy strand wrapped around her throat. Another strand continued upward, twisting around her arms until it stopped at her wrists.

"Daimon," she begged.

A slow smile stretched across his face, admiring his work.

"Should I bring you paints to make a portrait," said Evelina, huffing, "or are you actually going to touch me?"

But her words weakened as he stalked toward her.

Without a word, he slowly removed his shirt. Her eyes immediately fell to the scars that plagued his chest—they told stories of the pain he had endured. She wanted to kiss every scar until she replaced the memories with new ones.

He unbuttoned his pants and pushed them off, bringing her gaze to the knife tattooed across his hip. His shadows danced around her, caressing her skin as she struggled against the bindings still holding her hands above her head. He pulled her legs up around his waist, positioning himself against her and pushing in.

"Daimon," she gasped. Tension built inside of her, her body drinking in the delicious feel of him inside of her. The shadow around her neck pulled tighter, and he chased every gasp that came out of her mouth. She met every kiss, every stroke of his tongue against hers with equal urgency. Every moan, every gasp, pushed them closer to the edge.

"You are mine, Evelina," he rasped.

She screamed as the pressure between her thighs reached a tipping point, her vision blurring and body tightening. He groaned with her and gripped her waist, following her over the edge.

But she wasn't ready for it to be over yet. She needed more.

He pulled back, silently reading her needs. Her arms suddenly dropped, and he stilled inside of her.

"This won't be the only time you come for me tonight," he said with a smile.

She was lifted off the tree, and he walked them over to the window, the rain still pounding against the pane. He set her feet on the ground and spun her around. Her palms met cold glass as she pressed her hands to it. Thunder splintered across the sky, so loud that it rattled the glass beneath her palms.

Desperation washed over her, needy and breathless. She wanted to remember every second spent with him, every touch of his hands and kiss of his lips. She watched as streaks of lightning spread through the clouds like a splintering web.

The moment she inhaled, he pushed into her again. Their breathing was jagged and quick, full of longing as the reminder sunk in that this was just a dream, that they might never see each other again.

As they fell over the edge together once more, he pulled her close to him, turning her back around.

They pressed their foreheads together, their breath melding. He reached for her hand, pressing his palm against hers—scar to scar.

"Even if the lands die, my love will remain for you." It was a vow from him, a promise. "Until the stars collide and these wretched lands implode, my love will not falter."

SEVENTY-SIX

DAIMON

DAIMON COULDN'T BELIEVE HE WAS HERE WITH EVELINA. Vidaris might have tried taking everything from him, but she couldn't have this.

He held Evelina in front of the fire, a fuzzy blanket draped across her body as she lay on top of him. He never thought the day would come when he got to see her like this again, see her crinkle her nose when she thought too hard. She was the only thing tethering him to something good. The few glimpses he'd had of her on Harvest Moons had been the only thing keeping his head above water, reminding him there was someone who still cared about him.

His days were filled with darkness, and with every passing moment he could feel himself slipping closer to stepping into the Vale and fully giving himself over to Vidaris—if only to dull the pain. No matter how good he felt now, at the end of the night, he would have to go back to the darkness from which he came.

He shook his head. He wouldn't taint the one night he had with Evelina with such thoughts.

"I wish you were here," Evelina whispered. "*Really* here. I know you're suffering, Daimon. I can see it in your eyes."

Daimon sighed and looked away from her, his gaze set on the leaves above. Evelina reached over and turned his face back to her. She pressed her palm against his cheek, her gaze holding his.

It only made it hurt more that she could see past the words he wasn't saying. She was always so observant, so patient and willing to try and understand those around her. It just made it worse.

"Everyone deserves to know what you did," she said softly. "What you sacrificed to keep us safe."

He placed his hand over hers, moving it down to his chest. "Maybe one day."

But they both knew that day would never come. Not while Vidaris had a hold of his soul. He may have been able to travel outside of the Shadow Realm in the dream realm, but he'd never make it this far in the waking.

Daimon didn't want to think about all the things that would never be. Instead, he rolled over, sliding on top of Evelina and bracing his arms on either side of her head. He wanted to savor every inch of her, to hold her until the moon disappeared and it was time for them to wake back up.

She wiggled beneath him, her eyes brightening with hunger. "Is this where you make me remember your touch?" she said with a smirk. "It might be hard to top earlier."

He leaned down and whispered against her mouth, "I will never stop trying to top the time before."

She threw her arms around his neck, bringing her lips to his. He hiked the blanket up, bringing it over her knee and past her thigh. His eyes trailed the movement of his hand, savoring the feel of her skin. She shivered beneath his touch and scooted her hips closer, but he took his time.

He wanted to sear this into his memory, to be able to close his eyes and picture her naked beneath him. He grabbed her hips and squeezed, digging his fingers into her soft flesh.

With a torturously slow pace, he pushed into her. One of his hands roved down her body, gripping her breast and basking in the sounds he could draw out of her.

Their bodies melded together as he moved on top of her. She was everything to him—what he had sold his soul for. He would become the darkness for her time and time again.

The fireplace burned brighter, illuminating the shelves of books surrounding them.

"Quit thinking so much," Evelina whispered. "Stay here with me."

He kissed her, drinking in the taste of her skin. "Always."

She smiled against his mouth and he twisted, lifting her on top of him. She sat up, straddling his hips and spreading her hands across his chest. His eyes dropped to her breasts as she leaned forward, entranced by the way the firelight danced off them. He felt like he had entered the gates of Caelum, like he could lose himself between her legs and never come up for air.

He held her thighs as she rode him, their gazes colliding without breaking.

It was different this time, slower. He was eager to make it last, to watch each moan that came from her lips, to touch every inch of her before she came undone. They were both desperate at first, but now he wanted to draw every second out.

She leaned down, bringing her mouth to his. The kiss was deep and passionate, like they were making up for every missed kiss over the past three hundred years.

He came undone beneath her, squeezing her hips. She leaned her head back, her hair so long that it brushed across the tops of his thighs. He watched her in wonder as her mouth dropped open, her pace quickening and thighs clenching. She screamed his name, her hips slowing as she came back to her body.

Her eyes were closed but his were wide open. Being like this with her again—not the frantic touches against the tree—it almost broke him. To be reminded of how deep his love for her ran.

Leaving her to go back to the Shadow Realm would be torture. But he would make the deal again without hesitation.

She lay on top of him, her breathing returning to normal.

"I love you, Evelina," he whispered, pulling her close. "I am yours, forever."

She wrapped herself around him, her arms shaking. "And I yours."

They talked for hours, tangled together beneath the blanket, the fireplace crackling nearby. It was mostly Daimon listening and asking about her life, eager to avoid talking about the Shadow Realm. Evelina's happiness made it all worthwhile.

She told him about her daughter, Leda. How strong and brave she was.

"You should see her, Daimon. She sent *five* Aegis to the infirmary for touching her."

"She sounds incredible," he said softly.

Evelina shook her head, laughing fondly. "She's a force of her own."

His chest was tight with grief, but he smiled through it. He could never blame Evelina for moving on—for having a family. But it hurt all the same that it couldn't be with him.

A tear slid down her cheek as she told him all she had been through—everything she had lost. The jealousy stirring in his chest faded away, replaced with sadness. She was ruling by herself. Even if he wished it had been him at her side, it didn't make it better now that she was alone.

She talked about Annora, how she had a daughter named Avery who was the spitting image of her. How Annora became the council head for the Nocturna after Maliena and Neve retired.

"And I met a human—an artist that sells to Clara," she said quietly.

"A human that still lives in Penyth?" he asked. "They must have a hard time with that."

Evelina looked away from him, her eyes filling with sadness. The fire still burned beside them, keeping them both warm.

"I'm trying to show him that not all fae are so…difficult." She sighed.

Daimon smiled, watching her talk. She told him everything, from Leda's progress with her sword fighting lessons to Annora's career as the Nox leader. He would never tire of seeing her like this, with the glow of the fireplace lighting up her skin, how animated she got when telling a story.

Her arms flailed around, telling him about how Iris got under her skin like no other council member. Even when she drifted off to sleep, he watched her until the very last second.

He could feel the Harvest Moon lowering; his time was almost up. If he tried to hold on much longer, the dream would fall out of his hands, slipping through his fingers.

With one last kiss on her forehead, he separated their connection, ending the dream.

He didn't want to tell her goodbye—didn't want to see her cry. At least this way, he felt like it wasn't actually over.

SEVENTY-SEVEN

EVELINA

TWO MONTHS LATER

EVELINA HAD WOKEN UP ALONE, BARELY CERTAIN THE dream of Daimon had actually happened. She awoke in the Radix Room, tucked onto Ellerry's brightly colored couch with a blanket thrown over her. When she asked Ellerry how she ended up there, Ellerry just smiled and made her a cup of tea.

Evelina went to the Radix Room every night after, hopeful the connection would still be there. She tugged at the tether, but each time felt nothing.

So she was forced to go back to normal. As normal as she could feel after a night like that.

Today she was sitting in her room with Annora, eating lunch as they often did together.

Annora watched her closely, then hummed. "You seem different."

Evelina shrugged, her cheeks reddening. She *felt* different. There'd always been an empty loneliness that filled her chest, but after seeing Daimon, she felt a little less hollow.

"Do I?" she said around a mouthful of herb chicken.

She took another bite of food, but the moment she swallowed it down, it instantly soured in her stomach. She bolted out of the chair, running to the bathing room and emptying the contents of her stomach into a waste basket.

Annora rushed in after her and bent down to pull her hair out of the way. "Evelina?" She rubbed circles over her back as she heaved again. "Perhaps we should call for Gloriana. That's the third time this week you haven't been able to keep your food down."

"There's a lot going on." Evelina waved her off, wiping her mouth. "I'll be fine."

Annora shifted and gave her a pointed look, fully unconvinced.

Something Evelina didn't want to consider screamed in the back of her mind. She had been ignoring it all week, had ignored it when her cycle hadn't come and all the times she was forced to swallow down the nausea she felt with every scent that filled her nose.

"Evelina," Annora said gently.

She turned around and sat on the floor, her stomach settled for now. She leaned against the wall and closed her eyes. She couldn't be pregnant—refused to believe it. The only person she had been with was Daimon, and that was in a *dream*. Their bodies weren't there, just their minds. So it couldn't be possible…

A tear slipped down her cheek and she quickly wiped it away.

"Evie," Annora said gently. "It's more than just a lot going on, isn't it?"

Evelina dropped her head into her hands, her tears flowing steadily now. She didn't want to face the truth, couldn't say it out loud.

It was all too much, thinking about the possibility of having Daimon's child but not having Daimon.

Annora stayed quiet, letting her gather herself.

Finally, Evelina nodded. She opened her mouth, but nothing

came out. A tear slid down her cheek and she squeezed her eyes shut.

Annora must've seen the pain in her eyes, the overwhelm. She placed a hand over Evelina's and said, "There's only one way to know for certain. I'll get Gloriana."

She slipped out of the room, leaving Evelina to her thoughts. Her thoughts raced with fear of what would happen if she was pregnant. But a piece of her trembled—not from grief, but from joy at the possibility of it. To have a child with Daimon was a dream she had long ago given up. It felt as if her emotions had been cleaved into two, her joy warring with her fear.

She wished she could talk to Daimon. He would know what to do. But he wasn't here.

How would she explain it? To everyone, to Leda? Even if they could accept there was no father in the picture, there would be no hiding the child was severed from the father's Essence at the blessing ceremony.

It was a tradition the entire council would be present for. If she demanded things to change, it would raise too many questions, leaving people to think her child wasn't blessed by Eurydice.

Daimon's mother had been killed when the midwife saw what Nyx's Essence did to the child. If she were to conceive a child with someone also bound to that darkness…there would be no stopping it.

The council wouldn't understand.

All they would see was a child of a monster.

Annora returned with Gloriana, a handful of tinctures in a basket in her arms. Gloriana bustled over, looking her over from head to toe.

"How are you feeling?" she asked.

Evelina chewed on her lip. "Tired."

Gloriana hummed and set the basket down. "As a healer, you know it's a simple test to keep it discreet." She removed the lids from the jars she brought. "Sleep with this bundle beneath your pillow tonight. If it's blooming with flowers in the morning, then you are with child."

Annora walked over to Evelina, setting a hand on her shoulder. "How does that mean she's pregnant?"

Gloriana held up the bundle. "The stems have been cut from their roots, making it impossible for a flower to bud. When a Woodland is with child, her Essence will immediately begin to draw on nature to strengthen her body. Even without trying, her body will begin to do all that it can to keep the baby safe and healthy."

Annora took the bundle of cut stems from her, examining it.

"They've been dipped in a fertility tonic," Gloriana continued. "The flowers only form when a Woodland's Essence is behaving in that way. You will know by first light."

Annora passed the bundle to Evelina, her eyes curious.

"Thank you," Evelina said to Gloriana. There was no one else she would trust to prepare the test for her.

"I'll be back tomorrow to check on you," Gloriana said gently.

Once she left, Annora sat down on the bed beside Evelina.

"Do you want me to stay tonight?" she asked gently.

Evelina nodded, her body numb as she stared at the bundle, one she had prescribed and crafted dozens of times for others. She crawled into bed, setting the stems beneath her pillow as instructed.

Never had she thought this a possibility. She was only thankful she didn't have to do it alone.

She fell asleep first, Annora stroking her hair, and awoke to dawn's creeping light.

Annora was sound asleep beside her. Evelina took a deep breath and slowly pulled the bundle from beneath the pillow. Her breath caught as she looked down at it.

At the end of the stems, tiny little flowers bloomed.

SEVENTY-EIGHT

EVELINA

EVELINA WAS GOING TO HAVE DAIMON'S CHILD. WITHOUT him.

She threw the bundle across the room and screamed in frustration.

Annora stirred beside her, rolling over. "Evelina?" She quickly sat up, her throat scratchy from sleep. "What's—" Her breath caught. Slowly, she slid off the bed and walked over to the bundle of flowers. She picked it up and looked back at Evelina. "This means…"

Evelina nodded her head and pulled her knees to her chest. "I can't do this," she said into her hands. "I can't do this without him."

Annora placed a hand on her shoulder. "Who?" she said gently. Her voice was filled with understanding.

Evelina looked up at her. Her lip wobbled and she felt a rush of new tears threatening to spill over. She swallowed and answered, "Daimon."

Annora's bright gray eyes stared back at her, wide and filled with shock. "Daimon," she repeated slowly. "But Daimon is…"

Evelina took in a shaky breath and said, "He isn't dead, Annora."

Annora's brows pinched together as the words hung in the air. "Then where is he?"

Evelina never planned on telling anyone what Daimon had done, who he had become. But she could trust Annora more than she could trust anyone. She had grown up with Daimon, her parents taking him under their wing. If anyone could understand, it would be her.

"Daimon is the son of Nyx," Evelina finally said. "He became the ruler of the Shadow Realm to help secure the border, to try and keep the rebels from crossing. He bought us time to regroup, but he can never leave."

The last words felt like poison on her tongue.

Annora was quiet for a moment, her eyes bouncing between Evelina's. "But if he's there and you're here…"

"I've seen him on the Harvest Moon every year since Moros died," Evelina said slowly. "I thought it was a dream, my mind wanting to believe he wasn't lost to me forever. It was only in passing, small glimpses without any real contact before. But this past Harvest Moon…" She chewed on her lip as Annora gasped. "It was like he was here with me. I could hear him—touch him."

Annora sat heavily beside her and leaned against the wall. She blew out a long breath, processing the words.

"What am I going to do?" Evelina whispered. "Daimon is in the Shadow Realm. When it comes time for the child's Essence to be blessed at the temple, there will be no hiding it then."

People would fear the child. They wouldn't accept the magic inside it.

Annora crossed the room and sat beside her on the bed. She wrapped an arm around her shoulders and pulled her in close.

"I cannot lose this child." Evelina's voice cracked.

Annora squeezed her shoulder. "I'll do everything I can to make sure that doesn't happen," she said quietly. "We can say the father died?"

"But then the Essence would lift to the skies, to Caelum," Evelina whispered. "The way Daimon described it, the Essence that came out of him went to his mother, while the line that was supposed to seek out his father just…cut off."

Annora was quiet for a moment. Evelina could practically hear her trying to figure out what to do.

"His magic cut off," Evelina said slowly. "As if his father didn't have Essence at all."

Then her heart raced. It was possible the child only had *one* parent with magic.

She twisted toward Annora and gasped. "What if the father was human? We would still need a way to hide the shadows, but this would at least explain only my Essence surfacing."

Annora shook her head. "That's a big risk, Evelina. With the war, the rebels, the curse… Moros? It would be an outrage."

Evelina swallowed. "But having the child of the Lord of Shadows would be undeniably worse. He may as well be one of the dark gods now."

"Even if it worked, Eve…" Annora spoke slowly, clearly trying to dissuade her from the idea. "What human would even agree to this?"

Evelina only knew one human, really.

"I know one. He's been coming to the palace more recently. We're…friends."

"And the human you've been spending time with," Annora said slowly. "He'll just…agree to this?"

She would be asking the impossible from him. How could she expect Lawrence to go along with it? How could she even think to ask it?

But if it was her only chance at saving her child, she would do anything. Half-fae were not unheard of in the realm.

Evelina took a deep breath. "I don't know, but I have to try."

That night, Evelina went to the refugee camp outside of Astern. She donned her healer garb and secured a hood over her head. She walked through the camp, searching for the small green cottage.

She found him rocking in a wooden chair on the porch. His head was tilted back as he gazed up at the stars. Her heart pounded harder against her chest the closer she got.

He looked down, his eyes landing on her. She felt a twinge of guilt when he smiled and waved.

"And what have I done to deserve a visit so late?" he asked gently. He gestured to the rocking chair beside him, motioning for her to sit down.

She rocked, listening to the creak of the wood beneath her and the creatures of the wood singing.

"Lawrence." She hesitated and closed her eyes.

The sound of his chair rocking paused.

She took a deep breath and opened her eyes. He was watching her closely, fear in his eyes.

"What's happened?" he whispered.

She didn't know how to say it. They had become friends, but this…it went beyond friendship.

"Something happened that I didn't think was possible," she began. "I need your help."

His brows drew together. "What do you need?"

"I'm pregnant," she whispered. He drew in a sharp breath. "And no one can know who the father is. He—" She cleared her throat. "The child wouldn't be accepted."

Lawrence stared at her with his mouth open. He blinked a few times, processing what she had just said. "You're pregnant," he said slowly. "And you think I can help?"

She swallowed. "There's a ceremony a queen is subjected to when a new heir is born," she explained. "The child is born at the temple and the council gathers to watch the blessing of the child's Essence. The parents' magic will be returned to them after the birth, presenting in whatever form of magic the parent has."

Evelina's would present as light, just as it had with Leda. But this time, shadows would appear too, right before the connection severed, unable to find Daimon in the Shadow Realm.

She would need to find a way to hide the shadows, but if she could, then it would look as if there was simply no Essence going to the father at all.

"A piece of my magic will leave the child and return to me, but the father's…won't."

Lawrence pressed his mouth into a thin line. "So you need a human without magic to cover it up," he said slowly.

She nodded her head, her chest tightening. "I wouldn't ask it if there was any other option. You have every right to say no and I would never fault you for that. This is an impossible ask—"

"I'll do it," he said quickly. "I'll say I'm the father."

She blinked. "You will?"

"Of course I will." His voice was confident. Strong. "You're one of the only people to show me kindness in this world. Not only that, but you're my friend. I'm glad you asked me."

She still couldn't believe what she was hearing. She had been fully prepared for him to say no. He had no reason to say *yes*.

But he did.

"I don't know how to repay you," she said in disbelief.

He shook his head. "You've already done more for me than I thought a fae ever would for a human," he said. "Let me do this for you."

Tears welled in her eyes. "Thank you, Lawrence," she breathed.

Tomorrow, they would be telling the council she was pregnant, and a human was the child's father.

"Who knows, maybe a half-human heir could help change things here," he said with a small smile, glancing up at his cottage. "We could learn to live together again."

Hope swelled in her heart. "I'd love nothing more."

SEVENTY-NINE

EVELINA

EVELINA PACED BENEATH THE TWINKLING LIGHTS OF THE grove. She needed to see Daimon—to talk to him. It was supposed to be impossible, but so was having a child in the dream realm—so was everything that had happened up until now.

Dream orbs lined the forest floor, casting a warm glow through the dark trees. A memory crossed her mind of the attack that had left two Nox dead, when Evelina had been too late to save them.

But that was before she left to be a healer on the war front. Before she opened her heart up to Daimon again. Before she lost her mother and sisters and brother. Before she became queen and lost Daimon, too.

She wasn't afraid anymore—not of the shadows, or Nyx, or even Vidaris.

She was going to change their fate.

"Okay. This is going to work." Her voice was shaky as she closed her eyes.

This *had* to work.

"Nyx," she whispered, slightly unsure how to pray to a dark god. Praying to Eurydice was as easy as breathing, something she did before going to sleep at night or waking in the morning, but this was unfamiliar territory. "I need your help."

This was the last thing a Manor queen should be doing. Evelina herself had seen the punishment Carwyn had suffered for doing so.

But life had taught her things weren't always so simple. She was going to be raising this child alone.

Evelina needed to at least tell Daimon that she was having their child. To get his blessing to go forward with this plan.

So much had changed in ways she never expected. The pregnancy with Leda wasn't lonely; she had Senna by her side. He had sat with her through the days she couldn't keep food down, brought her water and warm broth when she couldn't get out of bed.

This time was going to be different.

She just hoped Nyx would be willing to help. *Please, Nyx,* she begged in her mind.

She had hoped coming to Nocturna territory would help, but as the minutes turned into hours, her hope began to fade. He wasn't coming.

With one last longing glance at the glowing dream orbs around her, she turned in the direction of the palace, thinking through how she would protect the child.

"Evelina Manor." A voice as thick as night snaked through the dark forest. "I'll admit, I was surprised to receive a prayer from you."

She slowly turned around, her heart beating wildly as her eyes landed on the God of Fear and Dreams. "Nyx."

A feline smile curled across his face, his eyes gleaming with delight. He looked just as he did in the Celestial Plane, his gaze holding the same look of knowing far more than she wished.

"Well, don't be shy." He tilted his head, watching her closely.

She steeled her spine. "I need your help." He nodded, waiting for more. "I need to speak with Daimon."

Nyx raised a brow. "That is not a wise idea."

"It doesn't have to be long," she rushed out. "If you could just help me get in contact with him—"

"And risk Vidaris sensing your bond?"

Evelina swallowed. "Maybe there's a way you could hide—"

Nyx laughed, a cruel and sharp sound that made the blood drain from Evelina's face. "There is no hiding from Vidaris," he said through another chuckle. "What could be so important to risk such a thing?"

Evelina instinctually placed her hand over her stomach. Nyx's eyes flicked down to her hand and the smile on his face disappeared.

"Evelina Manor," he said slowly, his face deadly serious. A chill ran down her spine at how intensely he watched her. "Please tell me you are not with child. *Tell* me you two didn't find a way to be together while he's under Vidaris's rule."

Tears welled in Evelina's eyes as she turned her head, unable to give him the answer he wanted. There was no point in lying.

Shadows fumed from his hands, brushing Evelina's skin, alarmingly close. But they were silky, cool, and did not harm her.

"I will not be making the connection for you to contact him." His voice was hard—unyielding. However, when his gaze met hers, she found pity.

Her chest tightened. "But—"

"I will not help you," Nyx repeated. "You cannot see each other again."

She froze. "Ever?" she whispered. At Nyx's unyielding gaze, she pleaded, "But Daimon said on the Harvest Moon it's safe. Vidaris can't see past the Vale while Eurydice's light is strong."

"I suggest you never see him again." Nyx's eyes hardened. Before she could protest, he continued, "Unless you want Vidaris to have a claim on the child."

The wind was knocked out of her, as if he had kicked her in the stomach.

"Claim?" she whispered, her voice shaking.

"Daimon made a deal when he became the Lord of Shadows," Nyx explained. "All that he is, all that he creates, and all that he owns belongs to Vidaris now. The bargain gives Vidaris free rein to claim the child as hers—to use it as she sees fit."

Evelina gasped and shook her head. "She can't." She didn't want to believe it. "This is *my* child. Mine and Daimon's."

Nyx sighed. "She can. She *will*."

Evelina never knew a heart could break so many times. Never knew there were a thousand ways her heart could feel pain. Her lungs emptied and she gasped, failing to take in more air. With one sentence, her entire world had come crashing down around her.

She couldn't risk Vidaris finding out who the father was. It wasn't just about keeping the kingdom from learning about the child's parentage—now it was about ensuring the Goddess of Vengeance didn't find out either.

"Which is why we can't see each other again," Evelina whispered.

She knew Daimon. He carried the weight of the entire realm on his shoulders, and he would blame himself—would wonder if Evelina regretted it too. All her actions would be affirming his shame in himself, of the shadows within him, when she wanted nothing more than to tell the kingdom the baby was his. That the father was the hero who slayed Moros.

That she could never regret this—only that she had to hide the truth to keep him and the baby safe.

Nyx nodded. "Exactly."

She knew what she had to do, but it didn't make it hurt any less. Her hands began to tremble. She wondered if, at some point, she would forget where the truth started and the lies ended.

"The blessing ceremony," Nyx continued formally. "You need to hide the connection to Daimon; it can't be shown as severed when it comes out of the child."

She nodded, her body numb. "A human has agreed to claim

it as his own." Pain stabbed at her chest. "If the father is announced as human and we find a way to hide the shadows, it wouldn't be odd if no magic came out."

"It could work," Nyx hummed. "He's simply agreed to this?"

"He wants to help." She still felt a well of guilt from asking Lawrence to do this, but she was out of options.

Nyx's eyes were blank, but his brows pulled together slightly. "When your light comes out of the child, you could use your affinity to make it brighter, to hide the shadows."

She nodded firmly. She would do anything to keep the child safe. A tear slid down her cheek as she realized she would truly have to face this alone.

"Thank you," she whispered. She still struggled to understand what Nyx had to gain in this. What price would she have to pay?

"Good luck, Evelina." He turned, already walking away.

"Why help me?"

Nyx paused, his back to her. He looked over his shoulder, his midnight eye landing on her briefly. "Because I didn't do it right the first time."

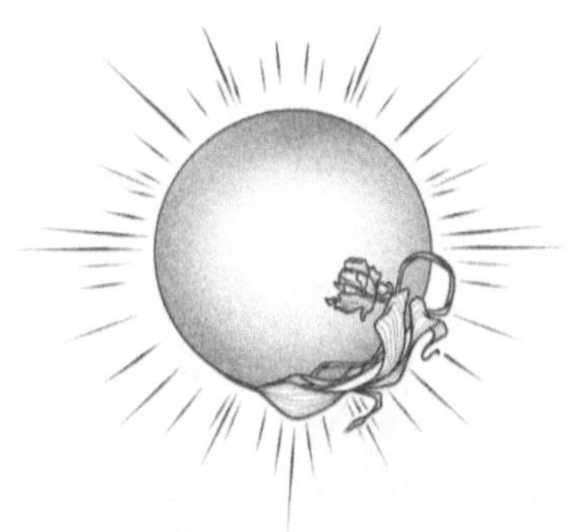

EIGHTY

EVELINA

EVELINA FOUGHT BACK HER NERVES, KNOWING WHAT HAD to happen today. She would tell the council she was pregnant and that a human was the father. Not Daimon.

She wished she could shout to the entire realm that he was the father. But there was more than that to think about. They had to protect their child, both from the cruelty of the world and from the Goddess of Vengeance.

She had called Lawrence to today's council meeting, prepping him out in the corridor for their questions. But there was only so much to say. They had to lie as best they could, and hope it was good enough. The council had filed in already, casting curious—or, perhaps, threatening—glances his way.

"We don't see humans much anymore. You'll have to forgive us," Annora said to Lawrence, shooting Seretha a pointed look.

Evelina glanced at the Undine council head, a feral smile stretched across her sharply angled face.

"And less often seated beside the fae queen herself," Seretha said with a smooth cadence of derision and charm.

"Queen Evelina has made me feel very fortunate to be in Penyth," Lawrence said quietly. He wouldn't look directly at Seretha.

Evelina was struggling to find the words to begin this conversation. She could feel the eyes of the council on her, wondering why she had called them here and brought a human with her. She knew what she had to do, but in this moment, all she wanted to do was throw the whole plan out the window.

"Is…everything all right?" Iris asked slowly.

No, it was very much *not* all right. But this was happening now whether Evelina wanted it to or not.

She got to her feet. Lawrence was by her side immediately, helping her up.

"I'm with child." She said it quickly, like ripping a bandage off.

Iris's eyes widened. So did the others'. They waited for more, but when none came, Cyprian prodded, "And the father…"

Seretha hissed at him, baring her teeth. "Does it matter right now, Cyprian?"

He shrugged. It was what they were all likely thinking. "It *will* matter when the kingdom finds out. I don't mean to be insensitive, Evelina. But the kingdom will want to know."

Iris's eyes dropped down to Evelina's stomach. "The child is strong. I can feel it."

Evelina's hands began to shake. Iris was talented with her mind-influencing affinity, one of the strongest she had ever seen. Evelina hadn't considered the possibility of her feeling something different within the child.

Lawrence placed a steadying hand on her arm.

Iris's head turned slowly to him. Her green eyes blazed, her lips twisting in disgust.

"It's me," Lawrence said quietly.

Evelina felt a dagger twist in her chest. The final crack in her heart broke entirely.

"Say that again, boy," Cyprian demanded.

Lawrence swallowed. "We were afraid that if anyone knew the father was human, it could cause discord within the kingdom."

"You." Iris nodded to Evelina, then to Lawrence. "Created a child with *him*?"

"Lawrence is the father," Evelina said with a sense of finality.

Seretha took a step forward, assessing Lawrence. "This will not go over well with the Undine," she said slowly. "Many of them fought alongside King Senna when he led the naval ships. They will not accept a human bastard."

Evelina bared her teeth at Seretha. "Then get them in line." Her patience was thin, her temper poorly restrained.

"Neither will the Aegis," said Iris, stepping forward. She glanced at Cyprian, who nodded.

"The Aegis fought the rebels for years before the curse," Cyprian continued. "They may be more willing to accept the child, but they will hate *him* for it."

Lawrence bristled and straightened his spine. "In time, they'll learn to—"

"No one will *learn* to accept you," Iris snapped. She turned to Evelina. "Is he to be king? To replace Senna?"

Evelina shook her head quickly. "No one is replacing Senna."

"This cannot be announced to the people with him still here," Seretha said. "The only way the Undine will accept news of a half-human heir is if there's no threat of a human king's claim on the throne."

Lawrence drew a sharp breath and took a step back. Evelina had been prepared for pushback, for disgust and derision. But humans and fae had once been the two essential parts of the united Valon Empire, a value she thought the council still held.

"No one is killing him," Evelina snarled.

"Then we banish him to Crea," said Seretha, as if it were a favor. "To be with the humans."

Iris hummed her approval.

"And we waste one of the last few portals to Crea for this?" said Cyprian. "It would be better to exile him in the wildlands."

"This is my home." Lawrence's voice trembled, but he held firm. "I won't leave my home or Evelina."

Annora stepped closer to Evelina, pressing her shoulder against hers. "We can't just send him to a land he's never been to," she reasoned. "It would be cruel."

"What was cruel," said Iris darkly, "was the thousands of fae lives lost at the hand of the last human king."

Evelina shuddered. If this was how they were reacting to a mere human—someone who had no power or Essence to threaten them—then she could only imagine what would have happened had she told the truth. A child of a dark god would have no place in this realm.

"We cannot blame the human for what Moros did," Seretha conceded. "But still, he would be safer among his own kind. It would also be cruel damning him to a land where we *know* those who fought in the war would gladly drive a sword through his chest."

Lawrence turned to Evelina, his eyes wide. "Evelina, please. Don't let them do this."

Evelina didn't know how to protect him. She had never foreseen the council going to such lengths, the fear of the past still so deep in their hearts.

Perhaps it was better if he left—if this was the world she had created as a ruler. One so cruel.

"Those in favor of banishing the human, raise your hand," Iris said.

Evelina closed her eyes. She'd always wanted their realm to be fairer. For each race to have equal say and vote when a disagreement arose.

She already knew what the vote would be.

"Evelina," Lawrence pleaded.

She opened her eyes, her vision blurring with the tears that filled them.

Iris, Cyprian, Seretha, and Warrick had their hands raised.

Evelina would owe Lawrence for her entire immortal life. Evelina from the past, the brave healer, might have stood up against them all and shielded him with her gift of light. Run away, far away from here.

But Leda was here. And she had a half-human child on the way. It wouldn't be safe for the child in either land, but she had to hope she could protect her here, as the queen bound to this land.

A queen who could not deny her council.

"I'm sorry," she breathed.

Lawrence's eyes widened as Cyprian stepped forward.

"Come with me," Lawrence pleaded. "We can go to Crea together."

Tears spilled down her cheeks. "You know I can't," she whispered.

Lawrence screamed as Cyprian dragged him out of the throne room. His cries echoed in Evelina's ears long after he was gone.

EIGHTY-ONE

EVELINA

THE PREGNANCY WAS FAR MORE DIFFICULT THAN IT HAD been with Leda. Evelina felt more of *everything*—nausea, exhaustion, pain. There was a newfound weakness growing in her every day. She was breathless from simple activities; even walking from her chambers to the throne room had become taxing.

And of course, people's judgment didn't help either. As opposed to her pregnancy with Leda, no one seemed eager to hear the baby kick or coo praises at her belly. They looked at it with fear.

Explaining to Leda was harder than anyone else, the flash of betrayal in her eyes piercing Evelina so deeply that she would remember it forever. But Leda was loyal and stood by Evelina's side every day, even if she seemed unwilling. It eased the pain of doing this without Daimon, but it didn't erase it. Nothing could erase that heartache.

Evelina didn't know how she would have their child without him. They could never meet, not if they wanted to keep the baby safe. He would never know if it was a girl or boy, never see them grow into an adult or discover what magic they might possess.

She began to realize how much those Harvest Moons had

meant to her, even those many fruitless years only catching glimpses of him through that shadowy haze. Then, she at least still had a piece of him left, a chance of seeing him again.

Now she had none.

The evening was a beautiful, temperate June night, moonlight streaming in through the window of Evelina's room.

"Mother, you should lie down," Leda pleaded. "Gloriana told you to take it easy."

Evelina shifted on her feet, pacing in front of the window. "This is taking it easy," she mumbled. In truth, she was restless, her fear of not being able to hide the babe's shadows haunting her the closer to full-term she got. The baby could come any day now.

Leda sighed and sat on the edge of the bed. "At least sit down. You're stressing me out."

Evelina propped a hand on her back and waved off Leda with the other.

Water rushed from between her legs, followed by a clenching deep in her swollen belly. She bent forward, breathing deeply in and out.

"Leda," she rasped.

Leda spun around, eyes wide when she saw the liquid on the floor. "The baby is coming," she gasped.

Evelina nodded and stood back up, rubbing a hand over her stomach. Leda rushed over to her, trying to lead her to the bed. Evelina shook her head, squeezing her eyes closed as the first wave came.

"Get Gloriana and Annora," she said through gritted teeth.

"I'm not leaving you."

Evelina paced the room, one hand on her back and the other still over her stomach. "Unless you want to deliver your sibling, you have to go get them."

Leda hesitated. Evelina screamed, the next wave stronger than the last. That was all it took for Leda to bolt from the room. Evelina braced her hands on the back of a wooden chair, breathing as deeply as she could.

"Your father and I love you so very much," she whispered. "One day, I'll find a way to tell you the truth. I promise."

The room was still, with only her ragged breaths filling the quiet. Soon, Leda returned with Annora and Gloriana. They rushed Evelina to the Celestial Temple, the waves of pain growing closer together.

By the time they reached the grounds of the temple, the Sacred was already waiting.

The baby was coming. Now.

Evelina exchanged a panicked look with Annora. This was it. She had to pray the darkness of night and her affinity for light would be enough to cover the severed shadows that presented in the child.

She had to trust in Annora, and in herself. Because right now, her child needed her to push.

Within the hour, she gave birth to a perfect little girl.

The pain of the birth subsided the moment she heard the baby take her first cry. Tears streamed down Evelina's face as she held her daughter in her arms. Her little cheeks were red, her eyes closed. Evelina dropped a kiss to her forehead, her heart swelling with pride at this perfect child.

The council gathered, eager to see the child and watch over the blessing of her Essence.

Evelina held her breath as the Sacred stepped forward. This was it.

"You have chosen to have your child on the sacred grounds of Eurydice's temple and your child will be blessed for it." As was tradition when the queen birthed a new heir, the Sacred laid a white rose in front of Evelina.

Light gathered at the baby's chest, and Evelina threw all of her focus into making it brighter, bright enough that no shadows could be seen. The Sacred turned her head to Evelina and tilted it to the side. Evelina's breath caught as her bright eyes seared into her.

The light lifted into the air and traveled over to Evelina, just as it had with Leda.

She held her breath and waited for the Sacred to say something, to say she could sense Evelina using her magic to make the light brighter. But the Sacred remained silent.

Eurydice, forgive me, she prayed.

What if it didn't work? She already knew she could never allow this child to be taken from her arms, and damn anyone that would try. She knew her council was loyal to her, but how far did that loyalty run? Even now, they believed they were responsible for the father's absence today.

Her exhausted muscles tensed, prepared to take the baby and run if needed.

The light flared brighter. She swore her heart stopped beating as she waited.

There were no shadows, no signs that pointed to Daimon being the father. No severed line to curse the child—no line from the father at all.

They had managed to cover the shadow before it showed, leaving it to look as if there was only magic returning to Evelina and none to a father. Just as it should if the father was a human, as the council believed.

She did it. Annora smiled and sat heavily on the ground.

"Glad to see she at least has some chance at having Essence," said Iris in a tone both pitying and curious. "Perhaps your light will be enough."

Seretha stared at the child, her brows furrowed. "Her name?" she asked.

Evelina thought about Daimon, about what they would decide if they could have this conversation together. Memories of their childhood came to mind first—of the safety she felt hiding between the shimmering pods of the lunaria garden, dreaming together. When he met her there morning after morning after her father died. When they played pretend and he took her mind off the bad days.

"Lunaria," she said with pride, looking down at the child they had created together. "Lunaria Manor."

She smiled at her beautiful little girl, her magic still flaring around her. She was safe in her arms.

But through the light, a small shadow flickered before it disappeared entirely.

EIGHTY-TWO

DAIMON

THERE WAS A TIME WHEN DAIMON COULD STAVE OFF THE darkness with the taste of Evelina's smile, with a breath of her lily scent. Her soft eyes and fierce mind could chase away the demons that threatened to pull him down, to fight off Vidaris's influence that surrounded him daily.

Evelina was always the thing that kept him going—kept him sane. But he didn't have that anymore. Not even in the dream realm, a place he always thought he would have her. The memories of her weren't enough to stave off the pit growing inside of him. There was nothing to fill the pain anymore. Nothing to make him feel worthy.

Could the purest of souls stay clean when surrounded by blood? He knew he was far from pure, his soul already tainted with the lives he had ended and the hate brewing in his heart. He harbored rage for what Vidaris had done to him and his people, and that rage could only stay buried for so long.

Now that he'd cut off his connection with Evelina, he questioned how long the memories of her would keep him from drowning. But as the darkness whispered into the depths of his soul, he knew it wouldn't be long now.

Never again would he see how Evelina's nose would crinkle

in the middle when her joy was at its highest, and the feeling of pure ecstasy that flowed through his body following that look. He wouldn't feel her in his arms again or taste her lips against his.

But Evelina was safe. Their *child* was safe. That was all that mattered. As long as Daimon stayed away from them, Vidaris would never know the child was his. When Nyx told him Evelina was having their child, he felt overwhelming joy, but it lasted only a split second before turning into dread. He knew he would never see her again—never see their child.

Daimon paced his empty castle. The black stone was cold and dark, so shiny that it reflected his frown back to him. He could feel his pain, wanting to welcome the vile shadows calling out to him from the Vale. They were different from his own, wilder and more untamed. His father had warned him about going into the Vale. Once he did, he would never be the same again.

But Daimon's soul, and everything bound to it, was already Vidaris's. If Vidaris were to ever learn he fathered a child beneath their deal, it would mean the child belonged to her. He couldn't have that—wouldn't let her take that too. Now that he had something to protect, he felt the call more than ever: to remove all connections and bindings and succumb his soul to utter darkness. It would keep them safe if none of his true soul was left, nothing calling out to them.

Selfishly, he hoped the magic would lessen his pain of never seeing Evelina again. Of never seeing his child. Would the baby have Evelina's smile and nose? Would it have anything of his? He clenched his jaw, knowing he would never see the life they had created together. He would never know the answers to his questions.

There was nothing left in this world for him.

Daimon could feel Vidaris in the back of his mind, waiting for the day he fully bent the knee to her. He had never had much hope in his father's plans, but what hope was left? Perhaps there would come a day when he really did take the Vale, and Daimon could be free.

"*The Vale will erase your pain, son of Nyx.*" Vidaris's gritty voice floated into the castle.

Over the years since the split of the empire, she had grown weaker. With the war over, people began to heal, to move on, and it left her weak, no longer able to hold a physical form in the living realm. If the living weren't giving in to their darker desires, her power dwindled. The Goddess of Vengeance was fueled by death, lust, anger, and pain. War was a breeding ground for these things, but that battle had long been lost.

Just like Daimon, she was shackled to the Shadow Realm.

"*I've seen your pain for centuries,*" she hissed. "*Why torture yourself? You have the power of a god.*"

He thought of Evelina, of how she would be having their child any day now, if she hadn't already. He hoped the child would grow up knowing the love he never had. That his child would never learn of him and his dark bloodline, would never experience the shame he fought his entire life.

Perhaps it was better this way. Evelina and Leda would be the only family the child ever needed. Leda was fierce, and he knew she would protect her younger sibling with everything she had. While Evelina would offer the child safe arms to always come home to... What more could a child need?

Even if he could be there, how could the son of a dark god ever be a worthy father?

With his heart bleeding memories of what he had lost, he fell to his knees.

They would be okay—better—without him. They had each other.

He had the darkness.

With his knees pressed against the icy stone, he closed his eyes. A single tear trailed down his cheek, dripping off his chin and landing on the ground beneath him. He opened his Essence to the one place he hadn't gone. To the shadows of the

Vale that had been banging on the door of his soul to be let in.

He used to try to hold on—to Maliena and Neve's soft presence in his life, the kindness of something like a home. To Keir's laughter over the fire as they tried to forget about the loves they left behind, the battle always a breath away. To the feeling of protection when his fleet surrounded him, or the soaring delight that filled his spirit when Zephyr spun above the clouds.

And then there was Evelina. His love. His soulbonded. A soul to which he was never good enough to be tied, but somehow was blessed enough to be loved by—even if their time together passed in the blink of an eye. She loved him when he didn't love himself, believed in him when he had no room in his heart to believe in himself. Her smile was brighter than the sun, her touch like every good feeling he'd ever had, all held in one person.

Every moment he spent with her in the camp was the happiest he had ever been. The afternoon he stole away to take her to the cave of glowing creatures, riding atop Zephyr together, holding her beneath the moonlight.

It all felt…so far from him now. Gone.

With one last flash of Evelina's smile in his mind, he finally let the darkness in.

"*Welcome home, Lord of the Shadows,*" Vidaris whispered, her voice bouncing off the walls and landing somewhere between the emptiness in his chest and his fading memories.

His pain was quickly replaced with delicious hunger. All he could feel was the need to find those cursed to Vidaris's realm, to seek them out and make them pay for their sins.

A slow smile spread across his face.

He felt nothing.

EPILOGUE

EVELINA

DAYS BLED INTO YEARS. EVELINA GENTLY COMBED HER daughter's hair, which was so long that it brushed her waist. The sun streamed through the window and warmed her skin. It was times like these that reminded her to thank Eurydice for the precious daughters she had been given. Even in all her anguish and years of grieving, she still had them.

They were the thing that kept her afloat, a lifeline to which she desperately clung.

More than grief, Evelina also had regrets. She often thought about Lawrence. All she could hope was that he had found happiness over the border in Crea.

There were so many mistakes she had made in her life that it was hard to keep track. But being Leda and Lunaria's mother was something she was certain she had done right.

She tried to trust in simply moving forward. But fear still prickled at the edges of her smiles. She had grown accustomed to losing the things she loved most. Fate had a pattern of giving her happiness, only to snatch it away. Deep down, she always felt as if her good days were numbered.

"Mommy?" Evelina felt a tug on her sleeve. "Are you playing pretend without me?"

Evelina laughed. "No, my love. I was thinking."

The little girl twisted around fully and looked up at her. Long lashes brushed her cheeks as they fanned out over big hazel eyes. She reached up and took her mother's face in her palms. Her tiny brows bunched together. With a voice far older than a five-year-old's should sound, she said, "Stop thinking so much."

"What do you propose I do instead?" Evelina laughed and pulled her in close.

Lunaria was different from her sister, wanting to explore everything. Evelina couldn't keep her out of any room in the palace or any garden nearby.

"Let's play in the glade!"

Leda snorted behind them from where she sat beneath the window. She skimmed through a book, a knowing smirk on her face.

Evelina smiled down at her younger daughter—wild and filled with life. The sadness that stayed bound around her heart lessened.

"How about you go with Leda today?" she whispered gently. "Annora and I are visiting Viridian this afternoon."

Her daughter's wide eyes swung to her sister. "Will you?" she squealed as she scrambled off Evelina's lap and over to Leda's side. She wrapped her tiny hands around Leda's leg, pleading.

Leda grumbled, but there was a small twitch of her lips turning up at the corners. "Only until sundown," she muttered.

No sooner were the words out of her mouth did her little sister squeal once more and take her hand in hers. Lunaria's head barely reached Leda's hip as she smiled a lopsided, toothy grin, pulling her toward the door, eager to go play in the grove.

Evelina smiled as she watched Leda begrudgingly move. Leda had a hard exterior, but there was a reserved softness she had only for her younger sister.

"Come on, Leda!" Lunaria stretched out her name to make it sound like it had five extra syllables.

Leda laughed, letting her sister drag her out of the room.

Evelina's eyes crinkled at the corners from the smile that stretched across her face.

"We'll be back this evening," Leda tossed over her shoulder. They'd reached the doors.

The sadness that plagued Evelina's chest thawed for several beats as she watched them, hand in hand. "I'll see you girls tonight."

But Lunaria paused, releasing Leda's hand. Her mouth quirked to the side and she flew across the room toward Evelina. She launched herself into her mother's lap, wrapping her small arms around her neck. "Love you, Momma," she whispered.

Evelina's chest warmed further as she squeezed her daughter back. She reached up and adjusted the medallion on her necklace, smiling at how it always seemed to get turned around or tangled in her hair.

"I love you always, Lunaria," Evelina replied. "Now go play before you lose daylight."

Lunaria squeezed her one last time before bounding over to Leda.

If this could be her life forever, it would have all been worth it. If she could just keep these two safe, that was all that mattered. Even as she watched Lunaria tuck her hand into Leda's and they walked out, she knew her kingdom was safe now.

In life, she had faced so much darkness—but in truth, it had only ever strengthened her light. She saw that in Leda and Lunaria. Where Leda saved her broken soul after the wedding and the losses during the split of the empire, Lunaria was her lifeline in the years following the pain of being without Daimon. She even saw a new strength in herself after all that she had lost. There was hope that still blossomed within her, a ray of light that broke through her deepest pain.

Still, not a day passed that she didn't think of Daimon. She would be eternally grateful that, no matter what pain lingered inside of her now, she would always feel lucky to have loved him. Especially to be loved *by* him. She and Daimon had found their soulbonded, had experienced a love that felt like basking in the light of Eurydice. A love she could never forget.

Even if Evelina couldn't dream of her happy ending now, maybe she would someday. And it would all have been worth it —because one day, she would dream again.

Dearest Reader,

Thank you for joining me on Daimon and Evelina's journey. You may have heard authors say they put pieces of themselves in each of their characters, and I am certainly among them. These two are especially close to my heart. Daimon, with his struggle to feel worthy and the sense that he never quite fit in with those around him. Evelina, for how she turns toward optimism because it's easier than facing some struggles.

Even through the heartache in this book, I hope a piece of you is able to relate to them as well. If there's ever been a time you've struggled with self-worth, I'm here to tell you that you're incredible. And if you've ever felt like putting on a smile because it was easier, know that you are not alone. This book's dedication was to those who had to learn how to heal themselves. You are so much stronger than you will ever know.

I'm eternally grateful for your support along the way. I'm still blown away each and every day by the thoughtfulness, kindness, and support from the reader community. And remember, *you* choose your own fate—you just have to be strong enough to take control of it.

Acknowledgments

The list of things to be thankful for could fill an entire book. I feel incredibly lucky to have such an amazing team by my side throughout this journey.

An overflowing amount of thank-yous to my husband, Tyler—none of this would be possible without you (and your quesadillas on late nights spent editing). Your endless support since the day I started writing has meant the world to me.

To my beta readers, street team, and ARC readers, thank you for dedicating your time and energy to supporting me and my books. Some of you have been on this journey since the ARC of *Lunaria* released, and it's kept me going having you all by my side over a year later.

To my beans, I couldn't do this without you. Without fail, you've been there for me on the hard days, the good days, and every day in between. You celebrate every win and pick me up with every failure. I love you with my entire heart.

A huge thank you to my proofreader, Erin, for helping me make it during the home stretch. You cheer me on when I need it the most and I can't say thank you enough.

And lastly, to my editor, Sophie. Thank you for being here since day one and reading my drafts before anyone else. You've helped me turn these books into something I can be proud of. You read my words when they're at their most vulnerable, and you somehow always find a way to make me feel safe.